NOVELISTS' AMERICA

Fiction as History, 1910–1940

NOVELISTS' AMERICA

Fiction as History, 1910-1940

NELSON MANFRED BLAKE

SYRACUSE UNIVERSITY PRESS

To my sister Pris

NELSON MANFRED BLAKE, Professor of History at Syracuse University, has written several books on the United States in the twentieth century and American social and cultural history. Among them: *Water for the Cities: A History of the Urban Water Supply Problem in the United States, A History of American Life and Thought, The Road to Reno: A History of Divorce in the United States.* He has also co-authored several important works in the field.

A series of lectures on the use of novels as sources of social history, says Professor Blake, was a trial flight that encouraged him to develop this idea further. To pursue the reading demanded by his subject, he was granted a semester's leave of absence. The task of writing that followed resulted in *Novelists' America.*

Professor Blake, who received his Ph.D. in history from Clark University in 1936, is a member of the American Historical Association, the Organization of American Historians, and the American Studies Association, as well as a frequent contributor to the journals in his field.

Preface

DURING the summer of 1963, I delivered the Charles E. Merrill Lectures on American Studies before kind and tolerant audiences at Stetson University, DeLand, Florida. I am grateful to my friends Professors John Hague and Gerald Critoph of the Stetson University American Studies Department for this opportunity to formulate some of my ideas about the use of novels as sources of social history. Other friends, Professor Rubin Weston of the North Carolina College at Durham and Professor William Askew of Colgate University, provided me with audiences for further exploration of the subject.

The lectures prepared for these occasions, however, constitute but a small part of the present text. I am indebted to Syracuse University for granting me the leave of absence necessary to extend my reading and prepare my manuscript.

The book, I hope, explains itself. Particularly in the first and last chapters, I tell what I have tried to do and why it seems worthwhile to me. I would only add that I make no pretension of being a literary critic. Let those who have the proper taste and training assess the artistic worth of these novels. I write always as a historian, searching for the information and insight that the novels provide for the understanding of the recent past, the prologue to our troubled present.

N. M. B.

Syracuse, New York
February, 1968

Acknowledgments

THE AUTHOR acknowledges with thanks the courtesies extended by the following authors and publishers who have granted permission to quote from their works:

Mr. John Dos Passos: From *Adventures of a Young Man* and *U.S.A.*

Harcourt, Brace & World, Inc.: From *Main Street, Babbitt,* and *Elmer Gantry* by Sinclair Lewis.

Random House, Inc.: From *Intruder in the Dust, The Town, Sanctuary, The Hamlet, Light in August,* and *Sartoris* by William Faulkner and *The Man from Main Street* by Sinclair Lewis.

Charles Scribner's Sons: From *The Letters of F. Scott Fitzgerald* edited by Andrew Turnbull; *This Side of Paradise, Tender Is the Night,* and *Flappers and Philosophers* by F. Scott Fitzgerald.

The Viking Press Inc.: From *East of Eden* and *The Grapes of Wrath* by John Steinbeck.

Quotations from the following works are protected by copyright and are reprinted by special permission of the publishers:

You Can't Go Home Again by Thomas Wolfe, copyright, 1940 by Maxwell Perkins as Executor; *Native Son* by Richard Wright, copyright, 1940 by Richard Wright; and *The God that Failed* by Richard Crossman; Harper & Row, Publishers.

Look Homeward Angel by Thomas Wolfe, *Thomas Wolfe's Letters to His Mother* edited by John Skally Terry, *The Letters of Thomas Wolfe* edited by Elizabeth Nowell; and *The Great Gatsby* and "Babylon Revisited" by F. Scott Fitzgerald; Charles Scribner's Sons.

Studs Lonigan: A Trilogy from "Studs Lonigan" by James T. Farrell. Copyright 1932, 1934, 1935, 1959, 1961, 1962, by James T. Farrell, The Vanguard Press.

Contents

Illustrations

Note: Illustrations have been selected from photographs and magazine covers of the period 1910
–1940, in order to give graphic emphasis to the
points made by the novelists in the accompanying
captions.

NOVELISTS' AMERICA

Fiction as History, 1910–1940

I

The Novelist as
Witness to History

He knew that there was scarcely a detail in George's book that was precisely true to fact, that there was hardly a page in which everything had not been transmuted and transformed by the combining powers of George's imagination; yet readers got from it such an instant sense of reality that many of them were willing to swear that the thing described had been not only "drawn from life," but was the actual and recorded fact itself. And that was precisely what had made the outcry and denunciation so furious.

THOMAS WOLFE, *You Can't Go Home Again* [1]

TO MOST PEOPLE *history* and *fiction* are contrasting words. History, they are told, is an account of what *really* happened; fiction is a literary work portraying *imaginary* characters and events. What could be more different? Yet the historian and the novelist have more in common than these definitions would suggest. At the most obvious level each has to have some of the other's quality. The historian who is a mere grubber for facts and has no imagination is seriously handicapped. He must select his material; he must give it a meaningful order and analysis; he must convey its color and drama to the reader. Such tasks require imagination—a properly disciplined and responsible imagination, to be sure. Similarly, the novelist who has nothing but imagination will be a mere spinner of tales; the serious author tries to convey

---

[1] Thomas Wolfe, *You Can't Go Home Again* (New York: Dell Publishing Co., 1960), 330.

1

to his reader what really might have happened—what, in the novelist's experience, is true.

But the interrelations of history and fiction do not end here. Consider the problem of the historian. What actually happened, and how does he know that it happened? Since the past no longer exists, the historian can never observe it directly. He infers what happened in a vanished world by the evidence that has chanced to survive. Certain kinds of events leave a plethora of evidence. Presidents and congresses produce a ceaseless flood of paper—treaties, proclamations, orders, messages, speeches, statutes, reports—and the writer of political history draws upon an overflowing reservoir of documents. With similar prodigality theologians, philosophers, and economists grind out a stream of articles and books, which the intellectual historian can use as sources. For political, diplomatic, constitutional, intellectual, and economic history the very processes of event-making produce the documentation that the historian needs.

Yet other happenings produce few records. What kind of life did a Chicago Irishman live in 1910, or a Mississippi Negro in 1920, or a California migrant in 1930? Poorly educated inarticulate people produce few written documents. An occasional bit of journalism or a government report may help, but it is a matter of chance whether even this type of evidence exists for any particular problem.

Must today's scholar be told that it is impossible to know about such matters because of the scarcity of evidence? To give up the search for knowledge too easily would be a pity. What after all do we most want to know in order to understand today's world? Do we not want to understand the origins of what Michael Harrington calls "the other America," the America of urban and rural poverty in the midst of an affluent society? Do we not want to understand the antecedents of the American Negro's mood of frustration and violence? Do we not want to know about the sources of decay in our cities and villages; about the corrosion of older values and moral standards? If history is to be relevant to the world we live in, we cannot afford to be content with conventional documents. We need to ask whether useful materials for understanding the past may not be found in works of fiction.

II

To suggest that the search for historical materials should be extended to the study of novels requires some courage. How can we rely upon works of imagination for knowledge about the real world?

Imagination never works in a vacuum. Even a child's daydreams are put together out of things he knows about, and the disciplined creations of the novelist have a much higher component of reality. Unless he makes his characters seem true to life and puts them into recognizable situations, he will not enlist the interest of his readers. This is more true of works that are realistic in intention than it is of those written in the tradition of romanticism. Yet even for the latter the novelist usually shores up his fantasy with sturdy beams of believable detail. Captain Ahab's mad pursuit of a legendary monster captures the reader's imagination all the more firmly because *Moby Dick* is heavily buttressed with facts about the actual life of whaling towns and whaling ships, facts grounded in Melville's own experience and observation.

Although almost any novel will yield meaningful information about the place and time in which it was written, three kinds provide particularly happy hunting for the historian. The first is the highly autobiographical novel—Herman Melville's *White Jacket,* Thomas Wolfe's *Look Homeward, Angel*—with characters modeled upon real people and incidents closely resembling real events. The second is the reminiscent novel—Edith Wharton's *The Age of Innocence,* Sinclair Lewis' *Main Street*—where the characters and incidents are largely imaginary, but the setting is one intimately known to the author through his own experience. The third is the documentary novel—Upton Sinclair's *The Jungle,* John Steinbeck's *The Grapes of Wrath*—in which the setting, although somewhat removed from his normal experience, gains authenticity from the novelist's search for facts.

Courts of justice cannot wait for ideal witnesses—impartial observers with 20/20 vision, acute hearing, and controlled emotions. Neither can students of history. Realistically, whoever has relevant information must be called to testify; the jury can then give the evidence whatever weight it deserves. As witnesses to history, novelists have certain great assets and certain serious liabilities. However, they do often treat just the thing that the student of history would like to know—what kind of people lived in certain communities, how did they treat each other, and what did they think of each other—often extending their observations to relationships inadequately documented elsewhere, like the relations of husbands and wives, parents and children, youths and maidens.

To make a more explicit point, the question of who's sleeping with whom is not a matter of prurient curiosity, but an issue of real significance, since it involves shifts in the community's operational morality. Kinsey-type investigations have sought an answer for recent years, although scholars may dispute their reliability. For earlier periods, however, the evidence is inevitably sketchy. Yet novelists usually have something to say about the matter—even in ages much more reticent than our own. The indexes of sexuality will read all the way from the extraordinary innocence of Howells' society, through the self-conscious sinning of Dreiser's characters, to the casual promiscuity of Kerouac's beatniks. In each case the personal predilection of the author colors his testimony, but actual shifts in the moral weather are nevertheless registered.

Good novelists have a fine sensitivity for observing the right things and putting their observations into appropriate words; they capture the quality of events. This gives their testimony a vividness that material culled from more prosaic sources often lacks.

Yet it must be conceded that the novelist looks at life from a special viewpoint. He differs from other people in his creative impulse, his imaginative powers, and his verbal skills. His writing is more like portraiture than photography, because it suppresses the less important details to emphasize dominant qualities. Manipulating his treatment of people and events, the novelist heightens the impact of his story. He is also likely to be a person of strong opinions and biases, liking or disliking businessmen, ministers, Jews, Negroes, or farmers—and his biases often color his writing. Above all, of course, the novelist injects his imagination, and his imagined episodes have a symbolic quality, differing radically from drab reality.

Students of history who venture to use novels as sources of history ought therefore to proceed with caution. They should ask in each case what kind of person the novelist was, what his prejudices were, how much opportunity for observation he had, and what other people thought of his accuracy. All this is much more important to the student of history than to the literary critic. To the latter, the novel is to a large extent an isolated object of criticism, whose worth is a matter of internal qualities of arrangement, meaning, and language; and to concentrate on the author and his background is to deal with things largely irrelevant to making judgments about the value of his work. But to the student of history, the novelist is a witness testifying about the past, and to judge the value of his testimony it is imperative to have some knowledge about the man himself.

III

If we wish to understand today's America, we will do well to take a close look at the forces that were moving through American society a generation ago. All division of history into periods is somewhat arbitrary——an attempt to impose a measure of order on the ceaseless flow of events——but there is a certain logic in regarding the years between 1910 and 1940 as a distinct epoch. Even before World War I, what was left of American innocence—both reality and myth—was in a state of disintegration. The process was accelerated both by the war itself and postwar developments. The businessman's America surged to a peak of confidence during the twenties, only to collapse in frightened disorder during the Depression. The thirties were marked by vast discontent on the part of the oppressed classes. There was no violent explosion, because the New Deal provided a safety valve; yet the old confidence in automatic progress was severely shaken. A new society, urbanized, sophisticated, yet troubled, was taking shape.

These years, in short, were years of change. And what, one might ask, is so remarkable about that? Is not all American history a record of change? This is true, of course, yet the changes of those years are closely linked to the shaping of our own society, a society of affluence and of poverty, of complacent suburbs and of decaying cities, of resentful Negroes and of stubborn whites.

As witnesses to the changing America of the years 1910 to 1940, a talented generation of American novelists is available. To name only eight from a list that might be made much longer, Sinclair Lewis, F. Scott Fitzgerald, John Dos Passos, William Faulkner, Thomas Wolfe, John Steinbeck, James T. Farrell, and Richard Wright all came to maturity during these years. This group began to produce notable books in 1920, when Lewis' *Main Street* and Fitzgerald's *This Side of Paradise* appeared. Although all but Wolfe and Fitzgerald were alive and still writing after World War II, they had already done most of their best work. Their novels, for the most part, dealt either with the years of their remembered youth, just before and during World War I, or with their years of adulthood in the twenties and thirties. All eight of them were acutely aware of the strong forces of change bearing down upon their familiar world.

Sinclair Lewis, brought up in a small Minnesota town, was torn between affection for the village virtues of simplicity and friendliness and distaste for the village vices of dullness and censoriousness. During the World War I period he saw the villages changing for the worse as the money-grabbing booster spirit took over. And in the rapidly growing American cities of the twenties Lewis saw the same corrupting forces at work. Realtors, physicians, clergymen—all shared the new passion for self-advertisement and monetary success.

F. Scott Fitzgerald witnessed within himself the demoralizing tendencies of the day. As a relatively poor boy in rich men's schools and colleges, he envied his more fortunate friends. He loved the good manners and gaiety of the rich. The stories and novels that he wrote about these people brought him the money to share briefly their style of living. Yet a melancholy feeling of doom hovered over Fitzgerald's personal life and his work. In the frenetic pleasure-seeking of the playboys and the flappers, in the selfish arrogance of the established rich, and in the vulgar ostentation of the newly rich, Fitzgerald saw a generation gyrating ever faster toward catastrophe.

The world of William Faulkner was far removed from those of Lewis and Fitzgerald. Yet even more disturbing winds were blowing through the decaying mansions of Mississippi. The old families were running out in idiocy and in futility; new clans of shifty and avaricious riffraff were displacing them. And beneath this jostling white world of change was the black world of impoverished sharecroppers and ill-paid servants, for the most part still biding its time, but showing ominous signs of potential violence.

Growing up in Asheville, North Carolina, Thomas Wolfe experienced the tensions of both South and North. Like Faulkner, he knew at firsthand the power struggle of the whites and the callous exploitation of the Negroes. Like Lewis, he saw greed for money take obsessive possession of his home town. He regarded the Great Depression as a classic retribution for the national sin of avarice.

Even more than Wolfe, John Steinbeck deplored the corrupting spirit of the times. By nature a romantic, he loved the California of his boyhood, a lush agricultural paradise where men lived close to nature in sturdy independence. All this was lost when great corporations bought up the land and hired migrant workers to harvest their vast estates. The migrants, as Steinbeck knew them, were a displaced people, sturdy yeomen impoverished by the commercialization of midwestern agriculture.

Between 1910 and 1940 American radicalism fed upon the abundant discontent of the times. Yet radicalism itself underwent a significant change during these years. The rebels of pre-World War I days found outlets for their energies in a dozen different channels. They were populists, single-taxers, socialists, anarchists, and syndicalists. They were passionate, idealistic, and sacrificial. At least they seemed so to the young John Dos Passos, never really poor himself yet alienated from affluent society. But the radicalism of eccentric individuality was engulfed by the Communist brand of radicalism, tightly-disciplined and cynically opportunistic. The affection that Dos Passos had recorded for the old left gave way to a bitter hatred of the changed and corrupted left of the thirties.

Sensitive novelists were alive to the explosive changes in the modern metropolis much earlier than the politicians were. James T. Farrell grew up in Chicago and watched his relatives and friends struggle futilely against the city's corrupting forces. He saw Irish neighborhoods complacently confident of the superior morality inculcated by family, church, and school speedily demoralized by bad liquor and brutal sexuality. He witnessed the growing violence as the Irish, the Germans, and the Italians struck out first against the Jews and then, much more brutally, against the Negroes.

The youngest of the novelists discussed in this book is Richard Wright, born in 1908. Appropriately, it is Wright, the Negro, who describes what was the most momentous change of all in the light of our contemporary experience. He writes of the great uprooting of southern Negroes who fled from the poverty and injustice of the South in quest of opportunity in the great cities of the North. He tells of their dangerous disillusionment when they discovered in their new home a system of white exploitation and discrimination, less explicit but even more frustrating than what they had known in the South. The blind violence of Wright's individual Negroes clearly foreshadows the collective fury of the Negro riots a generation later.

What follows is not history, but material for history. This is how sensitive and articulate observers described those aspects of American life which they knew best. In the testimony of the novelists there is much exaggeration and bias. But a consideration of each author's background will suggest the corrections that need to be made for his special angle of vision. Flawed though the mirror may be, the novels provide a vivid reflection of a significant age of social change.

2

Knockers and Boosters

Tell me, Mr. Pollock, what *is* the matter with Gopher Prairie?"

"Is anything the matter with it? Isn't there perhaps something the matter with you and me?

SINCLAIR LEWIS, *Main Street* [1]

IN 1920, Sinclair Lewis was a thirty-five year old man who had been practising the writing trade for a dozen years without success. His apprenticeship had included every menial task; he had been a sweeper of editorial offices, a cub reporter on provincial newspapers, a composer of fund-raising letters and advertisements, a reader of publishers' manuscripts, and a book reviewer. He had finally ventured to give up his meagre pay checks for the even more meagre rewards of selling short stories and articles to the magazines. Between 1914 and 1919, he published five novels—all of them, he himself said, dead before the ink was dry.[2]

And then came sudden fame with the appearance of *Main Street* in October, 1920. Most of the reviews were intensely favorable. The most respected critics of the day—men like Heywood Broun, Ludwig Lewisohn, Carl Van Doren, and Henry L. Mencken—praised the novel's acid honesty, and William Allen White wished that it might be made compulsory reading for Kansas school chil-

[1] Sinclair Lewis, *Main Street: The Story of Carol Kennicott* (New York: Harcourt, Brace and Company, 1920), 155.

[2] Sinclair Lewis, *The Man from Main Street: Selected Essays and Other Writings: 1904–1950,* edited by Harry E. Maule and Melville H. Cane (New York: Pocket Books, 1963), 53–54.

dren.[3] Across the country the book profited by that word-of-mouth advertising that provides any product, whether utilitarian or artistic, with its cheapest and most effective publicity. Even people who rarely read anything thought it necessary to have an opinion on *Main Street.*

Why the excitement? In later years Lewis explained it very simply. *Main Street,* he said, was "my first novel to rouse the embattled peasantry." [4] The unique nobility and happiness of village life had been one of the most treasured American myths, and Lewis had attacked the myth. The indignation of small town readers might have been expected; what was more remarkable was the condemnation voiced by many city readers who still clung to their nostalgic memories of rural life. In the *New York Times Magazine,* Catherine Beach Ely condemned the new novel as a "mud puddle of sordid tattle" and recorded her yearning for "a true picture of life as seen by a wholesome mind"—like that of Booth Tarkington.[5] Even Hamlin Garland, who had himself led the way toward a more realistic view of village life, grumbled that Lewis was "belittling" the descendants of the old frontier.[6] Hundreds of thousands, Lewis happily recalled, read the book "with the same masochistic pleasure that one has in sucking an aching tooth." [7]

From this triumph Lewis learned that he had one unique gift, that of writing books "which so acutely annoyed American smugness that some thousands of my fellow-citizens felt they must read these scandalous documents, whether they liked them or not." [8] His second attempt was equally successful. In *Babbitt,* published in 1922, Lewis pounced joyously on the myth of the self-made businessman. Not all Americans had regarded the businessman as a hero; indeed the populists had found in him a sinister villain. But at least the businessman had always been taken seriously. Lewis earned fat royalties by depicting him as a clown and a bore.

What should he do next? Readers and critics called upon him to outgrow his negativism and define his values. He met this chal-

---

[3] Mark Schorer, *Sinclair Lewis: An American Life* (New York: McGraw-Hill Book Company, Inc., 1961), 285.

[4] *The Man from Main Street,* 54.

[5] C. B. Ely, "A Belated Promenade on Main Street," *New York Times Book Review and Magazine* (May 8, 1921) 16.

[6] Schorer, *op. cit.,* 269.   [7] *The Man from Main Street,* 54.   [8] *Ibid.,* 53–54.

lenge with *Arrowsmith* (1925), a novel that idealized the true man of science. Yet even in this book he contrasted the dedicated hero with the fee-grabbing country-club doctors who dominated the medical profession. In *Elmer Gantry* (1927), Lewis returned to his old formula in a savage lampooning of the Protestant clergy.

Sinclair Lewis was not the first writer to gain fame by outraging his readers. In the eighteenth century Voltaire had provided a brilliant model; during the early twentieth century Henry L. Mencken was profitably attacking his fellow-countrymen as "boobs," "morons," and "yokels." Indeed Lewis sometimes seemed to be merely fictionalizing the stereotypes that Mencken had created.

Yet Lewis is a more interesting witness to history than Mencken for two reasons: first, Lewis had more opportunity and talent for first-hand observation than Mencken had; and second, Lewis had a saving affection for the very people he was ridiculing. In a curious way, Lewis himself was part village yokol and part hustling businessman. Indeed as he grew older his middle-class sympathies became more obvious. In *Dodsworth* (1929), the simplicity and genuineness of an American businessman is contrasted sharply with the sham of both American and European culture-snobs.

II

Although Sinclair Lewis innocently denied that he had any particular village in mind when he wrote *Main Street*, the residents of Sauk Centre, Minnesota, were not fooled. The new literary lion was the youngest son of their own town physician, Dr. Edwin Lewis. Young Harry, as he was then known, had spent his boyhood in Sauk Centre before leaving for eastern schools. The Gopher Prairie of the novel was clearly Sauk Centre. At first the town fathers condemned the book as an outrage, but they soon realized that it had brought a kind of fame, however invidious, to their community. Presently they were catering to the tourist trade at the "Gopher Prairie Inn" and the "Main Street Theater." When Sauk Centre's most famous son came home on occasional visits, he was greeted with appropriate jubilation.[9]

[9] Schorer, *op. cit.*, 270.

This is America . . .   Sinclair Lewis, *Main Street*

So heated was the discussion of *Main Street* that the novel's characters acquired a life of their own, and Americans debated the virtues and vices of Carol Kennicott and her husband, Dr. Will Kennicott. Many readers, especially women bored with their own bumbling husbands and dreary home towns, pronounced the rebellious Carol to be a thoroughly admirable person. But others, even those fully aware of Gopher Prairie's limitations, regarded Carol as a silly creature. Discontented and captious, she expended her energies in crusades to convert the village heathen to Georgian architecture, Strindberg plays, and classic dancing, leaving it to more prosaic citizens to work for better schools.

Who was Carol Kennicott? Inscribing a copy of *Main Street* to his first wife, the novelist wrote: "To Gracie, who is all the good part of Carol." [10] Undoubtedly Lewis had gained a new perspective on his home town by watching his young wife's reactions, when he first brought her there on an extended visit, in 1916. Yet Carol resembled Grace Lewis only superficially. Perceptive friends of the

[10] *Ibid.,* 286.

author proposed a much more challenging identification: was not Carol Kennicott really Sinclair Lewis himself? On at least one recorded occasion Lewis coyly admitted: "Yes . . . Carol is 'Red' Lewis: always groping for something she isn't capable of attaining, always dissatisfied, always relentlessly straining to see what lies just over the horizon, intolerant of her surroundings, yet lacking any clearly defined vision of what she really wants to do or be." [11] Mark Schorer, Lewis' perceptive biographer, suggests that Lewis projected one side of his personality in Carol and another in Will Kennicott. The conflict between Carol and her husband is thus a conflict within the author himself. At times Lewis seems to look at Gopher Prairie through the eyes of the rebellious Carol; at other times he appears to accept the viewpoint of the complacent Doctor Will.

When Carol Kennicott came as a bride to Gopher Prairie she was dismayed by the town's physical ugliness. Standing at the corner of Main Street and Washington Avenue, she saw the village as a dreary island in a drearier sea of harsh prairie. If the town had had the crowded houses and crooked alleys of a European village, she might have felt a sense of community, but this was impossible with the broad straight streets. Gazing down these wide gashes, the newcomer was overwhelmed by the vast open spaces of the surrounding country. Even the villagers' efforts to nurture shade trees and lawns gave a somewhat pathetic impression.[12]

In 1912, when Carol first saw Gopher Prairie, the town boasted eleven miles of concrete sidewalks but no paved roads. Main Street's wide expanse of mud was cluttered with Ford cars and lumber wagons. Its most pretentious building, the Minniemashie House, was "a tall lean shabby structure, three stories of yellow-streaked wood, the corners covered with sanded pine slabs purporting to symbolize stone." Inside, Carol could see a stretch of bare and dirty floor, a line of rickety chairs interspersed with brass cuspidors. The dining room beyond this dingy lobby was "a jungle of stained table-clothes and catsup bottles." [13]

Most of the Main Street business district consisted of shabby two-storey brick buildings. In one of these a grocery store invited customers with a window displaying overripe bananas and lettuce

[11] *Ibid.*, 286 n.   [12] *Main Street*, 33.   [13] *Ibid.*, 34.

on which a cat was sleeping. On the second floor were the lodge rooms of the Knights of Pythias and other fraternal orders. The meat market reeked of blood; the Greek candy store pulsated with the whine of a peanut roaster; the tobacco store was filled with young men shaking dice for cigarettes and ogling pictures of "coy fat prostitutes in striped bathing suits." Two garages stood on opposite sides of the street, one dedicated to the magic name of Ford and the other to Buick. Ugly though they were, the garages were "the most energetic and vital places in town." [14] Lewis explains:

"It was not only the unsparing unapologetic ugliness and the rigid straightness which overwhelmed her. It was the planlessness, the flimsy temporariness of the buildings, their faded unpleasant colors. The street was cluttered with electric light poles, telephone poles, gasoline pumps for motor cars, boxes of goods. Each man had built with the most valiant disregard of all the others." [15]

The domestic architecture of Gopher Prairie was equally depressing. The old family home to which Dr. Kennicott brought his bride was a square brown house at the end of a narrow concrete walk. It had a screened porch with pillars of thin painted pine surmounted by scrolls and brackets of jigsawed wood. Dr. Kennicott's friend, Sam Clark, lived in a recently-built house, one of the largest in town. Yet Carol found little to envy in this home. "It had a clean sweep of clapboards, a solid squareness, a small tower, and a large screened porch. Inside, it was as shiny, as hard, and as cheerful as a new oak upright piano." [16]

Yet Gopher Prairie's drab appearance was the least important count in Carol Kennicott's indictment of the town. Much more damning was the pettiness and monotony of small-town life. "I tell you it's dull," she complained to a sympathetic male visitor from the outside world. *"Dull!"* [17] Even the town's parties were dreary. At the one given to welcome Carol the guests sat in a rigid circle trying to talk to one another. "They sat up with gaiety as with a corpse." [18] Conversation as the exchange of ideas or even as lighthearted banter—Carol's kind—did not exist. Instead the talkers rattled on about trivial personalities, while the quiet ones listened. With the men the only sure-fire topic was automobiles. When con-

[14] *Ibid.*, 35–36.   [15] *Ibid.*, 37.
[16] *Ibid.*, 40.   [17] *Ibid.*, 284.   [18] *Ibid.*, 46.

versation of even this low order ran down, someone proposed stunts, and six of Gopher Prairie's more spirited citizens performed: Dave Dyer impersonated a Norwegian catching a hen, Ella Stowbody sang "Old Sweetheart of Mine," and the others parodied Mark Anthony's funeral oration, and told stories about Jews, Irishmen, and juveniles. During the following winter Carol had frequent opportunities to see these performances repeated.

The social structure of Gopher Prairie was less simple than these bucolic revels might suggest. As the wife of a physician, Carol easily gained admission to the "Jolly Seventeen." Composed mostly of young married women, the Jolly Seventeen met one afternoon a week to play bridge; once a month the husbands joined them for dinner and evening bridge; twice a year they had dances at the Odd Fellows Hall. Many members of the Jolly Seventeen also belonged to Thanatopsis, the women's study group. Despite this overlapping of membership the Jolly Seventeen sniffed at the dowdy earnestness of the other group. Eschewing the frivolity of bridge, the ladies improved their minds with papers on literary and artistic topics. To Carol's bewilderment, they undertook to review all the English poets in one afternoon. Shakespeare and Milton were lumped into one ten minute report; Byron, Scott, Moore, and Burns into a second; Tennyson and Browning into a third; and Coleridge, Mrs. Hemans, and other miscellaneous worthies into a fourth. Then reports Lewis, "Gopher Prairie had finished the poets. It was ready for next week's labor: English Fiction and Essays." [19]

The Jolly Seventeen and Thanatopsis drew their membership from Gopher Prairie's aristocracy, succinctly defined by Lewis as "all persons engaged in a profession, or earning more than twenty-five hundred dollars a year, or possessed of grandparents born in America." [20] Those who belonged enjoyed the privilege of looking down upon those who did not. Among the objects of their condescension were the German and Scandinavian farmers, the mechanics and wageworkers, and the domestic servants. When Carol developed a somewhat indiscreet friendship with Erik Valborg, an apprentice tailor, her offense was more against the town's sense of caste than against her marriage obligations.

[19] *Ibid.*, 127.   [20] *Ibid.*, 74.

Since it was the hall-mark of middle class respectability, in 1912, to have a maid, the members of the Jolly Seventeen loved to exchange complaints about their hired girls. Juanita Haydock moaned: "They're ungrateful, all that class of people. I do think the domestic problem is simply becoming awful. I don't know what the country is coming to, with these Scandinavian clodhoppers demanding every cent you can save, and so ignorant and impertinent, and on my word, demanding bath-tubs and everything—as if they weren't mighty good and lucky at home if they got a bath in the wash-tub." [21]

The Gopher Prairie aristocracy reserved their ultimate scorn for the poor. Still prevalent was the old Protestant conviction that poverty and unworthiness were synonymous terms. Sam Clark, one of the more likeable local citizens, explained that in Gopher Prairie "you don't get any of this poverty that you find in cities—always plenty of work—no need of charity—man got to be blamed shiftless if he don't get ahead." [22] Yet to Carol's anxious eyes, more than a few villagers seemed to be desperately poor. She proposed to Thanatopsis an effort to help these unfortunates with an employment agency and a home-building fund, but the Gopher Prairie ladies preferred to administer charity in their own way. The minister's wife hated to think of a world in which the more fortunate were deprived of all the pleasure of giving. "Besides, if these shiftless folks realize they're getting charity, and not something to which they have a right, they're so much more grateful." [23] The ladies gained a comfortable sense of virtue from giving their cast-off clothing to the poor and rejected with scorn Carol's suggestion that they ought at least to mend the garments before passing them on.

Supporting the social class system were pillars of economic fact. Although Gopher Prairie was in the heart of the Minnesota wheat-lands, the burghers were not themselves farmers. They made their money storing and processing crops; selling hardware, drugs, lumber, and dry goods; loaning money; and practicing medicine, law, and religion. No less devoted to money-making than their contemporaries in the large cities, the business and professional men of Gopher Prairie avidly speculated in land. In 1912, Dr. Will Kennicott was marveling at the recent rise in the price of wheatlands; six years later he was sharing in the prosperity of World War I.

The wheat money did not remain in the pockets of the farmers; the towns existed to take care of all that. Iowa farmers were selling their land at four hundred dollars an acre and coming into Minnesota. But whoever bought or sold or mortgaged, the townsmen invited themselves to the feast—millers, real-estate men, lawyers, merchants, and Dr. Will Kennicott. They bought land at a hundred and fifty, sold it next day at a hundred and seventy, and bought again. In three months Kennicott made seven thousand dollars, which was rather more than four times as much as society paid him for healing the sick.[24]

Comfortable and complacent, Gopher Prairie's ruling class hated any challenge to existing institutions. Even such mild threats to the local profit system as mail-order houses and farmers' cooperatives caused alarm. Before World War I Gopher Prairie, like most small American towns, had a few self-proclaimed radicals who refused to genuflect before the local aristocrats. These village rebels usually compounded their guilt by their religious agnosticism and by their Scandinavian or German-sounding names—like Miles Bjornstam, who was referred to as "that damn lazy big-mouthed calamity-howler that ain't satisfied with the way we run things." [25] The suspicious townsmen resented all evidences of disbelief. "Knockers" and "kickers" were regarded as scarcely less undesirable than socialists and anarchists. In her feeble efforts to reform the town, Carol Kennicott risked being branded as one of these knockers herself.

Gopher Prairie possessed many means to whip non-conformists into line. Carol perceived that the churches were the strongest of the forces compelling respectability. Although not a regular church-goer himself, Dr. Will asserted, "Sure, religion is a fine influence—got to have it to keep the lower classes in order—fact, it's the only thing that appeals to a lot of those fellows and makes 'em respect the rights of property." [26] But the repression of radicalism was not left entirely to the preachers. Carol learned from Ezra Stowbody, the most powerful local banker, that Swedes were not to

be trusted—if you didn't watch them they turned socialist or pop-
ulist on you in a minute. "Of course," Stowbody explained, "if they
have loans you can make 'em listen to reason. I just have 'em come
into the bank for a talk, and tell 'em a few things. I don't mind their
being democrats, so much, but I won't stand having socialists
around." [27]

The town punished non-conformity in behaviour even more
severely than heterodoxy in ideas. To Carol's indignation, the
school board fired Fern Mullins, a high school teacher whose only
real offense was that she was young and frivolous. During her early
days in Gopher Prairie, Carol had heard Dr. Will contrast the
independence of western towns with the servitude of eastern cities,
where one had constantly to be on guard against criticism. He
boasted, "Everybody's free here to do what he wants to." [28] But
later when he discovered that Carol was developing an affection
for Erik Valborg, he warned: "Course you like him. That isn't the
real rub. But haven't you just seen what this town can do, once it
goes and gets moral on you, like it did with Fern? You probably
think that two young people making love are alone if anybody ever
is, but there's nothing in this town that you don't do in company
with a whole lot of uninvited but awful interested guests." [29]

III

World War I disrupted life throughout America, and Gopher
Prairie illustrated the process. The young men went off to war; the
older men bought Liberty Bonds; the women made bandages and
did without sugar. Vicarious war-making was most evident in the
vigor with which the townsmen castigated the enemy. The village
librarian "raved that though America hated war as much as ever, we
must invade Germany and wipe out every man, because it was now
proven that there was no soldier in the German army who was not
crucifying prisoners and cutting off babies' hands." [30] Since the
Germans in Germany were far away, the Gopher Prairie militants
took out their vengeance on victims nearer at hand. One dissipated

[27] *Ibid.*, 49.   [28] *Ibid.*, 98.   [29] *Ibid.*, 395.   [30] *Ibid.*, 411.

local youth "got much reputation by whipping a farmboy named Adolph Pochbauer for being a 'damn hyphenated German.'" [31]

But small town America found its favorite scapegoats in suspected radicals. At the county seat, a mob of a hundred businessmen rode an organizer for the National Non-partisan League out of town on a fence rail, for defying the sheriff's ban against speaking at a farmers' political meeting. The worthies of Gopher Prairie applauded gleefully. "That's the way to treat those fellows—only they ought to have lynched him!" said Sam Clark.[32]

As Carol and Dr. Will both, in their own ways, perceived, the zeal with which radicals were harassed during the war bore some relationship to the money-making mania unleashed by the conflict. With high agricultural prices and unprecedented opportunities for quick profits in land speculation, Gopher Prairie businessmen were flush with optimism. The Commercial Club launched a Watch-Gopher-Prairie-Grow campaign at a banquet in the Minniemashie House, memorable for gold-printed menus, free cigars, and "oratorical references to Pep, Punch, Go, Vigor, Enterprise, Red Blood, He-Man, Fair Women, God's Country, James J. Hill, the Blue Sky, the Green Fields, the Bountiful Harvest, Increasing Population, Fair Return on Investments, Alien Agitators Who Threaten the Security of Our Institutions, the Hearthstone, the Foundation of the State, Senator Knute Nelson, One Hundred Per Cent Americanism, and Pointing with Pride." [33]

To Carol who measured progress in more gracious voices, more amusing conversation, more questing minds, the Watch-Gopher-Prairie-Grow campaign was the ultimate indignity. "She could, she asserted, endure a shabby but modest town; the town shabby and egomaniac she could not endure." [34]

And so in October, 1918, Carol sought escape by leaving her husband in Gopher Prairie and embarking for a career of her own in the city of Washington. Poor Kennicott, standing forlornly on the station platform as the train carried away his wife and son, was an unwilling witness to the woman's revolt, still another social change accelerated by World War I. "I could run an office or a

---

[31] *Ibid.*, 275.   [32] *Ibid.*, 419.   [33] *Ibid.*, 414.   [34] *Ibid.*, 417.

library, or nurse and teach children," Carol explained. "But solitary dish-washing isn't enough to satisfy me—or many other
women. We're going to chuck it. We're going to wash 'em by
machinery, and come out and play with you men in the offices and
clubs and politics you've so cleverly kept for yourselves! Oh, we're
hopeless, we dissatisfied women!" [35]

Although sketchily written, the Washington episode plays a significant part in *Main Street*. Here the identification of Carol Kennicott with her creator Sinclair Lewis is close. From October, 1918,
to June, 1920, Carol remained in the national capital; from September 26, 1919 to June 1, 1920, Sinclair Lewis and his wife were
living in a rented house in Washington while he finished the manuscript of the novel.[36]

The national capital was a singularly appropriate place for both
Carol and Lewis to gain a better perspective of Gopher Prairie. In
many ways Carol found the romance and excitement for which she
had yearned. Her job in a government war agency was routine and
monotonous, yet it gave her a feeling of independence. She also did
volunteer work addressing envelopes for the woman suffrage
headquarters, where she met interesting people. Scores of visitors
sat around her flat "talking, talking, talking, not always wisely but
always excitedly." [37]

Yet even while she was reveling in this different environment,
Carol recognized in Washington—as she had on an earlier trip to
California—"a transplanted and guarded Main Street." She noted
"the cautious dullness of Gopher Prairie" in gossipy Washington
boardinghouses, in the pews of the churches, in Sunday motor pro-
cessions, and at the dinners organized by the various state societies.
More important, Carol learned that Gopher Prairie was far from
being the worst small city in the nation. She heard of railroad towns
devoid of lawns and trees, of New England mill towns with ugly
rows of workers' cottages, of southern towns full of magnolia and
white columns, but hating the Negroes and obsequious to the Old
Families. Carol began to blame institutions rather than individ-
uals. Institutions "insinuate their tyranny under a hundred guises

[35] *Ibid.*, 421.   [36] Schorer, *op. cit.*, 259.   [37] *Main Street*, 428.

and pompous names, such as Polite Society, the Family, the Church, Sound Business, the Party, the Country, the Superior White Race; and the only defense against them, Carol beheld, is unembittered laughter." [38]

Having thus learned the gift of unembittered laughter, Carol returned to Main Street, Dr. Will Kennicott, and a new baby. Still a romantic, she now saw Gopher Prairie as a toiling new settlement. She sympathized with Kennicott's defense of its citizens as "a lot of pretty good folks, working hard and trying to bring up their families the best they can." She felt compassion for "their assertion of culture, even as expressed in Thanatopsis papers, for their pretenses of greatness, even as trumpeted in 'boosting.' " [39]

If Carol's conversion to Kennicott's set of values is unconvincing, it will help the puzzled reader to recall Sinclair Lewis's own divided feelings. One part of him was Carol Kennicott; the other Will. Although he allows Will to have the last word in the novel, he carries more conviction in those earlier passages where Carol spells out what is wrong with Gopher Prairie. "It is," she insists,

an unimaginative standardized background, a sluggishness of speech and manners, a rigid ruling of the spirit by the desire to appear respectable. It is contentment . . . the contentment of the quiet dead, who are scornful of the living for their restless walking. It is negation canonized as the one positive virtue. It is the prohibition of happiness. It is slavery self-sought and self-defended. It is dullness made God. A savorless people, gulping tasteless food, and sitting afterward, coatless and thoughtless, in rocking chairs prickly with inane decorations, listening to mechanical music, saying mechanical things about the excellencies of Ford automobiles, and viewing themselves as the greatest race in the world. [40]

Sinclair Lewis, in this bitter moment, was characterizing more than his home town of Sauk Centre, Minnesota. Doubtless all small towns, in all countries, in all ages, had a tendency to be not only dull but mean, bitter, and meddlesome. The American village, however, was uniquely menacing. "It is," Lewis wrote, "a force seeking to dominate the earth." American society functioned ad-

---

[38] *Ibid.*, 430.   [39] *Ibid.*, 442.   [40] *Ibid.*, 265.

mirably in the mass production of automobiles, watches, and safety razors. But it would not be satisfied until the entire world also admitted that the end and joyous purpose of living was to ride in flivvers. "And such a society, such a nation, is determined by the Gopher Prairies. The greatest manufacturer is but a busier Sam Clark, and all the rotund senators and presidents are village lawyers and bankers grown nine feet tall." [41] In the preface to *Main Street,* Lewis began with the words, "This is America . . ."

[41] *Ibid.,* 267.

It is an unimaginative standardized background . . .   Sinclair Lewis, *Main Street*

IV

Having attacked the American village so profitably, Sinclair Lewis planned his next campaign against the American city—not the gargantuan city, like New York or Chicago—but the city of intermediate size, more characteristic of the Middle West. In one of his notebooks he commented on the fact that American novelists had often written about the largest cities and about the villages, but had neglected the "enormously important type" of community that lay between these extremes—"the city of a few hundred thousand, the metropolis that yet is a village, the world-center that yet is ruled by cautious villagers." Only Booth Tarkington and a few local celebrities had dealt with these cities "which more than any New York, produce our wares and elect our presidents—and buy our books." [42]

Lewis was fascinated by the extent to which the character of Gopher Prairie had survived in these cities. "Villages—overgrown towns—three-quarters of a million people still dressing, eating, building houses, attending church, to make an impression on their neighbors, quite as they did back on Main Street, in villages of two thousand." [43] Yet these cities were "industrially magnificent." They supplied half the world with motor cars, machine tools, flour, locomotives, rails, electric equipment—"with necessities miraculous and admirable." [44]

After the publication of *Babbitt* in 1922, several American cities began to compete for the somewhat dubious distinction of having provided Lewis with his model. Duluth, where Lewis had spent several weeks in 1918, and Minneapolis, where he spent the following winter had plausible cases, but Cincinnati had the best claim of all. Early in 1921, Lewis made the Queen City Club in Cincinnati his headquarters while he made brief trips to lecture in other midwestern cities. All the while he was filling his notebooks with material for his new novel. To Alfred Harcourt, his publisher,

[42] *The Man from Main Street*, 27.　　[43] *Ibid.*, 24.　　[44] *Ibid.*, 23.

he wrote: "Bully time, met lots of people, really getting the feeling of life here. Fine for Babbitt. . . ." [45]

Yet Zenith was not Cincinnati in the same sense that Gopher Prairie was Sauk Centre. Zenith already existed in Lewis's imagination before he went looking for it. An earlier letter to Harcourt suggests the process: "Some time this winter I'm going to some Midwestern city—say Cincinnati or Dayton or Milwaukee—and complete the material for the next novel which I made a good beginning of gathering in Minneapolis, St. Paul, Seattle, San Francisco, New Haven, Washington . . . I want to make my city of 300,000 just as real and definitive in the novel as I made, or tried to make, Gopher Prairie." [46]

Unlike Gopher Prairie which lived in the imperishable memories of Lewis's youth, Zenith was created with cunning calculation. Mrs. Lewis wrote of her husband's "most astonishingly complete series of maps of Zenith, so that the city, the suburbs, the state [were] as clear as clear" in his mind.[47] Holed up in English inns with his typewriter, Lewis asked Harcourt's secretary to send him the material that he needed to fortify his novel with convincing detail——copies of *House Beautiful,* the *American Magazine,* the *Saturday Evening Post,* and real estate brochures. This process of synthesis does not necessarily detract from the historical value of *Babbitt* and subsequent novels about Zenith. How was Lewis so sure of the cities that he wanted to visit? Why did he collect these particular magazines and pamphlets? Was it not because he already knew Zenith and George F. Babbitt through his earlier wanderings?

For a man notorious for verbosity, Lewis was an extraordinarily acute listener. In a revealing self-portrait of 1930, Lewis wrote:

The fact is that my foreign traveling has been a quite uninspiring recreation, a flight from reality. My real traveling has been sitting in Pullman smoking cars, in a Minnesota village, on a Vermont farm, in a hotel in Kansas City or Savannah, listening to the normal daily drone of what are to me the most fascinating and exotic people in the world—the Average Citizens of the United States, with their friendliness to strangers

[45] Lewis to Harcourt, Feb. 16, 1921, Harrison Smith (ed.) *From Main Street to Stockholm: Letters of Sinclair Lewis, 1919–1930* (New York: Harcourt, Brace and Company, 1952), 63.
[46] Lewis to Harcourt, Nov. 12, 1920, *ibid.,* 44.
[47] Grace Lewis to Harcourt, July 20, 1921, *ibid.,* 79.

and their rough teasing, their passion for material advancement and their shy idealism, their interest in all the world and their boastful provincialism—the intricate complexities which an American novelist is privileged to portray.[48]

And so Lewis put together his composite picture of the city of Zenith, the city where George F. Babbitt sold real estate, Dr. Martin Arrowsmith served his internship, the Reverend Elmer Gantry preached, and Sam Dodsworth made a million dollars.

In 1920, the glossy and the shabby elbowed each other along Zenith streets. Piercing the morning mist were "austere towers of steel and cement and limestone, sturdy as cliffs and delicate as silver rods." But these recently-built cathedrals of commerce could not conceal the survivals from the nineteenth century: "the Post Office with its shingle-tortured mansard, the red brick minarets of hulking old houses, factories with stingy and sooted windows, wooden tenements colored like mud." [49]

This contrast between the new Zenith and the old became still sharper in the late 1920's. The general office of the Revelation Motor Company was "an immense glass and marble building" opposite the "flashing new skyscraper" of the Plymouth National Bank. The entrance to the executive offices was "like the lobby of a prententious hotel—waiting-room in brocade and tapestry and Grand Rapids renaissance." But to reach this marble palace Sam Dodsworth had to drive along Conklin Avenue with its "dreary rows of old red brick mansions, decayed into boarding houses," cheap grocery stores, dirty laundries, gloomy little undertaking parlors, and uninviting lunch rooms.[50]

By 1920, the more prosperous citizens of Zenith had already moved out of these depressing neighborhoods into pleasant residential districts on the outskirts. The Babbitts lived in Floral Heights, some three miles from the heart of the city. Twenty years earlier this hill had been a wilderness of ragged brush. Indeed, a few vacant lots with flowering apple and cherry trees still survived from the old orchards. But recently-built houses stood on most of the lots, each testifying to the architectural taste of the speculator

[48] *The Man from Main Street,* 55.
[49] Sinclair Lewis, *Babbitt* (New York: New American Library, 1961), 5.
[50] Sinclair Lewis, *Dodsworth* (New York: Dell Publishing Co., 1957), 19.

who had built it. The Babbitts' residence was a white and green
Dutch colonial, five years old. It had "a simple and laudable architecture" with all the latest conveniences and a multitude of elec-
trical outlets. Babbitt's neighbor on one side lived in "a comfortable house with no architectural manners whatever; a large
wooden box with a squat tower, a broad porch and glossy paint
yellow as a yolk." A more fastidious neighbor on the other side
owned "a strictly modern house whereof the lower part was dark
red tapestry brick, with a leaded oriel, the upper part of pale stucco
like spattered clay, and the roof red-tiled." [51]

Floral Heights was soon outshone by still glossier suburbs. Sans
Souci Gardens, for example, retained the beauties of forest, hill,
and river. Its roads were not broad straight gashes but byways wind-
ing through the hills. Here, masked among trees and gardens,
astonishing houses would spring up. "They were all imitative, of
course—Italian villas and Spanish patios and Tyrolean inns and
Tudor manor-houses and Dutch Colonial farmhouses, so mingled
and crowding one another that the observer was dizzy." [52]

V

In 1920, George F. Babbitt was the moderately prosperous head
of a Zenith real estate firm. "Mighty few fellows pulling down eight
thousand dollars a year," he exulted, "eight thousand good hard
iron dollars—bet there isn't more than five per cent of the people
in the whole United States that make more than Uncle George
does, by golly! Right up at the top of the heap!" [53]

In his office Babbitt expended his energies in the dictation of
incoherent letters and the drafting of high-powered advertisements. His style of authorship was "diligently imitative of the best
literary models of the day; of heart-to-heart talk advertisements,
'sales-pulling' letters, discourses on the 'development of Will-
power,' and hand-shaking house-organs, as richly poured forth by
the new school of Poets of Business." [54] Babbitt displayed his
generalship in issuing commands to his salesman and in over-
powering the feeble resistance of potential customers.

---

[51] *Babbitt*, 23–24.   [52] *Dodsworth*, 214.   [53] *Babbitt*, 46.   [54] *Ibid.*, 32–33.

They were all imitative, of course—Italian villas and Spanish patios and Tyrolean inns and Tudor manor-houses and Dutch Colonial farm houses, . . .   Sinclair Lewis, *Dodsworth*

For Babbitt, what a businessman did was less important than how he did it. He admired energy and drive—what he called "hustling." Not Babbitt alone, but all Zenith seemed to feel this compulsion.

Men in motors were hustling to pass one another in the hustling traffic. Men were hustling to catch trolleys, with another trolley a minute behind, and to leap from the trolleys, to gallop across the sidewalk, to hurl themselves into buildings, into hustling express elevators . . . Men who had made five thousand, year before last, and ten thousand last year, were urging on nerve-yelping bodies and parched brains so that they might make twenty thousand this year; and the men who had broken down immediately after making their twenty thousand dollars were hustling to catch trains, to hustle through the vacations which the hustling doctors had ordered.

And so, Lewis remarks, Babbitt hustled back to his office one afternoon "to sit down with nothing much to do except see that the staff looked as though they were hustling." [55]

Babbitt's place in Zenith's social structure was sharply defined. He had a good income by 1920 standards, but he did not have the wealth or breeding of the automobile manufacturer, Sam Dodsworth. Babbitt was a college graduate, but he was "a sound and standard ware from that great department-store, the State University" and not a "frivolous graduate" of Yale or Princeton.[56] He was a member of the Zenith Athletic Club, which, Lewis explained, "is not athletic and it isn't exactly a club, but it is Zenith in perfection." It had a billiard room, a swimming pool, and a gymnasium. "But most of its three thousand members use it as a café in which to lunch, play cards, tell stories, meet customers, and entertain out-of-town uncles at dinner." [57] It was the largest club in the city, but not as prestigious as the exclusive Union Club. In similar fashion Babbitt belonged to the Outing Golf and Country Club rather than to the elite Tonawanda Club and to the Presbyterian Church rather than to the Episcopal Church.

Babbitt was annoyed when the business of selling real estate was not granted due recognition. "Makes me tired," he said, "the way these doctors and profs and preachers put on lugs about being 'professional men.' A good realtor has to have more knowledge and finesse than any of 'em." He insisted upon being called a realtor instead of a real estate man—"sounds more like a reg'lar profession"—and pontificated on the "public service" and "trained skill" that were required.[58] Despite these admirable ideals Babbitt did not hesitate to grab a speculative profit whenever he could get inside information about future municipal needs.

Babbitt loved to make speeches and took particular delight in delivering the annual address at the Zenith Real Estate board. This windy piece of rhetoric was put together out of Pat and Mike jokes, mixed metaphors, and boastful tributes to the city. Zenith had the

---

[55] *Ibid.*, 128.   [56] *Ibid.*, 59.   [57] *Ibid.*, 47.   [58] *Ibid.*, 130–31.

"finest school-ventilating system in the country, bar none" and "the second highest business building in any inland city in the entire country." It had "an unparalleled number of miles of paved streets, bathrooms, vacuum cleaners, and all the other signs of civilization," as well as "one motor car for every five and seven-eighths persons in the city." The only threat to Zenith and to the nation came from the scoffers. "The American business man is generous to a fault, but one thing he does demand of all teachers and lecturers and journalists: If we're going to pay them our good money, they've got to help us by selling efficiency and whooping it up for national prosperity!" As for the "blab-mouth, fault-finding, pessimistic, cynical University teachers," it was "just as much our duty to bring influence to have those cusses fired as it is to sell all the real estate and gather in all the good shekels we can." [59]

Babbitt cheerfully confessed to being a "joiner." A decent man in Zenith, Lewis pointed out, was required to belong to one, preferably two or three, of "the innumerous 'lodges' and prosperity-boosting lunch clubs; to the Rotarians, the Kiwanis, or the Boosters; to the Oddfellows, Moose, Masons, Red Men, Woodmen, Owls, Eagles, Maccabees, Knights of Pythias, Knights of Columbus, and other secret orders characterized by a high degree of heartiness, sound morals, and reverence for the Constitution." To join was good for business. It also gave to Americans "such unctuous honorifics as High Worthy Recording Scribe and Grand Hoogow to add to the commonplace distinctions of Colonel, Judge, and Professor." And it allowed "the swaddled American husband" to stay away from home one evening a week. "The lodge was his piazza, his pavement café. He could shoot pool and talk man-talk and be obscene and valiant." [60]

Particularly congenial to Babbitt's temperament was the Boosters' Club, one of whose merits was "that only two persons from each department of business were permitted to join, so that you at once encountered the Ideals of other occupations—plumbing and portrait-painting, medicine and the manufacture of chewing gum." At their weekly meetings the Boosters all wore buttons giving their names, nicknames, and occupations. A ten-cent fine was imposed

[59] *Ibid.*, 154–55.   [60] *Ibid.*, 166–67.

upon any absent-minded Booster who addressed one of his brothers by any other appelation than his nickname. The members introduced their guests with genial insults, kidded each other noisily, and engaged in boyish pranks. But they took pride in their devotion to "service" and community welfare. For example, one Booster made a fervent appeal for support of a symphony orchestra. He boasted that he didn't "care a rap for all this long-haired music," yet Culture had become as "necessary an adornment and advertisement for a city to-day as pavements or bank-clearances." [61]

When Babbitt and his friends conversed, they were usually in emphatic agreement. They solemnly told each other that radicals should be silenced, labor unions opposed, immigrants restricted, and Negroes kept in their places. In his vigorous dogmatism Babbitt accepted unthinkingly the ideas that others formulated for him.

Just as he was an Elk, a Booster, and a member of the Chamber of Commerce, just as the priests of the Presbyterian Church determined his every religious belief and the senators who controlled the Republican Party decided in little smoky rooms in Washington what he should think about disarmament, tariff, and Germany, so did the large national advertisers fix the surface of his life, fix what he believed to be his individuality. These standard advertised wares—toothpastes, socks, tires, cameras, instantaneous hot-water heaters—were his symbols and proofs of excellence; at first the signs, then the substitutes, for joy and passion and wisdom.[62]

Even in his occasional dissipations, drinking bootleg liquor and visiting red light houses, Babbitt followed convention.

In his home, Babbitt took pride in his "altogether royal bathroom of porcelain and glazed tile and metal sleek as silver." [63] He enjoyed his sleeping porch and other comforts. But his family often fretted him. Mrs. Babbitt had become "so dully habituated to married life that in her full matronliness she was as sexless as an anemic nun." [64] Conversation between husband and wife consisted largely of his grumbling complaints about things in general and her soft grunts of feigned sympathy. At the breakfast and dinner

[61] *Ibid.,* 212.   [62] *Ibid.,* 80–81.   [63] *Ibid.,* 8.   [64] *Ibid.,* 10.

. . . the innumerous 'lodges' and prosperity-boosting lunch clubs [also gave to Americans] such unctuous honorifics as High Worthy Recording Scribe and Grand Hoogow to add to the commonplace distinctions of Colonel, Judge, and Professor.   Sinclair Lewis, *Babbitt*

table, the three Babbitt children squabbled noisily among themselves, and Babbitt nagged at them constantly.

Automobiles provided one of the few subjects of common interest to the Babbitts. Discussion progressed into matters of streamlined bodies, hill-climbing power, wire wheels, chrome steel, ignition systems, and body colors. It was much more than a study of transportation, Lewis pointed out.

It was an aspiration for knightly rank. In the city of Zenith, in the barbarous twentieth century, a family's motor indicated its social rank as precisely as the grades of the peerage determined the rank of an English

family. . . . The details of precedence we never officially determined.
There was no court to decide whether the second son of a Pierce Arrow
limousine should go in to dinner before the first son of a Buick roadster,
but of their respective social importance there was no doubt; and where
Babbitt as a boy had aspired to the presidency, his son Ted aspired to a
Packard twin-six and an established position in the motored gentry.[65]

Evenings at home were depressing. The two oldest children
escaped the house as soon as they could to amuse themselves with
their friends; the youngest went protestingly to bed; and Mrs.
Babbitt darned socks and flipped through her women's magazines.
Babbitt was happy as long as he could concentrate on the comic
strips of the evening paper, but reading the stories in popular
periodicals such as *The American Magazine* held his attention only
fitfully. After a little rambling conversation with Mrs. Babbitt, he
would retire to the second floor at an early hour and lounge lan-
guidly in the bathtub.

At least once a week Babbitt took his wife and youngest daughter to the movies. The American cinema was then entering its
golden age. Zenith's vast Chateau Theater had a palace-like lobby
with a rotunda ceiling, walls hung with pseudo-medieval tapestries,
parakeets sitting on lotus columns, and chairs upholstered in
embroidered velevet. To create the proper mood to accompany the
silent films, a fifty-piece orchestra played with alternating gusto
and pathos. As Babbitt so aptly remarked, "You got to go some to
beat this dump!" He liked three kinds of films: "pretty bathing
girls with bare legs; policemen or cowboys and an industrious
shooting of revolvers; and funny fat men who ate spaghetti." [66]

VI

What is the student of history to make of *Babbitt?* Was the
typical businessman of a middle-sized American city a person like
this Zenith realtor? H.L. Mencken said, yes; Lewis had depicted
the businessman "with complete and absolute fidelity." [67] But

[65] *Ibid.*, 63.   [66] *Ibid.*, 129–30.
[67] H. L. Mencken, "Portrait of an American Citizen," Mark Schorer (ed.) *Sinclair
Lewis: A Collection of Critical Essays*, (Englewood Cliffs, N. J.: Prentice Hall, Inc.,
1962), 21.

Mencken's judgment in this matter is not altogether reassuring, since the Baltimore sage was not one to explore Zenith for himself.

Lewis was really kinder to Babbitt than his Baltimore friend would have been. Having portrayed Babbitt through most of the novel as a thoroughly dull, stupid, and conventional fellow, Lewis provides a rather improbable turn of plot during which Babbitt kicks over the traces. He has a love affair, defends strikers, and refuses to join a new organization of vigilante patriots. To be sure, his rebelliousness soon peters out and he comes crawling back into his old rut, but Lewis certainly suggests that the businessman is a more complex person than the Mencken stereotype.

The fairest comment on Zenith is provided by the radical lawyer Seneca Doane who seems to speak for Sinclair Lewis himself. Doane makes the point that standardization is not necessarily bad:

When I buy an Ingersoll watch or a Ford, I get a better tool for less money, and I know precisely what I'm getting, and that leaves me more time and energy to be individual in . . . No, what I fight in Zenith is standardization of thought, and, of course, the traditions of competition. The real villains of the piece are the clean, kind, industrious Family Men who use every known brand of trickery and cruelty to insure the prosperity of their cubs. The worst thing about these fellows is that they're so good and, in their work at least, so intelligent. You can't hate them properly, and yet their standardized minds are the enemy.[68]

The purpose of Lewis' exaggeration thus becomes clear. He was really fond of middle-class America. Indeed, many critics have pointed out that there was much of Babbitt in Lewis himself. Yet he deplored the standardizing tendencies of middle-class life, and he caricatured them to make his point.

In *Dodsworth* (1929), Lewis handled the businessman much more tenderly. Sam Dodsworth's position in Zenith's social hierarchy was much higher than Babbitt's. The Dodsworths were one of the oldest and most esteemed families in the city. After an expensive education at Yale and the Massachusetts Institute of Technology, Sam went to work, in 1903, for the newly-organized Revelation Motor Company. He initiated the improvements in design and shrewd pricing policies that made Revelation one of the most

[68] *Babbitt,* 85.

profitable corporations in the field. By 1925, Dodsworth had become a bona fide captain of American industry and a true believer in the Republican Party, the high tariff, and the Episcopal Church. "He was the president of the Revelation Motor Company; he was a millionaire, though decidedly not a multimillionaire; his large house was on Ridge Crest, the most fashionable street in Zenith; he had some taste in etchings; he did not split many infinitives; and he sometimes enjoyed Beethoven." [69]

Dodsworth, according to Lewis, "was none of the things which most Europeans and many Americans expect in a leader of American industry. He was not a Babbitt, not a Rotarian, not an Elk, not a deacon. He rarely shouted, never slapped people on the back, and he had attended only six baseball games since 1900." In contrast to the scarcely literate Babbitt, Dodsworth "thought rather well of Dreiser, Cabell, and so much of Proust as he had rather laboriously mastered." He played a sound game of golf and enjoyed fishing in Canadian streams. "He was common sense apotheosized, he had the energy and reliability of a dynamo, he liked whiskey and poker and pâté de foie gras." [70]

An entrepreneur of a type already becoming scarce in 1925, Dodsworth resented the economic forces that were closing in on Zenith-owned industries. Although he wanted to fight to preserve Revelation's independence, his fellow-directors were afraid of "the imperial U.A.C. with its seven makes of motors, its body-building works, its billion dollars of capital." [71] Dodsworth reconciled himself to the deal whereby for a generous price U.A.C. would absorb Revelation, but he rebelled at becoming a salaried executive in the conquering giant's monopoly.

Dodsworth's friends were less boastful and vulgar than Babbitt's, yet they were men of limited sensibilities. Able to look at them more objectively after living a few months in Europe, Dodsworth could see "that none of his prosperous industrialized friends in Zenith were very much interested in anything whatever. They had cultivated caution until they had lost the power to be interested. They were like old surly farmers." They had much to say about money, golf, and drinking, but "these diversions were to the lords of Zenith not pleasures but ways of keeping so busy that they

[69] *Dodsworth*, 15.   [70] *Ibid.*, 15–16.   [71] *Ibid.*, 16.

would not admit how bored they were, how empty of ambitions."
Except for "a testy fear of the working class," they had no interest in
politics, which they turned over to "a few seedy professional vote-
wanglers." To Zenith's leading citizens, "women were only bed-
mates, housekeepers, producers of heirs, and a home audience that
could not escape, and had to listen when everybody at the office was
tired of hearing one's grievances." [72]

Dodsworth is thus depicted as a businessman with many attractive traits, a person of unusual entrepreneurial skill, genuine
honesty and decency, and a respectful tolerance for literature and
art. Lewis does not hide his limitations, but contrasts his basic
integrity to the shallow selfishness of most other men of his class
and the snobbish frivolity of his wife.

VII

The huckstering spirit of Zenith touched not only its businessmen, but its professional people as well. In *Arrowsmith* (1925),
Sinclair Lewis contrasted his hero's dedication to medical science
with the crass commercialism of many physicians. Dr. Martin
Arrowsmith lived only briefly in Zenith, where he married a nurse
and served an internship in the Zenith General Hospital. A few
years later he took a salaried post in the public health department
of Nautilus, Iowa. With its population of seventy thousand,
Nautilus was "a smaller Zenith but no less brisk . . . The only
authentic difference between Nautilus and Zenith is that in both
cases all the streets look alike but in Nautilus they do not look alike
for so many miles." [73]

Even in medical school Arrowsmith had been shocked at the
contrast between the honest researcher Dr. Max Gottlieb and the
money-grabbing Dr. Roscoe Geake, who told his students that
knowledge was the greatest thing, "but it's no good whatever unless
you can sell it, and to do this you must first impress your personality on the people who have the dollars." [74]

In Nautilus, Arrowsmith worked under the supervision of Dr.
Almus Pickerbaugh. His superior had a bristly mustache like

[72] *Ibid.*, 213.
[73] Sinclair Lewis, *Arrowsmith* (New York: New American Library, 1961), 186.
[74] *Ibid.*, 83.

Theodore Roosevelt's and cultivated Rooseveltian mannerisms. He was full of pep and heartiness and sold public health with atrocious jingles of his own composition.[75] He was a Rotarian, a Congregational Sunday School superintendent, a luncheon club speaker, and eventually a Congressman.

Yet for all Pickerbaugh's bombast, he had a passion for improving the health of the poor that seemed dangerous to another Nautilus physician, Dr. Irving Watters. Pickerbaugh, Watters complained, had "a bad socialistic tendency. These clinics—outrageous—the people that go to them that can afford to pay!" At medical school Watter's record had been mediocre, but marriage to a rich wife and an impressive professional manner had opened the way to success. He offered patronizing advice to Arrowsmith: "You want to join the country club and take up golf. Best opportunity in the world to meet the substantial citizens. I've picked up more than one high-class patient there." [76]

Arrowsmith compromised with Nautilus. He joined a variety of clubs and professional societies, but he did not yield enough to survive. He ran into trouble by enlarging the free clinics, devoting too much time to laboratory research, and condemning tenements owned by politically powerful landlords. Forced out of Nautilus, he found opportunities to pursue his research interests in the wealthy clinics and medical foundations of Chicago and New York. There too, the true scientist encountered corrupting influences but they were different from those of Zenith and Nautilus.

VIII

In *Babbitt* Sinclair Lewis had included some observations on Zenith religious life. Babbitt's theology was simple: he believed in a supreme being and in future rewards and punishments. "Upon this theology he rarely pondered. The kernel of his practical religion was that it was respectable, and beneficial to one's business, to be seen going to services; that the church kept the Worst Elements from being still worse; and that the pastor's sermons, however dull they might seem at the time of taking, yet had a voodooistic power

[75] *Ibid.*, 188.   [76] *Ibid.*, 204.

Rev. Mr. Monday, the Prophet with a Punch, has shown that he is the world's greatest salesman of salvation . . . Sinclair Lewis, *Babbitt*

which 'did a fellow good—kept him in touch with Higher Things.' " [77]

Zenith's clergymen were somewhat divided upon whether they should invite the sensational evangelist Mike Monday (obviously Billy Sunday) to the city. Certain Episcopal and Congregational clergymen had opposed the idea, but this opposition collapsed when the secretary of the Chamber of Commerce reported to a committee of manufacturers "that in every city where he had appeared, Mr. Monday had turned the minds of workmen from wages and hours to higher things, and thus averted strikes." The businessmen of Zenith subscribed forty thousand dollars to underwrite expenses, and a Mike Monday Tabernacle with fifteen thousand seats was erected on the County Fair Grounds. There the former prize fighter condemned "wooly-whiskered book-lice that think they know more about Almighty God and prefer a lot of Hun science

[77] *Babbitt*, 170.

and smutty German criticism to the straight and simple Word of God." He called upon his listeners to "come in, with every grain of pep and reverence you got, and boost all together for Jesus Christ and his everlasting mercy and tenderness!" [78]

All in all, Babbitt felt comfortable in his Christian faith. "I tell you, boy," he said to his son, "there's no stronger bulwark of sound conservatism than the evangelical church, and no better place to make friends who'll help you to gain your rightful place in the community than in your own church-home!" [79]

But Lewis had much more to say about this sector of Zenith life. Throughout 1926 he was hard at work on what he called his preacher novel. Eager to brief himself thoroughly, he visited the Reverend William L. Stidger, in Kansas City. Stidger was a vigorous Methodist, who had some years earlier criticized Lewis's treatment of religion in *Babbitt* and had urged the novelist to draw a more accurate picture of real clergymen. Through Stidger, Lewis met a number of other Kansas City clergymen and found, to his surprise, that he liked them. In a letter to Mencken he described Stidger as "a hell of a good fellow" and praised the intelligence of some of the more liberal ministers.[80]

Lewis soon returned to Kansas City, where he lived in a hotel suite for two months, filling his notebooks with tidbits of ministerial gossip and shop talk. Every Wednesday some fifteen to twenty clergymen had lunch with him. It was an unusual assemblage made up of not only assorted Protestants, but a Jewish rabbi and a Catholic priest. The meetings of what Lewis called his Sunday School class were lively affairs, where the host challenged his new friends to defend their activities. The novelist even accepted invitations to speak in the churches. "All of this damned fool preaching in pulpits and so on," Lewis explained to his publisher, ". . . has been largely to give me a real feeling of the church from the inside." [81] When he met with his Sunday School for the last time, Lewis said: "Boys, I'm going up to Minnesota, and write a novel about you. I'm going to give you hell, but I love every one of you." Then he embraced each man and said, "Good-by, old man; God bless you!" [82]

[78] *Ibid.*, 83–84.	[79] *Ibid.*, 182.	[80] Schorer, *op. cit.*, 454.
[81] Lewis to Harcourt, April 21, 1926, *From Main Street to Stockholm*, 207.
[82] Schorer, *op. cit.*, 454.

In *Elmer Gantry* (1927), Lewis' promise to give his minister friends hell was more than fulfilled. The title character was a moral monster whose fondness for alcohol and women led him from one early disaster to another. Nevertheless, the Reverend Mr. Gantry had no difficulty in getting admitted to the Methodist clergy and in winning the favor of his bishop. A man of handsome presence and calculating shrewdness, Gantry quickly learned how to succeed in the ministry. As described by Lewis, the formula was strikingly similar to that which Babbitt had learned in the real estate business. Gantry "discovered the art of joining, which was later to enable him to meet the more enterprising and solid men of affairs— oculists and editors and manufacturers of bathtubs—and enlist their practical genius in his crusades for spirituality." [83] He learned how to attract large congregations by advertising provocative sermon topics. And he saw the advantage of moving with the crowd. In 1918, for example, "he was one of the most courageous defenders of the Midwest against the imminent invasion of the Germans. He was a Four-minute Man. He said violent things about atrocities, and sold Liberty Bonds hugely." [84] He displayed the muscularity of his faith by felling a booze-dealer with a blow to the jaw.

When the bishop offered him the pastorate of Zenith's Wellspring Church, in 1920, Gantry glimpsed a golden opportunity. "He could see his Doctor of Divinity degree at hand, his bishopric or college presidency or fabulous pulpit in New York." [85] Yet the situation was a difficult one. The Wellspring Church had once been the most fashionable Methodist Church in Zenith, but the section had deteriorated, and membership in the church had declined from fourteen hundred to eight hundred. Gantry's disgusted eyes could see nothing in the neighborhood but "wops"—"nobody for ten blocks that would put more'n ten cents in the collection." He would probably have declined the bishop's offer had he not learned that the building of new apartment houses promised to revive the area. And so "he went to inform Bishop Toomis that after prayer and meditation he had been led to accept the pastorate of the Wellspring Church." [86]

[83] Sinclair Lewis, *Elmer Gantry* (New York: Dell Publishing Co., 1960), 315.
[84] *Ibid.*, 317.   [85] *Ibid.*, 321.   [86] *Ibid.*, 322.

In his new assignment, the Reverend Mr. Gantry put to work all the tricks of the trade. In a two-column spread, he advertised his first sermon topic: "Can Strangers Find Haunts of Vice in Zenith?" [87] Four hundred curious auditors were edified by the parson's explicit description of where he had observed scandalous bathing costumes, where he had been enticed by bad women, and where he had been told that he could buy bootleg liquor. There were reporters in the congregation eager to obtain titillating copy for their papers.

But Gantry's pulpit showmanship was matched by his energy in promoting church activities. "Wellspring Church had been carrying on a core of institutional activities and Elmer doubled them, for nothing brought in more sympathy, publicity and contributions. Rich old hyenas who never went to church would ooze out a hundred dollars or even five hundred when you described the shawled mothers coming tearfully to the milk station." There were study classes; there were troops of Boy Scouts and Camp Fire Girls; there were circles of sewing ladies; and there was a Men's Club, "for which the pastor had to snare prominent speakers without payment." [88]

The urban Methodists, as the sharp-eyed Sinclair Lewis could see, were changing during the 1920's. The "general bleakness" of the sect was passing, and Elmer Gantry found in the Wellspring Church "a Young Married Set, who were nearly as cheerful as though they did not belong to a church." These relaxed Methodists were not rich, "but they had Fords and phonographs and gin. They danced, and they were willing to dance in the presence of the pastor." [89]

The Reverend Mr. Gantry might look with indulgence upon the peccadilloes of his own flock, but he smote outside evil-doers with well-publicized indignation. He denounced vice in fiery sermons and personally led police raids against small-time bootleggers and scarlet women. However, he left the larger criminals with powerful political friends prudently alone.

Sinclair Lewis described many other clergymen in his preacher novel. Although none was as despicable as Gantry, each had some

---

[87] *Ibid.,* 327.   [88] *Ibid.,* 330–31.   [89] *Ibid.,* 346.

frailty. The Reverend Chester Brown was excessively enamored of flickering candles, robed choirs, and other touches of ritualism. The Reverend Dr. Otto Hickenlooper carried the proliferation of church activities to an absurd degree and opened his church forum to the most dangerous radicals, "who were allowed to say absolutely anything they liked, provided they did not curse, refer to adultery, or criticize the leadership of Christ." Dr. Philip McGarry exuded an exciting modernism. "He was accused of every heresy. He never denied them, and the only dogma he was known to give out positively was the leadership of Jesus—as to whose divinity he was indefinite." At the other extreme was the extraordinarily successful Dr. Mahlon Potts, who was "fat, pompous, full of heavy rumbles of piety." [90]

For only two of his fictional parsons did Lewis display any affection. Too gentle and old-fashioned ever to be elevated to a city pastorate, the Reverend Andrew Pengilly served cheerfully in country churches not far from Zenith.

If you had cut Andrew Pengilly to the core, you would have found him white clear through . . . To every congregation he had served these forty years, he had been a shepherd. They had loved him, listened to him, and underpaid him . . . Little book-learning had Andrew Pengilly in his youth, and to this day he knew nothing of Biblical criticism, of the origin of religions, of the sociology which was beginning to absorb church-leaders, but his Bible he knew, and believed, word by word, and somehow he had drifted into the reading of ecstatic books of mysticism.[91]

Much better educated than Pengilly, the Reverend Frank Shallard was tormented by twentieth-century doubts. Troubled by Baptist fundamentalism, he left his father's denomination and served as a common soldier during World War I. After the Armistice he accepted the pastorate of a Congregational Church in an unfashionable section of Zenith. For a time the traditional freedom of Congregationalism protected him, but his familiarity with the teachings of modern science made him increasingly skeptical. In an unguarded moment he admitted "that he did not accept Jesus Christ as divine; that he was not sure of a future life; that he wasn't

[90] *Ibid.*, 338–39.   [91] *Ibid.*, 252.

even certain of a personal God." Taunted as to why he didn't get
out of the ministry, Shallard explained: "Because I'm not yet sure
—Though I do think our present churches are as absurd as a belief
in witchcraft, yet I believe there could be a church free of supersti-
tition, helpful to the needy, and giving people that mystic something stronger than reason, that sense of being uplifted in common
worship of an unknowable power for good." [92]

Eventually Shallard was hounded out of his pastorate. Gantry
led the attack against him for the most despicable of reasons, to grab
for himself the patronage of Shallard's wealthiest parishioner. For a
moment, Shallard hoped that he might find comfort in the Roman
Catholic Church by accepting its dogmas as symbols only, but a
priest sternly rebuked him. Shallard wrote in his notebook: "The
Roman Catholic Church is superior to the militant Protestant
Church. It does not compel you to give up your sense of beauty,
your sense of humor, or your pleasant vices. It merely requires you
to give up your honesty, your reason, your heart and soul." [93]

Shallard finally found a cause to which he could dedicate himself. A liberal organization invited him to go on a lecture tour to
oppose the anti-evolution bills then being pushed through rural
legislatures. Thus it was that Shallard found himself in "a roaring
modern city in the Southwest," billed to speak on the subject "Are
the Fundamentalists Witch Hunters?" Ignoring telephoned warnings and menacing figures in the rear of the hall, Shallard began
his denunciation of religious obscurantism. His punishment was
swift and terrible. He was dragged from the building, hurried out
of town in a waiting automobile, and so savagely whipped that he
lost the sight of one eye. All this was done so that Shallard could
"tell his atheist friends it ain't healthy for 'em in real Christian
parts." [94]

Why was *Elmer Gantry* such an angry novel? Though he had
ridiculed the standardized minds of businessmen and chided the
commercialism of doctors, Lewis's mood had been one of urbane
satire, revealing his underlying affection for these Midwestern
Americans. But the Reverend Mr. Gantry had no redeeming qualities. While he thundered against vice from the pulpit, he con-

[92] *Ibid.*, 395.   [93] *Ibid.*, 403.   [94] *Ibid.*, 408.

tinued to practice shabby adulteries. In his ruthless quest for power, he crushed not only his rivals, but his relatives and friends. His religion was a complete sham. And most of the other ministers in the novel were petty men, jealous of each other and dishonest with themselves.

Perhaps Lewis's indignation is best understood if it is remembered that, as a youth, he went through a highly religious period. In Sauk Centre, he was an earnest young member of the Christian Endeavor, and at Oberlin Academy he joined the Y.M.C.A. and resolved to become a missionary. He taught a Sunday School class in a nearby country village to which he used to propel himself on a railroad handcar—in just the way in which Elmer Gantry commuted to his first church. The mature Lewis became an agnostic, but he never lost a measure of nostalgia for evangelical Protestantism. Hence, the eagerness with which he swapped ideas with the Kansas City ministers. According to one participant, Lewis would begin to preach with all sincerity, then he would bring himself up short, saying: "I have to stop this! I *could* have been a preacher." [95]

Trying to explain himself, in 1927, Lewis said that his only virtues were lasting affection for his friends, pyrotechnic conversation, and "a real, fiery, almost reckless hatred of hypocrisy—of what Americans call 'bunk,' from the older word 'buncombe,' and this may not be a virtue at all, but only an envy-inspired way of annoying people by ignoring their many excellent qualities and picking out the few vices into which they have been betrayed by custom and economic necessity." He hated politicians who indulged in banal eloquence, while they stole from the public; doctors who treated their patients for imaginary ailments; professors who perverted scholarship to the needs of war propaganda; and manufacturers who professed to be philanthropists, while they were underpaying their workmen. Said Lewis of himself, "Why, this man, still so near to being an out and out Methodist or Lutheran that he would far rather chant the hymns of his boyhood evangelicism than the best drinking song in the world, is so infuriated by ministers who tell silly little jokes in the pulpit and keep from ever admitting publicly their confusing doubts that he risks losing all

[95] Schorer, *op. cit.*, 499.

the good friends he once had among the ministers by the denunciations in *Elmer Gantry*." [96]

Having lost his own faith, Lewis saw only intellectual dishonesty in well educated men who were still preaching in terms of a personal God. The innocents like Pengilly still had his sincere respect, but the sophisticated modernists like McGarry irritated him. Even greater was his anger against the zealots, who were attempting to impose prohibition and other blue laws upon the nation. In their Puritanism he could see only a perverted lustfulness.

In his impatience Lewis overdrew the picture, especially in the incredible wickedness he attributed to Gantry himself. Yet with all its distortion, Lewis' novel has unusual interest for the historian. In many ways Lewis was an extraordinarily perceptive observer of the religious scene in the mid-1920's. He understood how the harshness of small-town Protestantism was being softened by the more secular culture of the cities. He noted the effort of the preachers to use newspaper and radio publicity to extend their influence. He understood the impact of changed theological training. He touched upon the problems of the urban churches occasioned by shifts of population, upon the new emphasis on ritualism among certain churches, and upon the vogue of the social gospel and the seven-day program.

Sinclair Lewis was a man with many flaws in character. He was strongly opinionated and often malicious in what he wrote. But the student of history cannot wait for the perfect witness. He can learn much from Sinclair Lewis, if he takes him as he finds him. Let the historian be on guard against Lewis' impulse toward exaggeration and caricature, but let him profit from the novelist's rich gifts for fact-gathering and mimicry.

[96] *The Man from Main Street*, 48.

3

The Pleasure Domes of
West Egg and Tarmes

> . . . and Gatsby was overwhelmingly aware of the youth and mystery that wealth imprisons and preserves, of the freshness of many clothes, and of Daisy, gleaming like silver, safe and proud above the hot struggles of the poor.
>
> F. Scott Fitzgerald, *The Great Gatsby* [1]

Like Jay Gatsby, F. Scott Fitzgerald was fascinated by wealth. His attitude was neither that of the securely rich man, who takes money for granted; nor that of the hopelessly poor man, able only to envy the rich. Fitzgerald lived most of his life on the periphery of the rich man's world. He was in frequent association with rich and fashionable people, he earned a great deal of money, and he spent still more. This situation created a tension that jeopardized his whole literary career. Fitzgerald had extraordinarily high literary standards; it was his ambition to write the great American novel of the twentieth century. Three times he came close—once with *The Great Gatsby* (1925), once with *Tender Is the Night* (1934), once with *The Last Tycoon* (1941), half-finished when he died. Yet the writing of the great novel was delayed and flawed by Fitzgerald's perennial need for money, not money to survive in the humble garrets of literary folklore, but money to live a rich man's life on Long Island, in Paris, and on the Riviera. It was for this that he expended so much time and energy writing trivial stories for *The Saturday Evening Post* and other popular magazines and grinding out still more ephemeral scenarios in Hollywood.

[1] F. Scott Fitzgerald, *The Great Gatsby* (New York: Bantam Books, 1945), 160.

No one condemned this prostitution of talent more than Fitz-gerald himself. As early as 1925, he wrote to the Scribner's editor, Maxwell Perkins: "I can't reduce our scale of living and I can't stand this financial insecurity. Anyhow there's no point in trying to be an artist if you can't do your best. I had my chance back in 1920 to start my life on a sensible scale and I lost it, and so I'll have to pay the penalty." [2]

In his origins, Fitzgerald belonged neither to the rich nor to the poor. Although descended from a Maryland family of some distinc-tion, Fitzgerald's father failed in business and did not earn enough as a salesman to support the household. The family was dominated by Fitzgerald's mother, the eccentric daughter of an Irish immi-grant, who had acquired a modest fortune in the wholesale grocery business. In St. Paul, Minnesota, where the future novelist was born and spent most of his early years, the Fitzgeralds moved fre-quently, living in rented houses on the fringes of the better resi-dential districts.

Fitzgerald went to good preparatory schools and to Princeton, a college chosen, not for its academic stature, but for its prestige in dramatics and athletics. Throughout these years, he was acutely conscious of the gulf between the marginal finances of his own family and the stable wealth of so many of his classmates. "Do you know what my own story is?" Fitzgerald asked Morley Callaghan, the Canadian novelist. "Well, I was always the poorest boy at a rich man's school. Yes, it was that way at prep schools, and at Princeton, too." [3]

Immediately after the war, Fitzgerald went through a period of real poverty and hated it. Unable to get established as a writer, he was slaving away at advertising copy in New York. This was all the more frustrating because he was engaged to the beautiful Zelda Sayre, daughter of a prominent judge in Montgomery, Alabama. He almost lost her because he didn't have money enough to get married. This confirmed him in a conviction that had long been forming: the rich men got the most beautiful girls.

The spectacular success of Fitzgerald's first novel, *This Side of*

[2] Fitzgerald to Maxwell Perkins, April 24, 1925, *The Letters of F. Scott Fitzgerald*, edited by Andrew Turnbull (New York: Charles Scribner's Sons, 1963), 180–81.
[3] Morley Callaghan, *That Summer in Paris: Memories of Tangled Friendship with Hemingway, Fitzgerald, and Some Others* (New York: Coward, McCann, 1963), 185.

Paradise (1920), changed all this. Zelda married him, and for the next few years they lived the life of a rich gay young couple in the environs of New York and in France. In 1924, Fitzgerald wrote an article entitled "How to Live on $36,000 a Year"—his approximate income during most of the 1920's. In 1929, he boasted to Morley Callaghan that he was the equivalent of a millionaire, since his annual earnings were $50,000.[4] Yet the high-living Scott and Zelda managed to spend it all and to fall continually into debt.

Earning powers capitalized in the literary market place of the 1920's were no more secure than Wall Street securities. After 1929, Fitzgerald's income went down rapidly. The mass-circulation magazines cut their rates, and Fitzgerald was particularly hard hit because the public associated him with frivolous themes inappropriate to the grim realities of the depression. But misfortune of a much more tragic character engulfed the Fitzgeralds. Zelda struggled with increasingly serious mental illness, while Scott alternated bouts of excessive drinking and depression with periods of rehabilitation. In 1937, when he began a stint of work in Hollywood he was $40,000 in debt.[5] The Fitzgeralds could no longer enjoy the luxuries of the 1920's, but the need to economize never completely destroyed Scott's feeling for the aristocratic proprieties. During one of his blackest periods in 1936, he took comfort that his daughter "Scottie" would be able—through a remission of tuition —to attend "a very expensive school where I wanted her to go." [6]

Loving to associate with rich and fashionable friends, Fitzgerald inevitably chose such people to write about. He ridiculed the inclination of some of his contemporaries to sing the virtues of simple inarticulate farmers, men close to the soil. "As a matter of fact," he wrote, "the American peasant as 'real' material scarcely exists. He is scarcely 10% of the population, isn't bound to the soil at all as the English and Russian peasants were—and, if he has any sensitivity whatsoever (except a most sentimental conception of himself, which our writers persistently shut their eyes to) he is in the towns before he's twenty." [7]

[4] *Ibid.*

[5] Arthur Mizener, *The Far Side of Paradise: A Biography of F. Scott Fitzgerald* (New York: Vintage Books, 1959), 297.

[6] Fitzgerald to Maxwell Perkins, Sept. 19, 1936, *Letters*, 267.

[7] Fitzgerald to Maxwell Perkins, (c. June 1, 1925), *ibid.*, 186–87.

Yet Fitzgerald's compulsion to live like a wealthy man and to write about the rich by no means blinded his eyes to the faults of the privileged class. Ironically, Fitzgerald was a man of great moral idealism. "Poor Scott," a friend said, "he never really enjoyed his dissipation because he disapproved intensely of himself all the time it was going on." [8] And in the same way, Fitzgerald the moralist continually condemned Fitzgerald the writer who was selling his literary soul to Mammon. The romance of his own life was flawed: to the struggling author, the girl of his dreams had been out of reach; only the jingle of money in his pocket had permitted him to marry her. The experience left him with what he described as "an abiding distrust, an animosity, toward the leisure class—not the conviction of a revolutionist but the smoldering hatred of a peasant." [9]

This Side of Paradise was patently autobiographical. It told the story of Amory Blaine, from birth to age 25. Like Fitzgerald, Amory had a weak, ineffectual father and a flamboyant Irish mother. Like Fitzgerald, Amory spent his boyhood in Minnesota; went to a fashionable prep school, where he sought popularity by playing sports, but antagonized his classmates with his egotism; chose Princeton as his college, because of its social prestige; and energetically threw himself into an effort to win campus leadership, through participation in dramatics and literature, only to ruin all he had achieved by getting into academic difficulties. And, also like Fitzgerald, Amory Blaine had a succession of youthful love affairs and aspired to write books.

Fitzgerald's later novels and short stories followed his personal experiences less closely, but continually made use of real episodes in which he had participated. He sometimes annoyed his friends by cross-examining them in obvious preparation for using them as characters in his fiction. The setting for *The Great Gatsby* was suburban Long Island, where the Fitzgeralds lived from 1922 to 1924. *Tender Is the Night* deals with Americans living on the French Riviera and in other places frequented by Scott and Zelda during the next few years. And *The Last Tycoon* was laid in the

---

[8] Mizener, *The Far Side of Paradise*, 93.

[9] F. Scott Fitzgerald, "Handle with Care," *The Crack-up* (New York: New Directions, 1945), 77.

Hollywood movie colony where Fitzgerald spent the final years of his life.

Fitzgerald's friends and critics were unanimous in praising the accuracy of his descriptions of his chosen world. Arthur Mizener, Fitzgerald's biographer, describes his first novel as "a kind of history, a remarkably accurate account of what happened, in feeling as well as fact, rather than an evaluating formal organization of things that might have happened." [10] Budd Schulberg, who knew Fitzgerald well during his last tragic years, says: "He was one of our better historians of the no-man's time between wars." [11] And John O'Hara, famous for the accuracy of his own fictional descriptions, says of Fitzgerald, that "the people were right, the talk was right, the clothes, the cars were real." [12]

II

Except for the stimulating friendship of Monsignor Darcy, the headmaster, Amory Blaine's two years at St. Regis Academy in Connecticut had little influence on him. "We have no Eton," Fitzgerald explained, "to create the self-consciousness of a governing class; we have, instead, clean, flaccid, and innocuous preparatory schools." [13] He achieved one brief moment of glory, when he scored the only touchdown of the day, in a game against Groton.

But St. Regis was only a short stopover for Amory, in his journey toward Princeton. For a boy of his aspirations, only three colleges were possible, and one of these, Harvard, was easily eliminated. All Harvard men, he believed, were sissies. Yale appealed to him, with its virile image of blue-sweatered pipe-smoking men, "but Princeton drew him most, with its atmosphere of bright colors and its alluring reputation as the pleasantest country club in America." [14]

When he entered college, in the fall of 1913, Amory was happy

[10] Mizener, *The Far Side of Paradise,* 117.

[11] Budd Schulberg, "Fitzgerald in Hollywood," Alfred Kazin (ed.) *F. Scott Fitzgerald: The Man and His Work* (Cleveland: World Publishing Co., 1951), 112.

[12] Arthur Mizener, "F. Scott Fitzgerald 1896–1940, The Poet of Borrowed Times," *ibid.,* 23.

[13] F. Scott Fitzgerald, *This Side of Paradise* (New York: Charles Scribner's Sons, 1920), 29.

[14] *Ibid.,* 40.

in his choice. "From the first he loved Princeton—its lazy beauty, its half-grasped significance, the wild moonlight revel of the rushes, the handsome, prosperous big-game crowds, and under it all the air of struggle that pervaded his class." The struggle was for campus recognition, and, as the only boy from St. Regis, Amory stood outside the earliest circle of power. The groups from the larger private schools elected their candidates to the freshman class offices, drawing to their support "the slightly less important but socially ambitious to protect them from the friendly, rather puzzled high-school element." [15]

When Amory murmered mildly against this injustice to the middle-class boys, a classmate set him right. After all, they had come to an Ivy League college for snobbish reasons: "We came to Princeton so we could feel that way toward the smaller colleges—have it on 'em, more self confidence, dress better, cut a swathe—" And Amory admitted that he didn't really object to "the glittering caste system." He liked having "a bunch of hot cats on top," but he must be one of them.[16]

To achieve the summit, Amory chose the most obvious path. He went out for freshman football. When an early injury blocked this route, he turned to campus journalism and dramatics. He found that writing for the *Nassau Literary Magazine* would get him nothing, "but that being on the board of the *Daily Princetonian* would get any one a good deal." [17] Achievement in the Triangle Club, which staged Princeton's famed musical comedies, would also be efficacious.

Amory's spirit and talents were well adapted to this kind of competition. For two years, all went according to plan. He survived the early cuts on the campus newspaper and earned a role in the Triangle show. The latter gave him one of the coveted college experiences, going on the Christmas tour. "They played through vacation to the fashionable of eight cities. Amory liked Louisville and Memphis best: these knew how to meet strangers, furnished extraordinary punch, and flaunted an astonishing array of feminine beauty. . . . There was a proper consumption of strong waters all

---

[15] *Ibid.*, 47.   [16] *Ibid.*, 50.   [17] *Ibid.*, 49.

along the line; one man invariably went on the stage highly stimu-
lated, claiming that his particular interpretation of the part
required it." [18]

In the spring of sophomore year, the upper class clubs made
their selections. Each had a distinctive image: "Ivy, detached and
breathlessly aristocratic; Cottage, an impressive melange of brilliant adventurers and well-dressed philanderers; Tiger Inn, broad-
shouldered and athletic, vitalized by an honest elaboration of prep-
school standards; Cap and Gown, anti-alcoholic, faintly religious
and politically powerful; flamboyant Colonial; literary Quad-
rangle; and the dozen others, varying in age and position." [19] The
factors influencing bids were fickle in the extreme. "In his own
crowd Amory saw men kept out for wearing green hats, for being 'a
damn tailor's dummy,' for having 'too much pull in heaven,' for
getting drunk one night 'not like a gentleman, by God,' or for
unfathomable secret reasons known to no one but the wielders of
the black balls." [20]

Surviving all these perils, Amory was elected to Cottage, and
everything seemed perfect. "Long afterward Amory thought of
sophomore spring as the happiest time of his life. His ideas were in
tune with life as he found it; he wanted no more than to drift and
dream and enjoy a dozen new-found friendships through the April
afternoons." [21]

But Amory's pursuit of happiness involved much more than
drifting and dreaming. He drank and gambled. He dated girls. He
was one of a convivial group that spent a riotous weekend in Atlantic City. "Mostly there were parties—to Orange or the Shore, more
rarely to New York and Philadelphia, though one night they mar-
shalled fourteen waitresses out of Childs' and took them to ride
down Fifth Avenue on top of an auto bus. They all cut more classes
than were allowed, . . . but spring was too rare to let anything
interfere with their colorful ramblings." [22]

The truth was that Amory liked everything about college except his courses. "Co-ordinate geometry and the melancholy
hexameters of Corneille and Racine held forth small allurements,

[18] *Ibid.*, 63.   [19] *Ibid.*, 49.   [20] *Ibid.*, 79.   [21] *Ibid.*, 80.   [22] *Ibid.*, 88–89.

and even psychology, which he had eagerly awaited, proved to be a dull subject full of muscular reactions and biological phrases rather than the study of personality and influence." [23]

This was the fatal flaw that ruined all his ambitions. Failure in his examinations made him ineligible for the junior posts on which he had set his heart. He idled through another year, then found a way out of his frustrations by enlisting in the World War I army.

Despite this fiasco, Amory claimed that he was "probably one of the two dozen men in my class at college who got a decent education." [24] He had discovered Bernard Shaw, quite by accident, browsing through the library. And his enthusiasm for Shaw had served to introduce him to a fellow freshman eager to discuss books with him. Amory now began to read "enormously every night— Shaw, Chesterton, Barrie, Pinero, Yeats, Synge, Ernest Dowson, Arthur Symons, Keats, Sudermann, Robert Hugh Benson, the Savoy Operas—just a heterogeneous mixture for he suddenly discovered that he had read nothing for years." [25] Through orgies of reading and rambling bull sessions, through experiments in writing poems and stories, Amory achieved an education in defiance of a system that seemed to make it impossible.

When *This Side of Paradise* became a best seller, Princeton's President, John Grier Hibben, was unhappy at the impression that it would convey to the public "that our young men are merely living for four years in a country club and spending their lives wholly in a spirit of calculation and snobbery." [26] In replying to Hibben's letter, Fitzgerald explained that he had written out of his own bitterness in discovering "that I had spent several years trying to fit in with a curriculum that is after all made for the average student. After the curriculum had tied me up, taken away the honors I'd wanted, bent my nose over a chemistry book and said 'No fun, no activities, no offices, no Triangle trips—no, not even a diploma if you can't do chemistry'—after that I retired." But he admitted that the book "does overaccentuate the gayety and country club atmosphere of Princeton. . . . It is the Princeton of Saturday night in May." [27]

---

[23] *Ibid.*, 88.   [24] *Ibid.*, 299.
[25] *Ibid.*, 57.   [26] Mizener, *The Far Side of Paradise*, 59.
[27] Fitzgerald to J. G. Hibben, [June 3, 1920], *Letters*, 462.

A Poor Fish Out of Water

ong afterward Amory thought of sophomore spring as the happiest time of his life.
. Scott Fitzgerald, *This Side of Paradise*

Even though Fitzgerald's playboy college was, by his own admission, something of an exaggeration, distorting what the university must have meant to more serious students, there can be no doubt that he had described the side of college life he knew best. This was the Princeton, where the students, not the professors, handed down the grades, and the cherished prizes were athletic celebrity, campus office, and the prettiest prom date.

III

Asked whether the nineteen-year-old Rosalind Connage behaved herself, her younger sister replied: "Not particularly well. Oh, she's average—smokes sometimes, drinks punch, frequently kissed—Oh, yes—common knowledge—one of the effects of the war, you know." [28] It was such passages that gave *This Side of Paradise* its delicious notoriety. Misbehaving males were an old story; misbehaving females—at least in upper class families— were something new.

Indeed, so great was the demand for Fitzgerald's stories about "the new American girl," that he soon grew weary of writing them. In December, 1920, he complained: "I'll go mad if I have to do another debutante, which is what they want." [29]

The girls described by Fitzgerald were beautiful, but in a different way from their mothers and grandmothers. Soft femininity was out, and figures were becoming almost boyish. Rosalind was "slender and athletic, without underdevelopment, and it was a delight to watch her move about a room, walk along a street, swing a golf club, or turn a 'cart-wheel.' " [30] Ardita Farnham, in "The Offshore Pirate," was "about nineteen, slender and supple, with a spoiled alluring mouth, and quick gray eyes full of radiant curiosity." [31] Jordan Baker, in *The Great Gatsby,* was "a slender, small-breasted girl with an erect carriage, which she accentuated by throwing her body backward at the shoulders like a young cadet." [32]

---

[28] *This Side of Paradise,* 182.

[29] Fitzgerald to Maxwell Perkins, Dec. 31, 1920, *Letters,* 145.

[30] *This Side of Paradise,* 184.

[31] F. Scott Fitzgerald, *Flappers and Philosophers* (New York: Charles Scribner's Sons, 1959), 17.

[32] *The Great Gatsby,* 19.

One defiant badge of modernity was bobbed hair. Gloria Gilbert, in *The Beautiful and Damned*, had bobbed hers as early as 1914. "It was not fashionable then. It was to be fashionable in five or six years. At that time it was considered extremely daring." [33] Gloria's friend, Muriel Kane, who prided herself on keeping up with the latest fashions, did not appear in bobbed hair until 1917.[34]

As late as 1920, there was still an assumption of recklessness in short hair. Fitzgerald received his first big mail—"hundreds and hundreds of letters"—after the May, 1920, publication of his *Saturday Evening Post* story, "Bernice Bobs Her Hair." [35] Bernice's bold step, which resulted from a dare, astonished the whole barber shop.

A man in the chair next to her turned on his side and gave her a glance, half lather, half amazement. One barber started and spoiled little Willy Shuneman's monthly haircut. Mr. O'Reilly in the last chair grunted and swore musically in ancient Gaelic as a razor bit into his cheek. Two bootblacks became wide-eyed and rushed for her feet. No, Bernice didn't care for a shine.

The results were disastrous.

Her hair was not curly, and now it lay in lank lifeless blocks on both sides of her suddenly pale face. It was ugly as sin. . . . Her face's chief charm had been a Madonna-like simplicity. Now that was gone and she was—well, frightfully mediocre—not stagy; only ridiculous, like a Greenwich Villager who had left her spectacles at home.[36]

Feeling that she had been tricked by her jealous cousin, Bernice took revenge by clipping off the rival's braids while she slept.

The one-piece bathing suit provided another weapon for challenging older ideas of propriety. "Honestly, there are only two costumes in the world that I really enjoy being in . . . ," Rosalind said. "One's a hoop skirt with pantaloons; the other's a one-piece bathing suit. I'm quite charming in both of them." [37] Ardita boasted: "I've got a one-piece affair that's shocked the natives all along the Atlantic coast from Biddeford Pool to St. Augustine." She recognized her legs as among her best assets. "A sculptor up at Rye

33 F. Scott Fitzgerald, *The Beautiful and Damned* (New York: Charles Scribner's Sons, 1922), 124.
34 *Ibid.*, 298.   35 "Early Success," *The Crack-up*, 87.
36 *Flappers and Philosophers*, 136.   37 *This Side of Paradise*, 184.

. . . a slender, small breasted girl with an erect carriage . . .   F. Scott Fitzgerald, *The Great Gatsby*

last summer told me my calves were worth five hundred dollars."[38] And Rosalind had a similar sense of pride. She didn't want to have to worry about pots and kitchens and brooms. "I want to worry whether my legs will get slick and brown when I swim in the summer."[39]

If Rosalind delighted in affronting prudery, she loved her scanty bathing suit for other reasons as well. A superb young swimmer, she emulated the famous Annette Kellerman by performing a beautiful swan dive off a thirty-foot summer house. Her male companion felt obligated to attempt the same feat. Telling about the episode, he complained: "Well, afterward Rosalind had the nerve to ask me why I stooped over when I dove. 'It didn't make it any easier,' she said, 'it just took all the courage out of it.' I ask you, what can a man do with a girl like that?"[40]

Rosalind was not the only girl to flaunt her athletic abilities. There was Marjorie Harvey, "who besides having a fairylike face and a dazzling, bewildering tongue was already justly celebrated for having turned five cart-wheels in succession during the last pump-and-slipper dance at New Haven."[41]

Even before World War I, the society girls had manifested a passion for dancing. "Gloria's out," her mother explained in 1914. "She's dancing somewhere. Gloria goes, goes, goes. I tell her I don't see how she stands it. She dances all afternoon and all night, until I think she's going to wear herself to a shadow."[42] Three years later, Muriel Kane exhibited the frenetic postures that jazz was stimulating. When the phonograph started, Muriel felt the compulsion "to rise and sway from side to side, her elbows against her ribs, her forearms perpendicular to her body and out like fins."[43] In 1919, sixteen-year-old Cecilia Connage could not resist the impulse to admire herself in the mirror and "to shimmy enthusiastically."[44]

The postwar dancing mania inspired musicians to extraordinary feats of exhibitionism. At the great Gamma Psi fraternity dance, in New York on May Day, 1919, "a special orchestra, special even in a day of special orchestras" provided the music. "They were headed by a famous flute-player, distinguished throughout New

[38] *Flappers and Philosophers*, 35.   [39] *This Side of Paradise*, 210.   [40] *Ibid.*, 203.
[41] *Flappers and Philosophers*, 117.   [42] *The Beautiful and Damned*, 39.
[43] *Ibid.*, 272.   [44] *This Side of Paradise*, 180.

York for his feat of standing on his head and shimmying with his shoulders while he played the latest jazz on his flute." Inspired by such virtuosity, Edith Bradin "danced herself into that tired, dreamy state habitual only with debutantes, a state equivalent to the glow of a noble soul after several long highballs." [45]

The index to a girl's popularity was the number of boys who cut in to dance with her. The custom of inviting extra men to the dances provided a stag line and guaranteed a rapid turnover in partners. Edith, dancing only a few steps with one boy before she found herself in the arms of the next, enjoyed a wonderful evening. Not so happy was the experience of Bernice, who at another dance suffered the humiliation of being stuck with one partner. "No matter how beautiful or brilliant a girl may be, the reputation of not being frequently cut in on makes her position at a dance unfortunate. Perhaps boys prefer her company to that of the butterflies with whom they dance a dozen times an evening, but youth in this jazz-nourished generation is temperamentally restless, and the idea of fox-trotting more than one full fox trot with the same girl is distasteful, not to say odious." [46]

Society girls had been smoking before World War I, but not without protest from the reformers. "Oh, Gloria, if you smoke so many cigarettes you'll lose your pretty complexion!" [47] After the war the practice became more common, conveying when necessary, just the proper degree of nonchalance. Ardita Farnham "took a carved jade case from her pocket, extracted a cigarette and lit it with a conscious coolness, though she knew her hand was trembling a little." [48] Quite good for a girl who believed that she was being kidnapped! Sixteen-year old Cecilia Connage, who preferred to indulge her rebellions in secret, stole one of Rosalind's cigarettes. "She lights it and then, puffing and blowing, walks toward the mirror." [49]

The girls were also drinking more. Seventeen-year old Eleanor Ramilly shocked her Baltimore relatives by traveling with a "rather fast crowd . . . who drank cocktails in limousines and were promiscuously condescending and patronizing toward older

---

[45] F. Scott Fitzgerald, *Tales of the Jazz Age* (New York: Charles Scribner's Sons, 1922) 97–98.

[46] *Flappers and Philosophers,* 119.　　　[47] *The Beautiful and Damned,* 59.

[48] *Ibid.,* 24.　　　[49] *This Side of Paradise,* 192–93.

, she's average—smokes sometimes, drinks punch, frequently kissed—Oh, yes—
nmon knowledge—one of the effects of the war, you know.   F. Scott Fitzgerald,
is Side of Paradise

people." [50] Attending a country club dance in a small Georgia city, Nancy Lamar surprised an admirer by eschewing ginger ale and drinking whisky straight from a bottle. "Taking out the cork she held the flask to her lips and took a long drink." [51]

Five minutes after Amory Blaine first met Rosalind Connage, in 1919, he asked for a kiss. After a bit of verbal sparring, they embraced. "Well, is your curiosity satisfied?" Amory asked. "Is yours?" Rosalind countered. "No, it's only aroused." Her next comment was disconcerting. "I've kissed dozens of men. I suppose I'll kiss dozens more." When Amory showed some discontent with this attitude, she said, "Most people like the way I kiss." And Amory replied, "Good Lord, yes. Kiss me once more, Rosalind." She protested that her curiosity was generally satisfied at one, but they soon repeated the experiment.[52]

The changing folkways of kissing bewildered not only the older generation, but many of the young males as well. Howard Gillespie reproached Rosalind because she hadn't kissed him for two weeks. "I had an idea," he said, "that after a girl was kissed she was—was —won." But Rosalind set him straight. "Those days are over. I have to be won all over again every time you see me." And she went on to explain that there used to be two kinds of kisses: "First when girls were kissed and deserted; second, when they were engaged. Now there's a third kind, where the man is kissed and deserted. . . . Given a decent start any girl can beat a man nowadays." [53]

Like other aspects of the feminine revolt, casual familiarity between the sexes had been apparent as early as 1914. On the Triangle Club Christmas tour, Amory "had come into constant contact with that great current American phenomenon, the 'petting party.' None of the Victorian mothers—and most of the mothers were Victorian—had any idea how casually their daughters were accustomed to be kissed. '*Servant*-girls are that way,' says Mrs. Huston-Carmelite to her popular daughter, 'They are kissed first and proposed to afterward.' " [54] Amory "saw the cities between New York and Chicago as one vast juvenile intrigue." [55]

A few years before, the "belle" had become the "flirt;" now the "flirt" had become the "baby vamp." The belle had been sur-

[50] *Ibid.*, 249.   [51] *Tales of the Jazz Age*, 15.   [52] *This Side of Paradise*, 188–89.
[53] *Ibid.*, 194.   [54] *Ibid.*, 64.   [55] *Ibid.*, 65.

A special orchestra, special even in a day of special orchestras.   F. Scott Fitzgerald,
Tales of the Jazz Age

rounded by a dozen men in the intervals between dances. The baby vamp simply disappeared during intermissions to pet with some boy in a limousine parked outside the country club. When the touring Amory remarked that it seemed rather odd to be embracing a girl whom he had never seen before and would never see again, the young lady was annoyed. " 'Oh, let's go in,' she interrupted, 'if you want to *analyze*. Let's not *talk* about it.' " [56]

All this kissing, however, did not imply similar promiscuity in sexual relations. Gloria Gilbert, who had been kissed from coast to coast, pushed a man down an embankment and broke his arm when "he began to think perhaps he could get away with a little more." [57]

[56] *Ibid.*, 66.   [57] *The Beautiful and Damned*, 181.

Even in the late 1920's, American girls played the game somewhat differently from Europeans. When Nicole Diver, beginning an extra-marital affair, asked the experienced European, Tommy Bardan, to kiss her on the lips, he protested. " 'That's so American,' he said, kissing her nevertheless. 'When I was in America last there were girls who would tear you apart with their lips, tear themselves too, until their faces were scarlet with the blood around the lips all brought out in a patch—but nothing further.' " [58]

Sexual mores reflected a class bias. Upper class men dated, kissed, and eventually married young women of their own set, but for sexual adventure they picked up working class girls. Amory Blaine became innocently involved in the escapade of a former Princeton classmate, who had taken a New York City girl to an Atlantic City hotel.[59] Anthony Patch, in an army training camp in the South, during World War I, drifted into an affair with a jewelry store clerk.[60] Gordon Sterett, waking up in a shabby hotel bedroom and realizing that he was "irrevocably married to Jewel Hudson," shot himself. It was the over-rouged Jewel who had boasted: "Well, let me tell you I know more college fellas and more of 'em know me, and are glad to take me out on a party, than you ever saw in your whole life." [61]

Yet in the relations of men and women of the same social class, the coming sexual revolution was clearly foreshadowed. There was no longer the old reticence in discussing such matters. In a Fitzgerald story published in 1920, a nineteen-year old girl, visiting her brother in a monastery, remarked upon the growing freedom in the matter of birth control. Seeing him wince, Lois said: "Oh, . . . everybody talks about everything now." [62] The new frankness was hastened by the Freudian fad, even though the great Austrian's teachings were poorly understood. One of Amory Blaine's girl friends said: "Oh, just one person in fifty has any glimmer of what sex is. I'm hipped on Freud and all that, but it's rotten that every bit of *real* love in the world is ninety-nine per cent passion and one little soupcon of jealousy." [63]

[58] F. Scott Fitzgerald, *Tender Is the Night* (New York: Bantam Books, 1950), 323.
[59] *This Side of Paradise*, 261–71.   [60] *The Beautiful and Damned*, 324–29.
[61] *Tales of the Jazz Age*, 100–01, 124–25.   [62] *Flappers and Philosophers*, 154.
[63] *This Side of Paradise*, 255.

It did not always stop with talk. The feverish excitement of World War I undoubtedly helped to undermine the old inhibitions. Daisy Fay, a rich Southern girl, gave herself to Jay Gatsby, whose humble origins were effectively concealed in an army uniform. "So he made the most of his time. He took what he could get, ravenously and unscrupulously—eventually he took Daisy one still October night, took her because he had no real right to touch her hand." [64] By the end of the decade the odds on virginity seem to have altered. "Looking at you as a perfectly normal girl of twenty-two, living in the year nineteen twenty-eight," said Dick Diver to Rosemary Hoyt, "I guess you've taken a few shots at love." [65]

Fitzgerald's relationship to the Jazz Age was a complicated one. Because of his early novels and stories, he embodied, for the general public, the very concept of flaming youth. Yet the social upheaval was bigger than he himself realized. In 1922, he exchanged letters with Maxwell Perkins on the advisability of using the title "Tales of the Jazz Age" for his latest collection of stories. The Scribner's sales force feared that the words "jazz" and "flapper" were fast becoming passé; Fitzgerald was inclined to agree, but decided to gamble with the Jazz Age title. "It is better to have a title and a title-connection that is a has-been than one that is a never-will-be. The splash of the flapper movement was too big to have quite died down —the outer rings are still moving." [66]

Actually the Jazz Age had seven more years to run. Fitzgerald felt competent to give it an exact dating. "The Jazz Age is over," he wrote in a later letter to Perkins. "If Mark Sullivan is going on, you might tell him I claim credit for naming it and that it extended from the suppression of the riots on May Day, 1919, to the crash of the stock market in 1929—almost exactly one decade." [67]

Fitzgerald claimed credit not only for naming the Jazz Age, but for fixing the image of the age's female incarnation. In 1925, he suggested a line that might be used on the jacket of *All the Sad Young Men:* "Show transition from his early exuberant stories of youth which created a new type of American girl and the later and more serious mood which produced *The Great Gatsby* and marked

[64] *The Great Gatsby*, 159.   [65] *Tender Is the Night*, 233.
[66] Fitzgerald to Perkins, May 11, 1922, *Letters*, 158.
[67] Fitzgerald to Perkins, [before May 21, 1931], *ibid.*, 225.

him as one of the half-dozen masters of English prose now writing in America." [68]

Did Fitzgerald in truth "create" a new type of American girl? Certainly in his earlier work he had thought of himself more as recorder than as innovator. Yet the important fact of the 1920's was not the sophistication of the country-club set, a sophistication already well advanced when World War I began, but the spread of this sophistication through a much larger sector of American society. The Fitzgerald stories played an important role in the democratization of the new mores—although Hollywood probably had even more influence.

Once again Fitzgerald, the moralist, was far from happy with what Fitzgerald, the hedonist, had helped to bring about. He wrote in 1925, "The young people in America are brilliant with second-hand sophistication inherited from their betters of the war generation who to some extent worked things out for themselves. They are brave, shallow, cynical, impatient, turbulent and empty. I like them not." [69]

The ambivalence of his feeling reflected itself in his work. "All the stories that came into my head, had a touch of disaster in them —the lovely young creatures in my novels went to ruin, the diamond mountains of my short stories blew up, my millionaires were as beautiful and damned as Thomas Hardy's peasants. In life, these things hadn't happened yet, but I was pretty sure living wasn't the reckless, careless business these people thought—this generation just younger than me." [70]

IV

"Let me tell you about the very rich," wrote Fitzgerald.

They are different from you and me. They possess and enjoy early, and it does something to them, makes them soft where we are hard, and cynical where we are trustful, in a way that, unless you were born rich, it is very difficult to understand. They think, deep in their hearts, that they

---

[68] Fitzgerald to Perkins, [c. June 1, 1925], *ibid.*, 189–90.
[69] Fitzgerald to Marya Mannes, [Oct., 1925], *ibid.*, 489.
[70] "Early Success," *The Crack-up*, 87.

are better than we are because we had to discover the compensations and
refuges of life for ourselves. Even when they enter deep into our world or
sink below us, they still think they are better than we are. They are
different.[71]

But if the rich differed from the poor, they differed from each
other as well. They differed in the age and respectability of their
fortunes. They differed in the manner of life considered appropriate to their station.

Still alive in World War I days were many first generation millionaires of the Rockefeller or Carnegie type. Such a man was Fitzgerald's Adam J. Patch, who had come home from the Civil War,
"charged into Wall Street, and amid much fuss, fume, applause,
and ill will . . . gathered to himself some seventy-five million
dollars." Retiring from money-making at the age of fifty-seven, old
Adam dedicated his declining years to the cause of moral reform.
"From an armchair in the office of his Tarrytown estate he directed
against the enormous hypothetical enemy, unrighteousness, a campaign which went on through fifteen years, during which he displayed himself a rabid monomaniac, an unqualified nuisance, and
an intolerable bore." [72]

In the second or third generations these families were more
likely to run to stuffy respectability than to eccentricity. The
Howard Tates were the most formidable people in Toledo. "Mrs.
Howard Tate was a Chicago Todd before she became a Toledo
Tate, and the family generally affect that conscious simplicity
which has begun to be the earmark of American aristocracy. The
Tates have reached the stage where they talk about pigs and farms
and look at you icy-eyed if you are not amused." [73]

Young men from these families attended the Ivy League colleges, where they avoided the follies of the Amory Blaines and enjoyed secure status. Tudor Baird was a Scroll and Keys man at Yale;
"he possessed the correct reticences of a 'good egg,' the correct notions of chivalry and *noblesse oblige*—and, of course but unfortunately, the correct biases and the correct lack of ideas . . ."

---

[71] F. Scott Fitzgerald, "The Rich Boy," *Babylon Revisited and Other Stories* (New
York: Charles Scribner's Sons, 1960), 152–53.
[72] *The Beautiful and Damned*, 4.   [73] *Tales of the Jazz Age*, 41.

Let me tell you about the very rich. They are different from you and me.   F. Scott
Fitzgerald, "The Rich Boy," *Babylon Revisited and Other Stories*

Gloria Patch kissed him one night, not because she loved him but "because he was so charming, a relic of a vanishing generation which lived a priggish and graceful illusion and was being replaced by less gallant fools." [74]

A coarser specimen was Tom Buchanan, who belonged to an enormously wealthy Chicago family. He had been "one of the most powerful ends that ever played football at New Haven—a national

[74] *The Beautiful and Damned*, 368–69.

figure in a way, one of those men who reach such an acute limited excellence at twenty-one that everything afterwards savors of anticlimax." He had married the beautiful Daisy Fay of Louisville; they had honeymooned in the South Seas, "spent a year in France for no particular reason, and then drifted here and there unrestfully wherever people played polo and were rich together." [75] Living on a beautiful Long Island estate during the early 1920's, Tom was "a sturdy straw-haired man of thirty with a rather hard mouth and a supercilious manner. Two shining arrogant eyes had established dominance over his face and gave him the appearance of always leaning aggressively forward." [76] Having recently read a book—a rare event—Tom was parroting its pseudo-scientific racial teachings. "It's up to us, who are the dominant race," he said, "To watch out or these other races will have control of things." [77] A cheap philanderer, who had begun having affairs with other women three months after his marriage, Tom had most recently become involved with the wife of a wayside auto repair man.

And finally there were men of recently acquired wealth such as Jay Gatsby. The sources of Gatsby's fortune were clothed in mystery because of their illegal character. All that his neighbor Nick Carraway was able to find out was that Gatsby had started life under the name of James Gatz on a poor North Dakota farm. At various times he had been a clam digger, the right-hand man for a flamboyant Western millionaire, an army captain, and the front man for an Eastern gangster. Out of postwar underworld activities, vaguely identified with bootlegging, gambling, and the handling of stolen bonds, Gatsby was enjoying enough income in the early 1920's to live in baronial splendor on Long Island.

Jay Gatsby lived in West Egg and Tom Buchanan in East Egg. The two villages lay within sight of each other, separated only by a placid inlet of Long Island Sound; both were populated with very wealthy people. Yet each had a clearly defined character. West Egg was "the less fashionable of the two, though this is a most superficial tag to express the bizarre and not a little sinister contrast between them." [78] The families of firmly established respectability lived in East Egg; the newly-rich and the adventurers lived in West Egg.

---

[75] *The Great Gatsby,* 14.   [76] *Ibid.,* 15.   [77] *Ibid.,* 21.   [78] *Ibid.,* 13.

Daisy Buchanan, attending one of Gatsby's parties, was "appalled by West Egg, this unprecedented 'place' that Broadway had begotten upon a Long Island fishing village—appalled by its raw vigor that chafed under the old euphemisms and by the too obtrusive fate that herded its inhabitants along a short-cut from nothing to nothing." [79]

In both villages the houses were impressively large, yet there were different standards of taste. The Buchanan's house in East Egg possessed quiet elegance—"a cheerful red-and-white Georgian Colonial mansion, overlooking the bay. The lawn started at the beach and ran toward the front door for a quarter of a mile, jumping over sun-dials and brick walks and burning gardens— finally when it reached the house drifting up the side in bright vines as though from the momentum of its run. The front was broken by a line of French windows, glowing now with reflected gold and wide open to the warm windy afternoon. . . .[80]

Jay Gatsby's residence in West Egg had a much more spectacular kind of magnificence. A "colossal affair by any standard," it was "a factual imitation of some Hotel de Ville in Normandy, with a tower on one side, spanking new under a thin beard of raw ivy, and a marble swimming pool and more than forty acres of lawn and garden." [81] A brewer had built it during the "period" craze just before World War I, "and there was a story that he'd agreed to pay five years taxes on all the neighboring cottages if the owners would have their roofs thatched with straw"—but they refused.[82] Inside the place, guests wandered through Marie Antoinette music-rooms, Restoration salons, and a Merton College library. Upstairs there were "period bedrooms swathed in rose and lavender silk and vivid with new flowers," and "dressing-rooms and poolrooms, and bathrooms with sunken baths." [83] Gatsby had his own private beach, his own hydroplane, and more than one automobile. His Rolls-Royce was "a rich cream color, bright with nickel, swollen here and there in its monstrous length with triumphant hat-boxes and supper boxes and tool-boxes, and terraced with a labyrinth of wind-shields that mirrored a dozen suns." [84] Green upholstery

---

[79] *Ibid.*, 115.   [80] *Ibid.*, 14–15.   [81] *Ibid.*, 13.   [82] *Ibid.*, 96.
[83] *Ibid.*, 99.   [84] *Ibid.*, 72.

ornamented its interior, and a three-noted horn gave forth bursts of melody.

Gatsby entertained lavishly. "There was music," said Nick Carraway,

from my neighbor's house through the summer nights. In his blue gardens men and girls came and went like moths among the whisperings and the champagne and the stars. At high tide in the afternoon I watched his guests diving from the tower of his raft, or taking the sun on the hot sand of his beach while his two motor-boats slit the waters of the Sound, drawing aquaplanes over cataracts of foam. On weekends his Rolls-Royce became an omnibus, bearing parties to and from the city between nine in the morning and long past midnight, while his station wagon scampered like a brisk yellow bug to meet all trains. And on Monday eight servants, including an extra gardener, toiled all day with mops and scrubbing-brushes and hammers and garden-shears, repairing the ravages of the night before.[85]

Most of Gatsby's guests came uninvited. They drove out to Long Island in their automobiles, and "somehow they ended up at Gatsby's door." Somebody introduced them, and after that they behaved as though they were in a public amusement park. "Sometimes they came and went without having met Gatsby at all, came for the party with a simplicity of heart that was its own ticket of admission." [86]

In the main hall "a bar with a real brass rail was set up, and stocked with gins and liquors and with cordials so long forgotten that most of his female guests were too young to know one from another." [87] In the garden there were buffet tables, "garnished with glistening hors-d'oeuvres, spiced baked hams crowded against salads of harlequin designs and pastry pigs and turkeys bewitched to a dark gold." [88] Two suppers were served—one early in the evening and the second after midnight.

Gatsby had hired an orchestra, "no thin five-piece affair, but a whole pitful of oboes and trombones and saxophones and viols and cornets and piccolos, and low and high drums." [89] The guests danced out of doors on a huge canvas floor spread out in the garden

[85] *Ibid.*, 47.   [86] *Ibid.*, 49.   [87] *Ibid.*, 48.
[88] *Ibid.*, 47–48.   [89] *Ibid.*, 48.

and illuminated with hundreds of colored lights. Old men pushed young girls backward "in eternal graceless circles;" superior couples held each other tortuously and fashionably, keeping in the corners; young girls danced individually or invaded the orchestra to take over the banjo or the traps. "By midnight the hilarity had increased. A celebrated tenor had sung in Italian, and a notorious contralto had sung in jazz, and between the numbers people were doing 'stunts' all over the garden, while happy, vacuous bursts of laughter rose toward the summer sky." [90] After scenes of maudlin drunkenness in which women fought with their escorts and men drove their cars into ditches, the party finally broke up.

But Long Island was only one of the playgrounds of the rich. Nick Carraway realized why the face of the tennis and golf playing Jordan Baker was familiar to him—"its pleasing contemptuous expression had looked out at me from many rotogravure pictures of the sporting life at Asheville and Hot Springs and Palm Beach." [91]

The wealthy escaped winter's rigors in Florida.

Palm Beach sprawled plump and opulent between the sparkling sapphire of Lake Worth, flawed here and there by house-boats at anchor, and the great turquoise bar of the Atlantic Ocean. The huge bulks of the Breakers and the Royal Poinciana rose as twin paunches from the bright level of the sand, and around them clustered the Dancing Glade, Bradley's House of Chance, and a dozen modistes and milliners with goods at triple prices from New York. Upon the trellised veranda of the Breakers two hundred women stepped right, stepped left, wheeled, and slid in that then celebrated calisthenic known as the double-shuffle, while in half-time to the music two thousand bracelets clinked up and down on two hundred arms.[92]

Pleasure-seeking Americans carried their quest beyond the national boundaries. "The gay elements of society," Fitzgerald explained, "had divided into main streams, one flowing toward Palm Beach and Deauville, and the other, much smaller, toward the summer Riviera. One could get away with more on the summer Riviera, and whatever happened seemed to have something to do with art." [93]

---

[90] *Ibid.,* 54–55.   [91] *Ibid.,* 26.   [92] "The Rich Boy," *Babylon Revisited,* 162.
[93] "Echoes of the Jazz Age," *The Crack-up,* 18–19.

In 1919, when Dr. Richard Diver, an American psychiatrist studying in Europe, married Nicole Warren, the psychotic daughter of a Chicago millionaire, they decided to make their home in the ancient hill village of Tarmes on the French Riviera. "We'll live near a warm beach," Nicole thought, "where we can be brown and young together." Ironically, one of the place's attractions was that it was quiet. "No one comes to the Riviera in summer, so we expect to have a few guests and to work." [94] Six years later, when the young movie actress, Rosemary Hoyt, and her mother visited Tarmes in June, the place was so dead they almost left. Even nearby Cannes was almost moribund. Rosemary became a little self-conscious, "as though people were wondering why she was here in the lull between the gaiety of last winter and next winter, while up north the true world thundered by." [95]

The Divers had taken care not to destroy the quaint charm of the setting. "The villa and its grounds were made out of a row of peasant dwellings that abutted on the cliff—five small houses had been combined to make the house and four destroyed to make the garden. The exterior walls were untouched, so that from the road far below it was indistinguishable from the violet gray mass of the town." [96]

It was a place far more conducive to relaxation than to work. Dr. Diver had no active practice and dawdled along on the ambitious work of scholarship on which he was supposedly engaged. The lazy routine of the days was broken by occasional nights of frivolity. "I want to give a really *bad* party," Dick told Nicole. "I mean it. I want to give a party where there's a brawl and seductions and people going home with their feelings hurt and women passed out in the *cabinet de toilette*." [97]

Between 1925 and 1930, the character of Tarmes completely changed, as more and more newcomers discovered the sensuous appeal of the summer Riviera. Dick Diver's hideaway was "perverted now to the tastes of the tasteless." The quiet beach on which he and Nicole had scavenged for odd pieces of glass was overrun with new paraphernalia, trapezes and swinging rings over the water, portable bathhouses, floating towers, searchlights from the

---

[94] *Tender Is the Night*, 177.   [95] *Ibid.*, 13.   [96] *Ibid.*, 27.   [97] *Ibid.*, 28.

nights' fêtes, and a modernistic buffet. "Now the swimming place was a 'club,' though, like the international society it represented, it would be hard to say who was not admitted." [98] The water was almost the last place to look for one's friends, "because few people swam any more in that blue paradise, children and one exhibitionistic valet who punctuated the morning with spectacular dives from a fifty-foot rock—most of Gausse's guests stripped the concealing pajamas from their flabbiness only for a short hangover dip at one o'clock." [99]

But the Riviera was only one of the European spots where rich Americans tried to escape boredom. Nicole Diver, heir to the Warren millions, saw to it that the family traveled in appropriate style. To help with the baggage, the children, and the dogs, she had her own maid, the governess, and the governess's maid. On the baggage car of the train the Divers had "four wardrobe trunks, a shoe trunk, three hat trunks and two hat boxes, a chest of servants' trunks, a portable filing-cabinet, a medicine case, a spirit-lamp container, a picnic set, four tennis rackets in presses and cases, a phonograph, a typewriter. Distributed among the spaces reserved for family and entourage were two dozen supplementary grips, satchels, and packages, each one numbered, down to the tag on the cane case." Nicole kept track of it all. "It was equivalent to the system of a regimental supply officer who must think of the bellies and equipment of three thousand men." [100]

Nicole shopped with the same regal flair. She bought from "a great list that ran two pages, and she bought the things in the windows besides. Everything she liked that she couldn't possibly use herself, she bought as a present for a friend." [101] One afternoon's plunder included colored beads, folding beach cushions, artificial flowers, honey, a guest bed, bags, scarfs, love birds, miniatures for a doll's house, prawn-colored cloth, a dozen bathing suits, a rubber alligator, a traveling chess set of gold and ivory, linen handkerchiefs, and two chamois leather jackets of kingfisher blue.

While Nicole practised conspicuous consumption in such ways as this, Dick Diver continued to indulge his passion for parties. In Paris, these affairs involved a great deal of carefree movement

---

[98] *Ibid.*, 306–7.   [99] *Ibid.*, 307.   [100] *Ibid.*, 280–81.   [101] *Ibid.*, 58.

from one part of the city to another; "Dick's parties were all concerned with excitement and a chance breath of fresh night air was the more precious for being experienced in the intervals of the excitement." The evening that Rosemary Hoyt went along, the party "moved with the speed of a slapstick comedy." The number of merrymakers varied. "People joined them as if by magic, accompanied them as specialists, almost guides, through a phase of the evening, dropped out and were succeeded by other people, so that it appeared as if the freshness of each one had been husbanded for them all day." They commandeered the Shah of Persia's limousine, convinced the concierge at the Ritz that General Pershing was one of their group, and ended up "riding along on top of thousands of carrots in a market wagon." [102]

Despite the psychological strains that were to destroy their marriage, the Divers lived with a kind of natural grace and gaiety that Fitzgerald admired. Not so appealing were other members of the fast international set. "Baby" Warren, Nicole's older sister, was a hard and calculating woman who thought that money would buy anything. She boasted of her close friendships with male members of the English aristocracy, but she never married. "Of course," she explained, "I know people say, Baby Warren is racing around over Europe, chasing one novelty after another, and missing the best things in life, but I think on the contrary that I'm one of the few people who really go after the best things. I've known the most interesting people of my time." [103] Different in background from Baby Warren, but similarly in search for excitement, was Mary North, the daughter of a Newark paper hanger. After the violent death of her first husband, a brilliant but alcoholic musician, Mary became the wife of the Conte di Minghetti, the fabulously rich ruler-owner of manganese deposits in southwestern Asia. "He was not quite light enough to travel in a pullman south of Mason-Dixon; he was of the Kyble-Berber-Sabaean-Hindu strain that belts across north Africa and Asia, more sympathetic to the European than the mongrel faces of the ports." [104] A more sinister form of European corruption involved Mary with Lady Caroline Sibly-Biers, an English Lesbian.[105]

[102] *Ibid.*, 82–85.   [103] *Ibid.*, 238.   [104] *Ibid.*, 282.   [105] *Ibid.*, 331–36.

Whether he wrote about West Egg or Tarmes, Fitzgerald continued to occupy his peculiar situation half in and half out of the class he was describing. As an insecure member of the leisure class, Jay Gatsby was not a little like Fitzgerald himself, and Gatsby's lavish entertaining resembled the parties that Scott and Zelda gave when they lived at Great Neck, Long Island. The Dick Divers in their most attractive moments—rich, handsome, gay, and charming—were modeled on Gerald and Sara Murphy, whose genius for informal entertaining made their home at Antibes a gathering place for American writers and artists visiting the Riviera. In their unhappier phases, drinking too much, fighting mental illness, and losing their capacity for creative work, the Divers resembled the Fitzgeralds.

Although Jay Gatsby, Tom and Daisy Buchanan, Dick and Nicole Diver, and Baby Warren were all too old to be still eligible for the flaming youth of Fitzgerald's earlier stories, they belonged to the same epoch of social history. The Jazz Age, Fitzgerald pointed out, became less and less an affair of the young. "The sequel was like a children's party taken over by the elders, leaving the children puzzled and rather neglected and rather taken aback. By 1923, their elders, tired of watching the carnival with ill-concealed envy, had discovered that young liquor will take the place of young blood, and with a whoop the orgy began. The younger generation was starred no longer." [106]

---

[106] "Echoes of the Jazz Age," *The Crack-up*, 15.

4

The Decay of Yoknapatawpha County

. . . And you stand suzerain and solitary above the whole
sum of your life beneath that incessant ephemeral spangling.
First is Jefferson, the center, radiating weakly its puny glow
into space; beyond it, enclosing it, spreads the County, tied
by the diverging roads to that center as is the rim to the hub
by its spokes, yourself detached as God himself for this moment above the cradle of your nativity and of the men and
women who made you, the record and chronicle of your native land proffered for your perusal in ring by concentric
ring like the ripples on living water above the dreamless
slumber of your past; . . .

WILLIAM FAULKNER, *The Town* [1]

"ALL MY LIFE," said William Faulkner, "has been lived
in a little Mississippi town." [2] This was not literally true, of course.
Faulkner ventured out of Mississippi on many occasions. When he
was about twenty, he spent several months in New Haven, Connecticut. After that, he received flight training in the Royal Canadian Air Force, although World War I was over before he could get
into combat. A few years later, he lived for a while in New Orleans,
working for a rum runner and doing some writing. He walked and
cycled for several weeks in Europe. First enticed to Hollywood
after *Sanctuary* (1931) achieved its scandalous success, Faulkner

[1] William Faulkner, *The Town* (New York: Random House, 1957), 315–16.
[2] Frederick L. Gwynn and Joseph L. Blotner (eds.) *Faulkner in the University:
Class Conferences at the University of Virginia 1957–1958* (Charlottesville: University of Virginia Press, 1959), 78.

75

made several later trips to the film capital, but only to earn the money to allow him to live in his own home town. On other occasions he worked brief stints in New York City, spent periods in residence at the University of Virginia, and crossed the Atlantic to receive the Nobel prize.

But Faulkner always returned to Oxford, Mississippi, to the house with the stately columns that he had purchased soon after his marriage. It was not the ancestral home of the Faulkners, but it looked as though it should have been. And this is what distinguished Faulkner from the other notable literary people of the day, most of them rootless people, alienated from their native towns and never establishing true homes elsewhere.

In his writing, Faulkner was similarly tied to home soil. Although, here too, he occasionally wandered. His earlier stories were laid in other settings, and the ambitious novel of his maturity, *A Fable* (1954), centered on European battlefields. But his fame is based on the fiction he wrote about Yoknapatawpha County and the town of Jefferson.

These places are not on any Mississippi map. In a playful attempt to persuade his readers that Jefferson was not his own home town, Faulkner sometimes mentioned Oxford in the novels as a separate place. On one occasion he set the distance between Jefferson and Oxford at fifty miles.[3] Yet the separateness of the two towns is not very convincing. When Hollywood moviemakers wanted to give *Intruder in the Dust* a setting of convincing realism, they moved their cameras to Oxford, and no one who saw the film failed to recognize the jail, courthouse, and square of Faulkner's description. And if Jefferson is Oxford only thinly disguised, Yoknapatawpha County is as clearly Lafayette County. Even the implausible name has its explanation. The Yocany River in the southern part of Lafayette County was once known as the "Yocanapatafa."[4]

Not only literary detectives, but Faulkner's neighbors have played the game of identifying the places and people mentioned in the novels. They have linked Frenchman's Bend with the real

[3] *The Town,* 290.
[4] Robert Coughlan, *The Private World of William Faulkner* (New York: Harper & Brothers, 1954), 82.

Dutch Bend, Garraway with Galloway, Seminary Hill with College Hill. The Sartoris family has close parallels with the Faulkner family; Gavin Stevens resembles Faulkner's lawyer friend Phil Stone. Many family names used in the novels, names like Armstid, Bunch, Bundren, De Spain, Hightower, and Varner are real family names in the region.[5] Episodes as pathetic as the idiot boy confined in the family yard or as comic as the mules tied to the railroad track bring back memories of real local events.[6]

Faulkner's fellow townsmen found the famous novelist a hard man to understand. Usually he kept by himself and repulsed all attempts at familiarity. Only in the easy comradeship of hunting trips did he let down the barriers. The few local folks who read his novels did not like them very much. John Cullen, one of Faulkner's hunting companions, could not understand why William objected to "dirty stories" in camp and yet wrote "dirty stories" in his fiction. Why did so moral a man write about "such completely immoral people?" Cullen complained that many of Faulkner's stories were distortions. "He exaggerates the ignorance of the poor whites, the nobility of the Negroes, and the decadence of the aristocrats. Many of his characters are freaks." [7] Shaking his head over Faulkner's treatment of the Snopeses, Cullen said sadly: "I wish that William had written more about some of the noble people here in our county whom I knew." [8]

To explain his friend's mysterious behaviour, Cullen could only suggest that Faulkner was writing these slanders upon the South "to sell to the Yankees." [9] And the novelist's younger brother John said much the same thing:

A great deal has been said about Bill writing about the kinds of people he did, always portraying their seamier side and their most outlandish doings. They say he presented the worst side of the South, when he could have presented its best. He himself said it better than I can, in *Intruder in the Dust*. In one passage he says that people will believe anything about the South if it is only bizarre enough. He wrote what people will

---

[5] John Cullen, in collaboration with Floyd C. Watkins, *Old Times in the Faulkner Country* (Chapel Hill: University of North Carolina Press, 1961), 64–69.

[6] *Ibid.*, 79, 104.   [7] *Ibid.*, 62.   [8] *Ibid.*, 107.   [9] *Ibid.*, 64.

believe, for that's what they will pay to read, and even a writer has to make money.[10]

Yet John Faulkner should have known better than this. Crude commercialism may account for the synthetic scandals of *Sanctuary*, but not for the indirectly revealed horrors of *The Sound and the Fury* and *Absalom, Absalom!* In his better books, Faulkner wrote not what he thought would be popular in Yankeeland, but what he felt compelled to say. Perverse and exaggerated though the novels often seem, they are Faulkner's attempt to tell a kind of truth not only about Mississippi, but about life itself.

Puzzling over Faulkner in 1936, Thomas Wolfe wrote to Stark Young: "I don't think I misunderstood you at all in what you said about Faulkner, and certainly no one who was present could have failed to understand that everything you said came from a feeling of true friendliness and admiration. And I agree utterly with your estimate in your letter—that what he writes is not like the South, but that the South is *in* his books, and in the spirit that creates them." [11]

Obviously, the historian must use the Faulkner novels with caution. He must realize that they are written not in the Howells tradition of meticulous realism, but in the older Melville spirit of romantic invention and rhetorical excess. Fortunately murder, suicide, rape, perversion, idiocy, and insanity are encountered less frequently in real life than in Faulkner fiction. Yet to ignore Faulkner would be to sacrifice a treasury of close observation. In no section of America are there more significant social tensions than in Mississippi, and, intelligently read, the Faulkner novels will reveal much that is literally true about that society as it evolved during the novelist's lifetime. "The artist," he wrote, "is influenced by all his environment. He's maybe more sensitive to it because he has to get the materials, the lumber that he's going to build his edifice with." [12] And the lumber of Faulkner's experience, his observation

---

[10] John Faulkner, *My Brother Bill: An Affectionate Reminiscence* (New York: Pocket Books, 1964), 245–46.

[11] Thomas Wolfe to Stark Young, March 7, 1936, *The Letters of Thomas Wolfe,* collected and ed. by Elizabeth Nowell (New York: Charles Scribner's Sons, 1956), 495.

[12] Floyd C. Watkins, Introduction to *Old Times in the Faulkner Country,* vii.

of how his neighbors acted and thought, helps us to understand a part of the recent past highly relevant to today's problems.

II

All Yoknapatawpha County stretched out beneath Gavin Stevens one beautiful spring evening as he drove onto a ridge beyond Seminary Hill. Under the stars he could see the alluvial river-bottom land, "the same fat black rich plantation earth still synonymous of the proud fading white plantation names." Here lived or had lived in the past the Sutphens, the Sartorises, the Compsons, the McCaslins, the Stevens, and the De Spains. Not all of them had actually owned plantations, but all had been proud and masterful people: "generals and governors and judges, soldiers (even if only Cuban lieutenants) and statesmen failed or not, and simple politicians and over-reachers and just simple failures, who snatched and grabbed and passed and vanished, name and face and all." [13]

Rising abruptly out of these fertile valleys was "the roadless, almost pathless perpendicular hill-country of McCallum and Gowrie and Frazier and Muir." Still scrabbling a living from this thin soil were the descendants of eighteenth century families that had been transported from the Scottish Highlands to the Carolina mountains and had later moved into Yoknapatawpha County. This Mississippi hill-country was in reality the western extension of the Appalachian Highland. Embarking upon the dangerous adventure related in *Intruder in the Dust,* young Charles Mallison and his companions invaded this region: "They were quite high now, the ridged land opening and tumbling away invisible in the dark yet with the sense, the sensation of height and space; by day he could have seen them, ridge on pine-dense ridge rolling away to the east and the north in similitude of the actual mountains in Carolina and before that in Scotland where his ancestors had come from but he hadn't seen yet. . . ." [14]

In a central location was the town of Jefferson, a place of some

[13] *The Town,* 316.
[14] William Faulkner, *Intruder in the Dust* (New York: Random House, 1948), 100.

3,000 inhabitants.[15] It was about the same size as Gopher Prairie, but of much greater importance because it was the county seat. Indeed the true heart of the whole region was the Square, along whose sides stood the courthouse, the banks, the drugstore, and various other businesses. These were "the edifices created and ordained for trade and government and judgment and incarceration where strove and battled the passions of men for which the rest and the little death of sleep were the end and the escape and the reward." [16] The courthouse was built in chastely traditional style with arched windows and a colonnaded portico. Above this stood a squat tower housing the great clock. As Faulkner describes the scene at night: "Now they could see the Square, empty too—the amphitheatric lightless stores, the slender white pencil of the Confederate monument against the mass of the courthouse looming in columned upsoar to the dim quadruple face of the clock lighted each by a single faint bulb with a quality as intransigeant against those four fixed mechanical shouts of adjuration and warning as the glow of a firefly." [17]

A more interesting building than the decorous courthouse was the jail. It was one of the oldest buildings in Jefferson, one of the few that had escaped destruction when Federal forces occupied the town during the Civil War. "It was of brick square proportioned, with four brick columns in shallow basrelief across the front and even a brick cornice under the eaves because it was old, built in a time when people took time to build even jails with grace and care. . . ." [18] A wooden porch across the front gave it the appearance of a residence. On the front of the second storey there was only one true window, a tall crossbarred rectangle, in which Negro prisoners could often be seen singing doleful songs or shouting down to Negro women idling along the fence below.

In the late 1920's, the contrast between townsman and countryman was still great. On Saturdays, the rural population would drive to Jefferson in their wagons and automobiles and crowd the streets around the Square.

The adjacent alleys were choked with tethered wagons, the teams reversed and nuzzling gnawed corn-ears over the tail-boards. The square

---

[15] *The Town*, 209.   [16] *Intruder in the Dust*, 85.   [17] *Ibid.*, 49.   [18] *Ibid.*

. . . the edifices created and ordained for trade and government and judgement and incarceration where strove and battled the passions of men. . . William Faulkner, *Intruder in the Dust*

was lined two-deep with ranked cars, while the owners of them and of the wagons thronged in slow overalls and khaki, in mail-order scarves and parasols, in and out of the stores, soiling the pavement with fruit- and peanut-hulls. Slow as sheep they moved, tranquil, impassable, filling the passages, contemplating the fretful hurrying of those in urban shirts and collars with the large, mild inscrutability of cattle or of gods, functioning outside of time, having left time lying upon the slow and imponderable land green with corn and cotton in the yellow afternoon.[19]

Phonographs and radios still possessed a fascinating novelty, and the farmers thronged about the doors of the stores listening to the blaring noise. "The pieces which moved them were ballads simple in melody and theme, of bereavement and retribution and repen-

[19] William Faulkner, *Sanctuary* (New York: Penguin Books, 1947), 64.

tance metallically sung, blurred, emphasized by static or needle—disembodied voices blaring from imitation wood cabinets or pebble-grain horn-mouths above the rapt faces, the gnarled slow hands long shaped to the imperious earth, lugubrious, harsh, sad." [20]

Beyond the Square lay the residential streets. Here, during the 1940's, the contrast between the old and the new Jefferson was striking. The big decaying wooden houses sat "deep in shaggy untended lawns of old trees and rootbound scented and flowering shrubs whose very names most people under fifty no longer knew." The old mansions no longer even faced the street but "peered at it over the day-after-tomorrow shoulders of the neat small new one-story houses designed in Florida and California set with matching garages in their neat plots of clipped grass and tedious flowerbeds, three and four of them now, a subdivision now in what twenty-five years ago had been considered a little small for one decent front lawn." In the new houses lived prosperous young married couples with two children each "and (as soon as they could afford it) an automobile each and the memberships in the country club/and the bridge clubs and the junior rotary and chamber of commerce and the patented electric gadgets for cooking and freezing and cleaning and the neat trim colored maids in frilled caps to run them and talk to one another over the telephone from house to house while the wives in sandals and pants and painted toenails puffed lipstick-stained cigarettes over shopping bags in the chain groceries and drugstores." [21]

The Negro sections had neither the drooping beauty of the old mansions, nor the glossy chic of the new bungalows. Not far from the Square was a street "bordered by negro stores of one storey and shaded by metal awnings beneath which negroes lounged, skinning bananas or small florid cartons of sweet biscuits." [22] Farther out, along the approaches to town, squalid cabins stood along the dusty unpaved road.

These decaying mansions and ramshackle hovels emphasized the Southernness of the town, yet in many ways Jefferson reminded one of Sinclair Lewis's Gopher Prairie. There was the same absorb-

---

[20] *Ibid.*, 64–65.   [21] *Intruder in the Dust*, 119–20.
[22] William Faulkner, *Sartoris* (New York: Signet Books, 1953), 154.

ing interest in other people's business. When Lawyer Gavin Stevens extended his friendship to young Linda Snopes, he worried much about what the town would say. "You know: in a little town of three thousand people like ours, the only thing that could cause more talk and notice than a middle-aged bachelor meeting a sixteen-year-old maiden two or three times a week would be a sixteen-year-old maiden and a middle-aged bachelor just missing each other two or three times a week by darting into stores or up alleys." [23] In this situation village meddlesomeness was amusing; in the case of another lawyer, Horace Benbow, attempting to help the ex-prostitute Ruby Lamar and her child, it became cruel.

Hearing the news that the hotel keeper had turned Ruby and her baby out after being waited upon by a committee of Baptist ladies, Benbow murmured bitterly, "Christians, Christians." [24] And elsewhere, Faulkner suggests that the County suffered from an overdose of Baptists and Methodists. Jefferson was "a town founded by Aryan Baptists and Methodists, for Aryan Baptists and Methodists." There was a small Episcopal church, the oldest extant building in town, and a Presbyterian congregation, also old. But these were insignificant,

. . . ours a town established and decreed by people neither Catholics nor Protestants nor even atheists but incorrigible nonconformists, nonconformists not just to everybody else but to each other in mutual accord; a nonconformism defended and preserved by descendants whose ancestors hadn't quitted home and security for a wilderness in which to find freedom of thought as they claimed and oh yes, believed, but to find freedom in which to be incorrigible and unreconstructible Baptists and Methodists; not to escape from tyranny as they claimed and believed, but to establish one.[25]

The town's only Oriental, a Chinese laundryman, and one of the town's two Jewish clothiers attended the Methodist church.

But the town's censoriousness applied more to open vice than to covert sinning. The former mayor and the banker's wife practiced adultery for eighteen years while the citizens discreetly averted their gaze.[26]

[23] *The Town*, 209.　　[24] *Sanctuary*, 106.
[25] *The Town*, 306–7.　　[26] *Ibid., passim.*

III

In 1919, a strong tradition of aristocracy still lingered in Yoknapatawpha County. Each afternoon, when the bank closed, a carriage driven by a Negro coachman waited at the curb to convey the bank president, Colonel Bayard Sartoris, to his estate four miles from Jefferson. The Colonel lived in a fine mansion built before the Civil War. "The white simplicity of it dreamed unbroken among the ancient sun-shot trees." From the colonnaded veranda, one stepped into a gracious hall. "The stairway with its white spindles and red carpet mounted in a tall slender curve into upper gloom. From the center of the ceiling hung a chandelier of crystal prisms and shades, fitted originally for candles but since wired for electricity. To the right of the entrance, beside folding doors rolled back upon a dim room emanating an atmosphere of solemn and seldom violated stateliness and known as the parlor, stood a tall mirror filled with grave obscurity like a still pool of evening water." [27]

In this beautiful home lived the Colonel, his eighty-year-old aunt, Miss Jenny, and his reckless grandson, young Bayard Sartoris, just returned from World War I. Serving their needs was a Negro family; the coachman Simon, who doubled as butler; his wife Elnore, the cook; his grandson Isom, who did odd jobs; and his son Caspey, recently discharged from the army and not in a mood to do much of anything.

When the Sartorises drove into Jefferson, they expected and received due deference. Old Simon imperiously ordered a Negro-chauffeured automobile away from the curb: "Don't block off no Sartoris ca'iage, black boy. . . . Block off de commonality, ef you wants, but don't invervoke no equipage waitin' on Cunnel or Miss Jenny. Dey won't stan' fer it." [28]

As Miss Jenny walked along the streets, merchants and others spoke to her "as to a martial queen." [29] Accompanying the reluctant Colonel to the doctor's office, she overawed the nurse who tim-

---

[27] *Sartoris*, 31.   [28] *Ibid.*, 45.   [29] *Ibid.*, 97.

idly inquired whether they had an appointment. "You go and tell
Dr. Alford we're here. . . . Tell him I've got some shopping to do
this morning and I haven't time to wait." [30] Not only the nurse,
but the doctor, meekly obeyed her command.

But the Sartorises were marked as belonging to the aristocracy
not so much by their spacious estate and their magisterial bearing
as by their consciousness of family tradition. They had an engross-
ment with the past quite foreign to even the wealthiest and most
pretentious families of Gopher Prairie. More alive than any Sartoris of the present generation was Colonel John Sartoris, who had
been shot to death by a political rival forty-five years earlier. It was
this earlier Colonel Sartoris who had built the family mansion and
developed the plantation, who had commanded Confederate
troops and outwitted the Yankees, who had killed two carpet-
baggers during a postwar election brawl, and who had built a railroad with Herculean effort. Readers of a more prosaic age are
likely to regard the masterful colonel as a stock character from the
pages of historical romance. Yet this Sartoris was, in sober truth, a
tolerably lifelike portrait of Faulkner's own grandfather, Colonel
William Falkner.

To the historian, the authenticity of the old Colonel is of less
concern than the impact of such traditions upon later generations.
Upper class people in Yoknapatawpha County knew a great deal
about their ancestors. Quentin Compson, desperately trying to
understand the disintegration of his own family, wondered
whether it was because "one of our forefathers was a governor and
three were generals and Mother's weren't." [31] Explaining the
background of Major Manfred De Spain, elected mayor of Jefferson in a minor political revolution of 1904, Faulkner says:

Jefferson, Mississippi, the whole South for that matter was still full at
that time of men called General or Colonel or Major because their
fathers or grandfathers had been generals or colonels or majors or maybe
just privates, in Confederate armies, or who had contributed to the campaign funds of successful state governors. But Major de Spain's father

---

[30] *Ibid.*, 98.
[31] William Faulkner, *The Sound and the Fury* (New York: Jonathan Cape and
Harrison Smith, 1929), 125.

had been a real major of Confederate cavalry, and De Spain himself was a West Pointer who had gone to Cuba as a second lieutenant with troops and came home with a wound. . . .[32]

Like most historic aristocracies, Jefferson's had shady origins. The military titles and the heroic exploits of family tradition were often spurious. Moreover, the proudest families could boast of gentle blood for only a few generations. Most of their eighteenth century ancestors had been dirt farmers in the Carolinas. The hard driving tactics by which the ancestral estates in Mississippi had been acquired gave rise to still another body of traditions such as those associated with Thomas Sutphen in *Absalom, Absalom!* or with Lucius Quintus Carothers McCaslin in *Go Down, Moses.*

The family legends were not so much of chivalric behaviour as of audacious deeds both good and bad. And deeds of this character became increasingly difficult to perform under twentieth century

[32] *The Town*, 10.

The white simplicity of it dreamed unbroken among the ancient sun-shot trees. William Faulkner, *Sartoris*

conditions. In the Faulkner novels, a social class is being liqui-
dated, not by violent revolution, but by forces of internal decay and
external social and economic change. The Compsons, in *The
Sound and the Fury,* provided an extreme case: the father was
ineffective and an alcoholic; the mother, a self-pitying neurotic;
one daughter had been ruined by promiscuity, and a grand-
daughter was starting along the same path; one son was an idiot,
another committed suicide, and a third became a villain of extraordinary meanness. The disintegration of young Bayard Sartoris was
as swift; unable to settle down after the death of his aviator brother,
he engaged in one escapade after another until he plunged to death
in a plane. Less dramatic, but truer to life were the cases in which
the old leaders of Yoknapatawpha society found themselves
shunted onto the sidetracks while the new masters rode past them
on the main express. This was the fate of Major de Spain, compelled to sell his bank stock and mansion to the scheming Flem
Snopes and to move out of town; of Horace Benbow whose languid
legal talents were too feeble to prevent the lynching of his client; or
of the more attractive lawyer, Gavin Stevens, doomed to soliloquize
over events he was unable to control.

IV

The great bulk of Yoknapatawpha people made no claim to
gentility. The "commonality," as the Sartoris coachman would
have described them, descended from people who had come into
the region from the northeast through the Tennessee mountains
"by stages marked by the bearing and raising of a generation of
children." More remotely, they had come from the Atlantic seaboard and before that from England and the Scottish and Welsh
Marches. They brought no slaves and no fine furniture; indeed for
the most part, they brought only what they could carry in their
hands.

They took up land and built one- and two-room cabins and never
painted them, and married one another and produced children and
added other rooms one by one to the original cabins and did not paint
them either, but that was all. Their descendants still planted cotton in
the bottom land and corn along the edge of the hills and in the secret

coves in the hills made whiskey of the corn and sold what they did not
drink. . . . They supported their own churches and schools, they married and committed infrequent adulteries and more frequent homicides
among themselves and were their own courts, judges and executioners.
They were Protestants and Democrats and prolific; there was not one
Negro landowner in the entire section. Strange Negroes would absolutely refuse to pass through it after dark.[33]

Despite similar ancestry the common people differed widely
from one another in economic activity, in education, and in aspirations. Gavin Stevens talked about one of these differences to his
young nephew Charles Mallison. Why did some of the people prefer to live in the hills and others in the valleys? In Gavin's probably too pat explanation, the hill people were of Scottish origin and
the valley people were English. The people who preferred to live in
the hills "on little patches which wouldn't make eight bushels of
corn or fifty pounds of lint cotton an acre even if they were not too
steep for a mule to pull a plow across (but then they don't want to
make the cotton anyway, only the corn and not too much of that
because it really doesn't take a great deal of corn to run a still as big
as one man and his son want to fool with) are people named Gowrie
and McCallum and Fraser and Ingrum. . . . who love brawling
and fear God and believe in Hell." Those who lived in the river
valleys "the broad rich easy land where a man can raise something
he can sell openly in daylight" were people with English names like
"Littlejohn and Greenleaf and Armstead and Millingham and
Bookwright." [34]

Another important difference was between those who owned
land and those who did not. This is what tipped the scales when
Zack Houston sought to marry Letty Bookright. "Although Zack
owned his place and was a good farmer, that's all he was: just a
farmer without no special schooling." [35] But this proved to be
enough and her father gave reluctant consent. The Faulkner novels
are thickly peopled with small independent farmers of the Houston
and Bookright type. Vernon Tull, who helped the improvident
Anse Bundren, was a hard-working man who lived on his own farm

---

[33] William Faulkner, *The Hamlet* (New York: Vintage Books, 1964), 4–5.
[34] *Intruder in the Dust*, 148–49.   [35] *The Town*, 78.

near the river. So too was Henry Armstid, who befriended the Bundrens in *As I Lay Dying* and Lena Grove in *Light in August*. In *The Hamlet*, Armstid fell for the swindles of Flem Snopes twice. The victim could ill afford these losses. Even though he owned his farm, he was a poor man. His wife complained: "Misters . . . we got chaps in the house that never had shoes last winter. We ain't got corn to feed the stock. We got five dollars I earned weaving by firelight after dark. . . ." [36] Gulled into believing there was buried treasure on the Old Frenchman's place, Armstid bought a third interest in the property by giving a mortgage on his farm.[37]

Less hard pressed were the MacCullums, with whom young Bayard Sartoris spent several days recuperating from his feeling of guilt in having contributed to Old Bayard's death. In a remote valley, nestled in the hills, lived the patriarchal Virginius Mac-Cullum and his six unmarried sons. The plebeian MacCullums had memories of the Civil War no less vivid than those of the aristocratic Sartorises. At the age of sixteen, Virginius had volunteered in Stonewall Jackson's brigade. After four years of service he "walked back to Mississippi and built himself a house and got married." This was the house in which Bayard found refuge more than a half century later. "The walls of the room were of chinked logs. On them hung two or three outdated calendars and a patent medicine lithograph in colors. The floor was bare, of hand-trimmed boards scuffed with heavy boots and polished by the pads of generations of dogs; two men could lie side by side in the fireplace." [38]

Farming, trading, hunting, and whisky-making provided the MacCallums with all they needed. Stuart was the most business-like member of the family. "He was a good farmer and a canny trader, and he had a respectable bank account of his own." [39] His older brother Henry was content to putter about the house and supervise the work of the Negro cook. "He visited town almost as infrequently as his father; he cared little for hunting, and his sole relaxation was making whisky, good whisky and for family consumption alone, in a secret fastness known only to his father and the negro

---

[36] *The Hamlet*, 296.   [37] *Ibid.*, 361.   [38] *Sartoris*, 263.   [39] *Ibid.*, 268.

who assisted him, after a recipe handed down from lost generations of his usquebaugh-bred forbears." [40]

The family ate in the kitchen, a separate building. At the long table there was only one chair, reserved for old Virginius; around the other three sides were backless benches. Food was abundant—"sausage and spare ribs, and a dish of hominy and one of fried sweet potatoes, and corn bread and a molasses jug of sorghum, and Mandy poured coffee from a huge enamelware pot." [41] The old man was contemptuous of his sons' intention of buying store food: "With a pen full of 'possums, and a river bottom full of squir'l and ducks, and a smokehouse of hawg meat, you damn boys have got to go clean to town and buy a turkey for Christmas dinner." [42]

Anse Bundren, the hill farmer in *As I Lay Dying,* was a man of much less competence. He and his ailing wife lived with four sons and a tomboy daughter in a house that tilted crazily. To assist the fat old country doctor up the perpendicular path Anse had to let down a rope. "What the hell does your wife mean," Dr. Peabody said, "taking sick on top of a durn mountain." [43]

Although his wife had worked herself close to death, Anse had taken no chances with his own health. "He was sick once from working in the sun when he was twenty-two years old, and he tells people that if he ever sweats, he will die. I suppose he believes it." [44] The Bundrens cared for nothing "except how to get something with the least amount of work." [45] They raised a little cotton, but the broken-roofed, dilapidated cotton house testified to their lack of success. Milk and turnip greens constituted an evening meal. They seldom visited Jefferson, the county seat; the youngest boy Vardaman remembered only the toy trains darting around the track in the store window. Such things were not for country boys, because flour and sugar and coffee cost so much. Bananas were his only treat. Stingy as well as lazy, Anse begrudged every dime of expenditure whether for taxes or medicine and wheedled away the pathetically small possessions of his own children.[46]

But even the Bundrens owned the infertile soil from which they scratched a living. Below them, in Yoknapatawpha eyes, was "that

[40] *Ibid.,* 266.   [41] *Ibid.,* 267.   [42] *Ibid.,* 283.

[43] William Faulkner, *As I Lay Dying* (New York: Vintage Books, 1957), 42.

[44] *Ibid.,* 17.   [45] *Ibid.,* 21.   [46] *Ibid.,* 3, 35, 58, 62–63, 181, 245.

nethermost stratum of unfutured, barely solvent one-bale tenant farmers which pervaded, covered thinly the whole county and on which in fact the entire cotton economy of the county was founded and supported." [47] The tenant was a man in overalls and tieless shirt "attached irrevocably by the lean umbilicus of bare livelihood . . . to the worn-out tenant farm." [48] Mink Snopes lived at the end of a rutted lane in "a broken-backed cabin of the same two rooms which were scattered without number through these remote hill sections. . . . It was built on a hill; below it was a foul muck-trodden lot and a barn leaning away downhill as though a human breath might flatten it." [49] He paid almost as much in rent, in one year, as the house had cost to build. It was not old, but already the roof leaked and the weather stripping had begun to rot away from the wall boards It was "just like the one he had been born in which had not belonged to his father either, and just like the one he would die in if he died indoors. . . ." [50] His corn was yellow and stunted because he had no money to buy fertilizer, and he owned neither the animals nor the tools to work the land properly. The tenants were people without roots. Mink had lived "in a dozen different sorry and ill-made rented cabins as his father had moved from farm to farm, without himself ever having been more than fifteen or twenty miles away from any one of them." [51]

Poorest among the tenants were the white and Negro share-croppers, chained by the crop mortgage system to the country merchants. Will Varner, who ran the store at Frenchman's Bend, rented out land to croppers compelled to buy all their provisions from him on credit. They delivered the entire crop to him, and once a year he sat at a desk "with the cash from the sold crops and the account books before him and cast up the accounts and charged them off and apportioned to each tenant his share of the remaining money." [52]

The common people of Yoknapatawpha County were both good and bad. Most were honest. The Varners could leave their store untended all day, trusting their customers to serve themselves and leave the money in a cigar box under the cheese cage.[53] Most were hospitable. Martha Armstid disapproved of the pregnant

[47] *The Town*, 280.   [48] *Ibid.*, 268.   [49] *The Hamlet*, 74.   [50] *Ibid.*, 223.
[51] *Ibid.*, 239.   [52] *Ibid.*, 90.   [53] *Ibid.*, 25.

. . . that nethermost stratum of unfutured, barely solvent one-bale tenant farmers . .
on which in fact the entire cotton economy of the county was founded and supportec
William Faulkner, *The Town*

Lena Grove, but took her in for the night and even gave her the egg
money.[54] The Bundrens, with their malodorous coffin, were unwelcome guests; but they had no trouble finding a barn to sleep in
each night. And they were also fed. Overriding Old Anse's feeble
refusal, the farmer Sampson asserted that "when folks stops with us
at meal time and won't come to the table, my wife takes it as a
insult." [55]

Quite apart from the foolhardy perseverance shown in braving
flood and fire to bury Addie in Jefferson, the Bundrens displayed
other virtues. They had their own brand of pride and independence. "We would be beholden to no man," said Anse at one point,
and on another occasion: "It's a public street. . . . I reckon we can
stop to buy something same as airy other man. We got the money to

[54] William Faulkner, *Light in August* (New York: Modern Library, 1950), 19.
[55] *As I Lay Dying*, 109.

pay for hit, and hit aint airy law that says a man cant spend his money where he wants." [56]

Many of the poor whites were ignorant, shiftless, quick tempered, and violent. A few were vicious and lawless. Vinson Gowrie was

the youngest of a family of six brothers one of whom had already served a year in federal penitentiary for armed resistance as an army deserter and another term at the state penal farm for making whiskey, and a ramification of cousins and inlaws covering a whole corner of the county. . . . [They were] integrated and interlocked and intermarried with other brawlers and foxhunters and whiskeymakers not even into a simple clan or tribe but a race a species which before now had made their hill stronghold good against the country and the federal government too, which did not even simply inhabit nor had merely corrupted but had translated and transmogrified that whole region of lonely pine hills dotted meagrely with small tilted farms and peripatetic sawmills and contraband whiskey-kettles where peace officers from town didn't even go unless they were sent for and strange white men didn't wander far from the highway after dark and no Negro at any time. . . .[57]

V

Social classes were by no means static in Yoknapatawpha County. The older families continued to lose their wealth and prestige. New families made money and exerted power. To point up this shift, Faulkner made the Snopeses leading characters in three of his novels and gave them a minor role in several others.

In 1919, Horace Benbow knew the Snopeses as "a seemingly inexhaustible family which for the last ten years had been moving to town in driblets from a small settlement known as Frenchman's Bend. Flem, the first Snopes, had appeared unheralded one day behind the counter of a small restaurant on a side street, patronized by country folk. With this foothold and like Abraham of old, he brought his blood and legal kin household by household, individual by individual, into town, and established them where they could gain money." Flem himself became successively manager of the city light and water plant, handy man to the municipal govern-

[56] *Ibid.*, 19, 193.   [57] *Intruder in the Dust*, 35–36.

ment, and—"to old Bayard's profane astonishment and uncon-cealed annoyance"—vice president of the Sartoris bank.[58]

In the train of the conquering Flem had come a whole legion of Snopes cousins. They spread to "small third-rate businesses of various kinds—grocery stores, barbershops (there was one an invalid of some sort, who operated a second-hand peanut roaster)—where they multiplied and flourished. The older residents from their Jeffersonian houses and genteel stores and offices, looked on with

[58] *Sartoris,* 157–58.

He owned most of the good land in the country and held mortgages on most of the rest.   William Faulkner, *The Hamlet*

amusement at first. But this was long since become something like consternation." [59]

This locust-like invasion of Snopeses into Jefferson had been preceded some years before by a similar infiltration of Frenchman's Bend. Where they came from originally, no one really seemed to know, although according to tradition, a man named Ab Snopes had been hanged as a horse thief during the Civil War. The first to appear in Frenchman's Bend was a later Ab Snopes, a share-cropper who never stayed long in one place—a fact apparently re-lated to mysterious fires in his landlords' barns. The relatives who followed him into the area had equally unsavory reputations: Isaac was an idiot; I.O. was a bigamous schoolmaster; Mink was sent to prison for murder.[60]

Flem Snopes was the son of the barn-burning Ab. By a succes-sion of shrewd *coups* he usurped control of Will Varner's rural fief and married the merchant's daughter, Eula. Having conquered Frenchman's Bend, Flem moved into Jefferson, where less than twenty years later, he achieved the presidency of the Sartoris bank. No less instructive than Flem's financial rise was his quest for respectability. He learned the advantages of keeping his manipu-lations within the letter of the law. When his relatives became in-volved in exhibiting pornographic pictures and initiating crooked damage suits, Flem hushed up the scandals and forced the offend-ing Snopeses to leave town.[61] To culminate his success, he bought the house of his vanquished rival, the aristocratic Major de Spain, and had it rebuilt in suitable grandeur. "It was going to have colyums across the front now," a shrewd local trader explained, "I mean the extry big ones so even a feller that never seen colyums before wouldn't have no doubt a-tall what they was, like in the photographs where the Confedrit sweetheart in a hoop skirt and a magnolia is saying good-bye to her Confedrit beau jest before he rides off to finish tending to General Grant." [62] Here Flem lived in comfortable wealth and Baptist sanctity, until the fateful day in 1946, when Mink Snopes killed him in an act of long delayed vengeance.[63]

---

[59] *Ibid.,* 158.   [60] *The Hamlet, passim.*
[61] *The Town,* 173–77, 251–57.   [62] *Ibid.,* 352.
[63] William Faulkner, *The Mansion* (New York: Random House, 1959), 416.

The Snopeses also infiltrated politics. Traveling by train to Jefferson one day, Horace Benbow encountered a fellow-passenger who introduced himself as "Senator Snopes, Cla'ence Snopes." Horace remembered him as he had been ten years before, "a hulking, dull youth, son of a restaurant-owner, member of a family which had been moving from the Frenchman's Bend neighborhood into Jefferson for the past twenty years, in sections; a family of enough ramifications to have elected him to the legislature without recourse to a public polling." [64]

Senator Snopes had obviously found many kindred spirits at the state capital. "There emerged gradually a picture of stupid chicanery and petty corruption for stupid and petty ends, conducted principally in hotel rooms into which bellboys whisked with bulging jackets upon discreet flicks of skirts in swift closet doors." [65] For relaxation the Senator made quiet excursions to Memphis, where he patronized only cut-rate brothels.[66]

A cheap political fixer, Clarence summed up his code and his prejudices: "I'm an American. . . . I don't brag about it, because I was born one. And I been a decent Baptist all my life, too. Oh, I ain't no preacher and I ain't no old maid; I been around with the boys now and then, but I reckon I ain't no worse than lots of folks that pretends to sing loud in church. But the lowest, cheapest thing on this earth aint a nigger: it's a jew. We need laws against them. Drastic laws. . . ." [67]

To the historian, the Snopeses have great interest. To what extent are they based upon real life in Oxford and Lafayette County? In the shrewd judgment of John Cullen, Faulkner's old hunting companion: "All the stories about the Snopeses are great exaggerations of actual persons and events. . . . Of course there are dishonest and cruel people here as in every community. But Faulkner has taken every crime and all the cheating and every instance of brutality he has remembered and told them all in his stories and novels, and time after time he has attributed these crimes and inhumanities to the Snopeses." [68] But having said this, Cullen had no difficulty in remembering several local episodes closely parallel to the exploits of the Snopeses.

---

[64] *Sanctuary*, 102–3.   [65] *Ibid.*, 103.   [66] *Ibid.*, 122.
[67] *Ibid.*, 157.   [68] Cullen, *op. cit.*, 99.

The idea of one vast family of rascals is clearly a whimsical Faulkner invention. But the general social movement thus symbolized is not. Faulkner's brother describes what happened in the case of sharecroppers who had a little more "git up and git" than their neighbors did. "They were not content to live out their lives as their forefathers had done, scrabbling out less than a living from some washed-out hill farm. They came to town for a better living for themselves and better education for their children, and by their initiative they secured both." Gradually they improved their status. "First they took menial jobs, then got into businesses of their own, like cafés and small grocery stores. At last they moved onto our Square and became merchants and town clerks and aldermen." [69]

William Faulkner's unflattering portrait of the Snopeses undoubtedly reflects something of the contempt with which the older Oxford families regarded the pushing newcomers. John Faulkner testifies to this: "Until then, our lives had been pretty well cut and dried. We were entrusted with our city government term after term and it coasted along in the same old rut that we considered good enough for us all. Our banks were in the hands of what we called our upper class, our more substantial citizens, and our department stores were handed down from father to son. When this new blood was infused into our daily circumscriptions, we didn't like it." [70]

But John Faulkner admits that the change was probably for the best. His class became "aware for the first time of the value of human endeavor." The new situation "made us hump along more lively than we had before in order to keep ahead or even to hold onto what we had. We still didn't like what we saw happening, really, but we didn't know what to do about it and we still don't." [71]

Was William Faulkner less understanding than his brother? Did he regard it as an unmitigated evil when some of the sharecroppers escaped from their dreary fate and made a new life for themselves in town? Not really, if his portrayal of the grocer, Wallstreet Snopes, is examined. From origins no less humble than those of Flem, Wall achieved a success almost as great. But Wall was as honest as he was hardworking. To be sure, this virtue suggested to Faulkner that he probably wasn't a Snopes at all. "His father's

---

[69] John Faulkner, *op. cit.*, 242.   [70] *Ibid.*, 243.   [71] *Ibid.*, 243–44.

mama," the author explained to a class at the University of Virginia, "may have done a little extra-curricular night work." But what difference does this sly Faulknerian suggestion make? The essential point is that Wall came from humble circumstances and achieved a deserved success. He wanted to be independent; he wanted to make money; "but he had rules about how he was going to do it. He wanted to make money by simple industry, the old rules of working hard and saving your pennies, not by taking advantage of anybody." [72]

Faulkner accepted the inevitability of the New South. His real nostalgia was for the older virtues that seemed to be in decay. He hoped for the survival of the cavalier spirit. "By cavalier spirit," he said, "I mean people who believe in simple honor for the sake of honor, and honesty for the sake of honesty." [73]

VI

The relationship between Negroes and whites in Yoknapatawpaha County was a far more complex thing than most Northerners realized. The white world and the Negro world were actually much less separated in the South than in the North. Whites were in daily contact with Negroes as servants, as workmen, as tenants, and as customers. Sometimes these relations were hostile and harsh; sometimes they were condescending or obsequious; sometimes they were affectionate even to the point of sentimentality.

Dilsey in *The Sound and the Fury* was a bizarre figure in her old age. "She wore a stiff black straw hat perched upon her turban, and a maroon velvet cape with a border of mangy and anonymous fur above a dress of purple silk. . . . She had been a big woman once but now her skeleton rose, draped loosely in unpadded skin that tightened again upon a paunch almost dropsical, as though muscle and tissue had been courage or fortitude which the days or the years had consumed until only the indomitable skeleton was left rising like a ruin or a landmark above the somnolent and impervious guts. . . ." [74] Yet this shabby Negro servant was the true mother of the tortured white family, providing the love and protec-

---

[72] Gwynn and Blotner, *op. cit.*, 246.   [73] *Ibid.*, 80.
[74] *The Sound and the Fury*, 330–31.

tion that the hypochondriac Mrs. Compson was too selfish to give.

If the nobility of Dilsey seems excessive, the affection of the Faulkner family for their own devoted servant may explain the novelist's feeling. The dedication of *Go Down, Moses* reads, "To Mammy Caroline Barr, Mississippi 1840–1940 Who was born in slavery and who gave to my family a fidelity without stint or calculation of recompense and to my childhood an immeasurable devotion and love." John Faulkner tells how William read the burial service over Mammy in his own parlor: "All of us loved Mammy, our shepherdess, at times an avenging angel. She appears in a great many of Bill's books. She it was who was faithful; she was the one who endured." [75]

But the relations of the white families with their Negro servants were not always so sweet. More than a dash of vinegar flavored the mixture. Dilsey served the Compsons with Christ-like patience, but she took no nonsense from them. When Mrs. Compson complained of the delay in breakfast and threatened to get the meal herself, Dilsey replied contemptuously: "En who gwine eat yo messin? . . . Tell me dat. . . ." and sent her mistress back to bed.[76] Dilsey conducted a running feud with the villainous Jason Compson. " 'Did you hear me?' Jason said. 'I hears you,' Dilsey said. 'All I been hearing, when you in de house. Ef hit ain't Quentin er yo maw, hit's Luster en Benjy. Whut you let him go on dat way fer, Miss Cahline?' " [77]

Nor was Dilsey unique in the easy familiarity with which she addressed her employers. Harry Mitchell accepted without protest some unsolicited marriage counseling from Rachel, the family's Negro cook. "Whut you let that 'oman treat you and that baby like she do, anyhow? . . . You ought to take and lay her out wid a stick of wood." [78] The advice was excellent and, if acted upon, would have saved both Belle Mitchell's husband and her lover from much trouble.

But white employers could address their Negro servants with the same roughness. "Drive on!" old Bayard shouted at Simon. "Drive on, damn your black hide." [79] And Miss Jenny stormed at the same garrulous old coachman: "You damn fool nigger! . . .

[75] John Faulkner, *op. cit.*, 42–43.   [76] *The Sound and the Fury*, 338.
[77] *Ibid.*, 346.   [78] *Sartoris*, 172.   [79] *Ibid.*, 30.

And you went and blurted a fool thing like that to Bayard. Haven't you got any more sense than that?" [80]

The gusty vigor of these interchanges can sometimes be explained by the fact that the relationships had extended over many decades. Simon's father and grandfather had been the slaves of old Bayard's father, Colonel John Sartoris, and Simon's earliest memories were of Civil War days. Walter Christian, Negro janitor at a Jefferson drug store, had a similar association with his employer, "Uncle Willy" Christian. "His grandfather had belonged to Uncle Willy's grandfather before the Surrender and he and Uncle Willy were about the same age and a good deal alike. . . . and if anything Walter was a little more irascible and short-tempered." [81]

In families with Negro servants, white and Negro children were often brought up in close association. Such was the case with Eunice Habersham and Molly Beauchamp. Molly had been the daughter of one of the slaves belonging to Miss Habersham's grandfather. She and Miss Habersham were "the same age, born in the same week and both suckled at Molly's mother's breast and grown up together almost inextricably like sisters, like twins, sleeping in the same room, the white girl in the bed, the Negro girl on a cot at the foot of it almost until Molly and Lucas married, and Miss Habersham had stood up in the Negro church as godmother to Molly's first child." [82] The young Compsons and Dilsey's brood played together, got into mischief together, and threatened to tell on each other. [83] The closest companion of young Charles Mallison was Aleck Sander, son of the Negro cook. [84] Similarly close was the relationship of the white Zack Edmonds with the Negro Lucas Beauchamp. "They had fished and hunted together, they had learned to swim in the same water, they had eaten at the same table in the white boy's kitchen and in the cabin of the negro's mother; they had slept under the same blanket before a fire in the woods." [85]

Still further contacts between the races arose through economic interdependence. White merchants sold to both white and Negro customers; Negro artisans maintained shops serving both races. The son of a blacksmith, Jabbo Gatewood had learned enough

[80] *Ibid.*, 52.   [81] *The Town*, 159.   [82] *Intruder in the Dust*, 87.
[83] *The Sound and the Fury*, 21–23.   [84] *The Town*, 244, 311.
[85] William Faulkner, *Go Down Moses* (New York: Modern Library, 1955), 55.

about automobiles to make himself indispensable to the first motorists in Jefferson. "Jabbo was the best mechanic in the county and although he still got drunk and into jail as much as ever, he never stayed longer than just overnight any more because somebody with an automobile always needed him enough to pay his fine by morning." [86]

Besides these accepted relationships there were occasional unsanctified contacts between whites and Negroes. Contrasting with the chivalrous family traditions of the Sartorises and the De Spains were the darker domestic histories of the McCaslins and the Sutphens, in which white plantation owners were the reputed fathers of children born to their female slaves. Nor did such connections cease with the abolition of slavery. Will Varner, the country merchant at Frenchman's Bend, was alleged to have had three mulatto concubines,[87] while Jack Houston at the age of fourteen was "the possessor of a mistress—a Negro girl two or three years his senior, daughter of his father's renter." [88] In the story "Delta Autumn" a Negro woman bore a child to Roth Edmonds, a white man who was actually her distant cousin since they were both descended from the lecherous old slaveowner Lucius McCaslin.[89]

Yet though Negroes and whites lived in close proximity and often on terms of easy familiarity and affection, the institution of segregation was no myth. Scores of petty conventions delimited the boundaries between the black and white worlds. All night long, Charles Mallison and Aleck Sander were close companions in dangerous adventure, yet in the morning the family "left Aleck Sander with his breakfast at the kitchen table and carried theirs into the dining room." [90] Even more extraordinary was the conduct of Joanna Burden, who admitted the mulatto Joe Christmas into her bed every night yet continued to set out his meals on the kitchen table.[91] When young Bayard Sartoris and two white companions embarked upon an evening of serenading girls, they loaded three Negro musicians and a bull fiddle into the back seat of the car. Since racial amenities required that whites and Negroes should not drink from the same vessel, the white men simply passed the whisky

[86] *The Town*, 68.   [87] *Ibid.*, 276.   [88] *The Hamlet*, 209.
[89] *Go Down Moses*, 357–61.   [90] *Intruder in the Dust*, 114.
[91] *Light in August*, 205.

jug from one to another and the Negroes drank from the cap to the
breather-pipe which Bayard had removed from under the car hood.
"It'll taste a little like oil for a drink or two. But you boys won't
notice it after that." [92] On this mellow evening, however, the traditional barriers eventually fell. The merrymakers lost the breather-
cap, "and, as they moved from house to house, all six of them drank
fraternally from the jug, turn and turn about." [93]

Most of the Jefferson Negroes lived in the squalor of The Hollow or Freedman Town.

A street turned off at right angles, descending, and became a dirt road.
On either hand the land dropped more sharply; a broad flat dotted with
small cabins whose weathered roofs were on a level with the crown of the
road. They were set in small grassless plots littered with broken things,
bricks, planks, crockery, things of a once utilitarian value. What growth
there was consisted of rank weeds and the trees were mulberries and lo-
custs and sycamores—trees that partook also of the foul desiccation
which surrounded the houses; trees whose very burgeoning seemed to be
the sad and stubborn remnant of September, as if even spring had passed
them by, leaving them to feed upon the rich and unmistakable smell of
negroes in which they grew.[94]

References to the smell of Negroes occur frequently in Faulkner's writings. In his earlier books he seemed to accept this as a racial characteristic; in his later ones he exhibited more understanding. Charles Mallison, befriended by Lucas Beauchamp after
falling into the creek, sat wrapped in a quilt in the Negro's cabin,

enclosed completely now in that unmistakable odor of Negroes—that
smell which if it were not for something that was going to happen to him
within a space of time measurable now in minutes he would have gone
to his grave never once pondering speculating if perhaps that smell were
really not the odor of a race nor even actually of poverty but perhaps of a
condition: an idea: a belief: an acceptance, a passive acceptance by them
themselves of the idea that being Negroes they were not supposed to
have facilities to wash properly or often or even to wash bathe often
even without the facilities to do it with; that in fact it was a little to be
preferred that they did not.[95]

---

[92] *Sartoris*, 136.   [93] *Ibid.*, 145.
[94] *The Sound and the Fury*, 362–63.   [95] *Intruder in the Dust*, 11.

If social conditioning rather than genetic determinism explained how Negroes smelled, other supposedly Negro characteristics might be similarly understood. Quentin Compson learned "that the best way to take all people, black or white, is to take them for what they think they are, then leave them alone. That was when I realized that a nigger is not a person so much as a form of behaviour; a sort of obverse reflection of the white people he lives among." [96] The Negro who would not behave as a Negro was resented. For years every white man in the region had been thinking about Lucas Beauchamp: "We got to make him be a nigger first. He's got to admit he's a nigger. Then maybe we will accept him as he seems to intend to be accepted." [97]

Since Negroes had to learn to act like Negroes and whites like whites, men who belonged exclusively in neither world were in a difficult, oftentimes tragic, situation. The admirable, but dangerous, pride of Lucas Beauchamp was rooted in his knowledge that his grandfather had been a plantation owner. The lighter the mulatto the greater the psychological tension. Both Joe Christmas, in *Light in August,* and Charles Bon, in *Absalom, Absalom!,* could pass as white, yet they were lost between the two worlds.

The conditioning process that made Negroes what they were had many unfortunate results. The Negroes of Yoknapatawpha County were oftentimes ignorant, superstitious, lazy, promiscuous, and brutal. Yet through an extraordinary process of compensation, sterling virtues had also evolved. Gavin Stevens admired the Negro,

because he had patience even when he didn't have hope, the long view even when there was nothing to see at the end of it, not even just the will but the desire to endure because he loved the old simple things which no one wanted to take from him; not an automobile nor flash clothes nor his picture in the paper but a little of music (his own), a hearth, not his child but any child, a God, a heaven which a man may avail himself a little of at any time, without having to wait to die, a little earth for his own sweat to fall on among his own green shoots and plants.

The Negro had, in short, the virtue that Faulkner most admired, the "capacity to wait and endure and survive." [98]

[96] *The Sound and the Fury,* 106.   [97] *Intruder in the Dust,* 18.   [98] *Ibid.,* 156.

To survive, the Negroes of Yoknapatawpha County had learned to avoid involvement in white affairs. The Negro boy Luster watched the rebellious Quentin Compson climb out of her bedroom window every night but said nothing about it. " 'Twarn't none o my business. . . . I aint gwine git mixed up in white folks' business." [99] Young Bayard Sartoris might have drowned, while two Negroes who discovered him in the creek, under his overturned car, debated the wisdom of doing anything about the situation. "Don't you tech 'im," the older and more prudent one said. "White folks be sayin' we done it. We gwine wait right here 'twell some white man comes erlong." [100] Fortunately the younger Negro was willing to run the risks of a Samaritan role.

This determinaion to stay out of trouble did not always work. Searching for information about the affairs of the murdered Joanna Burden, the sheriff showed little concern for the niceties of due process of law. " 'Get me a nigger,' the sheriff said. The deputy and two or three others got him a nigger. 'Who's been living in that cabin?' the sheriff said." [101] When the hapless Negro gave the characteristic answer that he didn't know, he was beaten by the deputy. "The strap fell again, the buckle raking across the Negro's back. 'You remember yet?' the sheriff said." [102] And the officers got the information.

The Negroes wanted to have as little to do with the law as possible. To a white man seeking a boy to carry a message to the sheriff, a Negro mother replied: "The sheriff? Then you come to the wrong place. I aint ghy have none of mine monkeying around no sheriff. I done had one nigger that thought he knowed a sheriff well enough to go and visit him. He aint never come back, neither. You look somewhere else." [103]

White men sometimes tried to pin their own crimes on Negroes. When a Negro of more than customary courage turned over to Sheriff Hampton the gun that would link Mink Snopes to a murder, Mink's cousin tried to involve the Negro himself. As he explained to Mink:

I throwed the suspicion right onto the nigger fore Hampton could open his mouth. I figger about tonight or maybe tomorrow night I'll take a

[99] *The Sound and the Fury*, 357.   [100] *Sartoris*, 184.
[101] *Light in August*, 254.   [102] *Ibid.*, 256.   [103] *Ibid.*, 381.

few of the boys and go the nigger's house with a couple of trace chains or maybe a little fire under his feet. And even if he dont confess nothing, folks will hear that he has done been visited at night and there's too many votes out here for Hampton to do nothing else but take him on in and send him to the penitentiary, even if he cant quite risk hanging him, and Hampton knows it.[104]

The Negro accused of killing or injuring a white person always stood in danger of lynching. Speaking of Joe Christmas, the Reverend Gail Hightower said: "Is it certain, proved, that he has Negro blood? Think, Byron; what it will mean when the people—if they catch . . . Poor man. Poor mankind."[105] When Lucas Beauchamp was arrested for murder, Mr. Lilley, one of the Jefferson grocers, represented a typical attitude. Lilley had nothing against Negroes, Gavin Stevens explained. All he required was that they act "like niggers." For a Negro to murder a white man was to be expected; equally to be expected was that the white people would "take him out and burn him." Both observed implicitly the rules: "the nigger acting like a nigger and the white folks acting like white folks and no real hard feelings on either side . . . once the fury is over." In fact, Mr. Lilley would probably be one of the first to contribute money to bury the lynch victim and support his widow and children, "which proves again how no man can cause more grief than one clinging blindly to the vices of his ancestors."[106]

In the end Lucas escaped lynching, but the danger had been there. Charles Mallison had seen the crowd before the jail.

He knew, recognized them all; some of them he had even seen and listened to in the barbershop two hours ago—the young men or men under forty, bachelors, the homeless who had the Saturday and Sunday baths in the barbershop—truckdrivers and garagehands, the oiler from the cotton gin, a sodajerker from the drugstore and the ones who could be seen all week long in or around the poolhall who did nothing at all that anyone knew, who owned automobiles and spent money nobody really knew exactly how they earned on week-ends in Memphis or New Orleans brothels—the men who his uncle said were in every little Southern town who never really led mobs nor even instigated them but were always the nucleus of them because of their mass availability.[107]

---

[104] *The Hamlet*, 237.   [105] *Light in August*, 87.
[106] *Intruder in the Dust*, 48–49.   [107] *Ibid.*, 42–43.

More dangerous still were the kith and kin of the murdered man, men from the lawless hill country.

Once again the Negro's instinct for self-preservation was dramatically in evidence. Although Lucas's arrest had occurred on a weekend when the streets would ordinarily have been filled with Negroes, there was not a colored face to be seen;

they were acting exactly as Negroes and whites both would have expected Negroes to act at such a time; they were still there, they had not fled, you just didn't see them—a sense, a feeling of their constant presence and nearness: black men and women and children breathing and waiting inside their barred and shuttered houses, not crouching cringing shrinking, not in anger and not quite in fear; just waiting, biding since theirs was an armament which the white man could not match nor —if he but knew it—even cope with: patience; just keeping out of sight and out of the way. . . .[108]

Hating trouble, the Negroes had little sympathy for those who had caused it. Noting that "they aint come for old Lucas yet," Aleck Sander commented: "It's the ones like Lucas makes trouble for everybody." [109] And the Sartorises' Caspey got no support from his father when he came home after World War I with uppity ideas. "Save dat nigger freedom talk fer town-folks: dey mought stomach it. Whut us niggers want ter be free fer, anyhow? Ain't we got ez many white folks now ez we kin suppo't?" [110]

Neither the aristocrats nor the poor whites could tolerate any challenge to the existing pattern of race relations. Miss Jenny was outraged by Caspey's arrogance: "Who was the fool anyway, who thought of putting niggers into the same uniform with white men?" [111] Whites with unorthodox ideas aroused even more resentment. Joanna Burden lived alone in a big house. "She has lived in the house since she was born, yet she is still a stranger, a foreigner whose people moved in from the North during Reconstruction. A Yankee, a lover of Negroes, about whom in the town there is still talk of queer relations with Negroes in the town and out of it, despite the fact that it is now sixty years since her grandfather and her brother were killed on the square by an exslaveowner over a question of Negro votes in a state election." [112]

[108] *Ibid.*, 96.   [109] *Ibid.*, 85.
[110] *Sartoris*, 89.   [111] *Ibid.*, 77.   [112] *Light in August*, 40–41.

There were a few whites of unimpeachable credentials who knew that change would have to come. "Sambo," Gavin Stevens told Charles Mallison, "is a human being living in a free country and hence must be free." [113] Yet even these quasi-liberals clung to the doctrine of gradualness. "Someday," Gavin said, "Lucas Beauchamp can shoot a white man in the back with the same impunity to lynch-rope or gasoline as a white man; in time he will vote any when and anywhere a white man can and send his children to the same school anywhere the white man's children go and travel anywhere the white man travels as the white man does it. But it won't be next Tuesday." [114]

VII

Gavin Stevens always coupled his dictum that the Negroes must be given their rights with an even stronger admonition that the North must not interfere. He insisted that he was defending "Sambo" from "the outlanders who will fling him decades back not merely into injustice but into grief and agony and violence too by forcing on us laws based on the idea that man's injustice to man can be abolished overnight by police." He did not excuse the bad treatment of the Negroes. "I only say that the injustice is ours, the South's. We must expiate and abolish it ourselves, alone and without the help nor even (with thanks) advice." [115]

Stevens argued that the attempt to use federal laws and federal police to abolish the Negro's shameful condition would divide the country at a time when it could not risk division. In a random sample of a thousand Southerners, he speculated, there might not be more than one with a genuine concern for the Negro's condition and not more than one who would participate in a lynching. Yet the full thousand would repulse "the outlander who came down here with force to intervene or punish" the lyncher. It would be folly for the Negroes to ally themselves with these outside elements, because on one side there would be only " a paper alliance of theorists and fanatics and private and personal avengers plus a number of others under the assumption of enough physical miles to afford

---

[113] *Intruder in the Dust*, 154.   [114] *Ibid.*, 155.   [115] *Ibid.*, 203–04.

a principle," while against them would be ranged not just "the concorded South" but a host of Northern recruits drawn both from the hinterland and from "the fine cities of your cultural pride your Chicagoes and Detroits and Los Angeleses and wherever else ignorant people who fear the color of any skin or shape of nose save their own and who will grasp this opportunity to vent on Sambo the whole sum of their ancestral horror and scorn and fear of Indian and Chinese and Mexican and Carib and Jew." [116]

In the brooding country lawyer's warning against Northern interference in the matter of Negro rights, he claimed that still larger values were involved. Stevens argued that the Southerners alone in the United States were "a homogeneous people." The rural New Englanders, to be sure, were similar, but there were not enough of them. Along the Atlantic seaboard lived "the coastal spew of Europe which this country quarantined unrootable into the rootless ephemeral cities with factory and foundry and municipal paychecks as tight and close as any police could have done it." The Southerners, he said, were not really resisting "what the outland calls (and we too) progress and enlightenment. We are defending not actually our politics or beliefs or even our way of life, but simply our homogeneity from a federal government to which in simple desperation the rest of this country has had to surrender voluntarily more and more of its personal and private liberty in order to continue to afford the United States." Returning to the Negro question, Stevens stated the paradox: "That's what we are really defending: the privilege of setting him free ourselves: which we will have to do for the reason that nobody else can since going on a century ago now the North tried it and have been admitting for seventy-five years now that they failed." Carrying his argument still further, Stevens argued that the Negro was a homogeneous man too.

We—he and us—should confederate: swap him the rest of the economic and political and cultural privileges which are his right, for the reversion of his capacity to wait and endure and survive. Then we would prevail; together we would dominate the United States; we would present a front not only impregnable but not even to be threatened by a

[116] *Ibid.,* 215–16.

mass of people who no longer have anything in common save a frantic greed for money and a basic fear of a failure of national character which they hide from one another behind a loud lipservice to a flag.[117]

Dislike and fear of the North found more venemous outlet in Jason Compson. Stealing from his own sister and niece to speculate in cotton, he blamed his market losses on New York and Washington. "Cotton is a speculator's crop. They fill the farmer full of hot air and get him to raise a big crop for them to whipsaw on the market, to trim the suckers with. Do you think the farmer gets anything out of it except a red neck and a hump in his back? You think the man that sweats to put it into the ground gets a red cent more than a bare living." It all went to the profit of "a bunch of damn eastern jews." [118] Jason's rancor against the North even extended to its sport heroes. He refused to bet on the Yankees because this was Babe Ruth's team; he could, he said, name a dozen men in either League who were more valuable than he was. " 'What have you got against Ruth?' Mac says. 'Nothing,' I says. 'I haven't got any thing against him. I don't even like to look at his picture.' " [119]

Touchy pride and suspicion of the North were sentiments strongly held in Yoknapatawpha County. Charles Mallison realized that such ideas were firmly implanted during childhood. The North was "not even a geographical place but an emotional idea, a condition of which he had fed from his mother's milk to be ever and constant on the alert not at all to fear and not actually anymore to hate but just—a little wearily sometimes and sometimes even with tongue in cheek—to defy." [120]

[117] *Ibid.*, 153–56. [118] *The Sound and the Fury*, 237. [119] *Ibid.*, 314.
[120] *Intruder in the Dust*, 152.

5

Lethal Gases in Altamont and Libya Hill

What happened in Wall Street was only the initial explosion which in the course of the next few years was to set off a train of lesser explosions all over the land—explosions which at last revealed beyond all further doubting and denial the hidden pockets of lethal gases which a false, vicious, and putrescent scheme of things had released beneath the surface of American life.

THOMAS WOLFE, *You Can't Go Home Again* [1]

EVEN MORE than most first novels, Thomas Wolfe's *Look Homeward, Angel* (1929) was transparently autobiographical. Like Wolfe, the fictional Eugene Gant was the son of a Pennsylvania-born maker of cemetery monuments and a strong-minded woman of Southern mountain stock who ran a boarding house and speculated in land. Gant's native city of Altamont in the state of Catawba was easily identified as Asheville, North Carolina, where Wolfe was born and raised. Major incidents in the book—Eugene's development and schooling, his education at the state university, his mother's complex business ventures, his father's tragic illness, his brother's death—were all paralleled in Wolfe's own early life.

To be sure, Wolfe made the usual disclaimer. In a note "To the Reader," he insisted that his book was "a fiction, and that he meditated no man's portrait here." Yet he acknowledged that he had

[1] Thomas Wolfe, *You Can't Go Home Again* (New York: Dell Publishing Company, 1960), 336.

"written of experience which is now far and lost, but which was once part of the fabric of his life." And a little later he laid down the principle: "Fiction is not fact, but fiction is fact selected and understood, fiction is fact arranged and charged with purpose." [2]

Maxwell Perkins, Scribner's great editor who did so much to encourage and discipline Wolfe's wild talent, denied that the novelist was slavishly literal in his treatment of these autobiographical materials. "He created something new and something meaningful through a transmutation of what he saw, heard, and realized." [3] Yet neither Wolfe nor Perkins could deny that the novels often transcribed real events with embarrassing fidelity. Laughing at himself in a later novel, Wolfe quoted the town souse as having said, "Why, hell! If George [Tom] wants to write about a horse thief, that's all right. Only the next time I hope he don't give his street address. And there ain't no use throwing in his telephone number, too." [4] Asheville found Wolfe's literalness far from amusing. During the early months after the publication of his first novel, Wolfe had to endure angry condemnation from old friends and hurt feelings from relatives. It was seven years before he dared to visit his home town. Eventually, of course, he was forgiven. Like Sauk Centre, Asheville learned to take pride in being so closely identified with a major work of literature, and Wolfe's family fiercely defended the son who had drawn such unflattering portraits of them.

Wolfe's second major work, *Of Time and the River* (1935), was equally autobiographical in following Eugene Gant's graduate training at Harvard, his university teaching in New York City, and his wanderings in Europe. Although the novel was well reviewed, certain critics began to deprecate Wolfe's inability to do more than write down at inordinate length the minutiae of his own experiences and thoughts. They attributed such form as the novels had achieved to the editorial genius of Maxwell Perkins, who had extracted the better passages from trunkloads of rambling manuscript. A sensitive man, Wolfe was upset by this attack. He informed Perkins that his next novel would be a completely objective

---

[2] Thomas Wolfe, *Look Homeward, Angel* (New York: Charles Scribner's Sons, 1952), xv.

[3] Maxwell E. Perkins, "Thomas Wolfe," *ibid.*, xiii.

[4] *You Can't Go Home Again*, 331.

non-autobiographical work. Apparently to dramatize this break
with the pattern of his earlier writing, Wolfe quarreled with Perkins on rather specious grounds and contracted with Harper's instead of Scribner's for his future books.

Such was the background for *The Web and the Rock* (1939)
and *You Can't Go Home Again* (1940) both published after Wolfe's
death in 1938. In his prefatory note to the first of these, Wolfe
assured his readers that this was "the most objective novel" he had
written. He had invented characters who were "compacted from
the whole amalgam and consonance of seeing, feeling, thinking,
living, and knowing many people." [5] The novel's theme was "the
innocent man" discovering life. Yet who was this innocent man?
His name, George Webber, was new, but his background was
strangely familiar. His father was a Pennsylvania man; his mother
was of Southern mountain stock; the aunt who raised him after his
mother's death, was strong-minded and garrulous. He spent his
boyhood in the city of Libya Hill in the state of Old Catawba. He
went to a regional college and then to the city, where he struggled
to become a writer. George Webber was as clearly Thomas Wolfe as
Eugene Gant had been. And in later passages of the two posthu-
mous novels, the parallel between Webber's experiences and
Wolfe's own was even closer. Each had a tempestuous love affair
with a wealthy married woman; each knew the exhilarations and
discouragements of authorship; each sought escape in Europe; each
had a traumatic quarrel with his editor and friend.

Literary critics will debate the extent to which Wolfe's compulsion to tell and retell the story of his own life detracts from his stature as an imaginative artist. But historians may well be grateful for
the record that he left. Like his mother, Wolfe had an extraordinary memory. His trouble, he said, was

that I might never make an end to anything because I could never get
through telling, what I knew, what I felt and thought and *had* to say
about it. That was a giant web in which I was caught, the product of my
huge inheritance—the torrential recollectiveness, derived out of my
mother's stock, which became a living, million-fibered integument that
bound me to the past, not only of my own life, but of the very earth from

[5] Thomas Wolfe, *The Web and the Rock* (New York: Dell Publishing Company,
1960), 20.

which I came, so that nothing in the end escaped from its inrooted and all-feeling explorativeness.[6]

This is not to say, of course, that all the episodes and characterizations of the novels were literally true. In height and weight, Wolfe was a preposterously big man, and this out-sized quality seemed to pervade all that he did. Everything in his novels seems a little larger than life-size; every action and every emotion contains a certain excess. Wolfe was not unaware of this: in the prefatory note to *The Web and the Rock* he recognized that the novel had a strong element of satiric exaggeration. It belonged, he believed, to the nature of the story, but it belonged also to "the nature of life, and particularly American life." [7] Certainly it belonged to the nature of Thomas Wolfe.

II

Asheville, North Carolina—called Altamont in Wolfe's first two novels and Libya Hill in the other two—was in many ways a unique community. Lewis's Gopher Prairie was not only Sauk Centre, Minnesota, but all American small towns. Faulkner's Jefferson could have been almost any county seat in the Deep South. But Wolfe's Altamont was different from most other places.

Altamont was a Southern city. As a sensitive boy, Eugene Gant absorbed a deep feeling for the region. This feeling was not so much historic as it was of "the core of dark romanticism"—an "unlimited and inexplicable drunkenness," a "magnetism" of the blood.[8] Obviously, the cult of Southernness was a mystique, not to be rationally explained. Yet Eugene recognized that it was a cult fortified by the romantic halo that his school history cast over the section and by the popular legend of beautiful mansions, chivalric colonels, gentle women, and happy slaves. In his adult years, George Webber chose to live in Northern cities or in Europe. He regarded his Southern heritage as more curse than blessing. He knew "that there was something wounded in the South. He knew that there was something twisted, dark, and full of pain. . . ." [9]

[6] *You Can't Go Home Again*, 667.   [7] *The Web and the Rock*, 20.
[8] *Look Homeward, Angel*, 127.   [9] *You Can't Go Home Again*, 307.

Yet Wolfe's South was a far different South from William Faulkner's. It was different, in the first place, because Altamont was located in Old Catawba (North Carolina). In one satiric passage, Wolfe contrasted Old Catawba with South Carolina. In South Carolina, village mobs took a savage pleasure in lynching Negroes; in Old Catawba the hill men might kill each other about a fence, a dog, or a boundary line, they might kill in drunkenness or lust. "But they do not saw off niggers' noses. There is not the look of fear and cruelty in their eyes that the people of South Carolina have." [10] Old Catawba was a place inhabited by humble folk. "There is no Charleston in Old Catawba, and not so many people pretending to be what they are not." [11] Old Catawba was neither too far south nor too far north; Old Catawba was just right.

Even in Old Catawba, Wolfe contended, some parts were better than others. The West was better than the East; the mountains were better than the Tidewater and the Piedmont. "The West is really a region of good small people, a Scotch-Irish place, and that, too, is undefined, save that it doesn't drawl so much, works harder, doesn't loaf so much, and shoots a little straighter when it has to." Kinder to his relatives and fellow townsmen in his later novels than in the earlier ones, Wolfe said of these people: "They are just common, plain, and homely—but almost everything of America is in them." [12]

But Altamont's special quality must be more sharply defined. Even before the Civil War fashionable people from Charleston and other parts of the South had sought relief from the summer heat in Altamont with its brisk mountain air and magnificent vistas of the Great Smokies. In the 1880's, rich men from the North began building hunting lodges near Altamont. One of them bought huge areas of mountain land and "with an army of imported architects, carpenters and masons," built "the largest country estate in America." [13] (This, of course, was George Vanderbilt's "Biltmore.") On the streets of Altamont one might see some of the most famous men of the country. In one of the novels William Jennings Bryan ambled through the streets exchanging heavy pleasantries with the local people.[14] Advertising itself as "America's Switzerland" and

[10] *The Web and the Rock*, 36.   [11] *Ibid.*   [12] *Ibid.*, 38.
[13] *Look Homeward, Angel*, 7.   [14] *Ibid.*, 279–81.

They are just common, plain, and homely—but almost everything of America is in them.   Thomas Wolfe, *The Web and the Rock*

patronized by rich and fashionable people, Altamont was much more sophisticated than most small American cities, either North or South.

But fashionable Altamont was not the Altamont of the Gant family. The Gants belonged to a rather seedy middle class composed of health-questing transients and avaricious innkeepers and merchants. In addition to eight de luxe hotels, Altamont had over 250 private hotels, boarding houses, and sanitariums.[15] As a boy, Eugene used to see the boarding-house keepers shopping in the public market. "They were of various sizes and ages, but they were all stamped with the print of haggling determination and a pugnacious closure of the mouth. They pried in among the fish and vegetables, pinching cabbages, weighing onions, exfoliating lettuce-heads." [16]

Eugene's own mother, Eliza Gant, ran a boarding house called Dixieland. As Eugene remembered the guests, they were a shabby lot. During the dull winter season only a few pathetic invalids from

[15] *Ibid.*, 157–58.   [16] *Ibid.*, 157.

the North occupied the rooms. During the summer there were boarders of a different kind—much more exciting to an adolescent boy—"slow bodied women from the hot rich South, dark-haired white bodied girls from New Orleans, corn-haired blondes from Georgia, nigger-drawling desire from South Carolina." [17]

III

Born in 1900, Eugene Gant remembered most vividly the Altamont of the years immediately preceding American entry into World War I. He remembered with particular vividness how the city looked on a beautiful April day in 1915, when he rambled through it with a schoolmate. They passed the Episcopal church, a new edifice in imitation Tudor; and the Presbyterian church, a sharp-steepled old building, rotting "slowly, decently, prosperously, like a good man's life, down into its wet lichened brick." [18] The boys looked into the Appalachian Laundry, where they had a moment's glimpse of "negresses plunging their wet arms into the liquefaction of their clothes." [19] Nearby on the second floor of a small brick building, housing lawyers, doctors, and dentists, they could see a white-jacketed figure working on a patient's tooth with a drill propelled by the rapid pumping of his foot. Eugene and George shivered as they peered into the flower-scented gloom of an undertaker's establishment. At the end of a dark central corridor, flanked by weeping ferns, they could just make out the form of a heavy casket, on a wheeled trestle, with rich silver handles and velvet covering.

On the principal business street, the boys encountered familiar figures. With the cruelty of adolescence they ridiculed the halting steps of the lonely old scholar, deaf and paralyzed, who lived in a room above the public library. They watched indifferently while other youths somewhat older than themselves pestered a feeble-minded pencil vendor. They laughed in glee as a terrified clothier scrambled out of the way of a careening roadster, driven by a misanthropic Virginian physician muttering curses against "the whole crawling itch of Confederate and Yankee postwar rabbledom, with a few special parentheses for Jews and niggers." [20]

[17] *Ibid.*, 116.   [18] *Ibid.*, 272.   [19] *Ibid.*, 273.   [20] *Ibid.*, 279.

Youth's rallying point was Wood's Drug Store. Young males, lounging around the door, hailed the girls who paraded in groups of three and four up and down the street. Establishing contact through an exchange of insults, the groups disappeared within the drugstore to continue their banter over "dopes," mint limeades, and chocolate milks. "Pert boys rushed from the crowded booths and tables to the fountain, coming up with a long slide. They shouted their orders rudely, nagging the swift jerkers glibly, stridently. . . . The jerkers moved in ragtime tempo, juggling the drinks, tossing scooped globes of ice-cream into the air and catching them in glasses, beating swift rhythms with a spoon." [21]

"The Square" was Altamont's civic nerve center. Here stood the city hall, the fire barn, and the public library; here the municipal fountain played; here the various street car lines had their junction point. To the local citizenry the Square was a source of pride, but to Eugene's father returning to Altamont one wintry morning after a long trip through other parts of the country it seemed small and dingy. "He got very definitely the impression that if he flung out his arms they would strike against the walls of the mean three-and-four-story buildings that flanked the Square raggedly." [22] Certainly Gant's own shop located in a grimy two-story building added nothing to the beauty of the scene. Near Gant's shop was the drayman's market—an old fashioned center of trade. On Gant's wooden steps the sprawling draymen would congregate, snaking their whips deftly across the pavement and wrestling in heavy horseplay.

Besides the upper-class city of the great hotels, and the middle-class city of the boarding houses, there was still a third Altamont, a city of ugly slums. Years later George Webber retained "a painful, haunting, anguished memory of the half-familiar, never-to-be-forgotten, white-trash universe" of Pigtail Alley and Doubleday, "that sprawled its labyrinthine confusion of unpaved, unnamed, miry streets and alleys and rickety shacks and houses along the scarred, clay-barren flanks of the hills that slope down towards the railway district in the western part of town." [23] In summer, the sun beat down "with impartial cruelty on mangy, scabby, nameless dogs, and on a thousand mangy, scabby, nameless little children—hideous

---

[21] *Ibid.*, 285.　　[22] *Ibid.*, 62.　　[23] *The Web and the Rock*, 79.

little scarecrows with tow hair, their skinny little bodies unrecognizably scurfed with filth and scarred with running sores." And the sun shone also on the Lonies, Lizzies, Lotties and Lenas of the district, the women who stood on the ramshackle porches, "tall and gaunt and slatternly, while their grimy little tow-haired brats scrabbled wretchedly around the edges of their filthy lop-sided skirts. They stood there, those foul, unlovely women, with their gaunt staring faces, sunken eyes, toothless jaws, and corrupt, discolored mouths, rilled at the edges with a thin brown line of snuff." [24]

Although Eugene seldom visited the poor-white section, boyish curiosity drew him continually to the Negro slums. Here he delivered newspapers; here he indulged the fantasies of adolescence. "He spent his afternoons after school combing restlessly through the celled hive of Niggertown. The rank stench of the branch, pouring its thick brown sewage down a bed of worn boulders, the smell of wood-smoke and laundry stewing in a black iron yard-pot, and the low jungle cadence of dusk, the forms that slid, dropped and vanished, beneath a twinkling orchestration of small sounds." [25] He found good, paying customers for his newspapers among decent and laborious Negroes—barbers, tailors, grocers, pharmacists, and ginghamed housewives—who greeted him "with warm smiles full of teeth, and titles of respect extravagent and kindly: 'Mister,' 'Colonel,' 'General,' 'Governor,' and so on." But it was the bad Negroes who really excited him, the "young men and women of precarious means, various lives, who slid mysteriously from cell to cell, who peopled the night with their flitting stealth." [26]

The relation of white to Negro was a matter of almost obsessive interest in Altamont. From early schoolmates Eugene learned the traditional attitudes. At night the boys would roar with laughter when they scared strolling Negro couples with make-believe snakes made of old black stockings. By day they would amuse themselves throwing stones at bicycling Negro delivery boys. They did not hate them; they regarded them as clowns. "They had learned, as well, that it was proper to cuff these people kindly, curse them cheerfully, feed them magnanimously. Men are kind to a faithful wagging dog, but he must not walk habitually upon two legs. They

[24] *Ibid.,* 80–81.   [25] *Look Homeward, Angel,* 250.   [26] *Ibid.,* 251.

knew that they must 'take nothin' off a nigger,' and that the beginnings of argument could best be scotched with a club and a broken head. Only you couldn't break a nigger's head." [27]

In Eugene's home these perverse ideas were reinforced. His mother, who had to employ Negroes in her boarding house, got along with them badly. "She had all the dislike and distrust for them of the mountain people. . . . She nagged and berated the sullen negro girls constantly, tortured by the thought that they were stealing her supplies and her furnishings, and dawdling away the time for which she paid them." [28] Consequently the girls were forever quitting, and it became increasingly difficult to recruit replacements. Gant's father contributed still further to Eugene's miseducation by trying to creep into the bed of a comely Negro cook, only to be repulsed with loud screams that aroused the whole household—an episode that Eugene and his brothers and sister found hilariously funny.

The adult George Webber of the later novels learned that the Negro might be a tragic as well as a comic figure. In *The Web and the Rock,* Wolfe told the story of Dick Prosser, the Bible-reading, athletic, ideal Negro servant, who was lynched by a mob after he went on a sudden wild spree of shooting and killing. To Webber, Dick Prosser became a symbol of man himself, "a projection of his own unfathomed quality, a friend, a brother, and a mortal enemy, an unknown demon—our loving friend, our mortal enemy, two worlds together—a tiger and a child." [29]

Webber perceived the injustice of the Negro's treatment. Describing the infamous Judge Rumford Bland who grew rich through usurious loans to the Negroes, Webber explained why his victims did not complain to the police. The Negro

stood in awe of the complex mystery of the law, of which he understood little or nothing, or in terror of its brutal force. The law for him was largely a matter of the police, and the police was a white man in a uniform, who had the power and authority to arrest him, to beat him with his fist or with a club, to shoot him with a gun, and to lock him up in a small dark cell. It was not likely, therefore, that any Negro would take his troubles to the police.[30]

---

[27] *Ibid.,* 79.   [28] *Ibid.,* 109.   [29] *The Web and the Rock,* 181.
[30] *You Can't Go Home Again,* 86–87.

Wolfe learned to feel pity for the Negroes and to see the frequent tragedy of their lot. But he never outgrew a kind of condescension in his attitude. In his correspondence it is evident that his real affection was for the deferential Negro of the South; he disliked well-educated northern Negroes who aggressively demanded their rights.

From his Altamont schoolmates Eugene Gant also learned to torture Jews.

The boys would wait on Jews, follow them home shouting 'Goose Grease! Goose Grease!' which, they were convinced, was the chief staple of Semitic diet; or with the blind acceptance of little boys of some traditional, or mangled, or imaginary catchword of abuse, they would call after their muttering and tormented victim: 'Veeshamadye Veeshamadye!' confident that they had pronounced the most unspeakable, to Jewish ears, of affronts.[31]

Later the teenaged Eugene compensated for his own lack of confidence by joining in the persecution of a boy unfortunately both Jewish and effeminate. "He never forgot the Jew; he always thought of him with shame." [32]

Ironically, the adult Eugene was destined to live in a city crowded with Jews and to teach in a university where most of the students were Jewish. Strangest of all, he was to become the ardent lover of a Jewish woman. Yet, as in his relations with Negroes, it seems likely that he never completely outgrew Altamont and that his feelings toward Jews were ambivalent to the end.

Altamont, as Eugene Gant remembered it, was a city of flourishing churches. Once a week he was sent to the Presbyterian Sunday School. "This starched and well brushed world of Sunday morning Presbyterianism, with its sober decency, its sense of restraint, its suggestion of quiet wealth, solid position, ordered ritual, seclusive establishment, moved him deeply with its tranquility." [33] He gathered something of the mystery and beauty of religion from the mellow gloom of the church, the rich distant organ, the nasal voice of the Scotch minister, and the interminable prayers. Yet he never felt that the disorderly Gant household really belonged in the se-

---

[31] *Look Homeward, Angel*, 79.   [32] *Ibid.*, 196.   [33] *Ibid.*, 115.

date Presbyterian fold. Most of the people in Gant's neighborhood were Baptists. "In the social scale the Baptists were the most populous and were considered the most common: their minister was a large plump man with a red face and a white vest, who reached great oratorical effects, roaring at them like a lion, cooing at them like a dove, introducing his wife into the sermon frequently for purposes of intimacy and laughing, in a programme which the Episcopalians who held the highest social eminence, and the Presbyterians, less fashionable, but solidly decent, felt was hardly chaste. The Methodists occupied the middle ground between vulgarity and decorum." [34]

For the other six days of the week Eugene lived in a far less pious world. The boarding house reeked with sin—or at least so it seemed to a hot-blooded teen-ager. At night "he heard the rich laughter of the women, tender and cruel, upon the dark porches, heard the florid throat-tones of the men; saw the yielding harlotry of the South." [35] Still more exciting was the unconcealed corruption of the Negro slums. One Saturday evening the fourteen-year-old newsboy on his round of collections made the acquaintance of Ella Corpening, a handsome mulatto of Amazonian proportions, who earned money by selling to white men a mysterious commodity known as Jelly Roll.

But neither covert adulteries nor bargain-rate prostitution threatened the moral integrity of Altamont as gravely as did the money-grabbing spirit of the more respectable citizens. Eugene Gant felt the corrupting influence on his own parents. To them industry and thrift were the pristine virtues. "It was not enough that a man work, though work was fundamental; it was even more important that he make money—a great deal if he was to be a great success—but at least enough to 'support himself.' This was for both Gant and Eliza the base of worth." [36] They sent all their boys out to earn money at a very early age. "It teaches a boy to be independent and self-reliant," said Gant.[37]

Eliza's own example provided the best lesson in the acquisitiveness that she sought to teach her sons. The Dixieland boarding house was not an end in itself; it was the means to an end. It pro-

[34] *Ibid.*, 114–15.   [35] *Ibid.*, 116.   [36] *Ibid.*, 94.   [37] *Ibid.*, 92.

vided a way to pay for a piece of real estate that would one day be very valuable. "Eliza saw Altamont not as so many hills, buildings, people: she saw it in the pattern of a gigantic blueprint." She knew the history of every piece of valuable property—who had bought it, who had sold it, what it was worth. She was sensitive to every growing-pain of the town, deducing the probable direction of its future expansion. "Her instinct was to buy cheaply where people would come; to keep out of pockets and *culs de sac,* to buy on a street that moved toward a centre, and that could be given extension.³⁸

Eliza's shrewdness and Gant's complaining co-operation pro-

³⁸ *Ibid.,* 104.

Dixieland was a big cheaply constructed frame house of eighteen or twenty drafty high ceilinged rooms: it had a rambling, unplanned, gabular appearance, . . .   Thomas Wolfe, *Look Homeward, Angel*

vided the couple with $100,000 by 1912, even before the intensive development of southern industry tripled Altamont's population. The great bulk of this was "solidly founded in juicy, well chosen pieces of property of Eliza's selection." [39] By the standards of the day, the Gants were rich. Yet to their children's disgust they continued to complain of poverty and to begrudge every dollar of expenditure.

American entry into World War I brought keen excitement to Altamont and to Eugene Gant. "The town and the nation boiled with patriotic frenzy—violent, in a chaotic sprawl, to little purpose. The spawn of Attila must be crushed ('exterminated,' said the Reverend Mr. Smallwood) by the sons of freedom. There were loans, bond issues, speech-making, a talk of drafts, and a thin trickle of Yankees into France." [40] Eugene Gant, now a college student at Pulpit Hill, was stirred by the spirit of adventure. "War is not death to young men; war is life. . . . In Eugene's mind, wealth, and love and glory melted into a symphonic noise: the age of myth and miracle had come upon the world again. All things were possible." [41] Too young for the armed services, he spent his summer vacation laboring in the Virginia embarkation ports.

But to Eliza Gant, the war meant only new opportunities to make money. Now in control of her stricken husband's property, she sold his old shop to a business syndicate as a site for Altamont's first skyscraper. With the money obtained from this and other transactions, she began to trade, buying, selling, obtaining options, "in an intricate and bewildering web." [42] She talked real estate unendingly, spending half her time talking to agents and driving off with them to look at property—all the time becoming more niggardly in personal expenditures. Although Eliza's children deplored her mania, they did not escape its contagion. Eugene's sister and her husband, Hugh Barton, were putting all the money they could scrape together into Altamont real estate.

IV

In *The Web and the Rock* and *You Can't Go Home Again*, Altamont became Libya Hill, the home town to which the writer

---

[39] *Ibid.*, 162.   [40] *Ibid.*, 354.   [41] *Ibid.*, 424.   [42] *Ibid.*, 505.

George Webber returned for occasional visits. Traveling back for his Aunt Maw's funeral in September, 1929, George Webber discovered that several Libya Hill luminaries were on the same train returning from a junket to New York. After mumbling their condolences, they resumed their favorite topic of conversation. "You ought to stay around a while, Webber," the banker Jarvis Riggs told him. "You wouldn't know the town. Things are booming down our way. Why, only the other day Mack Judson paid three hundred thousand for the Draper Block. The building's a dump, of course,—what he paid for was the land." After reporting other items of the same kind, he concluded, "That's the way it is all over town. Within a few years Libya Hill is going to be the largest and most beautiful city in the state. You mark my words." [43]

Forewarned though he was of the rising fever of speculation, George was still shocked by what he found in Libya Hill, "On all sides he heard talk, talk, talk,—terrific and incessant. And the tumult of voices was united in variations of a single chorus—speculation and real estate." The real estate men were everywhere. One could see them on porches unfolding blueprints and shouting enticements into the ears of deaf old women. Everyone seemed to be buying real estate—barbers, lawyers, grocers, butchers, builders, clothiers, "And there seemed to be only one rule, universal and infallible—to buy, always to buy, to pay whatever price was asked, and to sell again within two days at any price one chose to fix. It was fantastic." [44] When the supply of streets was exhausted, new streets were laid out in the surrounding wilderness, and even before the new streets were paved or a house had been built upon them, the tracts were being sold and resold for hundreds of thousands of dollars.

To the sensitive George Webber, a spirit of "drunken waste and wild destructiveness" seemed everywhere apparent. In the center of town there had been a beautiful green hill topped by an immense, rambling old wooden hotel. "It had been one of the pleasantest places in the town, but now it was gone." The hill had been leveled and paved with "a desolate horror of white concrete." Amidst a clutter of new stores and parking lots and office buildings, a new

---

[43] *You Can't Go Home Again*, 68.   [44] *Ibid.*, 117.

hotel was being built, sixteen stories high, of steel and concrete and pressed brick. "It was being stamped out of the same mold, as if by a gigantic biscuit-cutter of hotels, that had produced a thousand others like it all over the country. And to give a sumptuous—if spurious—distinction to its patterned uniformity, it was to be called The Libya-Ritz." [45]

The twenties were a time of super-salesmanship. Randy Shepperton, George's boyhood friend, was now the district agent for the Federal Weight, Scales and Computing Company. During George's 1929 visit to the Sheppertons, he met David Merrit, Randy's boss, who was in Libya Hill making one of his periodic visits of inspection. Ruddy, plump, and well kept, Merrit appeared to be the most amiable of men. Save for brief visits to the office, he spent most of his time promoting good will. "He would go around town and meet everybody, slapping people on the back and calling them by their first names, and for a week after he left the business men of Libya Hill would still be smoking his cigars." [46]

From Merrit, George learned the philosophy of "creative salesmanship." The old-fashioned founder of the company had set too modest a goal: he had only endeavored to place one of his scales in every store, shop or business that needed one. But, explained Merrit, "We've gone way beyond that! . . . Why, if we waited nowadays to sell a machine to someone who *needs* one, we'd get nowhere. . . . We don't wait until he needs one. If he says he's getting along all right without one, we make him buy one anyhow. We make him *see* the need, don't we Randy? In other words, we create the need." [47]

Merrit himself was only an archbishop in the vast hierarchy of the Federal Weight, Scales, and Computing Company. The reigning pope was Paul S. Appleton, III. He was the great man to whom had come the inspiration of creative salesmanship; he had also invented a special company heaven known as the Hundred Club. To this belonged all salesmen who sold 100 per cent of their individually assigned quotas. Those who qualified for the Hundred Club received generous rewards in commissions and bonuses. They also participated in "The Week of Play"—a magnificent annual out-

[45] *Ibid.*, 118.   [46] *Ibid.*, 133.   [47] *Ibid.*, 135.

ing paid for by the Company. Leaving their wives at home, the chosen salesmen assembled in Washington or Los Angeles or Miami; or they embarked on a chartered ship for Bermuda or Havana. Here some "twelve or fifteen hundred men, Americans, most of them in their middle years, exhausted, overweight, their nerves frayed down and stretched to the breaking point, met from all quarters of the continent 'at the Company's expense' for one brief, wild, gaudy week of riot. And George thought grimly what this tragic spectacle of business men at play meant in terms of the entire scheme of things and the plan of life that had produced it." [48]

But the Company had its hell as well as its heaven. Into outer limbo were cast all those lost souls unable to meet the insatiable demand for more sales. George was horrified to overhear Merrit castigating Shepperton in the privacy of the Company office. The boss was laying down a harsh ultimatum: "This district ought to deliver thirty per cent more business than you're getting from it, and the Company is going to have it too—or else! You deliver or you go right out on your can! See? The Company doesn't give a damn about you! It's after the business." [49]

Shepperton's frightened submissiveness was even more sickening than Merrit's savagery. Embarrassed to realize that George had overheard the conversation, Randy offered a feeble explanation: "Dave's a good fellow. . . . You—you see, he's got to do those things. . . . He—he's with the Company." [50] George had a sudden vision of toiling thousands dragging the stones for Pharaoh's Great Pyramid, with each lieutenant in the chain of command being lashed by his superior and applying the lash in turn to his underlings.

Libya Hill offered lessons in the interwoven webs of financial and political power. Jarvis Riggs appeared to be a living vindication of the American legend. The son of a poor but respectable local family, he had had to quit school at the age of fifteen to support his widowed mother. At eighteen he had gone to work for the Merchants National Bank, climbing from humbler posts to the position of teller. Because Riggs was bright and personable, he was offered the position of cashier in a new bank, the Citizens Trust

---

[48] *Ibid.,* 139.   [49] *Ibid.,* 140.   [50] *Ibid.,* 141.

Company, organized by a group of local businessmen in 1912. Rising rapidly in this infant organization, Jarvis Riggs soon became president.

Although it had been projected as a "progressive" and "young man's bank," the Citizens Trust Company followed a modest and conservative policy during its early years. But in the middle 1920's, Jarvis Riggs threw off his inhibitions. "The Citizens Trust began to advertise itself as 'fastest-growing bank in the state.' But it did not advertise what it was growing on." [51]

The bank was fattening on the paper values created through the manipulations of a clique of politicians and businessmen. To provide a front for their activities "The Ring" obtained the election of the popular and easy-going Mayor Baxter Kennedy. The city government floated enormous bond issues to finance new streets and public buildings. The proceeds were deposited in the Citizens Trust Company and flowed out again as a golden stream of easy credit to the politicians and their friends for private speculation. Thus was spun "a vast and complex web that wove through the entire social structure of the town and involved the lives of thousands of people. And all of it centered in the bank." [52]

The bigger the bubble of inflation was blown, the thinner its walls became. In the spring of 1928 Mayor Kennedy became frightened and sought to withdraw the city deposits, but Jarvis Riggs dissuaded him. He warned the mayor that any such step would close the bank and wreck the town. "You can't sell Libya Hill short," he said, using a phrase much in vogue at that time. "We've not begun to see the progress we're going to make. But the salvation and future of this town rests in your hands. So make up your mind about it. What are you going to do?" [53] And the unhappy mayor did nothing.

V

"Then it happened," Wolfe wrote. "March 12, 1930 was a day that will be long remembered in the annals of Libya Hill. The double tragedy set the stage as nothing else could have done for the

---

[51] *Ibid.*, 335.   [52] *Ibid.*, 336.   [53] *Ibid.*, 337.

macabre weeks to follow." [54]   Act One in the double tragedy opened at nine o'clock with the fearful news that the Citizens Trust Company was closed. As the word sped through the city, white-faced men and women rushed to the Square from every direction—housewives with their aprons on, mechanics with tools in hand, businessmen and clerks without their hats. In a desolate line they moved past the bank, seeing with their own eyes the locked and darkened doors. Some stared without a word, some wept, some muttered angrily.

"For their ruin had caught up with them. Many of the people in that throng had lost their life savings. But it was not only the bank's depositors who were runied. Everyone now knew that the boom was over." They knew that the closing of the bank had put an end to all their speculations. "Yesterday they could count their paper riches by ten thousands and by millions; today they owned nothing. Their wealth had vanished, and they were left saddled with debts that they could never pay." [55] What they did not yet know was that the city itself was bankrupt with six million dollars of its funds on deposit in the ruined bank.

Act Two in the Libya Hill tragedy was brief and unnerving. Less than three hours after the fateful news of the bank closing, the blind usurer Judge Rumford Bland stumbled across the body of Mayor Baxter Kennedy in a public toilet where the mayor had shot himself. "So it was that weak, easygoing, procrastinating, good-natured Baxter Kennedy, Mayor of Libya Hill, was found—all that was left of him—in darkness, by an evil old blind man." [56]

The days and weeks that followed deepened the gloom in Libya Hill. The mayor's suicide was followed by forty others during the next ten days and by still more later on. Those who did not take this way out of their troubles sought release in blaming each other and calling for vengeance, especially against Jarvis Riggs. Yet in reality they were all guilty. The town was suffering from "sublime, ironic, and irrevocable justice." What had happened in Libya Hill

went much deeper than the mere obliteration of bank accounts, the extinction of paper profits, and the loss of property. It was the ruin of men who found out, as soon as these symbols of their outward success had

---

[54] *Ibid.*, 338.   [55] *Ibid.*, 339.   [56] *Ibid.*, 340.

been destroyed, that they had nothing left—no inner equivalent from which they might draw new strength. It was the ruin of men who, discovering not only that their values were false but that they never had any substance whatsoever, now saw at last the emptiness and hollowness of their lives.[57]

Randy Shepperton, George's salesman friend, had no deposits in the defunct bank, nor had he been speculating in real estate. Yet the whirlpool of depression sucked him down relentlessly. A week after the bank closing Merrit fired him, thus carrying out the threat that George had overheard some months earlier. Randy refused to resent his dismissal, he accepted the idea that Merrit had no other course than to fire agents who could not get business. Yet there was no business to be had during Libya Hill's final spree. All the money in town had gone into real estate speculation, and now with the failure of the bank that too was gone.

Shepperton refused to worry about his plight. He repeated all the comforting catch phrases of the day. It was a big country and there was always a place for a good man. Did George ever hear of a good man who couldn't work? George was pessimistic, Randy argued, because he lived in New York. But New York was not America. Even if he couldn't find anything in Libya Hill, he could go elsewhere. There was one good thing about being a salesman: if you could sell one thing, you could sell anything. It was easy to switch products.

But this touching faith in the system went unrewarded. Randy was unable to find another job. He tried everything, but nothing worked. After eighteen months his savings were gone, and he had to sell the old family home for a pittance. He and his wife managed to scrimp along for a year or so on what the house had brought them. Then that too was gone. Randy fell ill, an illness more of the spirit than of the flesh. Moving at last from Libya Hill, the couple lived in a strange city, in the household of a relative. And as the final humiliation, Randy had to go on relief.

"And it seemed to George that Randy's tragedy was the essential tragedy of America. America—the magnificent, unrivaled, unequaled, unbeatable, unshrinkable, supercolossal, 99-and-44-one-

[57] *Ibid.*, 341.

hundredths-per-cent-pure, schoolgirl-complexion, covers-the-earth, I'd walk-a-mile-for-it, four-out-of-five-have-it, his master's voice, ask-the-man-who-owns-one, blue-plate-special, home of advertising, salesmanship, and special pleading in all its many catchy and beguiling forms." [58]

VI

This story of disaster at Libya Hill may sound a little too melodramatic. Is this really an authentic picture of Asheville during these years, or is it largely imaginary or symbolic?

Asheville did indeed have a notorious bank scandal. In November, 1930, the Central Bank and Trust Company failed. Amidst so many bank closings all over the country this would not have been a very unusual event, except for the political and economic ramifications that shook the community. Millions of dollars of public funds were tied up.[59] Wallace B. Davis, president of the bank and one of the city's leading citizens, was indicted and sent to prison for five years on a charge of violating the banking laws.[60] To Tom Wolfe, now slaving away at his writing in Brooklyn, this news had a certain grim fascination. On June 8, 1931, he wrote to his mother:

I have followed the general course of the bank trials and know that Davis has been sentenced to five years in prison. Have you been going to the trials? Write me about it, and save the newspaper clippings if you can. Davis of course is guilty as hell, but I think we shall live to see the day when he returns and becomes an honored pillar of the Methodist Church again. But I do not think that this generation will live long enough to forget the effect of his work—it has been ruinous. You used to say it was three generations from shirtsleeves to shirtsleeves—and I suppose that is what has happened to Asheville. When I was a child it was a little sleepy town, then it had its flare of glory, or thought it had, and now I suppose it will go back to its shirtsleeves once again.[61]

A particularly tragic victim of the bank scandal was the mayor of Asheville, blamed by his fellow-citizens for using public funds to

---

[58] *Ibid.*, 364.   [59] *New York Times*, Nov. 21, 23, 1930.   [60] *Ibid.*, June 4, 1931.
[61] Thomas Wolfe to Julia Wolfe, June 8, 1931, *Thomas Wolfe's Letters to His Mother, Julia Elizabeth Wolfe*, with an introduction by John Skally Terry (ed.) (New York: Charles Scribner's Sons, 1943), 206–07.

bolster up the tottering bank. In making the suicide of Baxter
Kennedy occur on the very morning of the bank closing, Wolfe
exercised his novelist's license to rearrange events to tighten the
drama. But the real mayor's fate was no less pathetic. Self-righteous
townsmen ran him out of office, and later—six months after the
failure of the bank—he did go to the second floor of the building
above his law office and shoot out his brains in the men's room. He
was even discovered by a blind man—much as Wolfe tells the
story.[62]

Finally, what about Randy Shepperton, the eager salesman who
lost his job and then went through one humiliating experience
after another as he was drawn into the vortex of the depression?
Wolfe's last editor, Edward C. Aswell of Harper's, regards Randy as
essentially a product of Wolfe's imagination—the projection of a
friend that he would like to have had.[63] Yet Wolfe attributes to
Randy certain experiences that came from real life. Two persons
closely related to Wolfe were salesmen. In 1930, his older brother
Fred was a sales engineer working for the Fairbanks, Morse Company, out of Jacksonville, Florida.[64] And Fairbanks, Morse, be it
noted, manufactured scales, as did the fictional company for which
Randy Shepperton worked. At the same time, Wolfe's brother-in-
law, Ralph Wheaton, was an agent for the National Cash Register
Company in Asheville. Both Fred Wolfe and Ralph Wheaton lost
their jobs during the depression; both were in difficult straits.[65]
Wheaton's case was a particularly distressing one, as Wolfe makes
clear in a letter of 1936.

To get back to Wheaton, I think he has been crushed by the catastrophe
of recent years. Furthermore, although I never had much feeling one
way or another about great corporations until this thing happened, I
think the way he was treated by the great corporation that employed
him after he had given his life, his strength, his youth and all his best
energies since his fourteenth year, was simply damnable and I for one do

---

[62] Jonathan Daniels, *Tar Heels: A Portrait of North Carolina* (New York: Dodd,
Mead & Co., 1941), 226–27.

[63] Edward C. Aswell, "A Note on Thomas Wolfe," in Thomas Wolfe, *The Hills
Beyond*, 358–59.

[64] Mabel Wolfe Wheaton with Le Gette Blythe, *Thomas Wolfe and His Family*
(New York: Doubleday & Co., 1961), 229.

[65] *Ibid.*, 229, 253, 310.

not propose to sit around silent and acquiesent in a society where such a situation exists and where such things happen.[66]

If Wolfe wrote with anguish about the great depression, it was because he was a close witness to the human suffering that it caused. And behind the depression he saw what he regarded as "hidden pockets of lethal gases"—gases produced by "a false, vicious, and putrescent scheme of things" lying beneath the surface of American life.[67]

[66] Thomas Wolfe to Margaret Roberts, May 20, 1936, *The Letters of Thomas Wolfe*, Elizabeth Nowell (ed.) (New York: Charles Scribner's Sons, 1956), 520.

[67] *You Can't Go Home Again*, 336.

6

The Lost Paradise

Thus they changed their social life—changed as in the
whole universe only man can change. They were not farm
men any more, but migrant men. And the thought, the plan-
ning, the long staring silence that had gone out to the fields,
went now to the roads, to the distance, to the West. That man
whose mind had been bound with acres lived with narrow
concrete miles. And his thought and his worry were not any
more with rainfall, with wind and dust, with the thrust of the
crops.

JOHN STEINBECK, *The Grapes of Wrath* [1]

VERSATILE almost to a fault, John Steinbeck has written
of many different things. His earliest novel was a swashbuckling
romance based upon the career of an English buccaneer. Later
writings have ranged over such diverse themes as marine biology,
the air force, the Nazi occupation of Norway, Mexican peasant life,
and village politics on Long Island. Steinbeck the man has wandered no less widely, having lived in many different places and
visited even more.

Yet Steinbeck's most memorable work has been focused on the
section of California where he was born and spent his earliest years.
The Steinbeck country, strictly defined, is the Salinas Valley, a
long narrow depression lying to the south of Monterey Bay. Bor-
dering the valley on the east are the golden foothills of the Galiban
Mountains; on the west tower the grim and forbidding Santa
Lucias standing like ramparts between the valley and the Pacific

---

[1] John Steinbeck, *The Grapes of Wrath* (New York: Viking Press, 1939), 267–68.

Ocean. Streams tumbling down the mountainsides form the Salinas River, an erratic stream that may swell to torrential size, trapping cows and pigs, toppling barns and houses, tearing away acres of good farm land or shrink until it goes completely underground. "It was not a fine river at all, but it was the only one we had and so we boasted about it—how dangerous it was in a wet winter and how dry it was in a dry summer. You can boast about anything if it's all you have. Maybe the less you have, the more you are required to boast." [2]

On the floor of the valley the topsoil lay deep and fertile, providing lush nourishment for the spring flowers that grew in wild profusion and for grains and vegetables planted by the farmers. But this fecundity did not extend to the uplands; over the foothills the soil was precariously thin, and the higher slopes were completely eroded.

Each major phase of California history had touched the Salinas Valley. The earliest inhabitants had been Indians of a primitive culture who neither hunted nor tilled the soil but lived on grubs, grasshoppers, and shell fish. Then had come Spaniards, who accumulated huge ranches and raised cattle for hides and tallow. Finally the Americans pushed in, settling first in the fertile valley and then along the slopes of the foothills. After the Civil War, California's masterful capitalists had thrust the Southern Pacific Railroad through the area and then promoted settlement with exuberant advertising. After reading this, says Steinbeck, "anyone who did not want to settle in the Salinas Valley was crazy." [3] Improved transportation and modern miracles of refrigeration ultimately encouraged the inhabitants to specialize in growing lettuce and other perishables for the national market.

Steinbeck's own forbears had participated in these historic events. His maternal grandfather, the patriarchal Samuel Hamilton, had emigrated from Ireland and homesteaded in the foothills east of King City. Unable to grow enough on his ample but barren acres, Hamilton had earned a precarious living drilling wells and blacksmithing while he sired nine children. One of his daughters, the spunky Olive Hamilton, began teaching in country schools at

---

[2] John Steinbeck, *East of Eden* (New York: Viking Press, 1952), 4.   [3] *Ibid.*, 134.

the age of eighteen and eventually married John Steinbeck, Sr., who had come from Florida and built a flour mill in King City. The couple subsequently moved to Salinas, where the husband continued in the milling business and served for many years as treasurer of Monterey County. It was into this moderately prosperous household that John Steinbeck, the future novelist, was born on February 27, 1902.

During his boyhood Steinbeck developed a love for nature and a sensitivity to the world of birds and animals. "The most tremendous morning in the world," he recalled was one "when my pony had a colt." [4] His schoolteacher mother instilled in him an enthusiasm for books and reading. At the Salinas high school, he participated in track and baseball and was elected president of his senior class. He spent vacations laboring as a hired hand on nearby ranches, and after graduation he worked for a year as an assistant chemist in a sugar beet factory.

Over a period of five years Steinbeck intermittently attended Stanford University, earning less than half the credits he needed for a degree. When he was not in attendance, he held a variety of jobs—clerking in a haberdashery store, working as a farm hand, and doing road work—all the while adding to the fund of observation and experience from which he drew later literary material.

In 1925, he spent several months in New York, in a premature attempt to launch a literary career. Supporting himself as a reporter and a laborer, he wrote short stories but was unable to get them published. He worked his way back to California as a deckhand on a ship passing through the Panama Canal. Still grinding out manuscript, he served for a time as caretaker of an estate on Lake Tahoe and as an attendant in a fish hatchery in the Sierras. In 1929, his first novel *Cup of Gold* appeared without creating any excitement either among the critics or with the general public.

Marrying for the first time in 1930, Steinbeck made his home in Pacific Grove, a coastal town near Monterey and his native Salinas Valley. Here he began an influential friendship with Ed Ricketts, the proprietor of a biological supply laboratory, and became acquainted with the carefree life of Monterey's Mexican-Americans.

[4] Peter Lisca, *The Wide World of John Steinbeck* (New Brunswick: Rutgers University Press, 1958), 22.

The novels and stories of these years, *The Pastures of Heaven* (1932), *To a God Unknown* (1933), "The Red Pony" (1933), exploited themes suggested by the traditions of the region and the author's own experience, but not until he published the roisterous *Tortilla Flat* (1935) did Steinbeck achieve an outstanding popular success. Although the early novels and stories often depicted acts of violence and cruelty, most of them were encased in a kind of romantic veneer. Steinbeck's depiction of brutal contemporary reality began with *In Dubious Battle* (1936) and *Of Mice and Men* (1937). His greatest success—both popular and critical—came with *The Grapes of Wrath*, published in 1939.

After 1940, Steinbeck spent less and less time in California. He sailed the seas with Ed Ricketts collecting marine specimens; he made excursions into Mexico; he reported the World War II battle fronts. After 1942, when his first marriage terminated in divorce, he no longer called California home. He lived for a number of years in New York City and then moved to Long Island. In some of his later books—*Cannery Row* (1945), *East of Eden* (1952), *Sweet Thursday* (1954)—he continued to use California materials but less successfully than in the novels of the 1930's.

From the standpoint of the historian, Steinbeck's greatest value lies in his feeling for the great transition in twentieth century agriculture. He remembers with nostalgia the comfortable agricultural society of his boyhood and youth; he understands the commercial forces that transformed agriculture after World War I; he shares the lot of the marginal farmers who lost their independence and became migrants during the Great Depression.

II

Steinbeck was not old enough to remember the great westward movement that had brought Americans into California. Yet the state was still so young that there were strong oral traditions of its heroic age. Weaving the saga of his own mother's family into the complex tapestry of *East of Eden*, Steinbeck wrote: "I must depend on hearsay, on old photographs, on stories told, and on memories which are hazy and mixed with fable in trying to tell you about the Hamiltons." [5]

[5] *East of Eden*, 8.

In the career of Samuel Hamilton, an Irish Protestant immigrant, both the opportunities and limitations of federal land policy were illustrated. When he arrived in the Salinas Valley, he recorded claims for 480 acres. He added to this, until in the end he acquired title to a total of 1760 acres.[6] If the land had been any good, such lavish governmental bounty would have guaranteed a fortune, but all the rich bottom land was gone when Hamilton arrived, and his acreage was in harsh and dry hill country.

Yet the more fortunate settlers enjoyed nature's bounty in lavish measure. Describing a district near the mouth of the Salinas Valley, Steinbeck wrote: "Rich vegetable land has been the result of the draining, land so black with wealth that the lettuce and cauliflowers grow to giants." [7] In the better years everything worked together for good. "It was a deluge of a winter in the Salinas Valley, wet and wonderful. . . . The feed was deep in January, and in February the hills were fat with grass and the coats of the cattle looked tight and sleek. In March the soft rains continued. . . . Then warmth flooded the valley and the earth burst into bloom—yellow and blue and gold." [8]

At its best the West was much more munificent than the East, but climatic conditions were so different as to require radical adaptation. Adam Trask, looking over his parched acres during a hot summer, "felt the panic the Eastern man always does at first in California." In Connecticut two weeks without rain is a dry spell and four is a drought. "But in California it does not ordinarily rain at all between the end of May and the first of November. The Eastern man, though he has been told, feels the earth is sick in the rainless months." [9]

Once the first hardships were overcome, the westerners enjoyed an idyllic existence—or so it seemed in romantic retrospect. The ranch described in "The Red Pony" provided a secure environment for the boy Jody. The human relationships were extraordinarily fine: a warm and tender mother, a strong father whose stern-

---

[6] Steinbeck attributes his grandfather's land acquisitions to homestead claims taken out in the name of himself, his wife, and nine children. This would not have been legal under the Homestead Act itself, but title to this much acreage might have been possible under other land laws with the aid of subterfuges then common.

[7] John Steinbeck, "Johnny Bear," *The Long Valley* (New York: Viking Press, 1939), 145.

[8] *East of Eden*, 310.   [9] *Ibid.*, 161.

ness was tempered by affection, a companionable ranch hand, rich
in practical knowledge. The lessons taught at the district school
were only a part of the boy's education. He did the chores appropriate to his age. When he was ten, he was filling the wood box and
feeding the chickens; a few months later he was driving a hay rake,
helping with the baling, and milking a cow. What might have been
the exploitation of child labor under different circumstances was
the purposeful activity of an excited boy earning his own pony.
Through vivid experience he learned not only the practical business of farming but was initiated into the mysteries of birth and
death. Shielded from nothing, he witnessed the whole process by
which his pony came into existence—the rough coupling of stal-
lion and mare, the course of the pregnancy, and the crude and
bloody operation necessary to deliver the foal.[10]

But agricultural America also valued its more formal agencies
of education. "In the country the repository of art and science was
the school, and the school teacher shielded and carried the torch of
learning and of beauty. The schoolhouse was the meeting place for
music, for debate. The polls were set in the schoolhouse for elec-
tions. Social life, whether it was the crowning of a May queen, the
eulogy to a dead president, or an all-night dance could be held nowhere else." [11]

Rural democracy had its own checks and balances. "Every town
has its aristocrats, its family above reproach. Emalin and Amy
Hawkins are our aristocrats, maiden ladies, kind people. Their
father was a congressman." [12] The respected spinsters provided
"the safe thing"—the place where a kid could get gingerbread and
a girl could get reassurance. "They're proud, but they believe in
things we hope are true." [13]

Attractive though they were, the simple values of the older society were forever threatened by the accelerating tempo of change.
Bemoaning the impact of the automobile, the village postmaster
said: "They'll change the face of the countryside. They get their
clatter into everything. . . . We even feel it here. Man used to
come for his mail once a week. Now he comes every day, sometimes
twice a day. He just can't wait for his damn catalogue. Running
around. Always running around." [14]

---

[10] "The Red Pony," *The Long Valley*, 203–79.   [11] *East of Eden*, 147.
[12] "Johnny Bear," *The Long Valley*, 154.   [13] *Ibid.*, 163.   [14] *East of Eden*, 370.

III

In the "Leader of the People," the grandfather persisted in long-winded stories about crossing the plains despite the obvious boredom of a younger generation that had heard all this before. Trying once more to explain himself, the old man said: "We carried life out here and set it down the way those ants carry eggs. And I was the leader. The westering was as big as God, and the slow steps that made the movement piled up and piled up until the continent was crossed." [15] To his grandson eager to do similar deeds he said sadly: "No place to go, Jody. Every place is taken. But that's not the worst—no, not the worst. Westering has died out of the people. Westering isn't a hunger any more. It's all done. Your father is right. It is finished." [16]

But the western movement was not really finished after all. During the 1930's, thousands of shabby automobiles and trucks crowded the roads leading to California. For some the old dreams were revived. Ma Joad liked to think how nice it was going to be. "Never cold. An' fruit ever'place, an' people just bein' in the nicest places, little white houses in among the orange trees." [17] Yet the woman's hopes were nourished more by her own nature than by the reality of her situation. The movement of which she was a part was more retreat than conquest. The highway west was "the path of a people in flight, refugees from dust and shrinking land, from the thunder of tractors and shrinking ownership, from the desert's slow northward invasion, from the twisting winds that howl up out of Texas, from the floods that bring no richness to the land and steal what little richness is there." [18]

It was this last pathetic westering that provided Steinbeck with his most memorable literary material. All his earlier years helped to prepare him for writing *The Grapes of Wrath*. In his own Salinas Valley he had seen the increasing specialization of agriculture and the growing reliance upon migrant labor. During his student days he had worked side by side with these poorly-paid laborers. When the agricultural workers revolted in a series of violent strikes, Steinbeck gathered the material for his grim strike novel *In*

---

[15] "The Leader of the People," *The Long Valley*, 302.   [16] *Ibid.*, 303.
[17] *The Grapes of Wrath*, 124.   [18] *Ibid.*, 160.

Dubious Battle. Instead of exhausting his interest in the problem, this piece of writing apparently intensified it. During the fall of 1936, Steinbeck lived in migrant camps and worked in the fields near Salinas and Bakersfield. In articles published in *The Nation* and the *San Francisco News* he reported upon the appalling poverty and dangerous discontent of the workers.

"My material drawer is chock full," Steinbeck wrote to his literary agent in October, 1936. Yet his experience was far more than a gathering of notes. To an extraordinary degree he was able to share the life and hardships of the workers. "I have to write this sitting in a ditch," he wrote a friend. "I'm out working—may go south to pick a little cotton. Migrants are going south now and I'll probably go along." [19] Even in the final stage of work on *The Grapes of Wrath,* Steinbeck felt compelled to leave his desk to aid the migrants. "I must go over into the interior valleys. There are five thousand families starving to death over there, not just hungry, but actually starving. . . . I'll do what I can . . . Funny how mean and how little books become in the face of such tragedies." [20]

Why had these suffering people come to California? In 1937, Steinbeck sought an answer. Having bought a car in Detroit, he drove to Oklahoma, where he saw for himself the combination of economic forces and natural disasters that were uprooting the farm population. He joined a group of migrants and shared their hardships on the long trek to the Pacific coast. The power and passion of *The Grapes of Wrath* is derived from this intense experience.

A weird league of furies bedeviled midwestern farmers during the 1930's. First, there was drought, parching the corn and cotton and drying out the top soil; then came the great winds, churning up the dust and blowing it across the countryside, in storms so violent that men and women huddled in the houses and wore goggles over their eyes and handkerchiefs over their noses when they went out. "Houses were shut tight, and cloth wedged around doors and windows, but the dust came in so thinly that it could not be seen in the air, and it settled like pollen on the chairs and tables, on the dishes." [21]

While calamities of nature were robbing the soil of its fertility,

[19] Lisca, *op. cit.,* 145.   [20] *Ibid.,* 146.   [21] *The Grapes of Wrath,* 5.

equally inexorable human forces were thrusting the farmers off the land. There had always been a substantial number of tenant farmers sharecropping the land belonging to large individual owners. Now the number of tenants was rapidly increasing, and the new owners were corporations—banks and finance companies. The process was simple. The hard-pressed farmer had to borrow money; the bank or finance company assumed title to the land; and the one-time owner became a sharecropper. The loss in status and security was painful: "Grampa took up the land, and he had to kill the Indians and drive them away. And Pa was born here, and he killed weeds and snakes. Then a bad year came and he had to borrow a little money. . . . The bank owned the land then, but we stayed and we got a little bit of what we raised." [22]

But even the pittance that the sharecropper retained was not safe. "Well, the folks that owns the lan' says, 'We can't afford to keep no tenants.' An' they says, 'The share a tenant gets is jus' the margin a profit we can't afford to lose.' An' they says, 'If we put all our lan' in one piece we can jus' hardly make her pay.' So they tractored all the tenants off a the lan'." [23] As the agent for the corporate owner explained: "The tenant system won't work any more. One man on a tractor can take the place of twelve or fourteen families. Pay him a wage and take all the crop. We have to do it. We don't like to do it." [24]

To the anguished tenants, the giant tractors were bloodless automatons destroying their familiar world. The driver seemed without a will of his own. "The man sitting in the iron seat did not look like a man; gloved, goggled, rubber dust mask over nose and mouth, he was a part of the monster, a robot in the seat." [25] He would drive straight across the country, cutting through a dozen farms and straight back. The human element seemed to have been removed from the whole planting process.

Behind the tractor rolled the shining disks, cutting the earth with blades—not plowing but surgery, pushing the cut earth to the right where the second row of disks cut it and pushed it to the left; slicing blades shining, polished by the cut earth. And pulled behind the disks, the harrows combing with iron teeth so that the lit-

[22] *Ibid.*, 45.   [23] *Ibid.*, 64.   [24] *Ibid.*, 44.   [25] *Ibid.*, 48.

The people came out from their houses and smelled the hot stinging air and covered their noses from it.   John Steinbeck, *The Grapes of Wrath*

tle clods broke up and the earth lay smooth. Behind the harrows, the long seeders—twelve curved iron penes erected in the foundry, orgasms set by gears, raping methodically, raping without passion.[26]

The evicted tenants belonged to a class that was usually quick to resort to violence, but in the present circumstances they did not know whom to fight. When the tractor driver, stopping for lunch, removed his goggles, he was recognized as Joe Davis's boy, one of themselves, who had taken the job to feed his wife and children. When the tenants protested that his tractor was depriving fifteen or

[26] *Ibid.,* 48–49.

they tractored all the tenants off a the lan'. John Steinbeck, *The Grapes of Wrath*

twenty families of their livelihood, the driver replied: "Can't think of that. Got to think of my own kids. Three dollars a day, and it comes every day. Times are changing, mister, don't you know? Can't make a living on the land unless you've got two, five, ten thousand acres and a tractor. Crop land isn't for little guys like us any more. . . ." [27] He confided that his employers gave him a two dollar bonus for every "accident" in which he plowed so near to a stubborn tenant's house that it fell down.[28]

To shoot the driver would do no good. "They'll just hang you, but long before you're hung there'll be another guy on the tractor,

[27] *Ibid.*, 50.　　[28] *Ibid.*, 51.

and he'll bump the house down." It would be equally futile to shoot the bank president and the board of directors. "Fellow was telling me the bank gets orders from the East. The orders were, 'Make the land show profit or we'll close you up.' " The driver's final comment was fatalistic: "Maybe there's nobody to shoot. Maybe the thing isn't men at all. Maybe, like you said, the property's doing it." But the tenant—perhaps Steinbeck arguing with himself—was not satisfied with this answer: "There's some way to stop this. It's not like lightning or earthquakes. We've got a bad thing made by men, and by God that's something we can change." [29]

Deprived of their means of livelihood, a few of the former sharecroppers took laboring jobs on the new giant farms. But there was no work for most of them, and the only spark of hope came in news of the opportunities for migrant labor in California. Reading about the Promised Land, Ma Joad scarcely knew what to think. "I seen the han'bills fellas pass out, an' how much work they is, an' high wages an' all; an' I seen in the paper how they want folks to come an' pick grapes an' oranges an' peaches. That'd be nice work, Tom, pickin' peaches. Even if they wouldn't let you eat none, you could maybe snitch a little ratty one sometimes. An' it'd be nice under the trees, workin' in the shade." But she was too shrewd a woman to be taken in completely. "I'm scared of stuff so nice. I ain't got faith. I'm scared somepin ain't so nice about it." [30]

Whatever their misgivings, thousands of families could see no other way of escape. They invested in second-hand cars and trailers, and set out on the great adventure. The heartbreaks began even before they left home. Often the only available buyer for their possessions was a junk dealer, who would purchase as scrap metal the farmer's still serviceable tools. "When everything that could be sold was sold, stoves and bedsteads, chairs and tables, little corner cupboards, tubs and tanks, still there were piles of possessions; and the women sat among them, turning them over and looking off beyond and back, pictures, square glasses, and here's a vase." [31]

They loaded what they could into their ancient automobiles and trucks, then burned the rest—the books and knicknacks that linked the family to the past. "Suddenly they were nervous. Got to

[29] *Ibid.*, 52.   [30] *Ibid.*, 122–23.   [31] *Ibid.*, 119.

get out quick now. Can't wait. We can't wait. And they piled up the goods in the yards and set fire to them. They stood and watched them burning, and then frantically they loaded up the cars and drove away, drove in the dust. The dust hung in the air for a long time after the loaded cars had passed." [32]

IV

The California Trail of the new westering was Highway 66—"the long concrete path across the country, waving gently up and down on the map, from the Mississippi to Bakersfield—over the red lands and the gray lands, twisting up into the mountains, crossing the Divide and down into the bright and terrible desert, and across the desert to the mountains again, and into the rich California valleys." [33]

Making their faltering way over this 1400 mile obstacle course were the jalopies of the migrants. Many were recently purchased from unscrupulous used car dealers, who had silenced moaning transmissions with sawdust and patched over dangerous wounds in the tires. Hour after hour these unreliable vehicles rolled slowly over the roads. "In the day ancient leaky radiators sent up columns of steam, loose connecting rods hammered and pounded. And the men driving the trucks and the overloaded cars listened apprehensively. How far between towns? It is a terror between towns. If something breaks—well, if something breaks we camp right here while Jim walks to town and gets a part and walks back and—how much food we got?" [34]

Filling stations and garages dealt warily with the wanderers. When the latter had cash, the operators took advantage of their necessities to sell them second-hand tires and used parts at bloated prices. When they ran out of money, the businessmen steeled themselves against their importunities. "Why," one filling station owner complained, "the folks that stops here begs gasoline an' they trades for gasoline. I could show you in my back room the stuff they'll trade for gas an' oil: beds an' baby buggies an' pots an' pans. One

---

[32] *Ibid.*, 121.   [33] *Ibid.*, 160.   [34] *Ibid.*, 161.

family traded a doll their kid had for a gallon. An' what'm I gonna do with the stuff, open a junk shop?" [35]

Yet the migrants did not always receive harsh treatment. Occasional acts of kindness—often brusquely performed—aided their passage. The operators of a roadside restaurant, touched by hungry faces, might sell a 15-cent loaf of bread for a dime, or two 5-cent candy bars for a penny. And rough truckdrivers, watching the scene, might double their tips as a way of making their own contribution to this shamefaced philanthropy.[36]

Eager to reach their destination some families might drive twenty-four hours a day, but most of the migrants camped by the roadside each night. During the day they traveled as separate families, but each evening they became part of a community. "And because they were lonely and perplexed, because they had all come from a place of sadness and worry and defeat, and because they were all going to a new mysterious place, they huddled together; they talked together; they shared their lives, their food, and the things they hoped for in the new country." One family might choose a campsite near a spring; a second family attracted both by the spring and the prospect of company, might stop; a third family, impressed by a site so favored, might join them. "And when the sun went down, perhaps twenty families and twenty cars were there." [37] Not forgetting their manners, each newcoming family gravely asked permission to stop from those already on the campsite.

The chosen places fulfilled certain requirements. Most important was access to water—"a river bank, a stream, a spring, or even a faucet unguarded." The campers also needed enough flat land to pitch their tents and a little brush or wood to build fires. A nearby dump was an advantage, since it could provide useful equipment—"stove tops, a curved fender to shelter the fire, and cans to cook in and eat from." [38]

Having adapted quickly to their gypsy life, the families knew what had to be done each night, and each member did his part without orders. The children gathered wood and carried water; the men pitched the tents and unloaded the beds; the women cooked and served the food. Chores performed and families fed, the itin-

---

[35] *Ibid.*, 172.   [36] *Ibid.*, 216–20.   [37] *Ibid.*, 264.   [38] *Ibid.*, 267.

erants fraternized with their neighbors. In nostalgic mood they swapped stories about the places they had come from; in anxious curiosity they compared conjectures about the mysterious country that lay ahead.

Sometimes a man would produce a guitar and start singing. Slowly the other campers would gather around and join softly in the old familiar ballads. "And now the group was welded to one thing, one unit, so that in the dark the eyes of the people were inward, and their minds played in other times, and their sadness was like rest, like sleep. . . . The children drowsed with the music and went into the tents to sleep, and the singing came into their dreams." [39]

In the morning the families would pack up and take to the road again. Each traveled at its own pace so that one night's fellow-campers were not identical with the next. Yet for all their transience, the migrant colonies were true communities. The travelers knew how they were expected to behave. "The families learned what rights must be observed—the right of privacy in the tent; the right to keep the past black hidden in the heart; the right to talk and to listen; the right to refuse help or to accept, to offer help or to decline it; the right of son to court and daughter to be courted; the right of the hungry to be fed; the right of the pregnant and the sick to transcend all other rights." [40]

Behavior that violated these rights would not be tolerated. No one must intrude upon privacy or be noisy while the camp slept. No one must rape or steal or murder. "And as the worlds moved westward, rules became laws, although no one told the families." It was unlawful to foul near the camp, or to foul the drinking water. It was unlawful to eat good rich food near a hungry man, unless he were asked to share. "And with the laws, the punishments—and there were only two—a quick and murderous fight or ostracism; and ostracism was the worst." [41]

The western movement of the 1930's with its ancient cars and trucks rattling over paved roads seemed far different than the earlier migration in covered wagons drawn across dusty trails by horses and oxen. Yet there were common features. In both, moun-

[39] *Ibid.*, 272.   [40] *Ibid.*, 265.   [41] *Ibid.*, 266.

tain and desert threatened the wayfarers with delay and hardship. In both, the various age groups followed their traditional patterns of behavior. Children lived each day in wide-eyed excitement; young couples made love and planned their future; middle-aged people struggled and worried; old folks grieved and died.

The death of the elders brought as much perplexity as sorrow. To migrating families, stretching every dollar to complete the long journey, even the simplest funeral rites might be too expensive. Sometimes under cover of night male survivors would hustle a body into a hastily-dug grave and take to the road again. Knowing full well the illegality of their action, the Joads explained their conduct on a piece of paper that they placed in Grandpa's grave: "This here is William James Joad, dyed of a stroke, old old man. His fokes bured him becaws they got no money to pay for funerls. Nobody kilt him. Jus a stroke an he dyed." [42]

V

The California toward which the migrants were making their painful way was far different from the frontier to which Steinbeck's grandfather had come. The first generation of Americans had often been lawless men, squatting on land that did not belong to them and guarding their stolen property with guns. But they had been real farmers with "stomach-tearing lust" for rich acres and for plows, windmills, and seeds. Their grandchildren were not really farmers at all, in Steinbeck's definition. They were little shop-keepers of crops. "No matter how clever, how loving a man might be with earth and growing things, he could not survive if he were not also a good shopkeeper. And as time went on, the businessmen had the farms, and the farms grew larger, but there were fewer of them." [43]

Farming had become an industry, "and the owners followed Rome, although they did not know it." They began to use Chinese, Japanese, Mexican, and Filipino laborers—paying them so little that they were almost slaves. Meanwhile, the crops were changing. Instead of grain, more and more fruit and vegetables were grown.

[42] *Ibid.*, 194.   [43] *Ibid.*, 316.

Many of these were "stoop crops." "A man may stand to use a scythe, a plow, a pitchfork; but he must crawl like a bug between the rows of lettuce, he must bend his back and pull his long bag between the cotton rows, he must go on his knees like a penitent across a cauliflower patch." [44]

As the giant properties grew, some became so large "that one man could not even conceive of them any more, so large that it took batteries of bookkeepers to keep track of interest and gain and loss; chemists to test the soil, to replenish; straw bosses to see that the stooping men were moving along the rows as swiftly as the material of their bodies could stand." Profits increased when the owner operated a store. Then he could pay the men, and afterwards sell them food and take the money back. Or even simpler, he could sell the food on credit and settle up when the wages were due. "A man might work and feed himself; and when the work was done, he might find that he owed money to the company." [45]

The owners could not depend exclusively on Mexicans and Orientals to meet their need for seasonal laborers. Some of the foreigners became disillusioned with harsh treatment and went home; some became dangerously defiant and were killed or driven out. Increasingly the owners sought to recruit native hands in the Middle West. Through agents they distributed thousands of handbills offering employment in picking oranges and other crops. The advertising found eager readers in the drought-stricken land. "And then the dispossessed were drawn west—from Kansas, Oklahoma, Texas, New Mexico; from Nevada and Arkansas, families, tribes, dusted out, tractored out. Carloads, caravans, homeless and hungry; twenty thousand and fifty thousand and a hundred thousand and two hundred thousand." [46]

Many more laborers were drawn to California than were needed. Steinbeck believed that this was a matter of cynical calculation on the part of the owners. Because of the surplus of workers and their desperate poverty, the employers could cut wages ruthlessly. As a disillusioned migrant explained to Tom Joad: "Know what they was payin', las' job I had? Fifteen cents an hour. Ten hours for a dollar an' a half, an' ya can't stay on the place. Got to

---

[44] *Ibid.*, 316–17.   [45] *Ibid.*, 317.   [46] *Ibid.*, 317.

We ain't foreign. Seven generations back Americans . . .
One of our folks was in the Revolution, an' they was lots of
our folks in the Civil War—both sides. Americans.   John
Steinbeck, *The Grapes of Wrath*

burn gasoline gettin' there. . . . That's why them han'bills was
out. You can print a hell of a lot of han'bills with what ya save payin'
fifteen cents an hour for fiel' work." [47]

Even at these starvation wages the work was short-lived. For
fifty weeks a year nine men might suffice to tend a mammoth peach
orchard. But for two weeks of harvest, the owners would need three
thousand hands. "Got to have 'em or them peaches'll rot. So what
do they do? They send out han' bills all over hell. They need three
thousan', an' they get six thousan'. They get them men for what
they wanta pay. If ya don't wanta take what they pay, goddamn it,
they's a thousan' men waitin' for your job. So ya pick, an' ya pick,
an' then she's done." [48]

[47] *Ibid.*, 334.   [48] *Ibid.*, 335.

And when one such job was done, all the jobs in that part of the country were likely to be done too. Because of the heavy specialization all the crops of a region were likely to ripen at the same time. As soon as the owners had completed the harvest, they forced the migrants to move on. They feared that the jobless strangers might resort to thievery or become involved in drunken brawls. They disliked the ugliness of their shabby camps. Most of all, they abhorred the prospect of higher taxes through additions to the local relief rolls. And so, willing or unwilling, the laborers would have to move on to scramble for whatever jobs might be available in some other section.

In dealing with the migrants the owners could count on the help of the public authorities. When migrants lingered too long, local boards of health would condemn their camps as health hazards. Sheriffs and their deputies would arrest as "reds" or "agitators" laborers who complained too loudly about their treatment. If harsher measures were required, private vigilantes would raid the camps at night, beating up the migrant leaders and burning down their shanties—all in connivance with the law enforcement officers.

By inducing so many hungry families to come to California, the owners had created a monster that they obviously feared. And the fear of the owners was shared by most other Californians. Storekeepers hated the migrants because they had nothing to spend; bankers hated them because they were unable to either save or borrow; laborers hated them as rivals in the job market. Although the strangers came from many other states besides Oklahoma, they were lumped together under the invidious label "Okies." In Steinbeck's description, the Okies were unschooled, poor, and violent; but they were also proud and independent. "We ain't foreign. Seven generations back Americans, and beyond that Irish, Scotch, English, German. One of our folks was in the Revolution, an' they was lots of our folks in the Civil War—both sides. Americans." [49]

The Okies avoided the payment of rent by huddling in shanty settlements that had sprung up on the outskirts of the California towns—each bearing the bitter generic name of Hooverville.

[49] *Ibid.*, 317–18.

"The man put up his own tent as near to water as he could get it; or if he had no tent, he went to the city dump and brought back cartons and built a house of corrugated paper. And when the rains came the house melted and washed away." [50]

Arriving in California after their long trip over the road, the Joads found shelter in one of these ugly villages. "There was no order in the camp; little gray tents, shacks, cars were scattered about at random." The first shanty the Joads saw was of bizarre construction: one wall was made of corrugated iron strips; a second of moldy carpeting; a third of tarred paper; a fourth of gunny sacking. The entrance was cluttered with equipment. "A five-gallon kerosene can served for a stove. It was laid on its side, with a section of rusty stovepipe thrust in one end. A wash boiler rested on its side against the wall; and a collection of boxes lay about, boxes to sit on, to eat on. A Model-T Ford sedan and a two-wheel trailer were parked beside the shack, and about the camp there hung a slovenly despair." [51]

In regions where there was little work, the migrants might be close to starvation. Cooking the Joad family's first California meal over an outdoor fire, Ma Joad found herself under hungry scrutiny. "The children, fifteen of them, stood silently and watched. And when the smell of the cooking stew came to their noses, their noses crinkled slightly. . . . The children were embarrassed to be there, but they did not go." [52] By quizzing them, she discovered that the children had had no breakfast and that their regular evening fare consisted of fried dough—nothing but flour and water. Although the Joads had scarcely enough stew for themselves, they felt a sense of guilt in eating it. They huddled miserably in the tent consuming their portions, while outside the hungry children scraped the pot with little sticks on Ma Joad's invitation. "A mound of children smothered the pot from sight. They did not talk, did not fight or argue; but there was a quiet intentness in all of them, a wooden fierceness. . . . There was the sound of scraping at the kettle, and then the mound of children broke and the children walked away and left the scraped kettle on the ground." [53]

In this Hooverville, the Joads received a painful initiation into

[50] *Ibid.*, 320.   [51] *Ibid.*, 328–29.   [52] *Ibid.*, 344.   [53] *Ibid.*, 352.

the harsh realities of the day. Soon after their arrival, a contractor and a sheriff's deputy made a joint visit to the camp. The contractor sought recruits for jobs in another county; the deputy arrested a migrant who asked too persistently how many men would be employed and how much they would be paid. By tripping up the deputy and kicking him in the neck, the men of the Joad party helped the culprit to escape, but such victories were Pyrrhic. The Joads had to take to the road again, while local vigilantes took their revenge by burning down the shacks.

After this experience, the Joads welcomed the security offered by a government camp—one of a few maintained as New Deal experiments. Behind a high fence they found a clean and orderly compound that contrasted sharply with the ramshackle Hoovervilles. "Tom walked down the street between the rows of tents. . . . He saw that the rows were straight and that there was no litter about the tents. The ground of the street had been swept and sprinkled." [54] A citadel of respectability was the "sanitary

[54] *Ibid.*, 393.

There was no order in the camp; little gray tents, shacks, cars were scattered about at random.   John Steinbeck, *The Grapes of Wrath*

unit"—a building low, rough, and unpainted on the outside, but admirably functional within. "The toilets lined one side of the large room, and each toilet had its compartment with a door in front of it. The porcelain was gleaming white. Hand basins lined another wall, while on the third wall were four shower compartments." [55] Investigating these mysteries, the Joad children ran away in panic, when the water roared through the toilet bowls.

Accustomed to arbitrary treatment from local law enforcement officers, the migrants exulted in the sanctuary provided by the government camps. "You mean to say they ain't no cops?" Tom Joad asked incredulously, and the watchman replied, "No sir. No cop can come in here without a warrant." The campers governed themselves. An elected central committee made the laws and enforced them. "Well, s'pose a fella is jus' mean, or drunk an' quarrelsome. What then?" For the first such offense, the watchman explained, the central committee warned the troublemaker. "And the second time they really warn him. The third time they kick him out of the camp." [56]

So seriously did the central committee take its responsibilities that the official camp manager was left with little to do other than to offer genial welcome to the newcomers. "The people here worked me out of a job," he happily explained. "They keep the camp clean, they keep order, they do everything. I never saw such people. They're making clothes in the meeting hall. And they're making toys. Never saw such people." [57]

In this environment Ma Joad felt a return of the self-respect that she had lost in her first encounter with California officialdom. "These folks is our folks—is our folks. An' that manager, he come an' set an' drank coffee, an' he says, 'Mrs. Joad' this, an' 'Mrs. Joad' that—an' 'How you gettin' on, Mrs. Joad?' . . . Why, I feel like people again." [58] In appropriate response, she took decisive steps to get the family clean. She ordered changes of clothing and washed the dirty overalls and dresses; she commanded that the children be scrubbed until they were red and shiny; she took a much needed shower bath herself.

On Saturday night the campers danced on an outdoor platform

[55] *Ibid.*, 409.   [56] *Ibid.*, 392.   [57] *Ibid.*, 415.   [58] *Ibid.*, 420.

that they had built and lighted with electric fixtures salvaged from the city dump. Men were garbed in freshly-washed overalls and girls in print dresses, stretched and clean, their hair braided and ribboned. They swung around vigorously in country-style dances to the accompaniment of fiddlers, guitars, and harmonicas. "And the girls were damp and flushed, and they danced with open mouths and serious reverent faces, and the boys flung back their long hair and pranced, pointed their toes, and clicked their heels. In and out the squares moved, crossing, backing, whirling, and the music shrilled." [59]

While most of the migrants relaxed, the camp leaders were patrolling the fence to keep out uninvited strangers and watching the dancers closely to remove any troublemakers. Thanks to a tip from a friendly farmer, the leaders knew that deputies were waiting outside, prepared to invade the camp on any plausible pretext. "If they can git a fight goin', then they can run in the cops an' say we ain't orderly. They tried it before—other places." [60]

The central committee's counter measures saved the day, but the situation remained dangerous. Why did the big farmers and their henchmen seek to destroy the federal projects? The guard in a crude camp maintained by one of the big fruit companies suggested one reason. Disgusted by a migrant's inquiry as to whether there was hot water, the guard commented: "It's them gov'ment camps. . . . I bet that fella been in a gov'ment camp. We ain't gonna have no peace till we wipe them camps out. They'll be wantin' clean sheets, first thing we know." [61] More serious perhaps was the issue recognized by one of the Okies: "They're scairt we'll organize, I guess. An' maybe they're right. This here camp is a organization. People there look out for theirselves." [62]

All that government camps could do was to maintain a minimum of decency in living conditions. The migrants still had to find their own jobs, and there was not much demand for labor in the Bakersfield area at the time the Joads were there. In his one short period of employment Tom Joad received sharp instruction in the power structure of California agriculture. The small farmer for whom Tom worked was a good man wanting to treat his workers

[59] *Ibid.*, 467–68.   [60] *Ibid.*, 453.   [61] *Ibid.*, 515–16.   [62] *Ibid.*, 406.

fairly, but he could not hold out against orders from above. Ashamed and humiliated, he explained why he had to cut wages from 30 cents to 25 cents an hour. The Farmers' Association to which he belonged had had a meeting the night before. "Now, do you know who runs the Farmers' Association? I'll tell you. The Bank of the West. That bank owns most of this valley, and it's got paper on everything it don't own. So last night the member from the bank told me, he said, 'You're paying thirty cents an hour. You'd better cut it down to twenty-five.' " The farmer had protested that he had good men who were worth what he was paying them, but the banker cut him off. " 'It isn't that,' he says. 'The wage is twenty-five now. If you pay thirty, it'll only cause unrest. And by the way,' he says, 'you going to need the usual amount for a crop loan next year?' " [63]

Small farmers could not afford the luxury of defying the banks. As victims of progress, they themselves were in a highly precarious position. The problems of Oklahoma were not those of California. In Oklahoma, crops were failing; in California, they were succeeding all too well. "All California quickens with produce, and the fruit grows heavy, and the limbs bend gradually under the fruit so that little crutches must be placed under them to support the weight." To the bounty of nature had been added the ingenuity of man. "Behind the fruitfulness are men of understanding and knowledge and skill, men who experiment with seed, endlessly developing the techniques for great crops of plants whose roots will resist the million enemies of the earth: the molds, the insects, the rusts, the blights." [64] Science had developed better wheat, better apples, better grapes, better walnuts. But the market mechanism did not keep pace with the leap in production. "Men who can graft the trees and make the seed fertile and big can find no way to let the hungry people eat their produce. Men who have created new fruits in the world cannot create a system whereby their fruits may be eaten. And the failure hangs over the State like a great sorrow." [65]

The depression's supreme irony came with the destruction of surplus crops. Oranges for which there was no market were squirted with kerosene; potatoes were dumped in rivers; pigs were

[63] *Ibid.*, 402.   [64] *Ibid.*, 473.   [65] *Ibid.*, 476.

slaughtered and buried. "There is a crime here that goes beyond denunciation. There is a sorrow here that weeping cannot symbolize. There is a failure here that topples all our success." [66]

In this over-productive economy the big producers stood a better chance of survival than the small. "The little farmers watched debt creep up on them like the tide. They sprayed the trees and sold no crop, they pruned and grafted and could not pick the crop." As the small operators went under, the banks and the great owners took over. They could still make a profit because they owned the canneries. "And four pears peeled and cut in half, cooked and canned, still cost fifteen cents. And the canned pears do not spoil. They will last for years." [67]

However pleasant the Joads found the government camp, they could not stay long. They needed money desperately and had to resume their journeying. In the orchards of Tulare County, they found what at first seemed to be a tolerable opportunity. The whole family, even twelve-year-old Ruthie and ten-year-old Winfield, picked and packed peaches at five cents a box. The first night the Joads dined on hamburg, potatoes, bread and coffee. Humble though the menu was, it was better food than they had eaten for many days.

Yet even in this rare moment of full employment, the migrants' life was still grim. The Joads were housed in a company shack— one of "fifty little square, flat-roofed boxes, each with a door and a window, and the whole group in a square." [68] The interior was filthy. "The floor was splashed with grease. In the one room stood a rusty tin stove and nothing more. The tin stove rested on four bricks and its rusty stovepipe went up through the roof. The room smelled of sweat and grease." [69] Unless they wanted to make a long trip to town, the migrants had to buy their provisions at the company store, a large shed of corrugated iron. Here Ma Joad purchased pale hamburg, full of fat and gristle, at five cents a pound more than in town, and other goods at similarly inflated prices.

Worst of all, the Joads discovered that they were being used as strike-breakers. Suspicious of the police motorcade that escorted them into camp and the armed guards patroling the premises, Tom

[66] *Ibid.*, 477.   [67] *Ibid.*, 476.   [68] *Ibid.*, 503.   [69] *Ibid.*, 504.

Joad slipped under the fence and learned the real situation. As the strike leader—the Reverend Jim Casy who had accompanied the Joads from Oklahoma—explained, "We come to work there. They says it's gonna be fi' cents. They was a hell of a lot of us. We got there an' they says they're payin' two an' a half cents. A fella can't even eat on that an' if he got kids—So we says won't take it. So they druv us off. An' all the cops in the worl' come down on us." [70]

The labor trouble erupted into savage violence that night. During an attack upon the pickets, a deputy killed Casy and was himself killed by Tom Joad. Having broken the strike, the owners promptly cut the rate to two and a half cents a box. This time there was no resistance. The migrants scrambled shamelessly for the work. As Uncle John reported, there was "a whole slew a new pickers so goddam hungry they'd pick for a loaf of bread. Go for a peach, an' somebody'd get it first. Gonna get the whole crop picked right off. Fellas runnin' to a new tree. I seen fights—one fella claims it's his tree, 'nother fella wants to pick off'n it. Brang these here folks from as far's El Centro. Hungrier'n hell." [71] The rate was too low to hold any but the most desperate men, yet the owners cynically calculated that the peaches would all be picked before the laborers quit again.

With Tom Joad a fugitive, the rest of the family resumed the search for jobs. The last agricultural task of the season was picking cotton. It was hard work, but it reminded the Joads of home. They found dry living quarters in one half of a converted freight car. "It's nice," Ma Joad said, "It's almost nicer than anything we had 'cept the gov'ment camp." [72]

But in the final pages of Steinbeck's novel, the rains descended, and a flood drove the Joads out of their box car haven. What became of them? They presumably survived, because they—or at least the indomitable Ma Joad—had the toughness to endure. Yet, even greater hardships certainly lay ahead. The great rain was the prelude to winter, and for three months there would be no employment of any kind. Residency rules prevented the granting of local relief. Hungry men crowded the alleys behind stores "to beg for bread, to beg for rotting vegetables, to steal when they could." [73]

---

[70] *Ibid.*, 522.   [71] *Ibid.*, 544.   [72] *Ibid.*, 558.   [73] *Ibid.*, 591.

Women sick with pneumonia gave birth in damp barns, and old people curled up in corners and died. Doctors were too busy to answer the frantic calls of the migrants. "The sheriffs swore in new deputies and ordered new rifles, and the comfortable people in tight houses felt pity at first, and then distaste, and finally hatred for the migrant people." [74]

Would the end be social revolution? Steinbeck did not think it impossible; "in the eyes of the hungry," he said, "there is a growing wrath. In the souls of the people the grapes of wrath are filling and growing heavy, growing heavy for the vintage." [75]

VI

The Grapes of Wrath was a shocker. Even in 1939, after a decade of depression, middle-class Americans were still clinging to the myth of unlimited opportunity. They wanted desperately to believe that honest and industrious people would not suffer—or not for long, that men who really wanted work would ultimately find it, that effort and thrift would provide adequate security, that employers would deal justly with their employees, that local authorities would dispense even-handed justice. Above all, they wanted to believe that small farmers were still God's special favorites, the proud and independent yeomen of venerated tradition. In denying these pieties, Steinbeck brought down upon his head a tempest of angry denial.

Although guardians of morality in many different parts of the country condemned the novel, the local patriots of Oklahoma and California were particularly indignant. Oklahoma Governor Leon C. Phillips refused to read the book, but denied its truth. "He said that he considered that the novel and the movie version of the book presented an exaggerated and untrue picture of Oklahoma's tenant farmer problem as well as an untruthful version of how migrants are received in California." [76] Oklahoma Congressman Lyle Boren denounced the novelist on the floor of the House of Representa-

---

[74] *Ibid.*, 592.   [75] *Ibid.*, 477.

[76] Martin Staples Shockley, "The Reception of The Grapes of Wrath in Oklahoma," E. W. Tedlock, Jr. and C. V. Hunter (eds.) *Steinbeck and His Critics: A Record of Twenty-five Years* (University of New Mexico Press, 1957), 237.

In the souls of the people the grapes of wrath are filling and growing heavy, growing heavy for the vintage.   John Steinbeck, *The Grapes of Wrath*

tives. "Today, I stand before this body as a son of a tenant farmer, labeled by John Steinbeck as an 'Okie.' For myself, for my dad and my mother, whose hair is silvery in the service of building the state of Oklahoma, I say to you, and to every honest, square-minded reader in America, that the painting Steinbeck made in his book is a lie, a black, infernal creation of a twisted, distorted mind." [77]

More serious than these knee-jerk reflexes were occasional challenges to Steinbeck's accuracy. The county agent for Sequoyah County, the scene of the novel's earliest episodes, denied that this was a dust bowl region or that it had many tractors.[78]

California boosters responded to *The Grapes of Wrath* with even greater resentment. Marshal V. Hartranft wrote a rebuttal under the euphoric title *Grapes of Gladness: California's Refreshing and Inspiring Answer to John Steinbeck's "The Grapes of Wrath"*. This told the story of a migrant family, to which California extended a most hospitable welcome including free land and loans of money. In a similarly reassuring narrative *The Truth About John Steinbeck and the Migrants*, George Thomas described how he had disguised himself as a migrant and made a good living. He had averaged four dollars a day in wages and had been invited by the growers to live in their ranch houses the year around. Thomas denounced *The Grapes of Wrath* as "a novel wherein naturalism has gone berserk, where truth has run amuck drunken upon prejudice and exaggeration, where matters economic have been hurled beyond the pale of rational and realistic thinking." [79]

But many witnesses volunteered testimony in support of Steinbeck. "I have been asked quite often if I could dig up some statistics capable of refuting the story of the *Grapes of Wrath*," said Professor O. B. Duncan, head of the sociology department at Oklahoma A & M College. "It cannot be done, for all the available data prove beyond doubt that the general impression given by Steinbeck's book is substantially reliable." [80] In a letter to the editor of the *Oklahoma City Times*, a rural reader ridiculed Congressman Boren and declared that Steinbeck had portrayed his characters "just as they actually are." [81]

---

[77] *Ibid.*, 237.   [78] *Ibid.*, 233.   [79] Lisca, *op. cit.*, 150.
[80] Shockley, *op. cit.*, 232–33.   [81] *Ibid.*, 238.

Before making his motion picture, the producer Darryl Zanuck sent private detectives out to test the novel's accuracy. These investigators reported that conditions among the migrants were even worse than Steinbeck had described. When the movie was released, controversy once again flared up, and *Life* magazine sent Steinbeck out with a photographer to make a new record of conditions among the migrants. The resulting picture story confirmed the essential truthfulness of both the novel and the film.[82]

Students of history may accept Steinbeck's findings of fact without sharing all his implied judgments. We may understand the sufferings of the migrants; we may visualize their pathetic Hoovervilles; we may see their moral disintegration under harsh adversities. At the same time we may suspect that Steinbeck's humaneness and anger sometimes distorted his focus. Perhaps he sentimentalized the Okies and dealt too harshly with the owners. Perhaps he attributed the latters' conduct too much to hardness of heart and not enough to the iron necessities of the depression. But such considerations as this are not too important. Students should be grateful that at a unique moment of history when a great upheaval had occurred, when the uprooted people made their weary way over the roads to California and struggled desperately to establish themselves in new surroundings, a writer abundantly endowed with keen observation and deep compassion was there to record what happened.

[82] Lisca, *op. cit.*, 150.

7

The Rebels

'It's funny, Don,' she was saying. 'I always go to sleep when
you talk about party discipline. I guess it's because I don't
want to hear about it.'

'No use being sentimental about it,' said Don savagely.

'But is it sentimental to be more interested in saving the
miners' unions?' she said, suddenly feeling wide awake
again.

'Of course that's what we all believe, but we have to follow
the party line . . .'

JOHN DOS PASSOS, *The Big Money* [1]

As A GUIDE through the confusing jungle of American
radicalism during the 1920's and 1930's, John Dos Passos possesses
unique qualifications. His own political compass was swinging
widely during those years. In the presidential campaign of 1932, he
voted for William Z. Foster, the Communist; in 1936 and 1940, he
voted for Franklin D. Roosevelt, the Democrat; and in 1944, he
voted for Thomas E. Dewey, the Republican.[2]

Yet this record is not as erratic as it appears. Dos Passos was always a liberty-loving man asserting his own declaration of independence against the prevailing oligarchy, whether represented by
the arrogant business community of the 1920's or the bureaucratic
liberalism of the latter-day New Dealers. In the 1920's he fraternized with Communists, both in Russia and America, but was too
skeptical to become a true believer. In the late 1930's, he staked his

---

[1] John Dos Passos, *The Big Money* (New York: Washington Square Press, 1946),
594.

[2] John H. Wrenn, *John Dos Passos* (New York: Twayne Publishers, 1961), 15–16.

hopes on the New Deal, but became disillusioned with manipulative politics. In the 1940's and 1950's, he retreated into history, finding heroes of more inspiring stature in figures like Tom Paine and Thomas Jefferson. He seems always to have had a compulsion to shock—to shock the conservatives of one decade by praising rebels like Bill Haywood and Joe Hill, to shock the liberals of another day by chipping away at Franklin D. Roosevelt and other idols.

Both the radicalism and the traditionalism may have their roots in Dos Passos's unusual background. At the age of twelve he was attending the Choate School. The respectability of this eastern academy testified to the aristocratic aspirations of the boy's father and mother; the false name—John Roderigo Martin—under which he was enrolled reflected the unhappy fact that these parents were not husband and wife.[3]

The future novelist was the product of an unusual liaison between two talented people. His father, John Randolph Dos Passos, was a self-made man, the son of an immigrant Portuguese shoemaker. Rising to prominence as a corporation lawyer and a writer of books, he had played a leading part in organizing the American Sugar Refining Company and other trusts; he was a supporter of McKinley and the author of *The Anglo-Saxon Century,* an imperialist tract. The novelist's mother was Lucy Addison Sprigg, a woman of refinement, whose father had been an engineer in the Confederate army. Unable to marry because of the lawyer's reluctance to divorce his invalid wife, the two conducted for years a bitter-sweet romance in out-of-the-way hotels and European resort towns. Their son, John Roderigo, was born in 1896, in a Chicago hotel.

The novelist's earliest memory, woven into a Camera's-Eye passage in *The 42nd Parallel* (1930), was of clutching his mother's hand, as they hurried along the streets of a foreign city enduring the insults of pro-Boer sympathizers.[4] "What a horrible childhood," Dos Passos wrote in another clearly autobiographical passage, "a hotel childhood." [5] It was not that he lacked affection. His gay and

---

[3] *Ibid.,* 13.

[4] John Dos Passos, *U. S. A.: The 42nd Parallel* (Boston: Houghton Mifflin Co., 1946), 4.

[5] John Dos Passos, *Chosen Country* (Boston: Houghton Mifflin Co., 1951), 26.

pretty mother lavished love upon him. His father, a mysterious figure who materialized from time to time, was a magnificently virile person spouting passages from Shakespeare, ordering Lucullan feasts, and sporting in the surf. But the boy felt his differentness—"of course Dandy was his father but he had never dared call him that, not even now." [6] A reader of books, the boy took lugubrious pleasure in "The Man Without a Country." "Lord I cried over that story and Ishmael the wanderer in deserts and Cain, that birthmark on the forehead the mark of the accursed like Cain, like all history's bastards . . ." He asked whether it was "the bar sinister or the nearsighted eyes that made him always fumble the ball—what a terrible tennis player, no good at football or even at soccer—or the foreign speech or the lack of a home that made him so awkward, tonguetied, never saying the right word, never managing to do the accepted thing at the accepted time." [7]

It was not until Dos Passos was almost ready for college that his parents were finally able to marry.[8] Despite the unconventionality of their own lives they tried to guide their son into the channels of safe conformity. When he entered Harvard at the age of sixteen, they admonished him to "be a good boy . . . get A's in some courses but don't be a grind be interested in literature but remain a gentleman don't be seen with Jews and Socialists." It was, Dos Passos felt, "four years under the ethercone." [9]

Yet the moment for independence was fast approaching. In April, 1916, Dos Passos's mother died, and the following June he graduated from college. When his father opposed his wish to join a foreign ambulance corps, he made a trip to Spain to study architecture. In 1917, he came of age in the fullest sense. One week after his twenty-first birthday his father died, and he returned to America to volunteer for ambulance service on the European battlefields.

For the next five years he rolled through the world tasting one adventure after another—ambulance duty in France and Italy, army training in Pennsylvania, medical corps service in France, writing in Spain and Portugal, field service with the Near East

---

[6] *Ibid.*, 29.   [7] *Ibid.*, 26.

[8] John Dos Passos, *The Best Times: An Informal Memoir* (New York: The New American Library, 1966), 16.

[9] *The 42nd Parallel*, 352.

Relief. His earliest books, published in 1921 and 1922, reflect the experiences of a rootless intellectual disgusted with the futility and stupidity of war and its aftermath.

From 1922 to 1925, Dos Passos lived mostly in New York's Greenwich Village gathering impressions of the city that he wove into the hard and brilliant novel *Manhattan Transfer* (1925). But he still felt the pull of faraway places. In the late 1920's, he was on the move again, traveling in Mexico, western Europe, Russia, and America.

Unlike his great contemporaries, Hemingway, Fitzgerald, and Faulkner, Dos Passos became deeply involved in left-wing politics. Rebelling against the warnings of his parents, he found excitement in the radical demonstrations of the day. He could remember a meeting in Madison Square Garden—probably in 1917—when from his seat in the gallery he could see only tiny black figures on the speaker's stand "and a man was speaking and whenever he said war there were hisses and whenever he said Russia there was clapping on account of the revolution I didn't know who was speaking somebody said Max Eastman and somebody said another guy but we clapped and yelled for the revolution and hissed for Morgan and the capitalist war . . ." [10]

From 1926 to 1934, Dos Passos often displayed his left-wing sympathies. In 1926, he helped launch *The New Masses*. He was a member of the executive board and contributed frequent editorials and articles. Although many non-Communists were included among the contributing editors, the new journal closely followed the Moscow line. In 1927, Dos Passos took a prominent part in the campaign to save Sacco and Vanzetti from the electric chair, searching for new evidence, picketing the State House, and writing articles and pamphlets. He was arrested and briefly jailed for his activities. In 1931, he became chairman of the National Committee to Aid Striking Miners Fighting Starvation. Together with Theodore Dreiser and other writers he went into Harlan County, Kentucky, to report on the bitter strife in the coal fields. Later a Kentucky grand jury indicted him and others on charges of violating the state's criminal syndicalism law, but the authorities made no

[10] *Ibid.*, 405. *Cf. The Best Times*, 46.

attempt to bring him back for trial. In 1932, he acted as treasurer of a committee collecting funds for the defense of the Scottsboro boys. And later that year he cast his defiant vote for the Communist presidential ticket.

Yet Dos Passos was neither faithful Communist nor Communist dupe. In his passionate advocacy of striking workers and victims of judicial oppression he often allied himself with the Marxists; but from the beginning he retained a healthy skepticism toward his radical friends. Malcolm Cowley recalls a night in a Greenwich Village restaurant when Dos Passos called out from a table where *The New Masses* was being planned: "Intellectual workers of the world unite, you have nothing to lose but your brains." [11] In his first editorial for the magazine, he warned against dogmatism from either right or left: "Particularly I don't think there should be any more phrases, badges, opinions, banners imported from Russia or anywhere else. . . . Why not develop our own brand?" [12]

When he visited the Soviet Union in 1928, he kept his eyes open. "I liked and admired the Russian people. I had enjoyed their enormous and varied country, but when next morning I crossed the Polish border—Poland was not Communist then—it was like being let out of jail." [13] Asked in 1932 whether it might deepen an author's work to become a Communist, he replied: "I don't see how a novelist or historian could be a party member under present conditions." [14]

Ashamed in earlier years of his middle-class origins, Dos Passos began to accept more willingly the role of bourgeois intellectual. After 1930, he wrote very little for *The New Masses,* contributing instead to *The New Republic* and *Common Sense,* an independent liberal journal that he helped found in 1932. He finally declared independence from his old allies in an "Open Letter to the Communist Party," signed by himself and twenty-four other liberals and published in *The New Masses* in March, 1934.[15]

In writing his novels Dos Passos borrowed heavily from his per-

[11] Maxwell Cowley, *Exile's Return: A Literary Odyssey of the 1920's* (New York: Viking Press, 1951), 223.
[12] *The New Masses,* I (June, 1926), 20.
[13] *The Best Times,* 196.   [14] Wrenn, *op. cit.,* 66.
[15] *The New Masses,* X (March 6, 1934), 8. Other prominent signers were Edmund Wilson, Clifton Fadiman, Lionel Trilling, and Robert Morss Lovett.

sonal experience. Despite the multiplicity of characters there were usually one or two in each novel whose background and point of view are much like Dos Passos's own. In *Manhattan Transfer,* the Dos Passos-like character is Jimmy Herf; in *1919* it is Dick Savage; in *Adventures of a Young Man* it is Glenn Spotswood. More important from the standpoint of social history is the way in which Dos Passos weaves into the novels descriptions of important·episodes that had fallen within the field of his own observation. This is certainly true of his treatment of radical activities in New York, the Sacco-Vanzetti demonstrations in Boston, and the bitter labor struggle in the coal fields. When he deals with the rebels of the 1920's and 1930's, Dos Passos uses the binocular vision of one who has been at the same time both insider and outsider.

II

Dos Passos well understood the process by which the American radical was produced. Ben Compton, the future Communist, made his first appearance in *The 42nd Parallel* as a gangling high school youth with heavy glasses, "who ate with his head hung over his plate and had a rude way of contradicting anything anybody said." Explaining this behavior, Ben's older sister told a friend not to mind the boy; "he was very good in his studies and was going to study law." [16]

The Comptons lived in frugal respectability in the Flatbush section of Brooklyn. Ben's father, a little old man with glasses on the end of his nose, worked as a watchmaker in a Fifth Avenue jewelry store. Ben's mother was "a fat pear shaped woman in a wig." They talked Yiddish among themselves. "In the old country their name had been Kompschchski but they said that in New York nobody could pronounce it. The old man had wanted to take the name Freedman, but his wife thought Compton sounded more refined." [17]

The Comptons had experienced the insecurities of urban life. When Ben was thirteen, his father had had to give up work for a year because of a long illness. The family lost a house that was al-

---

[16] *The 42nd Parallel,* 387.   [17] *Ibid.*

most paid for and had to move into a flat. Ben, the youngest child, worked evenings in a drug store; Sam took a job with a furrier in Newark; Izzy loafed around pool rooms and tried a little prize-fighting; Gladys helped support the family by doing stenography in a Manhattan office.[18]

Pathetically convinced that Ben's thick glasses guaranteed his success as a scholar, the old folks took great pride in his modest high school honors. He made the debating team and wrote a prize essay on "The American Government." The boy's ambitions were at first conventionally American. "Benny looked much older than he was and hardly ever thought of anything except making money so the old people could have a house of their own again. When he grew up he'd be a lawyer and businessman and make a pile quick so that Gladys could quit work and get married and the old people could buy a big house and live in the country." [19]

Ben's conversion from juvenile Babbitt to callow Marxist occurred the summer after he graduated from high school. Needing money for college, he located a road construction job in Pennsylvania, where he earned $10 a week driving a team and keeping books. He soon discovered that his boss, Hiram Volle, was a crook who cheated the workers in their accounts. Yet Ben felt little sympathy for the exploited "wops" until he struck up a friendship with a young worker named Nick Gigli.

Nick was from North Italy and all the men in the gang were Sicilian, so he was lonely. His father and elder brothers were anarchists and he was too; he told Benny about Bakunin and Malatesta and said Benny ought to be ashamed of himself for wanting to get to be a rich businessman; sure he ought to study and learn, maybe he ought to get to be a lawyer, but he ought to work for the revolution and the workingclass; to be a businessman was to be a shark and a robber like that sonofabitch Volle.[20]

Ben's first timid defiance of the capitalist system occurred on the morning when the Italian workers declared a sudden strike. Refusing to do what the boss ordered, Ben announced that he too was on strike. "Volle burst out laughing and told him to quit his

---

[18] John Dos Passos, *U. S. A.: Nineteen Nineteen* (Boston: Houghton Mifflin Co., 1946), 489.

[19] *Ibid.*, 491.   [20] *Ibid.*, 493.

kidding, funniest thing he'd ever heard of a kike walking out with a lot of wops. Ben felt himself go cold and stiff all over. 'I'm not a kike any more'n you are . . . I'm an American born . . . and I'm goin' to stick with my class, you dirty crook.' " [21]

But class solidarity collapsed at the first show of force. When Volle and his gang bosses brandished revolvers and threatened to fire anyone who didn't return to work when the whistle blew, all the other laborers submitted, leaving Ben and Nick to hit the road in search of new jobs.

After two weeks of dishwashing in a Greek restaurant in Scranton, Ben took the train back to the family hearth in Brooklyn. That fall, he entered the College of the City of New York. His father borrowed $100 from the Morris Plan to get him started, and Sam sent him $25 from Newark for books. He himself worked evenings in the drug store. But these bourgeois sacrifices were no longer dedicated to bourgeois goals. "Sunday afternoons he went to the library and read Marx's *Capital*. He joined the Socialist Party and went to lectures at the Rand School whenever he got a chance. He was working to be a wellsharpened instrument." [22]

Ben's college career was brief. Scarlet fever put him in the hospital for ten weeks and left his eyes in such bad shape that it gave him a headache to read. At a Cooper Union lecture he met Helen Mauer, a pale blond girl five years older than himself. She was a veteran of the labor wars who had been arrested and blacklisted, for her activities in the bitter Paterson textile strike. "She said there was nothing in the Socialist movement; it was the syndicalists had the right idea. After the lecture she took him to the Cosmpolitan Café on Second Avenue to have a glass of tea and introduced him to some people she said were real rebels." [23]

Ben's growing radicalism brought on a family storm. His father lectured on the obligations of sons towards their parents; Ben retorted that his first loyalty was to the working class. "The old man got to his feet, choking and coughing; he raised his hands above his head and cursed Ben and Ben left the house." [24]

The prodigal found convenient shelter with Helen, but was

---

[21] *Ibid.*, 494.   [22] *Ibid.*, 498.   [23] *Ibid.*, 499–500.   [24] *Ibid.*, 500.

careful not to get her pregnant because this would hamper their revolutionary activities. "There were bedbugs in the bed, but they told each other that they were as happy as they could be under the capitalist system, that some day they'd have a free society where workers wouldn't have to huddle in filthy lodging houses full of bedbugs or row with landladies and lovers could have babies if they wanted to." [25]

When Helen lost her job at Wanamaker's, the couple moved across the river to Passaic, New Jersey, where Ben took a job in a worsted mill. The employees soon went out on strike, and Ben and Helen were both on the committee. "Ben got to be quite a speechmaker. He was arrested several times and almost had his skull cracked by a policeman's billy and got six months in jail out of it. But he'd found out that when he got up on a soapbox to talk, he could make people listen to him, that he could talk and say what he thought and get a laugh or a cheer out of the massed upturned faces." [26]

After completing his jail sentence, Ben and Bram Hicks, another young radical, worked their way across the continent, arriving on the Pacific Coast just when strife between the Industrial Workers of the World and their vigilante foes was reaching a bloody climax. When Ben and Bram went with other "wobblies" on an organizing expedition to Everett, Washington, they were met on the docks by a drunken sheriff and an army of drunken deputies. Taken out into the woods, the unionists were forced to run the gantlet and cruelly beaten. "Ben was in the hospital three weeks. The kicks in the back had affected his kidneys and he was in frightful pain most of the time." [27] Thanks to $50 sent out by his faithful sister Gladys and a job on a freighter, Ben managed to get back home. "The sea trip and the detailed clerical work helped him to pull himself together. Still there wasn't a night he didn't wake up with a nightmare scream in his throat sitting up in his bunk dreaming the deputies were coming to get him to make him run the gantlet." [28]

Ben's parents took him in again and were delighted when he

---

[25] *Ibid.*, 501.   [26] *Ibid.*, 502.   [27] *Ibid.*, 508.   [28] *Ibid.*, 509.

was offered a chance to study law in the office of a radical lawyer named Morris Stein. In the evenings Ben addressed protest meetings about the Everett massacres.

His heart would always be thumping when he went into the hall where the meeting was and began to hear the babble and rustle of the audience filing in, garment workers on the East Side, waterfront workers in Brooklyn, workers in chemical and metalproducts plants in Newark, parlor socialists and pinks at the Rand School or on lower Fifth Avenue, the vast anonymous mass of all classes, races, trades in Madison Square Garden.

His stage fright would continue until he began to speak.

Then all at once he'd hear his own voice enunciating clearly and firmly, feel its reverberance along the walls and ceiling, feel ears growing tense, men and women leaning forward in their chairs, see the rows of faces quite clearly, the groups of people who couldn't find seats crowding the doors. Phrases like *protest, mass action, united workingclass of this country and the world, revolution,* would light up the faces under him like the glare of a bonfire.[29]

During these months Ben was a protégé of Morris Stein's sister Fanya, a wealthy woman of thirty-five who gave money to radical and pacifist causes. But the soft liberalism of the Steins could not withstand the fiercely patriotic wind that blew across the country after the declaration of war in 1917. Declaring that there was nothing to do but bow before the storm, Morris Stein quarreled with Ben who was determined to oppose the war at all cost.

Confronted by the war hysteria, Ben alternated between acts of bravado and moments of caution. On Stein's advice he had registered for the draft, but he had written "conscientious objector" on the card. He went back to Passaic to live with Helen Mauer, but the two found their familiar world collapsing around them.

The Rand School had been closed up, *The Call* suspended, every day new friends were going around to Wilson's way of looking at things. Helen's folks and their friends were making good money, working overtime; they laughed or got sore at any talk of protest strikes or revolutionary movements; people were buying washingmachines, Liberty

[29] *Ibid.,* 510–11.

Bonds, vacuum cleaners, making first payments on houses. The girls were buying fur coats and silk stockings.[30]

Ben took a factory job, but lost it after he refused to buy a Liberty Bond. Frightened by the growing pressures, he took Helen to a room in New York where they hid out under assumed names. He considered running away to Mexico, but news of the Bolshevik seizure of power in Russia shamed him into new revolutionary efforts. He and Helen raised funds from prosperous friends who didn't want their names used and organized a pro-Bolshevik meeting in the Bronx.

Defying the police cordon that surrounded the hall, the uniformed soldiers and sailors who packed the gallery, and two federal agents and a stenographer who sat in the front row taking down everything that was said, Ben launched into a typical Marxist harangue: "The capitalist governments are digging their own graves by driving their people to slaughter in a crazy unnecessary war that nobody can benefit from except bankers and munitions makers. . . . The American workingclass, like the workingclass of the rest of the world, will learn their lesson. The profiteers are giving us instruction in the use of guns; the day will come when we will use it." [31]

The police broke up the meeting and arrested Ben and a couple of other leaders. For three days they kept him in a vacant office in the Federal Building without anything to eat or drink. Relays of detectives badgered him with questions; they threatened to beat him with a rubber hose, but finally brought him some water and stale ham sandwiches instead. He was at last permitted to talk to a lawyer, his one-time patron Morris Stein. Stein and the prosecutor agreed on a deal: Ben should report for military duty and the government would quash all charges. But Ben refused to go along.

Ben's day in court was strangely anticlimactic. There was an almost genial atmosphere in which judge, prosecutor, and defense attorney all exchanged little jokes. Ben finally came to life when he addressed the court before his sentencing.

He made a speech about the revolutionary movement he'd been preparing all these weeks. Even as he said it, it seemed silly and weak. He

[30] *Ibid.*, 513.   [31] *Ibid.*, 516.

almost stopped in the middle. His voice strengthened and filled the courtroom as he got to the end. Even the judge and the old snuffling attendants sat up when he recited for his peroration, the last words of the Communist Manifesto: "In place of the old bourgeois society, with its classes and class antagonisms, we shall have an association, in which the free development of each is the condition for the free development of all." [32]

The judge sentenced Ben to twenty years' imprisonment, but Stein appealed the case. Free on bail again, Ben found himself the pampered ward of the Steins. He moved into a studio apartment with the love-stricken Fanya Stein, who nursed him through influenza and double pneumonia and clothed him in a new suit of English tweed. In the end, the circuit court denied the appeal, but reduced the sentence to ten years.

On the day that Ben finally surrendered to the federal authorities, New York was celebrating one of its many postwar holidays. The armistice had been signed; the Peace Conference had been held; returning American troops were parading through the cheering crowds along lower Broadway. "Everybody looked flushed and happy. It was hard to keep from walking in step to the music in the fresh summer morning that smelt of the harbor and ships. He had to keep telling himself: those are the people who sent Debs to jail, those are the people who shot Joe Hill, who murdered Frank Little, those are the people who beat us up in Everett, who want me to rot for ten years in jail." [33]

Accompanied by Stein still chirping about the possibilities of a presidential pardon, Ben turned himself in at the Federal Building. "It was a relief to have it all over, alone with the deputy on the train for Atlanta . . . Ben remembered it was his birthday; he was twenty-three years old." [34]

Dos Passos concludes Ben Compton's story in *The Big Money*. When he was released from federal prison, Ben was prematurely old. His face was white as a mushroom with brown bags under the eyes; he paced up and down with a strange dragging walk. His nerves were so frayed that he hated to sleep alone. Fortunately, he

---

[32] *Ibid.*, 518.　　　[33] *Ibid.*, 520.　　　[34] *Ibid.*, 523.

found a sympathetic bedmate in Mary French, a middle-class career girl with a passion for social protest movements. But as his strength returned, Ben spent less and less time with Mary and more and more in proletarian causes. "Once they decided they'd get married and have a baby, but the comrades were calling for Ben to come and organize the towns around Passaic and he said it would distract him from his work and that they were young and that there'd be plenty of time for that sort of thing after the revolution." [35]

Too fanatical to compromise, Ben went through periods of black despair when his organizing activities failed. After AFL officials from Washington "in expensive overcoats and silk mufflers" had taken a strike out of his hands and settled it, he sat for hours on the edge of Mary's bed, "telling her in a sharp monotonous voice about the sellout and the wrangles between the left-wingers and the oldline Socialists and labor leaders, and how now that it was all over here was his trial for contempt of court coming up." [36]

For the cause of social revolution, Ben Compton had given up his chance for a professional career, sacrificed the comforts of family life, been beaten almost to death, and spent years in prison. Yet in the end, the Communists rejected him. His stubborn outspokenness and refusal to trim antagonized the party yesmen. As he explained to Mary: "I've been expelled from the party . . . oppositionist . . . exceptionalism . . . a lot of nonsense. . . . Well, that doesn't matter, I'm still a revolutionist . . . I'll continue to work outside of the party." [37]

But it did matter. Expulsion from the party meant ostracism from the only world that he really knew. "I feel so lonely suddenly . . . you know, cut off from everything." [38] In a moment of exasperation Mary called him "a stoolpigeon" and "a disrupter"— two of the most cruel epithets in the radical vocabulary. "Ben Compton's face broke in pieces suddenly the way a child's face does when it is just going to bawl. He sat there staring at her, senselessly scraping the spoon round and round in the empty coffeemug." [39]

---

[35] *The Big Money*, 503–4.   [36] *Ibid.*, 506.   [37] *Ibid.*, 598.
[38] *Ibid.*, 599.   [39] *Ibid.*, 600.

III

One of Ben Compton's rivals, in the Communist Party, was Don Stevens, a radical given to big talk and sponging on his friends, particularly when they were women.

In 1917, Don was "a haggardlooking brighteyed young man" pushing his way into New York's left wing circles. He had been brought up in South Dakota where he had been a reporter on small town newspapers since his high school days. He had worked as a harvest hand and proudly displayed a red membership card in the IWW. He had come to New York to work on the Socialist *Call*, but had quit "because they were too damn lilylivered." [40]

Don's compulsion to talk extended even to the field of seduction. When Eveline Hutchins objected to his lovemaking on the ground that she'd known him only seven hours, he said

that was another stupid bourgeois idea she ought to get rid of. When she asked him about birthcontrol, he sat down beside her and talked for half an hour about what a great woman Margaret Sanger was and how birthcontrol was the greatest single blessing to mankind since the invention of fire. When he started to make love to her again in a businesslike way, she, laughing and blushing, let him take off her clothes. [41]

Don spoke at pacifist meetings and condemned the bankers' conspiracy that was threatening American neutrality. But after the declaration of war, he avoided the defiant course that had cost Ben Compton his freedom. He signed up with the Friends' Relief and spent the next few months in non-combatant duty in Europe.

Don's gray Quaker uniform by no means silenced him. When Eveline Hutchins, now with the Red Cross, met him in Paris, he was in a tremendous state of excitement about Bolshevik success in Russia and full of mysterious references to underground activities of his own. "Eveline, we're on the edge of gigantic events. . . . The workingclasses of the world won't stand for this nonsense any longer . . . damn it, the war will have been almost worth while if we get a new Socialist civilization out of it." [42]

Back in Paris again, in the spring of 1918, Don Stevens was in

[40] *Nineteen Nineteen*, 151.   [41] *Ibid.*, 153.   [42] *Ibid.*, 257–58.

civilian clothes. He had resigned from the Friends' Relief and was broke. He scoffed at Eveline's reluctance to take him in, teasing her "about her bourgeois ideas, said those sorts of things wouldn't matter after the revolution, that the first test of strength was coming on the first of May." [43] He was trying to practice free lance journalism, but was having a hard time getting stories because of the censorship and the failure of the French workers to carry through their predicted general strike.

After the Armistice, Don was still the same disagreeable person. As a result of his reporting for the radical press, he was arrested in Germany by the Army of Occupation. Eveline Hutchins pulled wires to get him released, but he preferred to give the credit to his own clever manipulations. At a party in Paris he drank too much and "kept making ugly audible remarks about parasites and the lahdedah boys of the bourgeoisie." He almost got into a fight with an army officer whom he called a "goddam fairy." [44]

Contentious and dogmatic, Don Stevens was well suited to play the role of Communist Party functionary. Drawn to Boston, in 1927, by the impending execution of Sacco and Vanzetti, he sought the largest possible advantage for the revolutionary cause even if it meant sacrificing the condemned men. When it was suggested that further demonstrations might weaken the chance of getting a commuted sentence, he opposed moderation. "He argued with trade-union officials, socialists, ministers, lawyers, with an aloof sarcastic coolness. 'After all, they are brave men. It doesn't matter whether they are saved or not any more, it's the power of the workingclass that's got to be saved,' he'd say." [45] Don expended his energies on a futile effort to organize a general strike of all the Boston workers. He excused his failure by blaming those who were trying to save the condemned men by other means. "We're not a couple of goddamned liberals," he told Mary French who was helping him. "Don't you hate lawyers?" [46]

The two Italians died in the electric chair, but Don Stevens had his moment of revolutionary glory. He marched in the front rank of the protest parade, was clubbed by the police, and carried off bleeding to jail.

[43] *Ibid.*, 366.   [44] *Ibid.*, 537.   [45] *The Big Money*, 515.   [46] *Ibid.*, 516.

" 'Comrades, let's sing,' Don's voice shouted.

"Mary forgot everything as her voice joined his voice, all their voices, the voices of the crowds being driven back across the bridge in singing:

"Arise, ye prisoners of starvation . . ." [47]

Stevens showed the same devotion to party advantage in dealing with a strike of the Pennsylvania coal miners. In contrast to Mary French, who wore herself out in efforts to solicit food and clothing for the starving families of the strikers, Don was principally interested in using the strike to extend control over the local unions. His chatter about "centralcommittee, expulsions, oppositionists, splitters" [48] rasped upon Mary's tired ears.

[47] *Ibid.,* 518.   [48] *Ibid.,* 594.

Hurrying along the stonepaved streets, she'd be whispering to herself, "They've got t
be saved, they've got to be saved."   John Dos Passos, *The Big Money*

In a behind-the-scenes struggle for power, Don Stevens had obviously chosen the winning side. Ben Compton told Mary French, "Stevens and me have never been friends, you know that. . . . Now he's in with the comintern crowd. He'll make the central committee when they've cleaned out all the brains." [49] Like a bishop honored by a summons to Rome, Don Stevens made a secret trip to Moscow and returned in obvious favor with the Kremlin. Appropriate to his more exalted status in the party was the new wife that he brought back with him after a marriage in Moscow. As a kind friend explained to Mary French: "She's an English comrade . . . she spoke at the big meeting at the Bronx Casino last night . . . she's got a great shock of red hair . . . stunning, but some of the girls think it's dyed. Lots of the comrades didn't know you and Comrade Stevens had broken up . . . isn't it sad things like that have to happen in the movement?" [50]

IV

Mary French, who shared her bed for a time with Ben Compton and then with Don Stevens, was not the strumpet that this conduct might suggest. She was a tender-hearted female of a type that Dos Passos must have often encountered in fraternizing with American rebels.

Mary's earliest memories were of quarreling parents. Her father practiced medicine, first in Denver, then in the mining town of Trinidad, and finally in Colorado Springs. Heedless in money matters, he exhausted his energies in caring for his poorer patients and neglected the richer ones who paid their bills. Mary's mother was a neurotic woman, who bullied her improvident husband and finally divorced him.

A sandy-haired, freckled child, wearing glasses and braces on her teeth, Mary escaped from unpleasant reality into the world of books. As an eighth grader, she won prizes in French, American history, and English. She continued to do well in high school and went east to college. "At Vassar, the girls she knew were better dressed than she was and had uppity finishingschool manners, but for the first time in her life, she was popular. The instructors liked her be-

[49] *Ibid.*, 599.   [50] *Ibid.*, 608.

cause she was neat and serious and downright about everything and the girls said she was as homely as a mud fence but a darling." [51]

But this happy interlude was soon over. During her second year in college, when she roomed with an over-dressed and talkative Jewish friend, Mary lost much of her popularity. She majored in sociology and dreamed of the good deeds she would do as a social worker. A summer job at Hull House, in Chicago, strengthened her commitment. In a Pullman berth one night she thought of

the work there was to be done to make the country what it ought to be, the social conditions, the slums, the shanties with filthy tottering back-houses, the miners' children in grimy coats too big for them, the over-worked women stooping over stoves, the youngsters struggling for an education in nightschools, hunger and unemployment and drink, and the police and the lawyers and the judges always ready to take it out on the weak; if the people in the Pullman cars could only be made to understand how it was; if she sacrificed her life, like Daddy taking care of his patients night and day, maybe she, like Miss Addams . . .[52]

When Mary was a junior, the excitement of the war made it hard for her to concentrate on her studies. After her mother's serious illness and her father's sudden death, she decided to quit college and work at Hull House. But institutional good deeds did not satisfy her and she gave up her job. After two unhappy weeks working as a countergirl in a Cleveland cafeteria, she traveled to Pittsburgh to try to get a clerical job in the steel mills. The employment offices looked upon former social workers with suspicion, but she finally found a position as a reporter on the *Times-Sentinel.*

Mary's career in journalism ended a few months later, after she handed in a special story on labor organizing activities. She had been given her assignment by Ted Healy, the managing editor, who had told her to conceal the fact that she was a reporter and to investigate union headquarters under the pretense of being a social worker trying to get both sides of the story on the impending strike. Healy was explicit in his instructions: "Well, I want to get the lowdown on the people working there . . . what part of Russia they were born in, how they got into this country in the first place . . . where the money comes from . . . prisonrecords, you know.

[51] *Ibid.*, 120.   [52] *Ibid.*, 125.

. . . Get all the dope you can. It'll make a magnificent Sunday feature." [53]

But Mary was too innocent to keep her newspaper connection concealed. Instead she confided in a husky young Polish unionist, who conducted her on a tour of the steel workers' squalid living quarters. At night she could see again

the shapeless broken shoes and the worn hands folded over dirty aprons and the sharp anxious beadiness of women's eyes, feeling the quake underfoot of the crazy stairways zigzagging up and down the hills black and bare as slagpiles where the steelworkers lived in jumbled shanties and big black rows of smokegnawed clapboarded houses, in her nose the stench of cranky backhouses and kitchens with cabbage cooking and clothes boiling and unwashed children and drying diapers.[54]

After this experience Mary's special story was hardly what her editor wanted. " 'Well, young lady,' he said, without looking up, 'you've written a firstrate propaganda piece for the *Nation* or some other parlorpink sheet in New York, but what the devil do you think we can do with it? This is Pittsburgh.' " [55]

Sacked by the newspaper, she took a job doing publicity for the union. During the great steel strike she worked harder than she had ever worked before and was paid only enough to cover her barest expenses. She wrote releases, got up statistics on health conditions, and visited the various mill towns. She saw "meetings broken up and the troopers in their darkgray uniforms moving in a line down the unpaved alleys of company patches, beating up men and women with their clubs, kicking children out of their way, chasing old men off their front stoops." [56]

After the steel strike failed, Mary had an opportunity to go to Washington as secretary for George Barrows, a windy liberal who made a good living as a lecturer and lobbyist. Barrows soon rounded out Mary's education. "He talked and talked about love and the importance of a healthy sexlife for men and women, so that at last she let him. He was so tender and gentle that for a while she thought maybe she really loved him. He knew all about contraceptives and was very nice and humorous about them. Sleeping

---

[53] *Ibid.*, 143–44.   [54] *Ibid.*, 147.   [55] *Ibid.*, 148.   [56] *Ibid.*, 150.

with a man didn't make as much difference in her life as she'd expected it would." [57] Evidently George was less expert in the practice of birth control than in its theory, because a few months later Mary had to pay for an abortion with money borrowed from her college roommate.

Mary found more congenial employment in New York, doing research for the International Ladies' Garment Workers. "She liked the long hours digging out statistics, the talk with the organizers, the wisecracking radicals, the workingmen and girls who came into the crowded dingy office she shared with two or three other researchworkers. At last she felt what she was doing was real." [58]

Mary's life became increasingly hectic after she took in Ben Compton. In addition to her regular job she did publicity for the strikes that he was organizing in the New Jersey mill towns. She solicited contributions from wealthy women; she induced prominent liberals to get themselves arrested on the picket lines; she coaxed articles out of newspapermen; she hunted up charitable people to put up bail.

The strikers, the men and women and children on picketlines, in soup-kitchens, being interviewed in the dreary front parlors of their homes stripped of furniture they hadn't been able to make the last payment on, the buses full of scabs, the cops and deputies with sawedoff shotguns guarding the tall palings of the silent enormously extended oblongs of the blackwindowed millbuildings, passed in a sort of dreamy haze before her, like a show on the stage, in the middle of the continuous typing and multigraphing, the writing of letters and workingup of petitions, the long grind of officework that took up her days and nights.[59]

After another abortion and a quarrel with Ben, Mary gave up her job and went to Boston to work for the committee of liberals trying to save Sacco and Vanzetti. Like Dos Passos himself, she struggled desperately.

She wrote articles, she talked to politicians and ministers and argued with editors, she made speeches in unionhalls. She wrote her mother pitiful humiliating letters to get money out of her on all sorts of pretexts. Every cent she could scrape up went into the work of her committee. There were always stationery and stamps and telegrams and phonecalls

---

[57] *Ibid.,* 159.   [58] *Ibid.,* 495.   [59] *Ibid.,* 504.

to pay for. She spent long evenings trying to coax communists, socialists, anarchists, liberals into working together. Hurrying along the stone-paved streets, she'd be whispering to herself, "They've got to be saved, they've got to be saved." [60]

But they could not be saved, and all that Mary French had to show for her months of labor was a new bedmate, the Communist Don Stevens, and a growing dependence on gin. Back in New York she threw all her strength into a campaign to send food and cloth-ing to the families of striking coal miners in Pennsylvania. Despite her indifference to Communist discipline, she was regarded as a kind of saint by humble rank-and-filers. As one of them said, "You feed Miss Mary up good, Comrade Stevens. We don't want her gettin' sick. . . . If all the real partymembers worked like she does, we'd have . . . hell, we'd have the finest kind of a revolution by the spring of the year." [61]

Good-hearted but muddle-headed girls like Mary French were casualties of the radical movement of the twenties. Mary emanci-pated herself from conventional sexual morality, only to squander her pathetically small capital of femininity on three selfish men— the labor faker George Barrows, the joyless zealot Ben Compton, and the self-seeking Don Stevens. When Dos Passos breaks off her story in *The Big Money,* she has been deserted by Stevens; she has been estranged still further from her rich and silly mother; she holds onto her wealthy friends only for what she can wheedle out of them for her causes; her most loyal friend in the radical movement has been killed. She is still young, but she is lost.

V

Dos Passos's treatment of the Communist Party, wry and satiri-cal in *The Big Money* (1936), becomes bitter and tragic in *Adven-tures of a Young Man* (1939). Mary French's flirtation with the left involves her with abortions and alcohol. Glenn Spotswood's dedi-cation dooms him to ostracism and death.

Glenn's rebellion sprang not from proletarian class origins but from middle-class humanitarianism. Glenn's father was an intel-

[60] *Ibid.,* 509.   [61] *Ibid.,* 597.

They must be made to see the significance of this strike . . . as part of the daily strug
gle of the world proletariat against the encroachments of the exploiting classes
John Dos Passos, *Adventures of a Young Man*

lectual who had lost his teaching post at Columbia because of pacifist activities during World War I, yet lacked any really heroic
quality. A sententious weakling, he gave little support, either
financial or moral, to his son after his wife's death.

Forced to fend for himself, Glenn started to work his way
through a small midwestern college, then transferred to Columbia
as the protégé of a young sociology instructor named Mike Gulick
and his wife Marice, a shallow dilettante, who chattered to him
about the wonders of psychoanalysis. Too naive to see Marice's real
interest in him, he confided his problem to a new friend Boris
Spingarn. If any woman talked this way to him, Boris advised, "he'd
lay her good and proper." When Glenn protested that she was the
wife of his best friend, Boris was impatient. He said that Glenn
ought to think of himself as a member of the revolutionary working

class and "stop associating with bourgeois liberals whose ideas were the main support of decaying capitalism. All this talk about sex was bourgeois liberalism and made him sick. What a workingman needed was plenty of bed exercise and to shut up about it, and revolutionary marxists ought to live like workingmen." [62]

Glenn was given a speedy indoctrination in revolutionary Marxism when he left the Gulicks and went to live with Boris and his wife Gladys. Gladys was an effervescent young hellion who wore tight skirts, slid down bannisters, sketched pictures, and allowed dust to accumulate in the attic apartment. The food was bad, the tea was worse, but the talk was intoxicating.

After they had eaten Gladys lay at full length on the couch smoking a Russian cigarette, with her head in Boris's lap, and the three of them argued for hours about whether the time had come for a revolutionary movement in America yet. Gladys said that the ruling class was beginning to commit atrocities like the Sacco-Vanzetti case and that was a sign that they were on their last legs, and that as things in Russia got better and better and they solved their economic problems, the American worker would turn more and more to the leadership of the Party.[63]

Driven almost daft by Glady who was willing enough to sleep with him but wouldn't leave Boris, Glenn escaped into a world of fantasy where he saw himself as a second Lenin swaying the masses. "The new Glenn Spotswood who was addressing this great meeting in this great hall was going on, without any private life, renouncing the capitalist world and its pomps, the new Glenn Spotswood had come there tonight to offer himself, his brain and his muscle, everything he had in him, to the revolutionary working class. Hands clapped, throats roared out cheers." [64]

Although he graduated from Columbia *cum laude,* Glenn took no pride in his achievement. To an old friend he talked about how he had wasted these years, putting himself through college just because nobody of the whitecollar class could think of anything better to do. "And all the time what he'd really wanted to be doing was beat his way around the country living like working people lived.

[62] John Dos Passos, *Adventures of a Young Man* (Boston: Houghton Mifflin Co., 1939), 99.
[63] *Ibid.,* 104–5.   [64] *Ibid.,* 127.

The whitecollar class was all washed up. It was in the working class
that real things were happening nowadays. The real thing was the
new social order that was being born out of the working class." [65]

To please his father and to earn money to pay off his college
debts, Glenn took a job in his uncle's bank in a small Texas town.
He salved his radical conscience by regarding himself as a spy in the
enemy camp. But the spy's secret loyalties soon betrayed him.
When the underpaid Mexican pecan shellers of the town went on
strike, Glenn became secretly involved. The police beat up the
pickets and threw them into jail, and the local judge set bail at
$10,000. Jed Farrington, a hard-drinking local lawyer, accepted the
unpopular cause of defending the prisoners, but needed money to
carry an appeal to a higher court. Acting as treasurer of the defense
fund, Glenn had an opportunity to observe two kinds of radical.
Frankie Perez, the local barber who called himself an anarchist but
talked like a Jeffersonian democrat, worked tirelessly and effectively to get the needed money from Mexican storekeepers, but
Irving Silverstone, a Communist emissary from New York City, insisted on tactics that only added to the strikers' troubles. "It doesn't
matter," he pontificated,

if we lose one case or a hundred cases as long as the workers are made to
realize the significance of revolutionary Marxism . . . what I am telling these comrades is that their historic position must be explained to
the workers of Horton. They must be made to see the significance of this
strike as the awakening of an exploited colonial minority, and as part of
the daily struggle of the world proletariat against the encroachments of
the exploiting classes. We must flood the city with leaflets. . . .[66]

Silverstone's activities gave the forces of reaction the only
excuse they needed. Early one afternoon the Ku Klux Klan put on a
menacing demonstration. "A line of closed cars packed with men in
white pointed hoods drove by fast while the cop held up traffic for
them. On the back of each car was a lettered banner: AGITATORS
BEWARE. The crowd of Mexicans turned as one man as the cars
passed them. Nobody said a word." [67] Silverstone discovered that
he had urgent business elsewhere. Spotswood lost his bank job and

---

[65] *Ibid.*, 138.   [66] *Ibid.*, 154–55.   [67] *Ibid.*, 166.

returned to New York. Only Jed Farrington was left to salvage what he could for the cowed Mexicans.

Despite Silverstone's unhelpful role in the pecan shellers' strike, Glenn allowed himself to become a Communist mouthpiece after his return to New York. He spoke of his southern experiences at street meetings and in small dingy halls. Not yet a party member, he explained his feelings during a reunion with Gladys Spingarn.

What he was going to do was get a job in a mine or mill or something, he wanted to get plain hard laborer's work, live, eat, sleep like a worker. He was sick of this whitecollar business. He hadn't any interest in the owning class, he was through with being a parlor pink. . . . He was going to join the Party as a worker and not as a whitecollar slave. When he was an honest to God worker he'd join the Party all right.[68]

Glenn never did become the hardy proletarian of his fantasies; he became instead a faithful Communist underling, using the party name of Sandy Crockett.

In an episode that must reflect some of his own observations in Harlan County, Kentucky, Dos Passos tells how Glenn Spotswood was sent on a dangerous mission into the lonely mountains. He was to help organize the American Miners Union as a more militant body than the older complacent Mineworkers Union. Glenn was touched by the prayer in which a grizzled old miner explained the issue.

O Lawd . . . bless this here house and this here meetin' of the 'Merican Miners like you blessed the Mineworkers in the old days before them organizers got to be traitors an' scallywags an' sold us out to the oppressors. . . . O Lawd, we need bread an' meat an' clothin' for our children, that's terrible sick of the flux an' can't sleep because they's so cold an' hongry, an' can't go to school to learn to be good citizens because they's so naked, an' they's likely to grow up the worst trash is ever been seen in these mountains.[69]

Conditions in the mines were grim. Coal prices were low, and the operators had cut wages to the point where the miners were in rebellion. Pearl Napier, the local strike leader, was not yet twenty-one but he was a married man with two children. He had started to

[68] *Ibid.*, 172–73.   [69] *Ibid.*, 192.

work in the mines at nine. Now his hungry family was kept alive by hand-outs from local sympathizers. The Communist fronts made their most effective move by sending in aid from the outside. "Then Glenn told about the soupkitchens the American Miners were going to organize and how the Workers' Defense was already shipping in clothes and flour and groceries with a girl comrade, Jane Sparling, who was a doctor and who'd tend the sick and ailing children as long as the strike lasted." [70]

The Coal Operators' Association controlled the local sheriff and his deputies and also maintained a private army of "gunthugs" to serve their interests. When the unarmed strikers attempted a protest march, the hirelings killed two of them. To the miners this was a cause for somber grief; to the undercover Communists it provided a precious opportunity for propaganda. " 'That's it,' said Irving. . . . 'A mass funeral for two classwar victims.' " [71] After the coffins were lowered into the graves, a big crowd of grim miners with their wives and children listened to a wide variety of speakers—embittered fellow-workers like Pearl Napier, outside organizers like Glenn Spotswood, earnest liberals like the Reverend James Breckenridge, "an Episcopal bishop interested in social conditions and the criminal syndicalism laws." [72]

The sheriff and his underlings allowed the meeting to run its course, although they took down a stenographic record of everything that was said. But afterwards, the inevitable outbreak of violence occurred. Two deputies were killed, and the sheriff's men retaliated with wholesale arrests of the striking miners. Glenn Spotswood and Pearl Napier were menaced by charges ranging from criminal syndicalism to murder.

The jailing of the strikers resulted in a confused situation in which radicals quarreled with radicals over tactics, politicians and unionists arranged cynical deals, and liberals fluttered about trying to help the oppressed. A few of the arrested miners belonged to the Communist-dominated American Miners Union; more were members of the OBU, One Big Union, a rival syndicalist group. Mutual suspicion hampered the defense. Irving Silverstone tried to get all the defendants to accept the services of a Communist front,

---

[70] *Ibid.*, 193.   [71] *Ibid.*, 204.   [72] *Ibid.*, 208.

the American Workers' Defense, which, he said, was "in a position to use mass pressure and to put this struggle in its true light as part of the international movement of the working class." [73] But the OBU men, mistrustful of Communist motives, stubbornly refused, and Pearl Napier and another of the American Miners group chose to join them in this independent course.

A third group involved in the affair was the Consolidated Mineworkers, the conservative old-line union. After Connolly, state president of the Consolidated Mineworkers, bailed out some of the arrested men, Herve Farrell, the OBU leader, was eager to arrange an alliance of the three organizations, but the Communists would not cooperate. " 'That social fascist,' said Irving, getting to his feet. 'If you want to help him sell out the workers you can; that's not what we came down here for.' " Farrell retorted that what the Communists had come down for was "to raise a big political stink and git yourselves a new crop of martyrs for . . . for your own mealtickets." [74]

Meanwhile Glenn Spotswood had been released from jail by means of a deal whereby the local authorities agreed to reduce his bail and the Communists promised to hustle him out of the state. Always the idealist, Spotswood hated to desert his new friend, Napier, and the other seven miners being held on murder charges, but Silverstone soothed his conscience with left-wing platitudes.

"They're all of them politically underdeveloped," said Irving as they were going back up in the elevator.

"I'd rely on Napier anywhere."

"I know," said Irving in a doleful tone. "Real proletarians . . . lovely people . . . but they lack marxist preparation. There's too much of the artist in you, Sandy. You are sentimental." [75]

The Communists sent Glenn on a secret mission back into the mountains to jack up the sagging morale of the American Miners Union, but the thugs of the Operators' Association were waiting for him. They caught him and Less Minot, the AMU organizer, took them out to a lonely parking area, and kicked them half to death. After being patched up in the local hospital, Glenn spent his con-

[73] *Ibid.*, 219.   [74] *Ibid.*, 223–24.   [75] *Ibid.*, 224.

valescence in the bed of Marice Gulick, his patronness of college days. Frivolous and faddish, Marice was one of the rich liberals eager to subsidize left-wing causes, during the 1920's and 1930's.

Glenn was still trying to help the eight miners who had been convicted of murder, but had been granted a new trial. Ideological feuds continued to hamper the defense. Late one night the head of the Communist Party gave Glenn his orders over the telephone. The Central Committee, he said, had decided to concentrate on getting out the two American Miners' Boys; "outside of that the trial was an educational demonstration and to be treated as such by the liberal lawyers: and as for cooperating with the O.B.U. he had every reason to believe it would be a mistake, after all we knew none of our boys had shot those deputies, no use trying to defend irresponsible elements, no time for Quixotic gestures." [76]

In obedience to these orders, Glenn got the AMU men to accept a separate trial and then attempted to testify for them. But a few minutes of cross-examination wiped out whatever influence his truthful account might have had upon the jury. Glenn admitted that he did not believe in God and that he considered "the Russian system of communism as practiced in red Moscow more conducive to the dignity of man . . . than belief in the Gospel, the sacredness of the home and private property and the Constitution of the United States." [77]

This confession of heresy so outraged local sentiment that not only Spotswood, but the big-name liberal lawyer who had been employed to defend the miners had to scramble out of the state in fear of their lives. Napier and his friend were found guilty and sentenced to twenty years in prison. Most disillusioning of all was the calloused reversal of policy by which the Communist Party suddenly deserted the American Miners Union and made a bargain with the Consolidated Mineworkers. As Less Minot, drunk and bitter, described the situation:

No more dual unions. What the hell had we been getting our blocks knocked off for, and letting the boys get their blocks knocked off for, but our own party union. Now the story was to go back and be good little boys and bore from within the good old Mineworkers. . . . No,

---

[76] *Ibid.*, 245–46.   [77] *Ibid.*, 253.

Mr. Connolly wasn't a crook or a socialfascist labor faker any more, he was a noble progressive fellow traveller, and we were going to work to bore from within him.[78]

Even after this experience, Glenn continued to dance on the party's puppet strings. His well-publicized strike activities had made him a hero, in liberal eyes, and he was sent on a cross-country speaking tour to raise funds for Workers' Defense. "Everywhere it was applause in halls crowded with faces of working people and professional people, and handshakings and little gatherings of comrades and sympathizers after the meetings or parties arranged for leading intellectuals by liberal hostesses." [79]

One day in Chicago, Glenn was shocked to read the news of Pearl Napier's death. He had been shot down while trying to escape from prison. Shortly afterwards, Glenn had a maudlin telephone call from Herve Farrell, the OBU organizer:

Had he read the news? . . . did he know who was responsible for that guy's death and the holy mess they made of the defense, well, he was, the sonofabitch, and if he was a man he'd come and get his dirty lying face smashed in. . . . And what was he doing now with all his speeches in defense of the classwar prisoners, . . . who was getting the money? The prisoners or his organization? Who was in jail? The working stiffs. Who was riding around the country staying in the best hotels making speeches and passing the plate? The comical commissars.[80]

Sick with guilt, Glenn defied party discipline, called off his speaking tour, and demanded that the Communists make an accounting of the Workers' Defense fund. Punishment followed speedily. Expelled from the party, he found that his former associates did not even dare to speak to him. When an old friend asked what he was doing now, he explained: "Running a little paper for working class unity . . . and campaigning to get guys out of jail that everybody else has forgotten. Have you heard about the splinter parties? Well, I'm a splinter." [81]

But the independent radical had no place to go. Troublemakers disrupted Glenn's meetings; his splinter movement soon collapsed. He went to Detroit to work for Ford, but was fired for promoting

[78] *Ibid.,* 257.   [79] *Ibid.,* 261.   [80] *Ibid.,* 262.   [81] *Ibid.,* 284.

unionism in the washrooms. Less Minot offered him a good job as a union organizer, but he refused to make the necessary promise to quit his anti-communist activities.

In a final effort to do something for the workers' cause, Glenn volunteered for service in the Spanish Civil War. The recruiter in Detroit shrugged off the political question. "We are all comrades . . . all of us who want to fight against . . . the enemies of the human race." [82] During his first hours in Spain, Glenn felt the lift of shared purpose with the Spanish Loyalists and the volunteers from other countries. But when he met Frankie Perez, whom he had known in the Texas pecanshellers' strike, he was soon set straight. "Here several different kinds of war. We fight Franco but also we fight Moscow . . . if you go to the Brigada you must not let them fight us. They want to institute dictatorship of secret police just like Franco. We have to fight both sides to protect our revolution." [83]

Frankie, it seems, had moved to Barcelona before the Civil War and was one of the anarcho-syndicalists who bitterly opposed the Communists. Jed Farrington, the Texas lawyer who had befriended Frankie in the old days, was now under Communist discipline as an officer in the International Brigade. Glenn tried to keep clear of these fratricidal politics: "I came here to try to help . . . I'll do any kind of work you people say, except tell other guys to go get their blocks knocked off. I'm fed up with that." [84]

But independent radicalism was even less possible in Civil War Spain than in New Deal America. Branded as politically unreliable, Glenn was first sidetracked into a mechanic's job and then imprisoned on absurd charges: "We are informed that you represent the Trotsky counterrevolutionary organization in America and were one of the channels of communication in actively preparing the Barcelona uprising." [85] Only when Franco's forces were overrunning the countryside did Glenn's Communist jailers finally release him from his cell and send him on an impossible mission: "Well, there are some of our boys with two machineguns in a pillbox to the left of hill 14. They got to have water. You got to take it to 'em. They are the only thing that's keeping the wops out of this

[82] *Ibid.*, 292.   [83] *Ibid.*, 305.   [84] *Ibid.*, 309.   [85] *Ibid.*, 315.

dump. Tell 'em to stick for another half hour, see, they got to cover us while we get some junk out of here." [86]

In a symbolic ending to the novel, Glenn sets out across no-man's land with two buckets of water. Fascist bullets pierce first one bucket, then the other, then the body of Glenn Spotswood himself.

VI

The American radicals of Dos Passos's description have ample reason for their rebellion. American employers deal harshly with their workers. Paid less than a living wage, the steelworkers, the textile mill employees, and the coal miners live in squalid tenements and shanties. Their wives are haggard and broken; their children are scrawny and rickety. When the workers attempt to strike, policemen and guards beat them up, and judges sentence them to prison.

Dos Passos sees heroic qualities in the honest rebels who struggle against these conditions, often at the risk of their lives. He deals kindly with the young coal miner Pearl Napier, whose attempts to better conditions for his family and fellow workers lead to unjust imprisonment and death; with the barber-anarchist Frankie Perez, whose sturdy independence ends when he is shot by rival leftists in Barcelona; and with the immigrant fish peddler, Bartolomeo Vanzetti, "hater of oppression who wanted a world unfenced" and died in the electric chair.

But the Communists do not qualify among Dos Passos's heroes of the left. The more attractive ones, such as Ben Compton and Glenn Spotswood, are sincere in their desire to help the workers, but they are corrupted by years of accepting party decisions instead of thinking for themselves. In the end, they rebel against this iron discipline, but their rebellion destroys them. Expelled from the party, they find themselves without jobs and without influence. The Communists who survive and prosper are unpleasant characters like Don Stevens and Irving Silverstone. They talk in Marxist clichés, take few risks, and slavishly follow the meandering party line.

[86] *Ibid.*, 320.

Dos Passos's unfavorable judgment does not result from the tensions of the Cold War. *The Big Money* and *Adventures of a Young Man* were published in the 1930's, when the Soviet Union still enjoyed a reasonably favorable American press. The novelist indicts the Communists not for their conspiracies against national security, but for their betrayal of the workers' cause, which they claim to be championing. They corrupt the authentic left, which Dos Passos still admires.

In Dos Passos's description, the Communists manipulate each situation for party advantage. In the Sacco-Vanzetti affair, they place more importance on demonstrating class solidarity than on saving the condemned men. In the coal strike, they first refuse to ally with the AFL union, when it might save the imprisoned miners and then reverse this policy and desert the men who have run great risks for them. The Communists, as Spotswood said, are always telling other guys to get their blocks knocked off.

Middle-class liberals also play an unheroic role in Dos Passos's novels. In their concern for social justice they are sincere, but blundering. They profess to love peace, but rush to enlist in Wilson's war. They wish to help the workers, but are guided more by sentimentality than by reason. Their willingness to give money, attend meetings, and serve on committees make them easy marks for the Communists.

Dos Passos's unflattering portrait of the American left may be too harsh, but it is based upon close observation. These were the people with whom he associated most closely during the 1920's and 1930's.

8

The World of
Fifty-eighth Street

> He wanted to be a writer. He didn't know how. He wanted to
> purge himself completely of the world he knew, the world of
> Fifty-eighth Street, with its God, its life, its lies, the frustra-
> tions he had known in it, the hates it had welled up in him.
>
> JAMES T. FARRELL, *The Young Manhood of*
> *Studs Lonigan* [1]

IN THE THREE NOVELS that James T. Farrell wrote about
Studs Lonigan, Danny O'Neill appeared occasionally as one of the
neighborhood boys, two or three years younger than Studs and
different enough from the other youths to be scorned as a "goof."
In *A World I Never Made,* and in four other Farrell novels, Danny
became the central character. The persistent reader can thus put
together the story of Danny's life, from his first memories as a
frightened child of three, until the day twenty years later, when he
left Chicago to seek a new life as a writer in New York.

Danny's father, a hard-working Chicago teamster, earned too
little to support his constantly increasing family. Three-year-old
Danny was therefore taken out of his parents' home in the Chicago
slums and cared for in the O'Flaherty household, composed of his
maternal grandparents, his unmarried uncle, and two unmarried
aunts. Anxious to protect their precarious foothold in the middle
class, the O'Flahertys moved several times to better addresses,

[1] James T. Farrell, *Studs Lonigan: A Trilogy Containing Young Lonigan, The
Young Manhood of Studs Lonigan, Judgment Day* (New York: New American
Library, 1958), 403.

finally taking an apartment near Fifty-eighth Street and Washington Park on Chicago's South Side. In 1915, when the O'Flahertys arrived, it was a respectable neighborhood, largely populated by lower-middle-class Irish families.

Danny O'Neill had a troubled childhood and youth. He did not lack affection; his fierce Irish grandmother and his neurotic Aunt Margaret pampered him shamelessly. Uncle Al was the only disciplinarian in the family, but he was on the road most of the time, selling shoes. Smothering love, however, could not give the boy security. He was ashamed of not being raised by his own parents. He hardly knew what to make of his unlucky struggling father, his shiftless superstitious mother, and his unkempt brothers and sisters. He was painfully aware of his own bespectacled goofiness. "What was the matter with him? Why did he seem different from other kids? He could fight, wrestle, play ball better than most kids. But many of them got respect for just being themselves. He had to fight kids to make them respect him or play ball better than they did. Well, he would." [2]

Danny attended parochial schools until 1923, when he graduated from high school and took a job with an express company. In 1925, he entered the University of Chicago, supporting himself by part time work in a filling station. His attendance was irregular and he finally dropped out without earning a degree, but this taste of college changed his life. His study of history, economics, and sociology gave him a new point of view toward the environment in which he had been reared, and his courses in literature and composition inspired a determination to become a writer.

The identity of Danny O'Neill has always been transparently clear. Step by step, Danny's early years parallel those of James T. Farrell himself. Farrell's father was an impoverished teamster; Farrell was raised in a household composed of grandparents, uncles, and aunts; the family lived in the Fifty-eighth Street neighborhood. Farrell went first to parochial schools, then for eight quarters to the University of Chicago, supporting himself by working in a filling station. Eventually he quit and went to New York to become a writer.

---

[2] James T. Farrell, *Father and Son* (Cleveland: World Publishing Co., 1947), 109.

By writing, Danny O'Neill said, he would purge himself completely of the world of Fifty-eighth Street. But for James T. Farrell, this purging took many years. Even after writing about the world of Fifty-eighth Street, in three Studs Lonigan books, five Danny O'Neill books, and a number of other novels and short stories, Farrell had by no means exhausted his fund of memories. In the late 1940's, he was writing novels about Bernard Carr, who had originated on the South Side of Chicago and was now living in the literary world of New York City. And in the 1960's, Farrell began a new series about one Eddie Ryan, who—strange to relate—was living near Fifty-eighth Street in Chicago with his grandmother, two uncles, and an aunt, while he worked in a filling station by night and attended the University of Chicago by day.

Sometimes Farrell seemed to exceed even Thomas Wolfe in obsessive interest in his own experience. Yet the differences between Wolfe and Farrell were more significant than the similarities. Wolfe was oversized in every way, a giant in height and weight, a glutton in eating, drinking, reading, writing, and roistering. Farrell was much less given to excess. He was not so much the tortured artist seeking a lost home as the struggling swimmer escaping dangerous waters. Farrell had genuine compassion for the ones who did not make it—for Studs Lonigan, brought to an early death by dissipation; for Jim O'Neill, beaten down by overwork and his wife's fecundity; for unhappy Aunt Margaret, Aunt Louise, and all the others whom life defeated.

Much more than Wolfe, therefore, Farrell sought to explain the environment in which these grim things happened. From the beginning, he knew that it would take thousands of pages to do the job. He talked in terms of twenty-five books, "which would contain, to the best of my ability, as complete a picture of the story of America as I knew it, of the hopes, the shames, the aspirations, of everything that it was possible for me to use as the legitimate material of literature." [3] And in the end he wrote even more books than he had planned.

In 1948, Farrell appeared on the witness stand of the Federal District Court in Philadelphia in a case involving police inter-

[3] James T. Farrell, "The Author as Plaintiff: Testimony in a Censorship Case," *Reflections at Fifty and Other Essays* (New York: Vanguard Press, 1954), 194.

ference with the sale of his work. Denying that the Studs Lonigan novels were obscene, Farrell swore to their essential truthfulness. Asked to what extent they were autobiographical, he replied, "I would say this: It is like the life I saw as a boy. It is like it in terms of the attitudes, the types, the thoughts, the types and patterns of language, the patterns of destiny." Studs embodied all that Farrell had decided that he would not be, "and in that sense it is a criticism of the conditions of youth in the city and in the neighborhood and in the times in which I grew up." [4]

"Did you see in your youth," his lawyer asked him, "characters of the kind portrayed in *Studs Lonigan?*" And Farrell replied, "I can say that I saw literally hundreds." "Did you live among many of them?" "I did." [5]

Critics have deplored Farrell's crudities of style, his repetitiousness, and his grimness, but they have always conceded his truthfulness. He is not "a pretty writer," Ralph Thompson pointed out, "but he is as sincere and conscientious a historian as can be found on the rolls of all the Irish-American societies combined." [6] J. Donald Adams wrote: "There is much that is sordid, much that is tragic, in the picture as Mr. Farrell has drawn it, but one has always the feeling that here is a writer who cannot compromise with what he sees. He must put it all down." [7] And Bernard De Voto preferred Farrell to Wolfe and Dos Passos: "Mr. Farrell makes his toughs live. Mr. Wolfe merely throws language at his without striking fire. . . . Mr. Dos Passos writes from theory, Mr. Farrell from life." [8]

II

In 1911, when seven-year-old Danny O'Neill was staying with the O'Flahertys, in the vicinity of Fifty-first Street, his father and mother were living on La Salle Street, some twenty-five blocks to the north. The contrast between the two households was stark. The

---

[4] *Ibid.*, 193–94.   [5] *Ibid.*, 194.

[6] Ralph Thompson, "Books of the Times," *New York Times*, Oct. 10, 1940, 23.

[7] J. Donald Adams, "Mr. Farrell's 'Father and Son' and Other Recent Fiction," *New York Times Book Review*, Dec. 1, 1940, VI, 7.

[8] Bernard De Voto, "Beyond Studs Lonigan," *Saturday Review of Literature*, Oct. 24, 1936, 5.

O'Flahertys enjoyed the comforts of electric lights, hot water, and indoor plumbing. The O'Neills lighted their shabby flat with kerosene lamps, drew their water cold from a single tap in the kitchen, and shared an ill-smelling backyard privy with Negro neighbors.

Burdened by frequent pregnancies and baby tending, Lizz O'Neill took no interest in housework. The clutter and dirt simply piled up until her husband attempted to clean it out in sporadic flurries of energy. Jim O'Neill fluctuated between moments of tenderness for his slovenly wife and feelings of disgust. "Jesus," he complained, "she wouldn't even wash her face." [9]

Jim goddamned his poverty, and he had good reason to do so. The bedroom that he shared with Lizz smelled musty even with the windows open. "He glanced around, junk all over, the dresser in the corner piled with it, rags, clothes, junk, and the table on the left with a slab of grocery box in place of one leg, it too, was piled and littered with every damn thing in the house." [10] The dining room was no better.

The torn papered walls appeared as if charging upon him to crush and compress him, to choke and smother the very breath of life within him. He looked at the table, with its dirty oilcloth covering, the papers and rags on it, the lamp burning with its funnel-shaped chimney smoked almost black. He wondered, as he was so often wondering these days, when, when would it change? When would he escape from this kind of life? When would he and his family be able to live decently? [11]

By 1914, the O'Neills had moved into a cottage at the corner of Forty-fifth Street and Wentworth Avenue. Lizz liked having a yard all her own, "not a yard to be shared with niggers like the one at Twenty-fifth and La Salle." [12] Yet if this was a step up in the world, it was only a small one. From the front room of the new home, one looked out on a street of "old wooden cottages, narrow sidewalks, dirt, garbage, wooden paving blocks." [13] The O'Neill cottage was unpainted and shabby. "The dining room and parlor . . . were connected by a doorless opening in which there stood a fat-bellied

[9] James T. Farrell, *A World I Never Made* (New York: Vanguard Press, 1936), 170.

[10] *Ibid.*, 21.   [11] *Ibid.*, 170–714.

[12] James T. Farrell, *No Star Is Lost* (New York: Vanguard Press, 1938), 161.

[13] *Ibid.*, 168.

stove. It usurped almost half the space of this opening. Both rooms smelled musty and were disorderly and strewn with papers." [14] For heat in the wintertime there was only this stove in the front part of the house and the range in the kitchen. The children "used to gather around the stove and take turns sticking their feet in the oven to get warm." [15]

When ten-year-old Danny O'Neill had to spend an occasional night in his parents' house, he was miserable. He and his older brother slept in the same bed, and a younger brother lay across the foot. "There was no room in the bed. He didn't like the darkness. He didn't like the smell of the room. The smell of the room was very different from the smell of the bedroom where he slept at home. The smell here was musty, and it made him feel dirty. He didn't know what made the smell except the bed and the dirty sheets and blankets, and it was musty." [16] The worst thing was the itching. "He scratched his legs again, and it felt as if he had scratched a bite until it was bleeding. In summer at home, mosquitoes did that, but never in winter. It must be bedbugs they had." [17]

To the O'Neill children, meat was a treat brought home by their father once or twice a week, usually on pay days. Even then there was not enough, and Jim rationed it out sternly. One of the younger boys warned his brother about the matter: "You watch yourself. Don't grab too much meat. Pa gets sore if you grab too much meat and don't let everybody else get any. He beat me up with his razor strap because I did it last time he brought meat home on payday." [18]

Living in poverty among neighbors whom she despised, Lizz O'Neill found her greatest solace in Catholicism. "Without the comfort of the Blessed Virgin," she said, "I don't know what I'd do." [19] Clad in a shabby man's coat, high shoes with knotted laces, and an unclean rag around her neck, she would make her way to the neighborhood church in the late afternoon. "She was able to be so alone with God, with Mary, with all of the angels and saints, with her father, her sister Louise, all her own dead children. . . . At home was the dirty house full of kids. Her man was out working

[14] *Ibid.*, 162.   [15] *Father and Son*, 3.   [16] *No Star Is Lost*, 234.
[17] *Ibid.*, 236.   [18] *Ibid.*, 220.   [19] *A World I Never Made*, 309.

hard, maybe straining himself, with his rupture. And here it was so peaceful, so like Heaven must be." [20] Lizz was a great dispenser of holy water. In the pangs of childbirth she demanded that her husband take the necessary precautions. "She asked him to get the small bottle of Easter holy water on the dresser and sprinkle some on her and around the room because when a child was born, the devils always came and tried to snatch the baby's soul before it was baptized. If the devils were not driven away, the child's soul might be possessed by them. And Easter holy water was especially good for chasing devils and making Satan hide his ugly head in fear." [21]

The escape that Lizz found in religiosity, Jim sought in occasional bouts of drinking. Ashamed of wasting the money needed by his large family, he would take the pledge of total abstinence again and again. But each time his resolution would weaken. In search of companionship he would drop into a corner saloon, intending to drink only one glass of beer. But once he started he found it impossible to stop, and he would drink until he came staggering home to face Lizz's bitter scolding. The morning after he would alternate between self-condemnation and self-defense. "What was wrong in getting drunk? When a man had worked as hard as he had worked all his life, he at least had earned the right to go on a bat now and then." [22]

During World War I the O'Neills seemed to make a little progress. Jim was promoted to a supervisory job in the Express Company, and Bill, the oldest son, was able to supplement the family income by going to work for the same firm. The family moved into a better house not far from the O'Flahertys in the Fifty-eighth Street neighborhood. There, for the first time, they enjoyed the blessings of an indoor bathroom, running hot and cold water, steam heat, and electricity. In one decisive gesture Jim bought Lizz a whole new wardrobe and threw away the dirty torn dresses she had been wearing. "She was going to be dressed up from now on. And if she was, she was a damned handsome woman. He didn't give a damn what she'd say about his having thrown away her old clothes. She was going to change her ways." [23]

But the O'Neills' toehold in the middle class was far from

---

[20] *Ibid.*, 148–49.   [21] *Ibid.*, 22.   [22] *Father and Son*, 79.   [23] *Ibid.*, 261.

secure. The family was large, and Lizz was a poor manager. "We've hardly a nickel in the bank," Jim complained, "and here again payday comes around and we've only got a couple of nickels in the house." [24] Lizz had to continue her appeals to her bachelor brother for help: "Please send me ten dollars if you can spare it. My expenses are so heavy and Jim is under the doctor's care and with the children in school and tuition and food and clothing things are hard." [25]

Jim's health deteriorated steadily. He suffered a series of strokes and eventually became a pitiful paralytic unable to work. The major burden of supporting the family fell upon Bill, the oldest son, who had to give up his night school classes. One bitter humiliation followed another. There was, for example, the bitter morning when two condescending Protestant ladies called on the family to leave a Christmas basket of food. " 'I have sunk so low, haven't I?' Jim said, his words throbbing, his voice on the verge of breaking, while he and Danny saw the women get into their automobile and drive off." [26]

Jim O'Neill died in 1923, the year Danny graduated from high school. The boy felt the tragedy of the event. "He told himself that his father was a man who'd never had a chance. His father had been a strong man, and a proud man, and he had seen that pride broken, and it had been a very sad spectacle to witness." [27]

III

Although Jim O'Neill passed his last years in a middle-class neighborhood, he didn't really belong there. He never made good his escape from the poverty of the Chicago slums. Much more representative of the world of Fifty-eighth Street were the traveling salesman, Al O'Flaherty, and the painting contractor, Paddy Lonigan. Both Al and Paddy took pride in the fact that they had risen above the level of their parents.

Al's father and mother had been born in Ireland and had come to America when they were young. Neither of them had ever learned to read, although in their old age they childishly concealed

[24] *Ibid.*, 170.   [25] *Ibid.*, 171–72.   [26] *Ibid.*, 453–54.   [27] *Ibid.*, 601.

And time was when he would be up before the crack of dawn and out in the cold on the wagon, and think nothing of it.   James T. Farrell, *The Face of Time*

the fact. "Well, I can read," Tom argued with his wife. "I can read a newspaper, Mary, but I can't read a telegram. That I never learned." [28] Old Tom had spent all his working days as a poorly-paid teamster. Facing death, he had the feeling "that he didn't belong here in America." [29]

Al O'Flaherty had no such doubts about his place in the world. Although he had had only a grammar school education, he had made the most of his opportunities. He had started by wrapping shoes in a State Street store; then he had become a retail clerk; and

[28] James T. Farrell, *The Face of Time* (New York: Popular Library, 1962), 30.
[29] *Ibid.*, 166.

finally he had risen to the rank of a traveling salesman selling shoes wholesale. He was proud of his progress. "And now he was a man of thirty-eight, and he had come along somewhat in life, come along on the power of his own ambition. And he was still climbing up the ladder." [30]

Al had never married. Between road trips he made his home with his widowed mother and a growing list of other O'Flahertys whom he helped to support. There was his unmarried sister Margaret, who worked as a cashier in a hotel; his brother Ned, a widower who was frequently unemployed; and first one, then two, and finally three of Al's nephews and nieces from the impoverished O'Neill family. Having no son of his own, Al focused his affection on Danny. His ambitions for the boy were typically middle-class Irish. He wanted him to be a lawyer and a politician. "The boy, yes, he would get all that Al O'Flaherty had never been able to get, a college education. He and Dan would go together, be like pals. He could see them together at, say, an O. of C. fourth degree banquet, or going to church on Sunday mornings, people pointing the boy out, saying that there was a smart young fellow who was beginning to amount to something." [31]

Al insisted on the dignity of his own vocation. He rebuked a fellow-huckster sharply. "Nix on it, Jack. Jack, the wise guy doesn't call himself a drummer. He's a salesman. It's only these bush leaguers who use a word like that. You're not a drummer. You're a salesman." [32]

In keeping with his painfully-won status, Al stayed in the best hotels and ordered expensive meals. He disapproved of many of the other traveling men. "There were some salesmen he didn't like, with their dirty jokes, their gambling, drinking, picking up women in their indiscriminate way." [33] Although in his loneliness, Al occasionally visited a brothel, he felt ashamed of such episodes. He spent most of his spare time in serious reading, attempting to make up for the deficiencies in his formal education. "Emerson, ah, there was a great philosopher! When Dan was older, he would have him read Emerson's beautiful and inspired thoughts on self-reliance, love, friendship, and compensation." [34]

---

[30] *A World I Never Made,* 83.   [31] *Ibid.,* 13.   [32] *Ibid.,* 88.
[33] *Ibid.,* 86.   [34] *Ibid.*

It was a happy day for Al when he purchased *The Letters of Lord Chesterfield*. "He was going to read every word of it. He lit a cigar and began reading through the introduction. Fine man, a gentleman, Lord Chesterfield was, and he only wanted to be as poised and educated a man. And he would make Danny into the kind of a poised and educated gentleman of the world that Lord Chesterfield had wanted to make of his son. He could envision himself writing letters to Danny like the ones Lord Chesterfield had written." [35]

Al never relaxed in his determination to be a gentleman. He was fastidious about his table manners and his grammar. He loved to display the new words he had learned through his reading. When he used the word *decorum* he explained proudly what it meant and emphasized its Latin derivation. "But say," exclaimed an admiring friend, "you must be a whizz to educate yourself and learn all them words you know without getting it in college." [36]

Al believed in all the traditional American pieties. He thanked God for beautiful mornings and was reassured to read that so great a scientist as Thomas Edison had retained a belief in "the eternal mind." He thought it was good for a man to be up and on the job early in the morning. "Watching people go to work, he could pick out the real ones just like the snap of a finger. If a man slouched along without any pep like that fellow across the street wearing a black derby, you'd be risking nothing in betting that he wasn't a live wire." Walking along the street, Al fought against the impulse to put down his heavy sample case for a moment's rest. He was convinced "that he shouldn't quit in the little things any more than he would quit in the big ones." [37]

O'Flaherty believed in saving his money and managed to do so despite all the demands made upon him by his family. He had a thousand dollar insurance policy, some Liberty bonds, a few public utility stocks, and some shares in the shoe company that employed him. He kept a thousand dollars in the bank to deal with any emergency. "God willing," Al humbly thought, he and his family "would all live for many years to come and enjoy the fruits of a fine, happy, and prosperous life together." [38]

But Al's yearning for happiness and respectability was contin-

[35] *Ibid.,* 93.　　[36] *Ibid.,* 101.　　[37] *Ibid.,* 175–76.　　[38] *Father and Son,* 22.

ually jeopardized by the excesses of the other O'Flahertys. His mother smoked a clay pipe, drank more beer than she should, and filled the air with picturesque profanity. His sister carried on with a married man—a black Protestant, to make matters worse—and had periods of wild drunkenness. "What he had always wished for in his own house was just a little peace, a warm hearth filled with love. And instead, look what his home was. . . . He himself, he had not had any too happy a childhood. He wanted both of the children to have a better childhood than his. And it would be if there wasn't so damn much fighting and drinking in the house. Oh, good Jesus Christ, couldn't anything be done to stop it?" [39]

Even young Danny was a disappointment. The college education that was to fulfill so many dreams alienated the youth from his elders. Danny lost faith in the two principal articles in his uncle's credo, the go-getter philosophy of the businessman and the truths of the Roman Catholic Church. Business itself failed Al. The factory whose shoes he had peddled so many years and in which he had invested much of his savings eventually closed, and in middle age, Al had to start life all over again, this time in California.

Paddy Lonigan, Studs's father, had done well as a painting contractor and had invested his savings in an apartment building. The Lonigans lived in middle-class neighborhoods and moved to better ones when the old ones deteriorated. Paddy was proud of his success. He remembered how poor his own childhood had been. "Often there had not been enough to eat in the house. Many's the winter day he and his brother had to stay home from school because they had no shoes. The old house, it was more like a barn or a shack than a home, was so cold they had to sleep in their clothes; sometimes in those zero Chicago winters his old man had slept in his overcoat." [40]

But all this was in the past; "he'd fought his way up to a station where there wasn't no real serious problems like poverty." He congratulated himself on being "a good Catholic, and a good American, a good father, and a good husband." [41] Paddy wanted his children to have more than he had had. He would encourage Studs to go to high school and then train him to take over the painting busi-

---

[39] *No Star Is Lost,* 472.   [40] *Studs Lonigan,* 18.   [41] *Ibid.,* 22.

ness. Martin, his second son, would be "a lawyer or professional man of some kind; he might go into politics and become a senator or a . . . you never could tell what a lad with the blood of Paddy Lonigan in him might not become." As for the girls, there would be plenty of time to make plans for them. "Anyway, there was going to be no hitches in the future of his kids." [42]

Paddy was sure that he and Mary had done their duty and been good parents. "They had given the kids a good home, fed and clothed them, sent them to Catholic schools to be educated, seen that they performed their religious duties, hustled them off to confession regularly, given them money for the collection, never allowed them to miss mass, even in winter, let them play properly so they'd be healthy, given them money for good clean amusements like the movies because they were also educational, done everything a parent can do for a child." [43]

Yet it all went for nothing. Paddy Lonigan was no more able than Al O'Flaherty to guarantee the happiness of himself and his family. Studs destroyed his health through dissipation and died before he was thirty. Martin seemed determined to repeat all Studs's mistakes. And old Paddy himself lost his business and savings during the Great Depression.

What defeated the Lonigans and the O'Flahertys? This was the question that James T. Farrell sought to answer in a dozen novels. His theme, he explained, was that of "spiritual poverty." If Farrell had written *Studs Lonigan* as a story of the slums, "it would then have been easy for the reader falsely to place the motivation and causation of the story directly in immediate economic roots. Such a placing of motivation would have obscured one of the most important meanings I wanted to inculcate into my story: my desire to reveal the concrete effects of spiritual poverty." [44]

IV

The world of Fifty-eighth Street, where Studs Lonigan and Danny O'Neill spent their formative years was a world centered

---

[42] *Ibid.*, 23.   [43] *Ibid.*, 24.
[44] James T. Farrell, "How Studs Lonigan Was Written," *The League of the Frightened Philistines and Other Papers* (New York: Vanguard Press, 1945), 86.

around the Roman Catholic Church. The Lonigans and the O'Flahertys never doubted that their first responsibility was to send their children to Catholic schools. On the occasion of Studs's graduation from St. Patrick's parochial school, portly Father Gilhooley extolled the benefits of Catholic education. He spoke touchingly of the nuns, "the modest, self-sacrificing, holy virgins who had pointed out the path of salvation for the children of St. Patrick's parish." He praised the parents "who had possessed the courage, the conscience and the faith to give their children a Catholic schooling." He contrasted them with "those careless, miserly and irreligious fathers and mothers who dealt so lightly with the

For what he had seen, for what he had been, for what he learned of these agonies, these failures, these frustrations, these lacerations, there would never be forgiveness in his heart.   James T. Farrell, *My Days of Anger*

souls of the little ones Gawd had entrusted in their care that they sent them to public schools, where the word of Gawd is not uttered from the beginning to the end of the livelong day." [45] He warned the parents about the future education of their children. They must send them to Catholic high schools.

At the Lonigan apartment after the graduation, Studs's parents exchanged felicitation with the Reilleys. The two couples rejoiced that they were Catholics. "And isn't the Catholic Church the grand thing?" Mrs. Reilley continued to ask, and the Lonigans each time agreed. "And isn't it the truth," Mrs. Reilley rattled on, "that a mother never need worry when she sends her byes and girls to the good sisters, the holy virgins." [46]

Yet the saintly nuns could not really provide envelopes of purity for the children. Catholic boys and girls were just as curious about forbidden topics as non-Catholic children were. Even while the adult Lonigans and Reilleys were complacently chatting over their ice cream in the dining room, the guests of honor, the graduating eighth graders, were elsewhere in the apartment, taking advantage of a childish game of Post Office to explore each others' bodies. "Take your hand off there," one girl whispered, "or I'll scream." [47] After the guests left, Studs found himself tortured by adolescent yearnings for his own sister. "Kneeling down at his bedside, he tried to make a perfect act of contrition to wash his soul from sin." [48]

The youngsters of Fifty-eighth Street did not always respect the priests and nuns. Studs and his friends called Sister Bertha, who taught them in the eighth grade, Battleax Bertha. " 'Well, Bertha always gave me a pain right here,' Weary said, pointing to the proper part of his anatomy." And of "Gilly," the parish priest Studs said: "He's always asking for the shekels. He's as bad as a kike." [49]

Yet the Church had a powerful hold upon them. The boys felt it important to go to confession and take communion before doing anything dangerous. "I'd never think of playing football without receiving communion. You never know what's going to happen to you in a Prairie football game like that one we've got scheduled tomorrow. And I always play safe." [50]

[45] *Studs Lonigan,* 30. [46] *Ibid.,* 44. [47] *Ibid.,* 49.
[48] *Ibid.,* 54. [49] *Ibid.,* 39. [50] *Ibid.,* 227.

The youthful Catholics felt themselves pulled first one way and then another in a rough tug-of-war between religious obligations and worldly temptations. Studs found it hard to keep his mind off girls while preparing himself for communion. "He hadn't thought of having these thoughts or willed them. They had just snuck up on him. He couldn't keep his eyes off the girl. He wanted to swear, do something. And he had to keep himself in the state of grace all day tomorrow, until Sunday morning." With difficulty he kept himself pure. "Studs went to the altar rail with a free conscience. He had gone to confession again on Saturday, even though everybody had kidded him. He was certain that he was in a state of grace, after the thoughts he'd had Friday night." But the state of grace was short-lived. That evening Studs and his friends got drunk. "They hung around until Slug talked them into going to a new can house, a small place. They went and had the girlies, and gypped them out of their pay. It was a big night." [51]

The Catholic boys of Fifty-eighth Street had no illusions about their own saintliness, but they continued to believe that Catholic girls were purer than the rest of the world. At the age of fourteen, Studs "guessed there was something in Catholic girls that made them different from other girls." [52] Ten years later Studs and his friends were still clinging to this idea. Rebuking the cynical assumption that any girl might be made if the right guy came along at the right moment, Red Kelly said: "No sir, you get a good Catholic girl, who has a decent home, the right kind of parents, and fear of God in her, like Studs's sisters, and they're decent, they're fine, they're amongst the finest things you can find in life." In the unlikely event that the Catholic girl did start to slip, Red explained, there were only two things to do. "The old man to give her his razor strap, and the old man or brother or somebody to give the clouts to the guys that try and fool around with her." [53]

Sinner though he was, Studs remained loyal to Catholicism. When he was initiated into the Order of Christopher, he felt strong emotions. "Seeing that, being one of those in it, he had been proud of his Church, proud to be entering an order of men so closely connected with the Church. Remembering his catechism from grammar school, he told himself that the Church was One, Holy, Catho-

[51] *Ibid.*, 400–401.   [52] *Ibid.*, 84.   [53] *Ibid.*, 375.

lic, and Apostolic, built upon the rock of Peter, and that it would last until Judgment Day. Yes, he was glad, damn glad, that he had been born on the right side of the fence." [54]

From time to time, there would be a preaching mission in St. Patrick's Church, to revive the sagging fervor of the faithful. Father Shannon, who conducted the mission in 1927, was a preacher with extraordinary gifts. He delighted the parishioners with sharp sallies of Irish wit and soaring flights of Irish eloquence. He labored to build Catholic defenses against all the worldly threats of the 1920's. He warned, "today there are afoot movements started by vicious men and women who philander with the souls of youth in order that they will receive their paltry profit, and their cheap, ephemeral notoriety. I refer to such movements as jazz, atheism, free-love, companionate marriage, birth-control. These, and similarly miscalled tendencies, are murdering the souls of youth (he slapped his hand on the pulpit)." [55]

Father Shannon poured out the vials of righteous wrath on Sinclair Lewis and *Elmer Gantry* ("a book that belongs in no decent household, a book that no self-respecting Catholic can read under the pain of sin, a book that should be burned in a garbage heap"), on Judge Ben Lindsay and the idea of Companionate Marriage ("This little man, this human atom, this intellectual midget, what does he preach—at a profit . . . ? I'll tell you in straight language without any fake pretense of those abused words, liberality and tolerance. In simple words this human rat, like the anarchistic, atheistic Bolsheviks in unhappy Russia, says . . . 'Away with the holy bonds of Matrimony!' "), on H. L. Mencken ("a noisy, vociferous, and half-baked little man"), and on H. G. Wells ("the biggest windbag of them all"). Father Shannon warned that the universities, "miscalled seats of learning, temples of truth," were full of enemies to the faith. He left no doubt that he was referring particularly to the University of Chicago. He told the story of a girl who had come to him for advice on whether she should read certain books assigned to her.

I told her what to do. I told her what every Catholic student should say in such circumstances. I told her to take the books back to her professor

[54] *Ibid.,* 526.   [55] *Ibid.,* 388.

and say that Father said she should tell him this: "I am a Catholic. I will
not read these books and endanger my holy faith. They are full of half-
truths, paradoxes, lies, and the men who wrote them are either ignorant
or else they are liars. You must put a stop to this sort of thing. You must
stick to what you know, to the limited field which you have studied, and
stop talking about or recommending books on morals and theology, because you are ignorant and biased." That is what every Catholic student
in a godless university should do.[56]

Although Father Shannon also condemned the familiar sins of
drunkenness and fornication, Studs Lonigan and his cronies applied the sermon more to other people than to themselves. They
were particularly edified to have the priest hand it out to "those
people who think they are too good for the human race like Young
O'Neill who goes to the University." [57] But Father Shannon's impact on Danny himself was far different. When he asked the priest
if he could talk to him, because he was a university student who had
lost his religion, Father Shannon replied that he was very busy.
"The incident had crystallized many things in Danny's mind. It
had made him feel that it was not merely ignorance and supersti-
tion. It was perhaps not merely a vested interest. It was a downright
hatred of truth and honesty. He conceived the world, the environment he had known all his life, as lies. He realized that all his education in Catholic schools, all he had heard and absorbed, had been
lies." [58]

In his bitterness Danny O'Neill probably blamed the Church
too much. Seeking to escape from the constricting environment, he
fed greedily on the ideas that he found in the books of Omar Khay-
yam, Algernon Swinburne, Walter Pater, Sinclair Lewis, and
Thorstein Veblen—all pagan writers in the eyes of the Church. In
his struggle for liberation, Danny turned savagely against the institution that had tried to fence him in. He exulted in his discovery
that he was really an atheist. "How meaningless had been the influence of the nuns who had taught him in grammar school, the priests
who had been his high-school teachers! How painless it was to lose
your faith! There was no regret. No sense of loss. The only pain he
had felt was a sympathetic one for his uncle." [59]

---

[56] *Ibid.*, 389–91.   [57] *Ibid.*, 397.   [58] *Ibid.*, 402.
[59] James T. Farrell, *My Days of Anger*, (New York: Vanguard Press, 1943), 222.

Yet the nuns and priests had probably taught Danny more than he realized. The rebellious Danny O'Neill became the compassionate James T. Farrell, a man whose concern for moral values showed the influence of Catholic indoctrination.

V

More critical than the inability of the Church to retain its hold on independent young thinkers like Danny O'Neill was its failure to keep faithful Catholic youths like Studs Lonigan from destroying themselves. Studs and his friends were not rebels. They went unquestioningly to mass and confession. They never doubted that American political and economic institutions were the best in the world. They saluted the flag with sentimental fervor and vigorously damned the socialists and labor union leaders. But they were peculiarly vulnerable to the corrupting influences of the pool room, the speakeasy, and the brothel—instruments of Satan that the Church seemed powerless to combat.

Fourteen-year-old Studs Lonigan liked to hang around the pool room on Fifty-eighth Street. This establishment had barber poles in front, and its windows bore the scratched legend, Bathcellar's Billiard Parlor and Barber Shop. The young men of the neighborhood congregated here, lounging about the entrance and crowding the interior. Juvenile "punks" like Studs were not allowed to play, but they sometimes got inside. "The pool room was long and narrow; it was like a furnace, and its air was weighted with smoke. Three of the six tables were in use, and in the rear a group of lads sat around a card table, playing poker. The scene thrilled Studs, and he thought of the time he could come in and play pool and call Charley Bathcellar by his first name. He was elated as he washed his hands in the filthy lavatory." [60]

A few years later Studs enjoyed full privileges. By this time shoe shine stands had displaced the barber chairs, and a long-suffering Greek named George ran the establishment. Studs and his cronies played pool for fifty cent bets, but this petty gambling was a minor vice compared with the other deviltry in progress. The boys drank

[60] *Studs Lonigan*, 113.

bootleg liquor in the men's room and rough-housed over the pool tables. On one occasion they started throwing billiard balls at dim-witted Vince Curley. "Vince, blushing, misunderstanding, asked Kelley why he would do such a thing to a good friend of his; and they roared. George the Greek nearby went into a fit of apoplexy, sobbing about his business." [61]

The pool room was a school for vice, where the older and more hardened denizens boasted about their exploits while the younger boys listened. They commented on the girls who went past the window. " 'That's a better one,' said Lee, pointing to a girl whom everybody marveled at because they said she was built like a brick out-house." They bragged about how "soused" they had been the night before. They exchanged suggestions on what to do about slightly pregnant girl friends. " 'All I hope is that that dope starts her like nobody's business,' Wills Gillen said." And Darby Dan Drennan consoled him: "If it don't, I know a doctor. I fixed up Sadie Prevost with him when she was knocked up by all you guys. She's all right, only to raise the dough she had to go out and hustle. She did so well hustling that she's in the business for good now." [62]

But the adolescents who hung around the pool room were not hearing about sex for the first time. In the world of Fifty-eighth Street the years of innocence were soon over. When Danny O'Neill was only seven, his eleven-year-old brother Bill told him in crude but explicit detail how fathers and mothers made babies.[63] Danny received an even more exciting lesson from his younger sister. "How do you know Papa and Mama do that?" Danny demanded skeptically, and four-year-old Margaret replied: "I saw them in bed when they thought I was sleeping." [64] Since little Margaret had to sleep at the foot of her parents' bed in the crowded flat, her precocity was scarcely to be wondered at.

At the age of fourteen Studs Lonigan had his sexual initiation. His opportunity came when teen-aged Iris entertained the boys of the neighborhood while her mother was out. At this "gang shag" the boys shot craps for turns, and Iris took them all on except Davey Cohen to whom she objected because he was Jewish. After it was over, Studs was conscience-stricken. He was afraid that Iris would

---

[61] *Ibid.*, 269.   [62] *Ibid.*, 115.
[63] *A World I Never Made*, 124.   [64] *Ibid.*, 427.

snitch or that he would die and go to hell. "He tried to pray, promising the Blessed Virgin that he wouldn't never fall into sin like that again, and he'd go to confession, and after this he'd go once a month and make nine first Fridays." To make matters worse, Studs was disappointed with the whole thing: "it didn't scarcely last a minute, and it wasn't as much fun as making a clean, hard-flying tackle in a football game, or going swimming like that day he and Kenny had gone; a double chocolate soda had it skinned all hollow." [65]

Although there was little satisfaction in loveless sex, Studs and his cronies could not leave the women alone, particularly as they grew older. Occasionally they went as a group to some can house; other times they stalked their prey at dance halls or on the streets. The girls they picked up were often very young. What one of these didn't know at the age of fourteen, "wasn't worth knowing," Studs discovered. She was insatiable; "she wanted an army." [66] There was another girl barely sixteen whom Studs assumed to be a virgin. He felt like "a bastard" for what he did to her, but he learned how mistaken he had been when he contracted a venereal disease. He went looking for her to "crack her one in the teeth," but she evaded him.[67]

Girls who flirted with the boys of Fifty-eighth Street and then tried to say no were playing a dangerous game. At a wild New Year's Eve party, in 1929, Weary Reilley overcame his date's refusal with savage force. "He half smothered her scream. He stuck his knee in her stomach, and slapped her viciously with his left hand. "Oh you will, will you!" he said, punching her jaw after she again flashed her teeth. He carried her unconscious to the bed." [68]

The temptations of the flesh took many forms. At the age of fourteen, Studs Lonigan detected something unnatural in the girlish behavior of the neighborhood music teacher. "He wondered why Leon was always placing his hands on a guy." [69] Bill O'Neill was even younger when he encountered men of this type. Coming out of the movies at the age of eleven, Bill was perplexed. "He felt funny. The man next to him grabbing at his pants that way. He knew that kids at school tried to stick their hands up under a girl's

[65] *Studs Lonigan*, 141–43.   [66] *Ibid.*, 206.
[67] *Ibid.*, 335, 348.   [68] *Ibid.*, 429.   [69] *Ibid.*, 60.

dress, and he tried it on Polack Mary once, and she had nearly scratched him for doing it . . . But he couldn't see why a man should try and do that to a kid. It had sent shivers running up and down his back." [70]

The wages of sin were all too literally death. Asked what was wrong with Paulie Haggerty, one of his friends explained: "every goddamn thing. Clap, gonorrheal rheumatism, his heart is shot, his lungs are gone, and he has ulcers of the stomach. The guy has just drunk and jazzed himself to death." [71]

The Irish of Chicago's South Side—or some of them, at least—had always had a weakness for the bottle. Jim O'Neill and Paddy Lonigan were occasionally drunk; Margaret O'Flaherty was frequently so. But the drinking of Prohibition days was more destructive than earlier drinking had been. Paddy Lonigan worried about Studs. The stuff that young people drank nowadays was "rat poison, that killed people like flies. If the young fellows kept up drinking stuff like that, they'd all be dead by the time they were twenty-five or thirty." [72] Studs himself acknowledged the danger in what he was doing. "A wave of self-disgust swept through him. It wasn't worth it. The stuff was generally strong enough to corrode a cast-iron gut. It was canned heat, rot-gut, furniture varnish, rat poison. When you drank it, you took your life in your hands, and even if it didn't kill you, it might make you blind, or put your heart, liver, guts or kidneys on the fritz for life." [73]

At the Cannonball Inn, a combination speakeasy and brothel where Studs Lonigan and his friends spent Christmas Eve in 1922, they asked the bouncer to let them look in on the worst drunks writhing in delirium in a secluded chamber. When their guide opened the door and snapped on the lights, "they saw a bare room where drunks were crowded all over the floor." One was snoring with open mouth in a corner; others rolled on the floor and raved. A thin guy was crawling over the others complaining because his feet wouldn't behave. A blonde boy, about eighteen, fell on his knees before them and begged to be saved from the snakes. "It was funny. He arose, clapped his hands to

[70] *A World I Never Made,* 224.   [71] *Studs Lonigan,* 216.
[72] *Ibid.,* 279.   [73] *Ibid.,* 292.

his ears, and yelled. He fell before the bouncer, and repeated his entreaties to be saved from the snakes; pointing dramatically in back of them. He crawled to the wall, still shrieking. The bouncer jerked out a blackjack and neatly put him to sleep." [74]

The boys from Fifty-eighth Street felt nothing but contempt for these wretched men, but they themselves were destined to end in piteous condition. On the train back to Chicago, after attending Shrimp Haggerty's funeral, the mourners philosophized over the sad event. " 'Poor Shrimp. He drunk himself under the sod. He was an alcohol fiend,' Les said." Though still in their late twenties or early thirties, many of the old gang were already dead. " 'Arnold Sheehan, the Haggertys and Tommy, Hink Webber who killed himself in the nut house. Slugs Mason beating the Federal Government Prohibition rap by dying of pneumonia, all our old pals. Lord have money on their souls. Here today and gone tomorrow, nobody ever spoke truer words,' Red said." Only for Weary Reilley did the boys have no sympathy. He deserved his ten years' term in the penitentiary. " 'That poor girl he raped at our New Year's eve party is paralyzed for life. Reilley was one first hand skunk,' Red said vindictively." [75]

Studs Lonigan had his own bitter memories of the notorious New Year's Eve party. It had been the ruin of him. "Weary Reilley pasting him when he was drunk, and then someone ditching him, letting him lay in the gutter and catch pneumonia." [76] Studs came out of the ordeal with a damaged heart that doomed him to early death in a second bout with pneumonia a few years later.

Danny O'Neill escaped the deadlier pitfalls of the neighborhood, but he had his moments of peril. After a night of drinking bootleg liquor with his high school fraternity brothers, he woke up in the hospital. One of his friends explained to him what had happened: "we had to take you. We thought you were gonna die. We took you to a restaurant and tried to feed you tomatoes and black coffee and it didn't do any good. You were vomiting and even coughing up blood. Christ, I was scared, Dan. I didn't know what to do, so I took you there. They pumped your stomach out." [77]

---

[74] *Ibid.*, 273.   [75] *Ibid.*, 439–40.   [76] *Ibid.*, 442.
[77] *Father and Son*, 467.

VI

Chicago's Irish hated and feared other groups. Despite her own poverty, Lizz O'Neill felt superior to her slum neighbors. She was second-generation—and therefore American— and they were not. "But, Mother," she complained, "I want to move and get out of this dump, and this dirty neighborhood. It's full of Germans, and Mother, never trust a German. . . . And there are Irish, and Polacks, and the dirty dagoes around, too, and Mother, I am a white woman! I'm a white woman, and I come from a fine family. Your father and mother owned land in Ireland, and they were the descendants of kings of Ireland." [78]

Whenever one of her brood got into trouble, Lizz took it for granted that clan loyalties would tip the scales of justice. In pre-World War I days, she placed her confidence in Irish policemen, Irish lawyers, and Irish judges. After a wagon driven by an Italian had run down her truant son, she looked forward with relish to the law suit. "When I go before the judge, I'll say to him, 'Judge, I was born in this country, and I'm an American. My mother came over here before Lincoln was shot. Judge, are you going to let a dago run over an American child in broad daylight and get away with it?' " Explaining her point still more forcefully, she said: "We Americans make laws for Americans, not for the wops." [79]

But the neighbors to whom Lizz objected most were the Negroes. " 'I'm a white woman, descended from kings of Ireland,' Lizz said, brandishing her arms, 'and I have to live with niggers in back of me, using the same toilet with us. My children can't go out in the back yard and play without smelling pickaninnies. I'm going to move out of this dump!' " [80]

Slum children picked up all the prejudices of their parents. Gangs of white boys crossed the railroad tracks to invade the Negro section. They fought with rocks, knives, razors, and whatever other weapons they could find. After one foray a tough white youngster boasted: "Hell, Mickey Galligan damn near druve a spike through one black bastard's eye. I wished he did get the eye instead of the

---

[78] *A World I Never Made,* 61.   [79] *Ibid.,* 305.   [80] *Ibid.,* 62.

cheek. Anything you do to a nigger is all right. Even my old man doesn't whale me when he knows I was fightin' with the blacks." [81]

During World War I days, there were no Negroes in the Fifty-eighth Street neighborhood, but the middle-class Irish complained of the encroaching Jews. Old Man O'Brian blamed the Jews for spoiling all the sports except baseball. "The kikes dirty up everything. I say the kikes ain't square. There never was a white Jew, or a Jew that wasn't yellow. And there'll never be one. Why, they even killed their own God." He lamented because the newcomers were spoiling the neighborhood. "We got them on our block. I even got one next door to me. I'd never have bought my property if I knew I'd have to live next door to that Jew, Glass's his name." [82]

Studs and his cronies beat up the Jewish boys for fun. They invaded the Jewish section looking for victims. They dragged two "hooknoses" down an alley and challenged them to battle. " 'Take that for killin' Christ,' said Benny." One of the Jews managed to run away, but the other was less fortunate. "They gave the guy the clouts, and left him moaning in the alley." [83] Ironically, one of the bullies was Davey Cohen, a Jewish boy who was trying desperately to pass as one of the gang. He didn't like fighting but what was he to do? "When he went with the guys smacking Jews, he sometimes got so sick he felt as if he'd puke. He didn't like it. He put himself off as a battler, and talked big and hard only because he had to. If you went around with the Irish and didn't make yourself out a scrapper, you had one hell of a time." [84] But Davey's false toughness didn't prevent his exclusion from the shag party at Iris's house, and he was bitter about this evidence of prejudice. "The goddamn Irish! Goddamn'em! Goddamn Studs Lonigan and the whole race of 'em. They got everything and deserved nothing. They were thickheaded. The dumbest Jew was smarter than the smartest Irishman. Well, some day." [85]

The Irish found it convenient to blame the Jews for any unwelcome social trend. The dynamics of urban change were pushing Chicago's Negroes farther and farther into hitherto all-white neighborhoods. As an intelligent radical tried to explain to "the

[81] *Ibid.*, 218.   [82] *Studs Lonigan*, 79.
[83] *Ibid.*, 130–31.   [84] *Ibid.*, 135.   [85] *Ibid.*, 137.

Bug Club" in Washington Park, the city could be divided into three concentric circles. The innermost circle contained the principal stores, offices, and commercial houses; the second ring housed factories, warehouses, slum tenements, brothels, and other dives; the outermost circle included the residential districts. The busy city grew at the center; as this pushed outward, it caused corresponding changes in the other concentric circles. "All these factors produced a pressure stronger than individual wills, and resulted in a minor racial migration of Negroes into the white residential districts of the south side. Blather couldn't halt the process. Neither could violence and race riots. It was an inevitable outgrowth of social and economic forces." [86] But the Irish insisted on blaming the Jews who were buying real estate and selling it to the Negroes. " 'Well, I tell you, once the kikes get into a neighborhood, it's all over,' said Red with unanswerable argument." [87] Lizz O'Neill wrapped up all her racial prejudices in one neat and convenient package: "Mother, you can never trust a nigger or a Jew. The Jews killed Christ, and the nigger is a Jew made black till the Day of Judgment as a punishment from God." [88]

When the Negroes ventured into sanctuaries that the whites claimed as their own, the Irish youths sometimes resorted to violence. Seeing two Negroes in Washington Park, Studs wished that his cronies would put in an appearance. "If the guys had come, they could have ganged the dinges. Niggers didn't have any right in a white man's park, and the sooner they were taught that they didn't, the better off they'd be." [89] Angered by the news that Negroes had killed a white boy during the race riots of 1919, Studs armed himself with a baseball bat, and the other fellows carried clubs, knives, and revolvers. "Studs said they ought to hang every nigger in the city to the telephone poles, and let them swing there in the breeze." But the only Negro they captured was a ten-year old boy. "They took his clothes off, and burned them. They burned his tail with lighted matches, made him step on lighted matches, urinated on him, and sent him running off naked with a couple of slaps in the face." [90] On other occasions they hazed the Negroes in a more amiable spirit. Drunk on jamaica ginger one evening,

[86] *Ibid.,* 364. [87] *Ibid.,* 376. [88] *A World I Never Made,* 60.
[89] *Studs Lonigan,* 183. [90] *Ibid.,* 201.

they had fun with a passing Negro hot-tamale man. "They slugged him and took the wagon. Red wheeled it and they marched down the street toward the park. They each had a hot tamale and debated what to do with the rest. Red caught a passing shine. They tossed him into the fountain by the curve in the boat-house path. He struggled to get out of the slippery fountain, and was shoved back, and pelted as long as they had hot tamales." [91]

Real Negroes were people to be hated and harassed, but black-faced whites acting out comedy skits on the radio were lovable characters. Paddy Lonigan's belly rolled with laughter as he told Studs about the latest Amos and Andy show. "They're so much like darkies. Not the fresh northern niggers, but the genuine real southern darkies, the good niggers. They got them down to a *T*, lazy, happy-go-lucky, strutting themselves out in titles and with long names and honors, just like in real life." [92]

Relentlessly the Negro tide moved closer to the Fifty-eighth Street neighborhood. The Irish hoped that the construction of a magnificent new church would stabilize the situation and halt the flight of the whites. But this did not happen. On the day in 1926, when the new building was consecrated, "four new and totally edified parishioners" stood at the rear of the church. "Their skin was black." [93] A year later, the Negroes were moving in rapidly, and Studs and his friends criticized Father Gilhooley for not doing anything to stop it. "If we had a pastor like Father Shannon, instead of Gilly that mightn't have happened. He wouldn't be the kind to build a beautiful new church, and then let his parish go to the dogs. He'd have seen to it that the good parishioners stayed, and that the niggers were kept out. He'd have organized things like vigilance committees to prevent it." [94]

In 1928, the Lonigans gave up and moved. The younger members of the family were happy to be leaving, but their parents were sorrowful. Paddy mourned that no home would be like this one had been. They had raised their children and spent the best years of their lives there. "Goddamn those niggers!" he fumed. And Studs offered the only comfort he could think of: "I guess it was the Jew real-estate dealers who did it." [95]

[91] *Ibid.*, 366. [92] *Ibid.*, 503. [93] *Ibid.*, 367.
[94] *Ibid.*, 385–86. [95] *Ibid.*, 405.

VII

The Irish prided themselves on their 100 per cent Americanism. They defended the nation's economic system as fervently as
they did its political institutions. Listening to radicals spout their
unorthodox ideas in Washington Park, Studs and his cronies were
bewildered and annoyed. When a Greek waiter at one of their hang-
outs criticized priests, politicians, and bankers, the gang was
indignant. They succeeded in getting the waiter fired. " 'I saw
Gus last night. He gave that radical bastard his pay when he came
down tonight, and he's through. There's a new man in there. I told
Mike we'd boycott the place, and that, if that wasn't enough, wreck
that bastard,' Red said." [96]

This faith in the eternal rightness of American institutions extended to a confidence that the price of common stocks would go
up forever. Like so many other Americans of the 1920's, the Irish
dreamed of gaining sudden wealth through the miracles of Wall
Street. Studs Lonigan invested most of his savings in Imbray Securities, acting on an inside tip. Solomon Imbray—by whom Farrell obviously meant Samuel Insull—was regarded with awe as a
financial wizard. "You know what's behind these stocks?" asked
Studs's friend, "Well, I'll tell you. All, or nearly all, the public util-
ities of the Middle West and the brains of a man like Solomon Imbray. What more security could you want?" [97]

But the price of Studs' stock kept falling, and he couldn't decide whether to take his loss or wait for a rise. Studs's tipster-friend
was in an even worse situation because he was still buying the stock
on an employee-stock agreement plan, at twice its market price. But
he refused to worry: "I got faith because I know you can't go wrong
on Imbray stock, and some day I know it's going to set me up sweet
and pretty on Easy Street." [98] So Studs held on and lost almost
everything.

Studs's father was caught even more cruelly. He had bought
heavily on margin and was ruined by the repeated calls of his

[96] *Ibid.*, 399.   [97] *Ibid.*, 468.   [98] *Ibid.*, 554.

broker. These losses in the stock market were matched by other disasters. Paddy's painting business had been largely dependent upon political pull and collapsed under the conditions of the depression. The city of Chicago was almost bankrupt, and the Irish no longer monopolized the few contracts that were still available. Paddy reported to Studs that one of his Irish political friends did nothing but cry all the time he saw him. "He was crying about the Polacks and the Bohunks. He says that they just almost cleaned out the Irish. He kept saying to me, "Paddy, if you want to get anything down at the Hall, you better put a *sky* on your name before you go down there.' " [99]

Paddy's real estate investments also failed. His depression-harassed tenants kept missing their rent payments, and it became increasingly difficult to hold on to his apartment building. On a black day in 1932—the very day when Studs came home mortally ill—Paddy's bank failed, and the old man lost the money he needed for his mortgage payment.

Despite their economic reverses, the Lonigans felt no temptation to listen to the blandishments of the Communists. Studs rebuffed a bitter unemployed man who was talking in terms of revolution. "I'm not a Bolshevik. It's against the country and the church." [100] And Paddy Lonigan shook his head in disbelief when he saw Irishmen marching in a Communist demonstration.

Paddy had his own ideas about what was wrong with the country. He blamed Hoover, of course; but beyond the President, he saw the sinister machinations of alien forces. He listened eagerly to the radio talks of Father Moylan (Farrell's name for Father Coughlin). Paddy told Studs: "He's one of the finest and smartest men in America, and he tells the people what's what. He lays into the bankers, too, and by God, they've got it coming to them." [101]

Lonigan could not see why so many troubles had come to him. He was a man who had always done his duty. "Hadn't he always provided for his family to the best of his abilities, tried to be a good husband and a good father, a true Catholic, and a real American?" And now Studs, his favorite son, was dying. "And he and Mary, after all their work and struggle, must come to such misery in their old

[99] *Ibid.*, 650.   [100] *Ibid.*, 562.   [101] *Ibid.*, 652.

age, be reduced almost to the state of paupers. It wasn't right. It wasn't fair. He had done nothing to merit this punishment. Why, why was it?" [102]

Once again, it was the Jews who had to take the blame. The "Jew international-bankers" were greedy for profits and didn't want America to collect its just debts from Europe. This was the reason for the depression. "And hadn't that radio priest, Father Moylan from the Shrine of The Little Rose of Jesus Christ, told the bankers where to get off at?" The Jews, Paddy grumbled, "queered everything they put their hands on." They had ruined the Fifty-eighth Street neighborhood by buying property and selling to the Negroes, forcing the Irish and the other white people to clear out. "Trickery, Jew trickery, had ruined this neighborhood. And the trickery of the Jew bankers was causing the depression and ruining him." [103]

In his hatred of Jews and Negroes, in his suspicion of fantastic conspiracy, Paddy Lonigan betrayed the spiritual poverty that James T. Farrell regarded as the real tragedy of Fifty-eighth Street. The true enemy was the narrow vision of the Irish themselves. Once again, Farrell speaks through the character of Danny O'Neill. As Danny prepared to leave Chicago to start a new life in New York, he resolved that "he would do battle so that others did not remain unfulfilled as he and his family had been. For what he had seen, for what he had been, for what he learned of these agonies, these failures, these frustrations, these lacerations, there would never be forgiveness in his heart. Everything that created these were his enemies." [104]

Did Farrell paint too black a picture of the neighborhood of his childhood? Probably yes. In later years he admitted that when he began to write he was "full of indignation because of the sorrows of this world." He was angry because of people's exploitativeness and coldness, "because of dirt, poverty, ignorance, aggressiveness, and the other things which ruin and sadden human lives." [105] In his anger he probably exaggerated the narrowness of Catholicism, the degeneracy of the streets and the pool rooms, the grubby materialism of the middle-class Irish. By so doing he pointed up the forces

---

[102] *Ibid.*, 735–36.   [103] *Ibid.*, 736.   [104] *My Days of Anger*, 401.
[105] "Reflections at Fifty," *Reflections at Fifty and Other Essays*, 61–62.

that destroyed Studs Lonigan and made the escape of Danny O'Neill miraculous.

In one of his essays, Farrell warns against the danger of confusing fiction with sociology. "The purpose of a novel, no matter how realistic it may be, is not that of being a literally true record of life. It is a re-creation, a concentrated image of what life is or may be like. It needs to be treated as such." Literature and sociology are different, he says, but "they can complement one another." [106] Certainly we may extend his statement to apply to the relations of literature and history. The Farrell novels may not provide a judiciously balanced picture of the American city during these years, but they provide the historian with a wealth of striking descriptions of the tendencies in family life, the conflicts of groups, and the forces of disintegration that would culminate in the urban problem of our own day.

[106] "Literature and Sociology," *ibid.*, 187.

9

The Volcano of Anger

He knew as he stood there that he could never tell why he
had killed. It was not that he did not really want to tell, but
the telling of it would have involved an explanation of his
entire life. The actual killing of Mary and Bessie was not
what concerned him most; it was knowing and feeling that he
could never make anybody know what had driven him to it.
His crimes were known, but what he had felt before he committed them would never be known.

RICHARD WRIGHT, *Native Son* [1]

THE ANGER that Bigger Thomas felt was the anger that
Richard Wright knew from his own experience. No more than
most American Negroes was Wright of pure African ancestry. The
harshly religious grandmother, who dominated the household in
which he was brought up, looked like a white woman. She came of
"Irish, Scotch, and French stock in which Negro blood had somewhere and somehow been infused." His father had Indian, white,
and Negro ancestry. "Then what am I?" Richard asked his
mother, and she mockingly replied: "They'll call you a colored
man when you grow up . . . Do you mind, Mr. Wright?" [2]

Actually, the percentage of red, white, and black blood in
Richard Wright's veins mattered not at all. What counted was that
he was born into the Negro world of Mississippi and experienced
all its cruelty and poverty, before he escaped to Chicago, only to
learn the bitter truth about that city's ghetto horrors.

[1] Richard Wright, *Native Son* (New York: Harper & Brothers, 1940), 261–62.
[2] Richard Wright, *Black Boy: A Record of Childhood and Youth* (New York:
Harper & Brothers, 1945), 43.

Wright's earliest memories were of living in a humble shack overlooking the Mississippi River near Natchez. From this rural environment, his parents moved to the city of Memphis, Tennessee, where they lived with their two children in a small tenement. Before Richard was six, his father deserted the family to go off with another woman. Until his mother could get a job Richard had very little to eat. "As the days slid past the image of my father became associated with my pangs of hunger, and whenever I felt hunger I thought of him with a deep biological bitterness." [3]

While their mother worked for meager wages, as a cook in white families, Richard and his brother ran the streets of Memphis, engaging in pastimes far from innocent. "I was a drunkard in my sixth year, before I had begun school. With a gang of children, I roamed the streets, begging pennies from passers-by, haunting the doors of saloons, wandering farther and farther away from home each day." [4] Ill and desperate, the mother placed the children in a Negro orphanage, a cheerless institution, where the boys were still hungry.

Redeemed from the orphanage, Richard and his brother accompanied their mother to Arkansas, where they lived for a time with relatives. In small Arkansas towns Richard became more aware of the frightening contacts between whites and Negroes. The morning after white ruffians murdered his uncle, to rob him of his profitable saloon, the rest of the family fled town without even trying to claim the body. Richard sensed the rising racial tensions of World War I days. "A dread of white people now came to live permanently in my feelings and imagination." [5] He participated eagerly in the stone-throwing wars between the white and Negro boys. "All the frightful descriptions we had heard about each other, all the violent expressions of hate and hostility that had seeped into us from our surroundings, came now to the surface to guide our actions." [6]

When Richard was twelve, he lost even the precarious security that his mother had tried to provide. She became a helpless paralytic, dependent upon relatives to care for her and the boys. After some unhappy attempts at other solutions to the problem, the

---

[3] *Ibid.,* 14.   [4] *Ibid.,* 19.   [5] *Ibid.,* 64.   [6] *Ibid.,* 72.

maternal grandmother took Richard and his mother into her home in Jackson, Mississippi.

Richard was already a rebel, but it was not for lack of discipline. One of his earliest memories was of being almost whipped to death by his terrified mother, after he had set the house on fire at the age of four.[7] From that time on, his mother, father, uncles, aunts, and school teachers all thrashed him whenever he violated their code of behavior. Nor did he lack for religious admonitions. His grandmother was a zealous Seventh Day Adventist, who wouldn't let him take jobs on Saturdays and imposed a stern Puritanical regime upon the family. Richard was repelled by this harsh faith.

Wright's relatives were respectable, hard-working people. Scarcely able to support themselves, they accepted with resignation the obligation to care for Richard's mother, his brother, and himself. Yet there was a grimness in the family environment that left its scars upon the boy. "After I had outlived the shocks of childhood, after the habit of reflection had been born in me," he wrote, "I used to mull over the strange absence of real kindness in Negroes, how unstable was our tenderness, how lacking in genuine passion we were, how void of great hope, how timid our joy, how bare our traditions, how hollow our memories, how lacking we were in those intangible sentiments that bind man to man, and how shallow was even our despair." Rather than being uninhibited children of nature, as whites liked to believe, the Negroes were actually confused, fearful, and uncertain. "Whenever I thought of the essential bleakness of black life in America, I knew that Negroes had never been allowed to catch the full spirit of Western civilization, that they lived somehow in it but not of it." [8]

By some miracle, the harsh environment neither crushed the boy's spirit nor made him a criminal. Under existing conditions in the South, where poorly-trained Negro teachers transmitted their pittance of knowledge to poorly-motivated Negro children, Wright's formal education was pathetically inadequate. He stayed in school through the ninth grade and graduated as valedictorian of his class. But his real education was in his own hands. A voracious reader of all kinds of books, he had already started writing stories while he was still a schoolboy.

[7] *Ibid.*, 6.   [8] *Ibid.*, 33.

Wright's keen intelligence and touchy independence made it difficult for him to hold a job. Most white employers demanded of their Negro employees a grinning deference that Wright found it difficult to simulate. On one job, white fellow-employees hazed him until he quit; on another carousing whites brained him with an empty whiskey bottle because he forgot to say "sir"; on a third a white watchman threatened him with a revolver because Wright showed his distaste for the watchman's fanny-slapping ways with the Negro maids. "I had begun coping with the white world too late," Wright wrote. "I could not make subservience an automatic part of my behavior." He could see how other Negroes adapted, how they "acted out the roles that the white race had mapped out for them." [9] These Negroes found an outlet for their frustrations in gambling, drinking, and wenching, but Wright could not settle for these shabby substitutes for real achievement.

Escape from the South became imperative, and eventually Wright was able to move northward. In order to get the necessary cash he stole from a white employer. For many Negroes such thefts were taken for granted; since the days of slavery Negroes had registered their silent protest against white exploitation by petty thievery. But Wright had prided himself on his honesty. Aboard a train speeding north he discovered tears on his cheeks. "In that moment I understood the pain that accompanied crime and I hoped that I would never have to feel it again. I never did feel it again, for I never stole again: and what kept me from it was the knowledge that, for me, crime carried its own punishment." [10]

The first lap of Wright's northward exodus took him only as far as Memphis, but two years later he and his aunt ventured to Chicago, found jobs, and sent for his mother and brother. Thus during the late 1920's the Wrights became part of that enlarging Black Belt which so alarmed the Lonigans and the O'Flahertys.

Even in Chicago a young Negro found it difficult to keep employed. Wright worked for brief stints as a porter in a Jewish delicatessen store, as a dishwasher in a North Side café, and as a temporary clerk in the post office. With the onset of the depression jobs became still harder to find. With his mother, aunt, and brother all ill at home, Wright wandered the streets looking for work. "Unem-

[9] *Ibid.,* 172.   [10] *Ibid.,* 181.

ployed men loitered in doorways with blank looks in their eyes, sat dejectedly on front steps in shabby clothing, congregated in sullen groups on street corners, and filled all the empty benches in the parks of Chicago's South Side." [11]

Wright finally took a position selling life insurance policies for Negro burial societies and collecting the weekly premiums. This gave him a sickening insight into how Negroes in Chicago lived in hundreds of "dingy flats filled with rickety furniture and ill-clad children." To Wright's disgust, the Negro insurance business depended on Negroes swindling other Negroes, taking advantage of their ignorance to sell them over-priced and trickily-worded policies. Many of the customers were females, and the agents knew how to capitalize on this situation. Wright himself had "a long tortured affair with one girl by paying her ten-cent premium each week." [12]

The deepening depression finally forced Wright onto relief. At first, he felt deep humiliation at making a public confession of his hunger. For hours he sat waiting at the relief station, resentful of the hungry people about him. But he slowly became conscious that something significant was going on. The waiting Negroes had at first very little to say to each other. Each was a troubled individual, somewhat fearful of the others and thinking only of his own problems; each was "staunch in that degree of Americanism that had been allowed him." Gradually their isolation broke down, and they began to talk and exchange experiences. Wright marveled at the blindness of the ruling classes in setting up relief machinery so potentially dangerous. "Had they understood what was happening, they would never have allowed millions of perplexed and defeated people to sit together for long hours and talk, for out of their talk was rising a new realization of life. And once this new conception of themselves had formed, no power on earth could alter it." For Wright himself the experience was an illumination. "The day I begged bread from the city officials was the day that showed me I was not alone in my loneliness; society had cast millions of others with me. But how could I be with them? How many understood

---

[11] Richard Wright, "The Man Who Came to Chicago," *Eight Men* (Cleveland: The World Publishing Co., 1961), 227.
[12] *Ibid.*, 228.

what was happening? My mind swam with questions that I could not answer." [13]

The relief officials eventually assigned Wright to a job as an orderly in a medical research institute in a large Chicago hospital. With three other Negroes he cleaned operating rooms and cared for the animals that were used for experimental purposes. During a brawl one wintry afternoon, two of his fellow-orderlies knocked over dozens of cages releasing their assorted inmates. The Negroes repaired the damage as best they could, putting rats, mice, guinea pigs, and rabbits back into the various receptacles. But which were the tubercular animals? which were the cancerous ones? which had been inoculated? which had not? In the segregated organization of the hospital, the white doctors had never bothered to explain their research to the lowly orderlies, and the Negroes were too much afraid for their jobs to tell what had happened. "I earned thirteen dollars a week," explained Wright, "and I had to support four people with it, and should I risk that thirteen dollars by acting idealistically?" In retrospect, Wright could only guess how many scientific hypotheses had been upset by this random scrambling of the experimental data. The episode was rich in symbolic meaning. "The hospital kept us four Negroes as though we were close kin to the animals we tended, huddled together down in the underworld corridors of the hospital, separated by a vast psychological distance from the significant processes of the rest of the hospital—just as America had kept us locked in the dark underworld of American life for three hundred years—and we had made our own code of ethics, values, loyalty." [14]

In the political climate of the 1930's, it was inevitable that the Communist Party would appeal to a Negro like Richard Wright, so highly intelligent and so resentful of the injustices of American society. "It was not the economics of Communism," he wrote, "nor the great power of trade unions, nor the excitement of underground politics that claimed me; my attention was caught by the similarity of the experiences of workers in other lands, by the possibility of uniting scattered but kindred peoples into a whole. It seemed to me that here at last, in the realm of revolutionary

[13] *Ibid.*, 234–35.   [14] *Ibid.*, 250.

expression, Negro experience could find a home, a functioning value and role." [15] Wright discovered, in the Communist movement, themes for his poems and short stories, outlets for publication, and comradeship with other artists and writers.

As a Negro in largely white organizations, Wright became at first unwittingly, later consciously, a tool of the Communists. He was elected executive secretary of the Chicago John Reed Club and signed a Communist Party membership card. He helped to make the club a useful front for Communist agitation.

Wright embraced the Communist gospel with fervor. Stalin's *Marxism and the National and Colonial Question* captivated him. He made "the first total emotional commitment" of his life when he read how the Soviet leaders had dealt with their nationality groups. "I had read how these forgotten folk had been encouraged to keep their old cultures, to see in their ancient customs meanings and satisfactions as deep as those contained in supposedly superior ways of living. And I had exclaimed to myself how different this was from the way in which Negroes were sneered at in America." [16]

Wright's eventual disillusionment with the Communist Party was equally inevitable. A man of his prickly independence had not escaped from dependency in the South only to become the complacent slave of an authoritarian party in the North. To be feared as an intellectual, when he had to earn his daily bread by cleaning streets at thirteen dollars a week, was obviously absurd, yet Wright found his fellow-Communists, both Negro and white, regarding him with suspicion because he wanted to write books. When he sought literary material in the early experience of other Negro Communists, he was feared as a police spy. When he opposed the Communists' cynical dissolution of the John Reed clubs, he was denounced as a "petty bourgeois degenerate," an "incipient Trotskyite," and accused of holding an "anti-leadership attitude" and "seraphim tendencies." [17] When he sought to avoid hack party assignments to protect his writing time, he was condemned for insubordination.

Wright tried to get out of the movement, but was told that "no

---

[15] Chapter by Richard Wright in Richard Crossman, ed., *The God That Failed* (New York: Harper & Brothers, 1949), 118.
[16] *Ibid.*, 130.   [17] *Ibid.*, 140–41.

one can resign from the Communist Party." [18] One could only be expelled in disgrace. Wright and the party leaders carried on a cold war. Wright stopped attending party functions; the leaders punished him in a variety of ways. During periods of work for the Federal Negro Theater, the Writers' Project, and other WPA agencies, he found himself shunned by many of his associates and frustrated in his projects. He suffered a final indignity when he was roughly ejected from a May Day parade. "The rows of white and black Communists were looking at me with cold eyes of nonrecognition. I could not quite believe what had happened, even though my hands were smarting and bleeding. I had suffered a public, physical assault by two white Communists with black Communists looking on." [19]

Wright's quarrel was with the party, not with the ideology. "I wanted to be a Communist," he wrote, "but my kind of Communist. I wanted to shape people's feelings, awaken their hearts." [20] When this proved impossible, he felt deep grief. He knew that he "should never be able to feel with that simple sharpness about life, should never again express such passionate hope, should never again make so total a commitment of faith." Heading home after being thrown out of the May Day parade, he felt "alone, really alone," telling himself "that in all the sprawling immensity of our mighty continent the least-known factor of living was the human heart, the least-sought goal of being was a way to live a human life." [21]

Wright's political education was bitter, but his knowledge of the Chicago Black Belt was increasing all the while. He had, he said, been in "three-fourths of the Negroes' homes on the South Side," peddling insurance or doing other errands. The relief agency had placed him in a job at the South Side Boys' Club, and he found it an engrossing experience to work with Negro boys between eight and twenty-five. "They were a wild and homeless lot, culturally lost, spiritually disinherited, candidates for the clinics, morgues, prisons, reformatories, and the electric chair of the state's death house." [22] For hours, Wright listened to their talk of planes, women, guns, politics, and crime. He kept pencil and paper in his

[18] *Ibid.*, 149.   [19] *Ibid.*, 161.   [20] *Ibid.*, 145–46.   [21] *Ibid.*, 162.   [22] *Ibid.*, 134.

pocket to jot down their colorful figures of speech. Out of the anger of these Negro boys, and out of his own anger, Richard Wright wrote *Native Son* (1940).

II

On the last page of *Native Son*, Bigger Thomas says good-bye to Boris Max, his Jewish lawyer, one of the few human beings who has ever tried to befriend him. In a few minutes the attendants will conduct him to the death chamber and the executioner will throw the switch that will bring Bigger's twisted life to an end.

Technically there has been a miscarriage of justice. The court has imposed the death penalty for a homicide in which there was no malice aforethought or accompanying crime. Putting to bed Mary Dalton, the drunken daughter of his new employer, Bigger had pressed a pillow into her face to keep her quiet, when her blind mother unexpectedly entered the room. He had not raped her, as the State alleged. Nor was Bigger's subsequent conduct the confession of guilt that it seemed. Having suffocated the girl unintentionally, he cut off her head and stuffed her body into the furnace because of panicky fear.

Yet Bigger's innocence was itself an accident. As Richard Wright makes clear, Bigger was at heart a murderer. After the deed was done, he felt exultation rather than remorse. During his attempt to escape, he killed Bessie, his Negro girl friend, in cold blood. As Max explained to the judge: "This Negro boy's entire attitude toward life is a *crime!* The hate and fear which we have inspired in him, woven by our civilization into the very structure of his consciousness, into his blood and bones, into the hourly functioning of his personality, have become the justification of his existence." [23]

Bigger Thomas was the youth that Richard Wright might have become if he had not saved himself. Like Wright, Bigger had passed his boyhood in Jackson, Mississippi. His father had been killed during a riot, and his mother—a hard working, hymn-singing

[23] *Native Son*, 335.

woman like Wright's mother—had brought up the family as best she could. They had moved from Mississippi to South Side Chicago when Bigger was fifteen.

Bigger's troubles with the law had begun at an early age. In the unfriendly description of a Mississippi newspaper editor: "Thomas comes of a poor darky family of a shiftless and immoral variety. He was raised here and is known to local residents as an irreformable sneak thief and liar. We were unable to send him to the chain gang because of his extreme youth." [24] Bigger had been accused of stealing tires and sent to a Southern reform school. He hadn't really done anything wrong, he claimed; he had been with some boys and the police had picked them up.[25]

Bigger quit school in the eighth grade because he had no money. In trying to earn a living, he suffered the frustration that Richard Wright knew so well from his own experience. "You get a little job here and a little job there. You shine shoes, sweep streets; anything. . . . You don't make enough to live on. You don't know when you going to get fired. Pretty soon you get so you can't hope for nothing." [26]

The Thomases lived in a single rat-infested room. Even during the depression, empty flats were scarce in the Black Belt. Whenever Bigger's mother wanted to move she had to put in her request many weeks in advance. She once made Bigger tramp the streets for two months looking for a place to live. "The rental agencies had told him that there were not enough houses for Negroes to live in, that the city was condemning houses in which Negroes lived as being too old and too dangerous for habitation." He remembered the time when the police had driven his family out of a building that had collapsed two days later. Bigger had heard it said "that black people, even though they could not get good jobs, paid twice as much rent as whites for the same kinds of flats." [27] He knew that Negroes could not find tenements outside the Black Belt; they had to live on their side of the "line." No white real estate man would rent a flat to a Negro in any section other than that which had been condemned to their use. Most of the houses in the Black Belt were "ornate, old, stinking; homes once of rich white people, now inhab-

[24] *Ibid.*, 239.   [25] *Ibid.*, 43.   [26] *Ibid.*, 299.   [27] *Ibid.*, 210.

That was the way most houses on the South Side were, ornate, old, stinking; homes once of rich white people, now inhabited by Negroes . . .
Richard Wright, *Native Son*

ited by Negroes or standing dark and empty with yawning black windows." [28]

The parents of the white girl slain by Bigger Thomas thought of themselves as friends of the Negro race. They gave millions of dollars to Negro schools; they were supporters of the National Association for the Advancement of Colored People; they treated their Negro chauffeurs generously. Yet Henry Dalton was one of the landlords who kept the Chicago Negroes penned in the ghetto. Dalton owned the South Side Real Estate Company, and the South Side Real Estate Company owned the house where the

[28] *Ibid.*, 155.

Thomases paid eight dollars a week for one shabby room. "Even though Mr. Dalton gave millions of dollars for Negro education, he would rent houses to Negroes only in this prescribed area, this corner of the city tumbling down from rot." [29]

There could be little privacy for four people living in a single room, but the Thomas family respected a code of decency. "The two boys kept their faces averted while their mother and sister put on enough clothes to keep them from feeling ashamed; and the

[29] *Ibid.*, 148.

Even though Mr. Dalton gave millions of dollars for Negro education, he would rent houses to Negroes only in this prescribed area, this corner of the city tumbling down from rot.   Richard Wright, *Native Son*

mother and sister did the same while the boys dressed." [30] An un-
easy tension was inevitable. When Bigger absent-mindedly looked
at his sister at an inopportune moment, she hysterically threw her
shoe at him and accused him of trying to look under her skirt.[31]

These pathetic efforts at modesty were largely futile. Slum
children learned about sex through raw experience. Holed up in
an empty apartment house during his flight, Bigger could look
through shadeless windows into a nearby tenement. In the morning sunlight, he could see three naked Negro children sitting on a
bed, watching a man and a woman, both naked, who lay on another
bed. "There were quick, jerky movements on the bed where the
man and woman lay, and the three children were watching. It was
familiar; he had seen things like that when he was a little boy sleeping five in a room. Many mornings he had awakened and watched
his father and mother." [32]

To the women, the rodents who gorged on garbage and invaded
the tenement were a special terror. Mrs. Thomas and Vera climbed
onto a bed and clung to each other in hysterical fright while Bigger
and Buddy chased a foot-long rat around the room, finally killing
him with an iron skillet. "The two brothers stood over the dead rat
and spoke in terms of awed admiration. 'Gee, but he's a big bastard.'
'That sonofabitch could cut your throat.' " [33]

In pleading for Bigger in the court room, Boris Max used a provocative argument. To send this Negro to prison instead of the
electric chair would not be merely to spare his life, but to confer life
upon him. He would be brought for the first time within the orbit
of American civilization. "The very building in which he would
spend the rest of his natural life would be the best he has ever
known. Sending him to prison would be the first recognition of his
personality he has ever had. . . . The other inmates would be the
first men with whom he could associate on a basis of equality." [34]

Institutionalized virtue could not touch boys like Bigger. One
of Henry Dalton's deeds of kindness had been to give a dozen ping-
pong tables to the South Side Boys' Club; but Bigger asked bitterly,
"What the hell can a guy do with ping-pong?" When Lawyer Max
asked him if the Boys' Club kept him out of trouble, Bigger replied:

[30] Ibid., 3–4.   [31] Ibid., 88.   [32] Ibid., 209.   [33] Ibid., 6.   [34] Ibid., 338.

"Kept me out of trouble? . . . Naw; that's where we planned most of our jobs." The church was even less effective. All the church-goers did, Bigger complained, was to sing and shout and pray all the time. "And it didn't get 'em nothing." Nobody but poor folks got happy in church.[35]

Bigger much preferred the camaraderie of the pool room. In this he obviously resembled Studs Lonigan. Farrell and Wright, in truth, are interlocking novelists. They both deal with Chicago's South Side and mention many of the same streets. Farrell makes the explicit point that as the Negroes took over the neighborhoods evacuated by the Irish, they became exposed to the same corrupting influences. In the last page of *The Young Manhood of Studs Lonigan,* he describes an unnamed fourteen-year old Negro boy hanging around a corner crap game and snitching a half-pound of butter left on a chain store counter by an absent-minded clerk. That boy could easily have been Bigger Thomas. Yet despite the striking parallels, Bigger's world was a harsher and more brutalizing one than that of Studs Lonigan.

III

The Thomases were an unhappy family. Vera was a fearful adolescent, who seemed "to be shrinking from life in every gesture she made." [36] She burst into tears at every unkind remark and bickered continually with her brothers. Buddy idolized Bigger, but the latter scorned his puppylike affection. The overworked mother could not cope with the wrangling children. She nagged at them all, but centered her most bitter reproaches on the shiftless and trouble-prone Bigger. Bigger hated his family because he knew that they were suffering and that he was powerless to help them. "He knew that the moment he allowed himself to feel to its fulness how they lived, the shame and misery of their lives, he would be swept out of himself with fear and despair. So he held toward them an attitude of iron reserve; he lived with them, but behind a wall, a curtain." Toward himself, Bigger was even more tyrannical. "He knew that the moment he allowed what his life meant to enter fully

---

[35] *Ibid.,* 301.   [36] *Ibid.,* 93.

into consciousness, he would either kill himself or someone else. So he denied himself and acted tough." [37]

Bigger vented his anger not only on his family, but upon other Negroes. In the pool room one afternoon he provoked a quarrel with his friend Gus, kicked him to the floor, punched him in the head, and threatened to cut his throat with an open knife. When Gus finally escaped, Bigger wantonly ruined a pool table by slashing the green top with his knife, much to the indignation of Doc, the Negro proprietor. Fear drove him to do these things. His gang had planned to rob a white pawn broker that afternoon, and the brawl in the pool room saved him from going through with the job. "His confused emotions had made him feel instinctively that it would be better to fight Gus and spoil the plan of the robbery than to confront a white man with a gun." But he did not admit this truth even to himself. He was sure that he had turned on Gus, because Gus arrived late at the pool room. He felt no other responsibility to his co-conspirators. "As long as he could remember, he had never been responsible to anyone. The moment a situation became so that it exacted something of him, he rebelled. That was the way he lived; he passed his days trying to defeat or gratify powerful impulses in a world he feared." [38]

Bigger's subconscious fear extended only to robbing whites. Stealing from Negroes was easy. The gang had filched from newsstands, fruit stands, and apartments. "They had always robbed Negroes. They felt it was much easier and safer to rob their own people, for they knew that white policemen never really searched diligently for Negroes who committed crimes against other Negroes." [39]

The Negro world in which Bigger played this rebellious role was a narrowly constricted one. Even within the ghetto, Negroes had few opportunities for legitimate moneymaking. "Almost all businesses in the Black Belt were owned by Jews, Italians, and Greeks. Most Negro businesses were funeral parlors; white undertakers refused to bother with dead black bodies." White businessmen demonstrated their contempt for their black customers by petty profiteering. Chain stores in the Black Belt charged five cents a loaf

---

[37] *Ibid.*, 9.   [38] *Ibid.*, 36.   [39] *Ibid.*, 12.

for bread, "but across the 'line' where white folks lived, it sold for four." [40]

In this jungle each individual took what he could for his own survival and gave to others only grudgingly. Bigger and his girl friend Bessie needed and used each other. Bigger's need was elemental; he was an unmarried twenty-year old male. Bessie's was equally simple. After a week of slaving in the kitchen of a white employer, she wanted release. "She worked long hours, hard and hot hours seven days a week, with only Sunday afternoons off; and when she did get off she wanted fun, hard and fast fun, something to make her feel that she was making up for the starved life she led." Most nights she was too tired to go out; all she wanted was to get drunk. "She wanted liquor and he wanted her. So he would give her the liquor and she would give him herself." [41] In the end, this sordid affair reached its appropriate culmination. Bigger found gratification in Bessie's embrace one final time, and then he beat her brains out with a brick. He could not allow her to live longer, because this would threaten his own slim chance of escape. How could Bigger do such a terrible thing? Did he not love Bessie? In arguing for Bigger's life, Max explained that love was impossible for such a couple. "Love grows from stable relationships, shared experience, loyalty, devotion, trust. Neither Bigger nor Bessie had any of these." All they had was a physical dependence upon each other, and that dependence engendered savagely mixed feelings. "Their brief moments together were for purposes of sex. They loved each other as much as they hated each other; perhaps they hated each other more than they loved." [42]

Not all Negroes behaved as these two did. Religion was to Bigger's mother what whiskey was to Bessie. In a passage that probably reflects Wright's own internal struggle, he describes the fugitive Bigger, lonely and afraid, watching the singing, clapping men and women in a nearby church. "Would it not have been better for him had he lived in that world the music sang of? It would have been easy to have lived in it, for it was his mother's world, humble, contrite, believing. It had a center, a core, an axis, a heart which he needed but could never have unless he laid his head upon a pillow

[40] *Ibid.*, 211.   [41] *Ibid.*, 118.   [42] *Ibid.*, 336.

of humility and gave up his hope of living in the world. And he would never do that." [43]

Negroes who chose the path of accomodation hated the rebellious Negroes whose misdeeds intensified the racial prejudice of the whites. During his flight Bigger overheard a conversation in which a hard-working Negro laborer complained bitterly at being laid off because of the murder of Mary Dalton. "Yuh see, tha' Goddamn nigger Bigger Thomas made me lose mah job. . . . He made the white folks think we's all jus' like him!" When another Negro protested that he would die before he would betray Bigger to the police, the realist pointed out that this was crazy talk. The Negroes were so far outnumbered that it would be futile to fight; the whites could kill them all. "Yuh gotta learn t' live 'n' git erlong wid people." [44]

Asked by Max why he had not appealed for help to the leaders of his race, Bigger showed how little the Negro masses trusted the small Negro elite. Bigger felt that these successful ones wouldn't listen to him. They were rich. "They almost like white people, when it comes to guys like me. They say guys like me make it hard for them to get along with white folks." [45]

The most frightening thing about Bigger Thomas was his complete divorce from the values of common humanity. Feeling no remorse for his terrible deeds, he was humiliated by the sight of his sobbing mother and terrified brother and sister. "They ought to be glad! It was a strange but strong feeling, springing from the very depths of his life. Had he not taken fully upon himself the crime of being black? Had he not done the thing which they dreaded above all others? Then they ought not stand here and pity him, cry over him; but look at him and go home, contented, feeling that their shame was washed away." [46]

IV

Although the Chicago Negroes were forced to live in their own section of the city, many of them entered the white world every day as employees. Slaving for meager wages, they often felt no com-

---

[43] *Ibid.,* 215.   [44] *Ibid.,* 213.   [45] *Ibid.,* 303.   [46] *Ibid.,* 252.

punction about stealing from their bosses. When Bigger was trying to involve a reluctant Bessie in a scheme for exacting a large sum of money from the Daltons, he taunted her: "You scared? You scared after letting me take that silver from Mrs. Heard's home? After letting me get Mrs. Macy's radio? You scared now?" [47] Bessie's response was sensible. She saw the difference between pilfering and extortion. "They'll look everywhere for us for something like this. It ain't like coming to where I work at night when the white folks is gone out of town and stealing something." [48]

Bigger's secret visits to the homes of Bessie's employers scarcely prepared him to go to work for such people himself. The truth was that he knew very little about rich whites except the misinformation to be picked up from movies. He had recently seen a picture called *The Gay Woman*, "in which, amidst scenes of cocktail drinking, dancing, golfing, swimming, and spinning roulette wheels, a rich young white woman kept clandestine appointments with her lover while her millionaire husband was busy in the offices of a vast paper mill." [49] In his day dreams, Bigger imagined himself working for people like this, and his friend Jack helped to feed his fantasies. "Ah, man, them rich white women'll go to bed with anybody, from a poodle on up. Shucks, they even have their chauffeurs. Say, if you run into anything on that new job that's too much for you to handle, let me know . . ." [50]

The Daltons did not fit Bigger's preconceived notions. They prided themselves on being enlightened people. They gave millions for Negro education and took a paternal interest in the Negroes who worked for them. They had encouraged Bigger's predecessor to go to night school and prepare himself for a government position. Mrs. Dalton, blind and saintly, began at once to urge Bigger to follow this good example. Henry Dalton promised to pay Bigger $25 a week instead of the bare $20 specified by the relief agency. He was to have $5 to spend as he liked, while contributing $20 to support his mother and keep his brother and sister in school. In all their actions, the Daltons ran true to the description given by Peggy, the Irish housekeeper: "They're Christian people and believe in everybody working hard and living a clean life." [51]

[47] *Ibid.*, 123.   [48] *Ibid.*, 124–25.   [49] *Ibid.*, 26.
[50] *Ibid.*, 27.   [51] *Ibid.*, 48.

To middle-class whites, these values were axiomatic; but to Bigger, they were not so obvious. His own mother had steered by these beacons, but this had not saved her from the shoals of bleak poverty. Moreover, he sensed a kind of hypocrisy. The Daltons who wanted to help him were the same Daltons who drew tribute from their Negro tenants.

The older Daltons merely puzzled Bigger, but the twenty-two year old daughter, Mary Dalton, scared him. The first time he met her, she asked him whether he belonged to a labor union and referred to her father as a capitalist—a term which Bigger did not understand. Peggy the housekeeper explained that Mary ran around with a crazy bunch of reds, but that she didn't "mean nothing" by it. "Like her mother and father, she feels sorry for people and she thinks the reds'll do something for 'em." [52]

Mary Dalton continued to bewilder Bigger by her defiance of all the familiar taboos. She cut the University lecture that she was supposed to be attending and had Bigger drive her to a rendezvous with Jan Erlone, her Communist boy friend. Mary and Jan tried to offer friendship to Bigger, but he could not believe that they meant it. As Jan gripped his hand in a prolonged greeting, Bigger asked himself, "Were they making fun of him? What was it they wanted? Why didn't they leave him alone." He was more conscious than ever of his blackness.

He felt he had no physical existence at all right then; he was something he hated, the badge of shame which he knew was attached to a black skin. It was a shadowy region, a No Man's Land, the ground that separated the white world from the black, that he stood upon. He felt naked, transparent; he felt that this white man, having helped to put him down, having helped to deform him, held him up now to look at him and be amused. At that moment he felt toward Mary and Jan a dumb, cold, and inarticulate hate.[53]

Mary, Jan, and Bigger sat in the front seat of the car together. To the young Negro it was an exciting experience. "Never in his life had he been so close to a white woman. He smelt the odor of her hair and felt the soft pressure of her thigh against his own." [54] When his white companions insisted on going to a Negro restau-

---

[52] *Ibid.,* 49.   [53] *Ibid.,* 58.   [54] *Ibid.,* 59.

rant, Bigger directed them to Ernie's Kitchen Shack on the South Side. Rather than endure the stares of his Negro acquaintances, Bigger would have preferred to wait in the car, but he went in and sat at the same table with them after Mary began to cry. "Good God! He had a wild impulse to turn around and walk away. He felt ensnared in a tangle of deep shadows, shadows as black as the night that stretched above his head. The way he had acted had made her cry, and yet the way she had acted had made him feel that he had to act as he had toward her. In his relations with her he felt that he was riding a seesaw; never were they on a common level; either he or she was up in the air." [55]

The strange evening pushed toward its tragic climax. The white couple drank heavily themselves and urged their Negro comrade to drink with them. They had Bigger drive them around Washington Park while they cuddled together in the back seat and drank still more. After Jan left to catch a street car home, Bigger found himself with a very tipsy girl on his hands. "He watched her with a mingled feeling of helplessness, admiration, and hate. . . . But she was beautiful, slender, with an air that made him feel that she did not hate him with the hate of the other white people. But, for all of that, she was white and he hated her." [56]

Desire alternated with hate as Bigger finally deposited his helpless charge on the bed of her own room. He placed his hands on her breasts and kissed her. What would have happened if the blind mother had not entered the room and if Bigger had not sought to keep Mary quiet with a pillow? He himself did not know. Struggling to explain his feelings to Max, his lawyer, Bigger admitted that he was "feeling that way" when he was with Mary. He craved the white girl's body because he knew that he wasn't supposed to. It was the very strength of the taboo that made Mary Dalton's proximity to Bigger so dangerous, to her and to him. Long after it was all over he still hated her. "I didn't know nothing about that woman," he told Max. "All I knew was that they kill us for women like her. We live apart. And then she comes and acts like that to me." [57]

Bigger knew that his hatred of the tender-hearted white girl

---

[55] *Ibid.*, 62.   [56] *Ibid.*, 71.   [57] *Ibid.*, 297.

made no sense, yet he tried to explain it to himself. "He felt that his murder of her was more than amply justified by the fear and shame she had made him feel." But what had she really done to make him feel this way? He didn't know. "It was not Mary he was reacting to when he felt that fear and shame. Mary had served to set off his emotions, emotions conditioned by many Marys. And now that he had killed Mary he felt a lessening of tension in his muscles; he had shed an invisible burden he had long carried." [58]

When had he started hating Mary? Max wanted to know, and he replied: "I hated her as soon as she spoke to me, as soon as I saw her. I reckon I hated her before I saw her. . . ." Mary stood for the white people who wouldn't let him do the things he wanted to do. They wouldn't let him go to aviator school and learn to fly a plane. They wouldn't even let him be a real soldier or a real sailor. "Hell, it's a Jim Crow army. All they want a black man for is to dig ditches. And in the navy, all I can do is wash dishes and scrub floors." [59]

However unfair Bigger was in blaming Mary Dalton for his constricted life, he had abundant reason to feel that most whites were his enemies. Britten, the private detective employed by Dalton after Mary's disappearance, questioned Bigger roughly from the start. Bigger knew "that the hard light in Britten's eyes held him guilty because he was black." The detective was familiar to him; "he had met a thousand Brittens in his life." [60] As soon as Mary's body was found and suspicion centered on him, Bigger could see that he was doomed. The newspapers carried inflammatory headlines: AUTHORITIES HINT SEX CRIME. "Those words excluded him utterly from the world. To hint that he had committed a sex crime was to pronounce the death sentence; it meant a wiping out of life even before he was captured; it meant death before death came, for the white men who read those words would at once kill him in their hearts." [61]

After Bigger was captured, the newspapers took his guilt for granted. The stories referred to him as a "Negro rapist" and a "Negro sex-slayer." They described his appearance as ape-like. "All in all, he seems a beast utterly untouched by the softening influences of modern civilization. In speech and manner he lacks the

---

[58] *Ibid.*, 97.   [59] *Ibid.*, 299–300.   [60] *Ibid.*, 138–39.   [61] *Ibid.*, 206.

charm of the average, harmless, genial, grinning southern darky so beloved by the American people." [62] In an orgy of hate, white mobs broke the windows in Negro homes and gathered threateningly around the jail and court house. The politically ambitious district attorney fed the flames by accusing Bigger of all recent unsolved rapes and murders. The State hurried Bigger's case to trial while the popular indignation was still at a peak.

Attempting to save Bigger's life by the tactics employed by Clarence Darrow in the Loeb-Leopold case, Lawyer Max had Bigger plead guilty. But the Negro did not win the same compassion from the judge that the rich white boys had. Max's patient attempt to explain why Bigger had struck out in violence against the white world was overborne by the district attorney's lurid reconstruction of the crime. "Your Honor, must not this infernal monster have burned her body to destroy evidence of offenses *worse* than rape? That treacherous beast must have known that if the marks of his teeth were ever seen on the innocent white flesh of her breasts, he would not have been accorded the high honor of sitting here in this court of law! Oh suffering Christ, there are no words to tell of a deed so black and awful!" [63] He reminded the judge of the waiting mob. "Your Honor, millions are waiting for your word! They are waiting for you to tell them that jungle law does not prevail in this city! They want you to tell them that they need not sharpen their knives and load their guns to protect themselves. They are waiting, Your Honor, beyond that window!" [64]

When the judge announced that he would pronounce sentence in an hour, Max knew that passion had outweighed reason and that Bigger would have to die.

V

The only noble characters in Richard Wright's disturbing novel are the two Communists, Jan Erlone and Boris Max. What are we to make of this?

Bigger Thomas knew very little about Communists and accepted the stereotypes of the day. "He remembered seeing many

---

[62] *Ibid.*, 238.   [63] *Ibid.*, 344.   [64] *Ibid.*, 346.

cartoons of Communists in newspapers and always they had flaming torches in their hands and wore beards and were trying to commit murder or set things on fire. People who acted that way were crazy. All he could recall having heard about Communists was associated in his mind with darkness, old houses, people speaking in whispers and trade unions on strike." [65]

Jan Erlone, Mary Dalton's boy friend, scarcely fitted this description. Pressing his friendship on the suspicious Negro, he had remonstrated when Bigger called him "sir." When he learned that Bigger's father had been killed in a southern race riot, Jan explained that this was what the Communists were fighting. "Don't you think," he asked Bigger, "if we got together we could stop things like that." Bigger was unimpressed. "There's a lot of white people in the world," he pointed out.[66]

Although Mary and Jan didn't really know many Negroes, they sentimentalized over them. "They have so much emotion!" Mary said. "What a people! If we could only get them going. . . ." And Jan replied, "We can't have a revolution without 'em. . . . They've got to be organized. They've got spirit. They'll give the Party something it needs." Mary began to sing "Swing low, sweet chariot," and Jan joined in. Bigger smiled derisively. "Hell, that ain't the tune, he thought." [67]

After he killed Mary, Bigger concocted a scheme for pinning the blame on Jan. He deliberately left in his room some Communist pamphlets on the race question that Jan had given him. He planned to show them to the police if he were ever questioned. "He would say that he had taken them only because Jan had insisted. . . . Yes, he would tell them that he was afraid of Reds, that he had not wanted to sit in the car with Jan and Mary, that he had not wanted to eat with them. He would say that he had done so only because it had been his job. He would tell them that it was the first time he had ever sat at a table with white people." [68] When he wrote the kidnap note, Bigger drew a crude hammer and sickle on it and signed it with the word "Red."

Bigger's plan was dangerous, because Britten became convinced that Jan and Bigger were both Communists. Pushing Bigger's head

---

[65] *Ibid.*, 57.   [66] *Ibid.*, 65.   [67] *Ibid.*, 66–67.   [68] *Ibid.*, 84.

against a wall, the detective shouted: "You *are* a Communist, *you goddamn* black sonofabitch! And you're going to tell me about Miss Dalton and that Jan bastard!" [69] Henry Dalton intervened to protect Bigger from this rough interrogation, but Britten took up the idea again later. In questioning Peggy the cook, he proceeded on the assumptions that most Communists were Jews and that they corrupted Negroes. When Bigger talked, did he wave his hands around a lot, as though he'd been around a lot of Jews? Did he call anybody *comrade?* Did he sit down without being asked? Did he take off his cap? "Now, listen Peggy," Britten said, "Think and try to remember if his voice goes *up* when he talks, like Jews when they talk. Know what I mean? You see, Peggy, I'm trying to find out if he's been around Communists. . . ." [70]

Things went better for Bigger when Britten began to try to build a case against Jan alone. The detective was ready to believe the worst of a Communist, and Bigger took advantage of this. "Bigger knew the things that white folks hated to hear Negroes ask for; and he knew that these were the things the Reds were always asking for. And he knew that white folks did not like to hear these things asked for even by whites who fought for Negroes." [71] But in the end, the discovery of the body and Bigger's panicky flight upset his scheme to pin the crime on Jan.

After Bigger was captured, the young Communist came to see him. Despite the fact that the Negro had killed the girl he loved, Jan still offered his friendship. "I'm not angry," he said, "and I want you to let me help you. I don't hate you for trying to blame this thing on me. . . . Maybe you had good reasons. . . . I don't know. And maybe in a certain sense, I'm the one who's really guilty." He had never done anything against Bigger or his people in his life. "But I'm a white man and it would be asking too much to ask you not to hate me, when every white man you see hates you." [72]

Bigger wondered whether this was a trap. "He looked at Jan and saw a white face, but an honest face. This white man believed in him, and the moment he felt that belief he felt guilty again; but in a different sense now. . . . For the first time in his life a white man

---

[69] *Ibid.*, 137.   [70] *Ibid.*, 163.   [71] *Ibid.*, 166.   [72] *Ibid.*, 244.

became a human being to him; and the reality of Jan's humanity came in a stab of remorse: he had killed what this man loved and had hurt him." [73]

In Boris Max, Bigger found a second white man whom he could trust. Max was a Communist and a Jew. In undertaking Bigger's defense he defied the world of white respectability. "They hate me because I'm trying to help you," Max told Bigger. "They're writing me letters, calling me a 'dirty Jew.'" [74]

When he entrusted his defense to the Communist lawyer, Bigger Thomas deliberately rejected the advice of his mother's pastor, Reverend Hammond. The old Negro preacher warned that dragging Communism into the case would simply stir up more hate. Bigger's only course was to put his trust in God. "There ain' but one way out, son, 'n' tha's Jesus' way, the way of love 'n' fergiveness. Be like Jesus. Don't resist." [75] But Bigger accepted Max's help and threw away the cross that the preacher had given him.

Visiting Bigger in jail, Max drew out a halting explanation of how the young Negro felt toward life. The whites owned everything. "They don't even let you feel what you want to feel. They after you so hot and hard you can only feel what they doing to you. They kill you before you die." [76] His crimes had given him a sense of accomplishment. "Maybe they going to burn me in the electric chair for feeling this way. But I ain't worried none about them women I killed. For a little while I was free. I was doing something. It was wrong, but I was feeling all right." He killed them because he was scared and mad. "But I been scared and mad all my life and after I killed that first woman, I wasn't scared no more for a little while." [77]

After unburdening himself to Max, Bigger felt good. "He could not remember when he had felt as relaxed as this before. He had not thought of it or felt it while Max was speaking to him; it was not until after Max had gone that he discovered that he had spoken to Max as he had never spoken to anyone in his life; not even to himself. And his talking had eased from his shoulders a heavy burden." [78]

Pleading for Bigger's life, Max cast some of his argument in

---

[73] *Ibid.*, 246.   [74] *Ibid.*, 295.   [75] *Ibid.*, 243.   [76] *Ibid.*, 299.
[77] *Ibid.*, 300.   [78] *Ibid.*, 305.

Marxist terms. He attributed the threatening mob to capitalist incitement. The men of power wanted to oppress not only Negroes, but workers and unionists. The state's attorney had promised the Loop bankers that relief demonstrations would be stopped; the governor had promised the Manufacturers Association to use troops against strikers; the mayor had told the merchants that no new taxes would be imposed on behalf of the needy.

There is guilt in the rage that demands that this man's life be snuffed out quickly! There is fear in the hate and impatience which impels the action of the mob congregated upon the streets beyond that window! All of them—the mob and the mob-masters; the wirepullers and the frightened; the leaders and their pet vassals—know and feel that their lives are built upon a historical deed of wrong against many people, people from whose lives they have bled their leisure and luxury. . . . Fear and hate and guilt are the keynotes of this drama! [79]

By the time that he wrote *Native Son* Richard Wright had become disillusioned with the Communist Party, but the novel does not reflect this disillusionment. Why not? Presumably because Wright still believed in the vision of a world where color barriers would fall and men would deal with each other on the basis of their common humanity. He had found such idealism in individual Communists, and he drew his Communist characters as he wanted them to be, free of the duplicity and calculation so often encountered in the party bureaucrats of real life.

As historical evidence, the role Wright assigns to his Communists is worth serious thought. During the 1930's, where were the other whites? Many of them, like the Lonigans and the O'Flahertys, were treating the Negroes with undisguised hostility. A few, like the Daltons, were salving their consciences by giving ping-pong tables to boys' clubs. A few more were supporting the moderate programs of the National Association for the Advancement of Colored People and the Urban League. But only the Communists were championing the Negro cause with any high degree of visibility. Had the Marxists taken maximum advantage of the situation, the post-World War II rights movement might have taken a much more revolutionary form than it did. But in real life not all

79 *Ibid.*, 326–27.

Communists were as humane and selfless as Jan Erlone and Boris Max, nor were all non-Communist Negroes as spineless as the Reverend Hammond.

Yet the novel's Communist rhetoric is far less impressive than its grim warning of future violence. More than twenty-five years before rioting Negroes took to the streets in Watts and Detroit, Richard Wright wrote a better explanation of the burning and the looting than has appeared in the ponderous reports of the investigating committees. The problem, as Boris Max somberly told the judge, was the Negro's alienation from American society. "This boy

. . . they constitute a separate nation, stunted, stripped, and held captive *within* th nation, devoid of political, social, economic, and property rights.   Richard Wrigh *Native Son*

represents but a tiny aspect of a problem whose reality sprawls over a third of this nation." Would the white daughters of America be made any safer by killing Bigger? "No! I tell you in all solemnity that they won't! The surest way to make certain that there will be more such murders is to kill this boy. In your rage and guilt, make thousands of other black men and women feel that the barriers are tighter and higher! Kill him and swell the tide of pent-up lava that will some day break loose, not in a single, blundering, accidental, individual crime, but in a wide cataract of emotion that will brook no control." [80] America's twelve million Negroes constituted "a separate nation, stunted, stripped, and held captive *within* this nation, devoid of political, social, economic, and property rights." [81] Another civil war is not impossible, "and if the misunderstanding of what this boy's life means is an indication of how men of wealth and property are misreading the consciousness of the submerged millions today, one may truly come." [82]

[80] *Ibid.,* 330. [81] *Ibid.,* 333. [82] *Ibid.,* 338.

IO

Fiction as History

Reporting the extreme things as if they were the average
things will start you on the art of fiction.

F. Scott Fitzgerald [1]

Suppose that in some freak disaster of the future, all
conventional historical records were destroyed and only novels and
short stories survived. How much would it be possible to learn
about American history of the early twentieth century from fiction
alone—from the writings, let us say, of Sinclair Lewis, F. Scott
Fitzgerald, William Faulkner, Thomas Wolfe, John Steinbeck,
John Dos Passos, James T. Farrell, and Richard Wright?

Without works of reference, the readers of the novels would
find much to perplex them. Why, for example, did the Americans
of that distant day drink something called "bathtub gin," or live in
settlements called "Hoovervilles"? Yet these minor mysteries
would not prevent earnest scholars from learning a great deal about
these ancient Americans and their society.

Suppose the future investigators began with Sinclair Lewis's
Main Street. From this they would learn that many Americans in
the early twentieth century were living in small towns. These
places had a kind of monotony to them. Along their main streets
stood a few business buildings with dreary brick fronts, decrepit
town halls and court houses, and barn-like churches. On the residential streets, the houses were either Victorian Gothic horrors or
new bungalows of unimaginative sameness. In these ugly towns

[1] F. Scott Fitzgerald, "The Note-Books," *The Crack-up* (ed.) Edmund Wilson
(New York: New Directions Paperbook, 1956), 178.

lived people who were decent and hard-working, but nevertheless dull, conforming, and gossipy. The quality of American small town life seemed to be declining, and sensitive people were rebelling against its constricting influence.

If these future students went on to read Sinclair Lewis's later novels—*Babbitt, Arrowsmith, Elmer Gantry, Dodsworth*—they would discover that after World War I, the American cities of intermediate size grew rapidly. This expansion provided profits and prestige for a pot-bellied clan called the realtors. These smooth-talking operators anticipated future urban trends by timely speculations in land; they developed grassy suburbs to serve the needs of business executives and professional men who made their money in the cities, but did not want to live in them. Sharp dealing and acquisitiveness dominated life in these cities, and the money-making spirit corrupted not only the realm of business, but that of medicine and the church. In the cities, as in the small towns, there was a strong pressure toward conformity. Men earned the praise of their fellows by "hustling" in their personal affairs and "boosting" their home towns. The non-conformists who "knocked" the existing order of society were ostracized. National advertisers, national columnists, and national politicians supplied the catch phrases that made independent thought unnecessary.

Yet there were many paradoxes in this complacent society, and some of these would be reflected in the novels and short stories of F. Scott Fitzgerald. The rich, Fitzgerald liked to say, were different. They received their education at playboy colleges like Princeton and Yale. They spent their money in gracious living and gay parties on Long Island and the Riviera. American females had been restless even before World War I, according to Fitzgerald, and in the early 1920's they were in happy revolt. They were bobbing their hair, reddening their lips and cheeks, and shortening their dresses. They were puffing on cigarettes and taking slugs of bootleg whiskey from their escorts' flasks. More frequently than in earlier generations they were sleeping with men who were not their husbands. This moral upheaval had begun with youth, but was rapidly invading older groups in the population.

The fictional South, described in the novels of Thomas Wolfe and William Faulkner, reflected many of the national trends. There was the same provinciality in the small towns, the same conformity of thought, the same money-grabbing spirit. Yet the South was at the same time different. Still living in rundown mansions were the elderly gentle folk, who cherished a tradition of aristocracy; but these old families were withering away. They were surrendering leadership to greedy traders and demagogic politicians. The children of the gentry were futile failures. More vital were the white farmers—ignorant, but tough and shrewd—and the Negroes—mistreated, but enduring. The South of fiction was a maladjusted South, as full of dangerous tension as a coiled spring.

Future readers of the novels of John Steinbeck would learn that American agriculture had been in the process of a mighty change. In many parts of the country the medium-sized farm, operated by its owner with his sturdy sons and a few hired hands, was becoming a nostalgic memory. In California, farm corporations owning thousands of acres were growing fruits and vegetables for the canneries; in the Middle West, debt and dust storms were depressing the small farmers into the status of tenants, and the tenants in turn were being forced off the land by giant tractors and the need for consolidating acreage. Through a tragic metamorphosis, the displaced farmers of Oklahoma became the migrant workers of California.

In the books of James T. Farrell, the scholar of the future would learn that a growing malignancy seemed to be eating into the vitals of the great American cities. Even for middle class whites, urban life was demoralizing during the 1920's. Bored youths hung around cheap pool rooms, drank poisonous liquor, and consorted with diseased girls. Bored fathers worked at monotonous jobs, came home to quarreling households, read trashy newspapers, listened to trivial radio programs, and went on occasional drinking sprees. Young and old shared the same violent prejudices against Jews and Negroes. The great city was depicted as a place of ruined lives, interracial assaults, and stunted intellects.

From his reading of the novels, the investigator would conclude that in the 1920's and 1930's most Negroes lived lives of poverty and desperation. In the South, they tilled the soil as tenants of white landlords, bought their provisions and sold their produce in white-owned country stores, cooked in white kitchens, and chauffeured the cars of white employers. Convinced of their own magnanimity, the white patrons expected their Negro retainers to maintain a smiling deference and to accept their paltry wages without complaint. In the new slavery, arising out of poverty and ignorance, the Southern Negroes lived in dirty tumbledown shacks on rubbish-cluttered patches of land. The occasional rebel, guilty of some act of crime or gesture of disrespect, was harshly punished, either by the one-sided justice of some Southern court or by a night of torture at the hands of a Southern mob.

Attempting to escape these conditions in the South, thousands of Negroes were crowding into the great cities of the North. But here—as described in the novels of Richard Wright—they suffered new tribulations. The invisible hand of the real estate interests dictated the sections where they would be allowed to live; in these ghettos they paid high rent for small flats in crumbling old buildings. Even in good times there were not enough jobs open to Negroes, and during the depression there were fewer still. Negro families—often fatherless—lived on relief doles; Negro youths drifted into lives of idleness, dissipation, and petty crime. Throughout Negro America, a great anger was building up, an anger all the more dangerous because so few whites were conscious either of the anger itself, or of the terrible injustices on which the anger fed.

Although the depression hurt the Negroes more cruelly, its impact on the whites was devastating enough. Seen through the eyes of Wolfe and Farrell, the depression meant the loss of jobs and savings, demoralizing months of unemployment, and the foreclosure of mortgages. Most serious of all, it shattered the complacent optimism and faith in American institutions that had been characteristic of the 1920's.

To the reader of these novels, it might seem strange that social protest during the 1920's and 1930's did not take more violent form than it did. All the combustible materials seemed to be there—exploited workers in the steel mills and textile plants, ruined victims of the depression, exploited migrant laborers, and desperate Negroes. Yet there was no major explosion. The Communists who had the most to gain missed their opportunity. As depicted in the novels of John Dos Passos, the Marxists, even more than the capitalists, seemed to be digging their own graves; their leaders were heartless manipulators much more interested in building up the party than in saving the people. What matter if Sacco and Vanzetti went to the electric chair, or strikers were killed, or Negroes were lynched, so long as their deaths contributed to proletarian solidarity? In dealing with middle-class liberals and with anarchists, syndicalists, and socialists, the fictional Communists played a cynical game, sometimes extolling the glories of the popular front, sometimes maneuvering to destroy all factions except their own.

Obviously, our imagined antiquarian could discover much about a lost world of American life by reading the few novels that had survived. Even without the conventional documents of history, he could learn how in the early twentieth century rural America had been declining in importance, as urban America grew with arrogant pride. He could learn about changes in the dress and behavior of women and about rebellious youngsters and frustrated parents. He could learn about the passing of an old heirarchy of rank in the South and the growth of a new agricultural feudalism in the West. He could learn of the unhappy plight of American Negroes and the growing violence in the great American cities. He could learn how the great depression undermined American complacence, but how the impulse to social protest was dissipated by radical factionalism. All these things would be not only true, but so significantly true that the trends depicted for the 1920's and 1930's would still be in process a generation later—during the 1960's.

But would the description of the novelists be the whole truth, and nothing but the truth?

II

If this scholar of the future should unexpectedly add to his little library of novels a few documents of a radically different kind, his picture of the lost America might be modified and extended. Suppose, for example, he happened upon the convenient summary issued by the Bureau of the Census called *Historical Statistics of the United States*. By exploring the many columns of figures in this massive book, he would get a more accurate idea of how many Americans there had been, where they had lived, at what rate they had reproduced and died, how they were employed, how many years of schooling they obtained, and how much their education cost the taxpayers. But would the knowledge of twentieth century America thus obtained be more truthful than the picture derived from the novels?

Statistics are facts; novels are fiction. But are facts and fiction in quite the polar relationship that we usually assume? Because one is true, is the other false? According to the statistics, the average young man of the 1920's should have lived past the age of sixty. Was James T. Farrell distorting the truth to have Studs Lonigan die at half that age? The obvious answer is that some men die young, some die old; the statistics on life expectancy represent an averaging of experience, an abstract way of stating a certain truth. But is not Farrell's treatment of the character Studs Lonigan a way of stating another truth, the truth that many young men in the world of Farrell's observation came to early and tragic deaths?

Statistical tables and works of fiction both contain truths, but their truths are of a different kind. The truths of statistics— always provided the statisticians are honest men—are highly objective. They are truths that can be expressed in numbers and neatly arranged in columns. In this collection and measurement of data, hundreds of observers have participated. Their names and personalities do not matter, because neither color, nor ancestry, nor loves, hates, hopes, and fears of the statisticians will color the truth contained in their chaste numbers. Since this kind of truth is passionless, it may be called cold truth.

How different are the truths contained in works of fiction! This kind of truth is highly subjective. Looking at small town life, Sinclair Lewis will see one thing; Booth Tarkington will see another. It will do no good to say that one man's view is true, and the other's is false, because each is saying what he thinks. The real truth in *Main Street* is not that American small towns were ugly in appearance and that their citizens were dull. By what yardstick is ugliness or dullness to be measured? All we can say is that a fictional Gopher Prairie *seemed* ugly and dull to a fictional Carol Kennicott, and undoubtedly the reason why it did was deeply rooted in Sinclair Lewis's own memories of his home town of Sauk Centre, Minnesota. If Lewis's writing is true to his own experience and feeling, it is a truth that the historian should recognize. Unlike the *cold truth* of the statistician it is a *hot truth,* highly charged with the passions of the observer.

The historian would not want to be restricted to either the cold truths of the statistician, or the hot truths of the novelist. If history were simply the drawing of inferences from columns of figures, it would be thin and lifeless. The growth of Chicago's Negro population by 557 per cent between 1910 and 1940 is an impressive piece of data, but it will not tell us how it felt to be one of those Negroes. On the other hand, a history derived entirely from the novels would be subjective to a dangerous degree. Are the violent resentments described in Richard Wright's *Native Son* the products of just one Negro intellectual's imagination, or were they shared by many real life Negroes? The historian needs both statistics humanized by individual testimony and individual testimony measured against statistics.

The fiction writer's testimony about his times is written from his own angle of vision. In this he is like the rest of us. Who is disinterested as he passes through life? Certainly not the priest, nor the dentist, nor the sharecropper, nor the professor. Each looks at the world from his own point of view, shaped not only by the work that he has to do but by a score of other conditioning factors.

The historian's task is a delicate one. He is attempting to construct an account of the past that will be inclusive enough to accommodate these particular views and abstract enough to find patterns of meaning in this welter of particulars. For a divine scribe looking down at struggling humanity from some insulated heaven, the task of writing history would not be easy; for the all-too-human historian, who is himself involved in the very processes he is trying to describe, it is almost impossibly difficult. What can he do? The scientific method—the collection of data, the formulation and testing of hypotheses—will help him. But he has to go beyond science to venture speculations about the significance of the events he is describing. Here he has much in common with the novelists. Yet the historian must always be aware that the novelist is a decidedly special person looking at experience in a way that needs to be understood.

The writer of fiction is a man who has put his imagination to work. He creates people, names them, describes their appearance, reveals their personalities, and manufactures their thoughts and speeches. He puts these imaginary people onto imaginary streets in imaginary towns and cities. He describes their imaginary experiences. Like the Calvinist God, the novelist predestines his creatures to salvation or damnation.

The historian also has to use his imagination. If he is to write convincingly about the depression, he must get beyond the economists' figures on gross national product, to imagine how it felt to lose one's life savings in a bank failure, to go without work for months, or to stand in a soup line. The historian must try to feel within himself what it would have been like to be Franklin D. Roosevelt hearing the news of Pearl Harbor, or Lyndon Johnson flying back to Washington after President Kennedy's assassination. History has its moments of high drama, and the historian must feel and convey its excitement and tension. The historian must also use his imagination in selecting from the great mass of past happenings the particular events he chooses to record. These, he says, are the significant things that happened; let me tell you their meaning. Even though he writes about real people and real events, the requirement that he must ignore most people and most events gives his work an abstract or symbolic character. Without imagination the historian could not see any patterns of meaning in past occurrences.

Despite this similarity, the roles of the historian and the novelist are clearly different. The historian's imagination must be rigorously disciplined. In the days of Herodotus and Thucydides, the historians acted as ghost writers for dead statesmen, putting into their mouths orations appropriate to the occasion. We no longer permit this. Grover Cleveland must say only what the evidence shows he did say. Grover Cleveland may not even think thoughts that cannot be documented. The novelist's imagination is not under leash. His characters may say anything and do anything their creator wants them to, subject only to the rebuke of his readers if the imagined episodes become too improbable.

How is the historian to deal with this unreal world of fiction? It will help him if he realizes that the novelist is not as capricious as he seems. He creates his characters with a purpose in mind. William Faulkner manufactured a whole clan of Snopeses. The particular antics of these sly, thieving, and avaricious cousins are of no great significance to the historian, but their general role in Faulkner's world is a highly important one. The Snopeses represent an intrusion of the rural poor whites into the southern towns. Southern society was becoming more mobile: tenant farmers rose to the status of storekeepers; bank clerks became bank presidents. Losing ground in politics and business, the older aristocrats sneered at the newcomers. Their attitude, as revealed in the Faulkner novels, was partly one of jealous vexation, and partly one of sincere regret at the loss of the old code of gentlemanly conduct.

Fictional characters are likely to differ from the people of real life in the accentuation of key traits. George F. Babbitt was probably a more fanatic hustler than most urban businessmen; he probably accepted conventional ideas more unquestioningly and made more asinine speeches. Certainly Elmer Gantry was more sensational, more lecherous, and more hypocritical than most ministers. The cautious historian will discount Sinclair Lewis's testimony, but he ought not to ignore it. Caricature is ineffective unless the traits being exaggerated have some reality. The reader finds satisfaction in the satire only when he recognizes similarities to people he has known in his own experience.

Even when the novelist writes about characters taken from real life, he is likely to exaggerate to make his point. Eliza Gant was clearly Thomas Wolfe's own mother, but she was nevertheless compelled to serve his literary purposes. He needed to dramatize the destructive materialism of his native city, and he therefore accentuated the avariciousness in Julia Wolfe's personality. Danny O'Neill is clearly James T. Farrell himself, yet Danny too must serve as a dramatic foil. He is Studs Lonigan's opposite number, subjected to a worse home situation than Studs, brought up in the same demoralizing urban environment, yet saved by timely repudiation of his constricting Irish faith and escape to the world of literature. The historian will discount the purposeful overstatements and look for the underlying social facts.

Like the historian, the novelist must select his material. He cannot write about all human experience. But the two will follow different standards of selection. The historian looks for the usable past, the past that will help him to understand our present world in all its complexity—political, economic, social, intellectual. The novelist will reject a purpose so inclusive and so utilitarian; by selection and arrangement he aspires to produce a work of art. Even a novel as long and comprehensive as Dos Passos's *U.S.A.* selects and arranges its material to produce a kaleidoscopic impact upon the consciousness of the reader.

The novelist selects from the past the themes that he can accommodate to literary purposes. He ignores as too prosaic many trends that the historian would want to stress. Who, for example, writes a novel about electricity? Yet the spreading network of power lines between 1910 and 1940 transformed many aspects of American life. It made factories cleaner and safer places to work; it lightened the labor of farmers and farmers' wives; it displaced domestic servants and gave housewives more time for independent careers and bridge clubs. Who writes a novel about the Standard Oil Company of New Jersey? Yet the changes in the organization, control, and function of American corporations has been one of the most significant trends of twentieth century American history.

Who, if the truth be bluntly stated, writes a novel about most of us? We do our jobs with only the usual grumbling; we marry and have children; we have our moments of joy and sorrow. As characters in a novel, most of us would not do. We do not shine like silver as did Fitzgerald's Daisy Buchanan; we do not eat with the prodigious appetite of Wolfe's Eugene Gant; we do not avoid work with the pertinacity of Faulkner's Anse Bundren. We are too commonplace for fiction, but in the aggregate we are history.

When the historian uses novels as sources, he must always remember that the novelist has his own angle of vision. The novelist is blind to many prosaic aspects of life, yet what he does see, he sees with striking clarity. He senses the pettiness of village society, the demoralizing tendencies within the great cities, the restlessness of modern women, the mercenary goals of business and professional people, the sullen anger of exploited groups. The novelist is almost never a neutral observer. He feels life with intensity. His emotions range the whole width of the spectrum from anger to compassion. Sometimes he is convulsed by the humor of the human situation;

sometimes he is appalled by its tragedy. As witnesses to history, novelists are prejudiced and willful, but, nevertheless, they have much to tell.

Fortunately, the historian can draw upon many sources intermediate between this hot truth of fiction and the cold truth of statistics. So long as future disasters spare his records, the historian can continue to deal with the lukewarm truths contained in letters, diaries, memoirs, newspapers, and government records. To write a well-rounded view of history, the historian will need to use all the truth he can find.

Bibliography

I. NOVELS AND OTHER FICTION USED IN THIS STUDY

For the convenience of the reader, publishing information about both the original edition and (in brackets) the edition—usually paperback—used for the citations in this book has been included. In cases where no later edition is listed, I have used the original one.

By JOHN DOS PASSOS:

Adventures of a Young Man. Boston: Houghton Mifflin Co., 1939.

Chosen Country. Boston: Houghton Mifflin Co., 1951.

Manhattan Transfer. New York: Harper & Brothers, 1925. [New York: Sentry Edition, 1963.]

U.S.A.: The Big Money. New York: Harcourt, Brace & Co., 1936. [New York: Washington Square Press, 1961.]

U.S.A.: The 42nd Parallel. New York: Harcourt, Brace & Co., 1930. [Boston: Houghton Mifflin Co., 1946.]

U.S.A.: Nineteen Nineteen. New York: Harcourt, Brace & Co., 1932. [Boston: Houghton Mifflin Co., 1946.]

By JAMES T. FARRELL:

The Face of Time. New York: Vanguard Press, 1953. [New York: Popular Library, 1962.]

Father and Son. Cleveland World Publishing Co., 1947.

My Days of Anger. New York: Vanguard Press, 1943.

Studs Lonigan: A Trilogy Containing Young Lonigan, The Young Manhood of Studs Lonigan, Judgment Day. [New York: New American Library, 1958.] Original editions: *Young Lonigan.* New York: Vanguard Press, 1932. *The Young Manhood of Studs Lonigan.* New York: Vanguard Press, 1934. *Judgment Day.* New York: Vanguard Press, 1935.

No Star Is Lost. New York: Vanguard Press, 1938.

The Silence of History. Garden City, N.Y.: Doubleday & Company, Inc., 1963.

A World I Never Made. New York: Vanguard Press, 1936.

By WILLIAM FAULKNER:

As I Lay Dying. New York: J. Cape & H. Smith, 1930. [New York: Vintage Books, 1957.]

Big Woods. New York: Random House, 1955.

Go Down, Moses. New York: Random House, 1942.

The Hamlet. New York: Random House, 1940. [New York: Vintage Books, 1964.]

Intruder in the Dust. New York: Random House, 1948.

Light in August. New York: H. Smith & R. Haas, 1932. [New York: Modern Library, 1950.]

The Mansion. New York: Random House, 1959.

Sanctuary. New York: J. Cape & H. Smith, 1931. [New York: Penguin Books, 1947.]

Sartoris. New York: Harcourt, Brace & Co., 1929. [New York: Signet Books, 1953.]

The Sound and the Fury. New York: J. Cape & H. Smith, 1929.

The Town. New York: Random House, 1957.

By F. Scott Fitzgerald:

Babylon Revisited and Other Stories. New York: Charles Scribner's Sons, 1960.

The Beautiful and Damned. New York: Charles Scribner's Sons, 1922.

Flappers and Philosophers. New York: Charles Scribner's Sons, 1920. [New York: Charles Scribner's Sons, 1959.]

The Great Gatsby. New York: Charles Scribner's Sons, 1925. [New York: Bantam Books, 1945.]

The Last Tycoon: An Unfinished Novel. Ed. by Edmund Wilson. New York: Charles Scribner's Sons, 1941.

Tales of the Jazz Age. New York: Charles Scribner's Sons, 1922.

Tender Is the Night. New York: Charles Scribner's Sons, 1934. [New York: Bantam Books, 1950.]

This Side of Paradise. New York: Charles Scribner's Sons, 1920.

By Sinclair Lewis:

Arrowsmith. New York: Harcourt, Brace & Co., 1925. [New York: New American Library, 1961.]

Babbitt. New York: Harcourt, Brace & Co., 1922. [New York: New American Library, 1961.]

Dodsworth. New York: Harcourt, Brace & Co., 1929. [New York: Dell Publishing Co., 1957.]

Elmer Gantry. New York: Harcourt, Brace & Co., 1927. [New York: Dell Publishing Co., 1961.]

Main Street: The Story of Carol Kennicott. New York: Harcourt, Brace & Co., 1920.

By John Steinbeck:

East of Eden. New York: Viking Press, 1952.

In Dubious Battle. New York: Viking Press, 1938. [New York: Bantam Press, 1961.]

The Grapes of Wrath. New York: Viking Press, 1939. [New York: Compass Books, 1958.]
The Long Valley. New York: Viking Press, 1939.
Of Mice and Men. New York: Viking Press, 1937.

By THOMAS WOLFE:

The Hills Beyond. New York: Harper & Brothers, 1941.
Look Homeward, Angel. New York: Charles Scribner's Sons, 1929. [New York: Charles Scribner's Sons, 1952.]
Of Time and the River. New York: Charles Scribner's Sons, 1935.
The Web and the Rock. New York: Harper & Brothers, 1939. [New York: Dell Publishing Co., 1960.]
You Can't Go Home Again. New York: Harper and Brothers, 1940. [New York: Dell Publishing Co., 1960.]

By RICHARD WRIGHT:

Eight Men. Cleveland: The World Publishing Co. 1961.
Native Son. New York: Harper & Brothers, 1940.

II. SUPPORTING WORKS

On JOHN DOS PASSOS:

Davis, Robert G. *John Dos Passos.* Minneapolis: University of Minnesota Press, 1962.
Dos Passos, John. *The Best Times: An Informal Memoir.* New York: The New American Library, 1966.
Potter, Jack. *A Bibliography of John Dos Passos.* With an Introduction by John Dos Passos. Chicago: Normandie House, 1950.
Wrenn, John R. *John Dos Passos.* New York: Twayne Publishers, 1961.

On JAMES T. FARRELL:

Branch, Edgar M. *James T. Farrell.* Minneapolis: University of Minnesota Press, 1963.
Farrell, James T. *The League of the Frightened Philistines, and Other Papers.* New York: Vanguard Press, 1945.
Farrell, James T. *Literature and Morality.* New York: Vanguard Press, 1947.
Farrell, James T. *Reflections at Fifty and Other Essays.* New York: Vanguard Press, 1954.

On WILLIAM FAULKNER:

Bachman, Melvin. *Faulkner: The Major Years; a Critical Study.* Bloomington: Indiana University Press, 1966.
Brooks, Cleanth. *William Faulkner: The Yoknapatawpha Country.* New Haven: Yale University Press, 1963.
Coughlan, Robert. *The Private World of William Faulkner.* New York: Harper & Brothers, 1954.

Cowley, Malcolm. *The Faulkner-Cowley File: Letters and Memories, 1944–1962*. New York: Viking Press, 1966.

Cullen, John B. in collaboration with Floyd C. Watkins, *Old Times in the Faulkner Country*. Chapel Hill: University of North Carolina Press, 1961.

Dain, Martin J. *Faulkner's County: Yoknapatawpha*. New York: Random House, 1964.

Faulkner, John. *My Brother Bill: An Affectionate Reminiscence*. New York: Pocket Books, 1964.

Gold, Joseph. *William Faulkner: A Study in Humanism, from Metaphor to Discourse*. Norman: University of Oklahoma Press, 1966.

Gwynn, Frederick L. and Blotner, Joseph L. (eds.). *Faulkner in the University: Class Conferences at the University of Virginia, 1957–1958*. Charlottesville: University of Virginia Press, 1959.

Hoffman, Frederick J. *William Faulkner*. New York: Twayne Publishers, 1961.

Hoffman, Frederick J. and Vickery, Olga W. (eds.). *William Faulkner: Decades of Criticism*. East Lansing: Michigan State University Press, 1960.

Howe, Irving. *William Faulkner: A Critical Study*. 2nd ed., revised and expanded. New York: Vintage Books, 1962.

Longley, John L. *The Tragic Mask: A Study of Faulkner's Heroes*. Chapel Hill: University of North Carolina Press, 1963.

Malin, Irving. *William Faulkner, an Interpretation*. Stanford: Stanford University Press, 1957.

Meriwether, James B. *The Literary Career of William Faulkner: A Bibliographical Study*. Princeton: Princeton University Library, 1961.

Millgate, Michael. *The Achievement of William Faulkner*. New York: Random House, 1966.

Miner, Ward L. *The World of William Faulkner*. Durham: Duke University Press, 1952.

Slatoff, Walter. *Quest for Failure: A Study of William Faulkner*. Ithaca: Cornell University Press, 1960.

Swiggart, Peter. *The Art of Faulkner's Novels*. Austin: University of Texas Press, 1963.

Vickery, Olga W. *The Novels of William Faulkner: A Critical Interpretation*. Rev. ed. Baton Rouge: Louisiana State University Press, 1964.

Waggoner, Hyatt H. *William Faulkner: From Jefferson to the World*. Lexington: University of Kentucky Press, 1959.

Warren, Robert Penn (ed.). *Faulkner: A Collection of Critical Essays*. Englewood Cliffs, N.J.: Prentice-Hall, 1966.

Webb, James W., and Green, A. Wigfall (eds.). *William Faulkner of Oxford*. Baton Rouge: Louisiana State University Press, 1965.

On F. Scott Fitzgerald:

Brucoli, Matthew J. *The Composition of Tender Is the Night: A Study of the Manuscripts*. Pittsburgh: University of Pittsburgh Press, 1963.

Callaghan, Morley. *That Summer in Paris: Memories of Tangled Friendships with Hemingway, Fitzgerald and Some Others.* New York: Coward-McCann, 1963.

Fitzgerald, F. Scott, *The Crack-Up: With Other Uncollected Pieces, Note-Books and Unpublished Letters.* Edmund Wilson (ed.). New York: New Directions Book, 1945.

Goldhurst, William. *F. Scott Fitzgerald and His Contemporaries.* Cleveland World Book Publishing Co., 1963.

Graham, Sheilah. *College of One.* New York: Viking Press, 1967.

Graham, Sheilah and Frank, Gerold. *Beloved Infidel: The Education of a Woman.* New York: Henry Holt & Co., 1958.

Kazin, Alfred (ed.). *F. Scott Fitzgerald: The Man and His Work.* Cleveland: World Book Publishing Co., 1951.

Lehan, Richard D. *F. Scott Fitzgerald and the Craft of Fiction.* Carbondale: Southern Illinois Press, 1966.

Miller, James E. *F. Scott Fitzgerald, His Art and His Technique.* New York: New York University Press, 1964.

Mizener, Arthur. *The Far Side of Paradise: A Biography of F. Scott Fitzgerald.* New York: Vintage Books, 1959.

Mizener, Arthur (ed.). *F. Scott Fitzgerald: A Collection of Critical Essays.* Englewood Cliffs, N.J.: Prentice-Hall, 1963.

Perosa, Sergis. *The Art of F. Scott Fitzgerald.* Translated by Charles Matz and the Author. Ann Arbor: University of Michigan Press, 1965.

Turnbull, Andrew (ed.). *The Letters of F. Scott Fitzgerald.* New York: Charles Scribner's Sons, 1963.

Turnbull, Andrew, *Scott Fitzgerald.* New York: Charles Scribner's Sons, 1962.

On SINCLAIR LEWIS:

Lewis, Grace. *With Love from Gracie.* New York: Harcourt, Brace & Co., 1955.

Lewis, Sinclair. *The Man from Main Street: Selected Essays and Other Writings: 1904–1950.* Harry E. Maule and Melville H. Cane (eds.). New York: Pocket Books, 1963.

Schorer, Mark. *Sinclair Lewis, an American Life.* New York: McGraw-Hill Book Co., 1961.

Schorer, Mark (ed.). *Sinclair Lewis: A Collection of Critical Essays.* Englewood Cliffs, N.J.: Prentice-Hall, 1962.

Smith, Harrison (ed.). *From Main Street to Stockholm: Letters of Sinclair Lewis, 1919–1930.* New York: Harcourt, Brace & Co., 1952.

Sheean, Vincent. *Dorothy and Red.* Boston: Houghton Mifflin Co., 1963.

On JOHN STEINBECK:

French, Warren. *John Steinbeck.* New York: Twayne Publishers, 1961.

Gannett, Lewis. *John Steinbeck: Personal and Bibliographical Notes.* New York: Viking Press, 1939.

Lisca, Peter. *The Wide World of John Steinbeck.* New Brunswick, N.J.: Rutgers University Press, 1958.

Moore, Harry T. *The Novels of John Steinbeck: A First Critical Study.* Chicago: Normandie House, 1939.

Tedlock, E. W., Jr. and Hunter, C. V. (eds.). *Steinbeck and His Critics: A Record of Twenty-Five Years.* Albuquerque: University of New Mexico Press, 1957.

On THOMAS WOLFE:

Daniels, Jonathan. *Tar Heels: A Portrait of North Carolina.* New York: Dodd, Mead & Co., 1941.

Holman, C. Hugh. *Three Modes of Southern Fiction: Ellen Glasgow, William Faulkner, Thomas Wolfe.* Athens: University of Georgia Press, 1966.

Johnson, Elmer D. *Of Time and Thomas Wolfe: A Bibliography with a Character Index of His Works.* New York: Scarecrow Press, 1959.

Johnson, Pamela H. *Hungry Gulliver: An English Critical Appraisal of Thomas Wolfe.* New York: Charles Scribner's Sons, 1948.

Muller, Herbert J. *Thomas Wolfe.* Norfolk, Conn.: New Directions Books, 1947.

Nowell, Elizabeth (ed.). *The Letters of Thomas Wolfe.* New York: Charles Scribner's Sons, 1956.

Nowell, Elizabeth. *Thomas Wolfe: A Biography.* Garden City, N.Y.: Doubleday & Company, Inc., 1960.

Pollock, Thomas C. and Cargill, Oscar (eds.). *Thomas Wolfe at Washington Square.* New York: New York University Press, 1954.

Raynolds, Robert. *Thomas Wolfe: Memoir of a Friendship.* Austin: University of Texas Press, 1965.

Rubin, Louis D. *Thomas Wolfe: The Weather of His Youth.* Baton Rouge: Louisiana State University Press, 1955.

Terry, John Skelly (ed.). *Thomas Wolfe's Letters to His Mother, Julia Elizabeth Wolfe.* New York: Charles Scribner's Sons, 1943.

Walser, Richard (ed.). *The Enigma of Thomas Wolfe: Biographical and Critical Selections.* Cambridge: Harvard University Press, 1953.

Wheaton, Mabel Wolfe, with Le Gette, Blythe. *Thomas Wolfe and His Family,* New York: Doubleday & Company, Inc., 1961.

On RICHARD WRIGHT:

Crossman, Richard (ed.). *The God That Failed.* New York: Harper & Brothers, 1949.

Wright, Richard. *Black Boy: A Record of Childhood and Youth.* New York: Harper & Brothers, 1945.

Wright, Richard. *12 Million Black Voices: A Folk History of the Negro in the United States.* New York: Viking Press, 1941.

III. GENERAL WORKS ON AMERICAN FICTION, 1910–1940

Aaron, Daniel. *Writers on the Left: Episodes in American Literary Communism.* New York: Harcourt, Brace & World, 1961.

Aldridge, John W. *After the Lost Generation: A Critical Study of the Writers of Two Wars.* New York: McGraw-Hill Book Co., 1951.

Beach, Joseph W. *American Fiction, 1920–1940.* New York: Russell & Russell, 1960.

Boynton, Percy H. *America in Contemporary Fiction.* Chicago: Chicago University Press, 1940.

Blotner, Joseph. *The Modern American Political Novel, 1900–1960.* Austin: University of Texas Press, 1966.

Cowley, Malcolm (ed.). *After the Genteel Tradition: American Writers Since 1910.* New York: W. W. Norton & Co., 1937.

Cowley, Malcolm. *Exile's Return.* New York: Viking Press, 1951.

Fiedler, Leslie A. *Love and Death in the American Novel.* New York: Criterion Books, 1960.

Frohock, Wilbur M. *The Novel of Violence in America, 1920–1950.* Dallas: Southern Methodist University, 1950.

Geismar, Maxwell. *The Last of the Provincials: The American Novel, 1915–1925.* Boston: Houghton Mifflin Co., 1947.

Geismar, Maxwell. *Writers in Crisis: The American Novel Between Two Wars.* Boston: Houghton Mifflin Co., 1942.

Gelfant, Blanche H. *The American City Novel.* Norman: University of Oklahoma Press, 1954.

Hoffman, Frederick J. *The Modern Novel in America.* Chicago: Gateways Editions, 1956.

Hoffman, Frederick J. *The Twenties: American Writing in the Post-War Decade.* New York: Collier Books, 1962.

Rideout, Walter B. *The Radical Novel in the United States, 1900–1954.* Cambridge: Harvard University Press, 1956.

Thorp, Willard. *American Writing in the Twentieth Century.* Cambridge: Harvard University Press, 1960.

Index